PRAISE FOR FIONA McIN

'Skilful storytelling and compelling
that leap from the page.' BOOKS+PUBLISHING

'Elegantly written, yet with no shortage
of satisfying thrills.' APPLE BOOKS

'Flawless.'
AUSTRALIAN WOMEN'S WEEKLY

'Will keep you second-guessing until the very end.'
BETTER READING

'McIntosh's riveting, page-turner style makes this book
an ideal poolside summer holiday read.'
SYDNEY MORNING HERALD

'Will have you hooked from page one . . .
a fast-paced romance filled with secrets, adventure,
and plenty of twists.' WEEKENDER

'A blockbuster of a book that you won't
want to put down.' BRYCE COURTENAY

'She's so prolific, you wonder how
Fiona McIntosh does it.' THE AGE

'A fast-paced and enchanting page-turner.'
KIRKUS REVIEWS

'Fiona McIntosh is an extraordinary storyteller.'
BOOK'D OUT

The Fallen Woman

Fiona McIntosh is an internationally and million-copy bestselling author of novels for adults and children across several genres. Alongside her highly successful historical fiction titles, for which she has been nominated at the Australian Book Industry Awards for commercial fiction book of the year, her popular Detective Jack Hawksworth series will soon be released across the UK. Several of her historical titles as well as the 'world of Hawksworth' crime novels have been optioned for the screen. Her debut children's picture book, *Harry and Gran*, will be published in 2025. Fiona roams the world for her research and lives between Adelaide in South Australia and Wiltshire in England.

FIONA McINTOSH

The Fallen Woman

PENGUIN BOOKS

UK | USA | Canada | Ireland | Australia
India | New Zealand | South Africa | China

Penguin Books is part of the Penguin Random House group of companies
whose addresses can be found at global.penguinrandomhouse.com

Penguin
Random House
Australia

First published by Penguin Books, 2024

Cover image by Alexey Kazantsev/Trevillion Images
Inside cover image by Zane Lee/Unsplash
Cover design by Louisa Maggio Design © Penguin Random House Australia Pty Ltd
Typeset in 11/16 pt Sabon LT Pro by Midland Typesetters, Australia

Printed and bound in Australia by Griffin Press, an accredited
ISO AS/NZS 14001 Environmental Management Systems printer

 A catalogue record for this
book is available from the
National Library of Australia

ISBN 978 1 76104 929 3

penguin.com.au

*We at Penguin Random House Australia acknowledge that Aboriginal and Torres Strait Islander
peoples are the Traditional Custodians and the first storytellers of the lands on which we live
and work. We honour Aboriginal and Torres Strait Islander peoples' continuous connection
to Country, waters, skies and communities. We celebrate Aboriginal and Torres Strait Islander
stories, traditions and living cultures; and we pay our respects to Elders past and present.*

*For our beloved Henry, who arrived
into our family amid much joy,
while I was writing this book.*

1

Jane Saville's gasp conveyed her shock as her mother's words landed like small blows.

'It's the least you can do under the circumstances,' Eugenie spat, straightening her back against the sofa and pinching her lips in a tight pout of finality.

Jane looked between her mother and her sister Charlotte, older by three years, who at least had the grace to look uncomfortable, avoiding her gaze. Only moments ago Jane had thought there couldn't be worse news than the King's coronation being cancelled due to illness. A year of mourning had been observed for the much-loved Queen Victoria, but the country was looking forward to her popular son Edward being crowned, releasing everyone from grief to start a new era. In her dismay at the news that the coronation was in jeopardy, Jane had decided to paint. It helped her to focus on something other than the disappointment of hundreds of thousands of people, who were now cancelling their street parties and special celebrations. The country's collective anxiety for the dangerously ill new king would silence the excitement. All the joy flattened with a single proclamation from the palace.

But that news paled as her mother had arrived. She had been seated in the orangery, a whimsical addition to their London home, which her grandfather had made in his later years. Her father had added to its romance by installing a tiny stone fountain and fish pond. Jane was the one who, after his death, had tended to the pond and to the many plants he had grown. The greenhouse was now resplendent with sweet-scented jasmine, plumbago, pelargoniums, ferns and a citrus tree that was struggling but surviving. She loved the constant changing landscape of colours and textures as the various plants came into season. They were her friends in this quiet space, where the soft sound of water was soothing as much as cooling.

Her mother's arrival instantly destroyed the peace of Jane's painting session. The garden's first summer irises had opened fully that morning, and Jane had decided to make a study of one of the blooms. She had dipped her paintbrush into a snowish white made from ground Carrara marble and calcium stearate and was poised to mix the tiniest hint of porcelain earth pigment into the white, which would gently bring the petals into vivid life from their soft pencil sketch. She would need many layers to achieve the vibrant purple of the flower petal, and she had not yet made a single mark when her mother burst into the orangery to make the announcement that Charlotte was pregnant to Edmund Cavendish, a man Jane considered a scoundrel but who her sister was convinced simply hadn't committed to the right woman. He was wealthy, no doubt, but his money belonged to his mother and she likely doled it out as a favour. Jane didn't blame her. Edmund, as far as she was concerned, was a wastrel who preferred pleasure to business, carousing to family, and any number of adoring women to taking a wife. But Charlotte and her mother had decided Edmund was the right catch, especially because Melba Cavendish wanted very badly what their family already had: high social standing and respect in the coveted royal circle. And Charlotte simply couldn't look past the money that might be at her disposal if she became Mrs Edmund Cavendish.

Pregnant and unmarried, though. That news had felt like a crack of lightning, sparkling an incandescent cyan in her mind, searing through her tranquil mood to split it in two: one shocked and speechless, the other horrified and galvanised, running for smelling salts. They were required for her mother, who had swooned with an agonised and repeated muttering: *a baby out of wedlock.*

Her mother had revived, thanks to Jane's ministrations with the salts. Charlotte had appeared, mute and pale. Jane might have felt sorry for her then if her mother hadn't ordered tea, forbidden anyone to talk until Mrs Poole had served it, and in that ten minutes come up with an audacious and dark plan that was, her mother thought, the only way forward. Now they were knee-deep in the argument around her ghastly, ill-conceived idea. Everyone was on the attack, including Jane, who hated that she had allowed them to upset her, making her defensive.

'Under what circumstances, Mother?' Jane's tone was as reasonable as she could contrive in the moment.

'What are you talking about?'

'You said it was the least I could do under the circumstances. I want to know what those circumstances are, given Charlotte is the one who has behaved in a way unbecoming to a Saville. I would even go so far as to say she might earn a title other than Lady Cavendish.'

'Take that back!' Charlotte snapped.

Jane was too angry to respond, but she inhaled silently and calmed herself. Years of these sorts of arguments, in which her two closest relatives ganged up on her, had taught her to never raise her voice, not even take a tone, for it was useless. She did not want to waste her life feeling like she was filled with boiling blood or had a catty tongue. This, however, was a whole new level of angst. What her mother was proposing was outrageous. They couldn't possibly be serious, and yet her mother's chins were set as far back into her fleshy neck as they could go, while Charlotte's thin lips had all but disappeared. If not for her nervous tongue licking those lips, Charlotte's mouth would have gone missing in her anguish, waiting for her mother to solve this catastrophic turn of events.

Eugenie answered. 'I was referring to our impoverished circumstances through your father's ill-timed death, not your sister's poor decision-making.'

'Well, his death five years ago was an accident. He didn't die in order to vex you,' Jane replied.

'Of course you'd take that attitude, Jane. You and our father were like a precious couple who let no one else in.'

Jane turned to her sister at the caustic remark. 'I think you should save your petty jealousy for another time. Don't make this about our father, rest his soul. This is about you. You're all about ambition, but you have very little care for whom that ambition might hurt.'

Her mother took up the fight again. 'None of this bickering solves the fact that we are running out of funds as a family. Charlotte marrying Eddie is our chance to change things – all our problems solved. But the pregnancy will ruin everything. Don't you care about what happens to us? Where's your conscience?'

'Couldn't *she* have let her conscience serve her before she climbed into bed with him?' Jane pointed at Charlotte. Both her mother and sister gasped, and Jane took the moment to press her point. 'I don't use much of the funds you have, Mother, and soon I shall be earning my own income from my art, so I'll be glad to pay my way.'

'Your *art*.' Eugenie sneered. 'Well, you need to make *some* sort of income, Jane, because heaven alone knows it's not going to be easy to settle you on a prospective husband.'

'I don't need one,' Jane said, her tone firm.

Eugenie and Charlotte made fresh sounds of disapproval.

'One day I may want one,' she qualified, 'and then I'm sure I shall find him for myself.' She managed a smile.

Both women laughed now.

'How funny you are, Jane,' Charlotte said. 'Father named you well. You're as plain as one of your canvases before you begin one of your little "studies".' She loaded the final word with disdain.

'I'll remind you that Jane was his beloved grandmother's name, and I wear it proudly. Incidentally, those new canvases to which you refer promise endless possibility, colour, ambition and joy,' Jane replied, deliberately cool. She mustn't lose control of this conversation. 'Anyway, Mother, Charlotte's decision was made as an adult and hardly without the knowledge of the repercussions. This is not my mess to clear up.'

'You'd be doing this for all of our sakes, not just Charlotte's. Don't you care about this family?'

'I care enough to live quietly, asking for very little financially, while supporting both of you in a manner that is, let's be honest now, just shy of service. I'm like a maid to you both. I contribute more than my share.'

Her sister ignored that truth, going instead on the offensive. 'Your stupid little paintings aren't going to keep us in food.'

'Perhaps not, but at least I didn't resort to acting like a slut.'

The insult hung in the air. Jane hadn't meant to say it, but she'd been hearing the word in her mind since her mother had made the announcement.

'I'm going to forgive you that terrible slur against your sister, Jane,' her mother said, 'because we need to be a family now. We must work as one.'

'That's not true, though, is it? This may be about *family*, but are you considering what your suggestion will do to my name? To my wellbeing? To my future? You were joking about no one wanting to marry me, but this really will mean that. I'll be an outcast.'

'Jane,' her mother started, as though speaking to a simpleton, 'if Charlotte does not marry Edmund Cavendish, there is no future for anyone in this family, including the child growing in her belly. We must make this marriage happen.'

'The answer is no. Simply no. This is not happening. I will not pretend that Charlotte's child – her *illegitimate* child – is mine. There will be men who will marry her because they long for marriage, for an heir, for—'

'But they'll be old and desperate,' Charlotte spat.

'So what? They might also be very wealthy and, frankly, I know that's what matters here to the two of you.'

'You're so selfish,' Charlotte said.

Jane had to close her eyes against all the retorts she wanted to hurl at her sister, who had no genuine awareness of anyone else's needs but her own. It had always been like this. *Don't be so surprised, Jane*, she said to herself. *This kind of self-centred approach is nothing new.* 'No, Charlotte, you're being selfish, asking me to ruin my life because you were short-sighted to the point of being simple. What were you thinking?'

'Without this marriage, Jane . . .' Charlotte began in the same wearied tone that her mother had used a moment earlier, but Jane would not hear it.

'I know all that, Charlotte. I want to know what you were thinking by allowing Edmund Cavendish to take advantage of you like that. What did you think might possibly happen?'

'Well, our mother asked me to ensure he was bound to me.' Charlotte dared to smile, unaware of her mother's pursed lips, which told Jane she hadn't asked Charlotte to go quite this far.

'It was a moment in time,' she said almost dreamily. 'One day it might visit you, Jane . . . although that's doubtful, given your plain presentation, propensity for isolation and the paint on your apron.'

That was a lot of alliteration, Jane thought, but kept it to herself. 'Is that the best you can do to make a man want you? I don't pretend to understand or get involved in matchmaking or courting; I don't know how to flirt or catch the eye of a man. You know all those things, and you're good at them, plus you're beautiful, and that alone will always attract men. But I'm certain you also know that to let Eddie be so intimate with you risked everything you're surely aiming for. What you've given him was the ultimate prize. Now he has it, why is he going to—'

'Because, Jane,' their mother said, enunciating the words so they felt like daggers, 'Melba Cavendish wants this marriage too, and Eddie Cavendish is scared of his mother. He's terrified of being cut off, so he will keep the secret if we do.'

'What exactly is the secret we're keeping? How on earth do we pretend the child is mine, when clearly Charlotte is the pregnant one?'

'Haven't I made myself clear? We will say that you have got yourself pregnant out of wedlock and that your good sister Charlotte is postponing her wedding to accompany you somewhere out of London, away from society, where you can have your child . . . where the air is fresh and the countryside will revive you. Then Charlotte can return to London and marry Edmund, as planned . . .'

Jane had rarely seen eye to eye with her mother in recent years, but she never thought she could stoop this low. Truly? Was she mad? No, Jane could see her mother was thinking lucidly and with her usual cunning. In a blink, Eugenie Saville had come up with a clever but twisted way in which to release Charlotte from all responsibility for her carelessness.

Jane was surprised she could find the words to reply. 'What a hateful plan! What a cruel pair you are. Can you in all good conscience actually carry this out? What about *my* life?'

'Certainly. We are protecting our livelihood, including yours, you little fool!' Eugenie snapped, reaching again for the foul-smelling salts. Their powerful restorative vapours were supposedly covered by lavender, but Jane could smell the horrid ammonia from where she stood nearby. She watched her mother sniff and momentarily look dizzy before rallying. 'Melba Cavendish wants this marriage because our name offers her the entry to society and the royals that she so desperately wants. She knows we'll never readily accept her vulgar American ways—'

'Happy to accept her money, though,' Jane murmured with a savage look Charlotte's way.

'Money is money,' Eugenie dismissed. 'She has it, we need it. And we have what she wants in return. But!' She pointed at Jane. 'She might be American, but she has standards. Melba will not tolerate a child out of wedlock for her beloved son as she tries to integrate into English society. She wants everything to be perfect, with no stain against the family name. Charlotte being pregnant would ruin everything.'

'Charlotte *is* pregnant. And Eddie does a pretty good job of tarnishing the family name all on his own. He's louche!' Jane snapped, barely recognising herself, being so waspish.

'You sound jealous of my fiancé,' Charlotte said airily.

'Hardly. Let me be honest, as we're all being so candid today. Eddie will let you down time and again, Charlotte. He already has. Clearly he knows about the child?'

'I told him this morning.'

'And?'

Charlotte looked away. 'He said bad news comes in threes.'

Jane blinked. 'Why would he respond like that?'

'Well, Yorkshire are apparently losing to the Australians, and in Eddie's mind Yorkshire might as well be England – we're all united when the old enemy arrives to play cricket.'

Jane breathed out with frustration. 'What else did he say?'

'That the second bad news was the cancellation of the King's coronation.'

'Postponement,' Jane corrected. 'We must be optimistic for his recovery.'

'It's pneumonia, apparently,' Eugenie chimed in. 'We heard that direct from the palace,' she said, putting a finger to her lips as though it were secret.

'Jennifer Gantry told me it's something that requires surgery. And her parents are part of the inner sanctum,' Charlotte remarked.

'Just days away from that crown being put on his head.' Her mother tutted.

Jane couldn't take a second more of this. 'Charlotte!'

Her sister rolled her eyes. 'Yes?'

'What did Eddie say about you being with child?'

Charlotte shrugged. 'Well, he hated the way I was crying and bundled me out into the garden. That's when he said it was the third piece of bad news.'

'That's it? Just superstition?' Jane was aghast.

'No. He said it had to be kept secret and that his mother must never ever get the tiniest whiff of it, or the wedding would be off. He was very cross with me and sent me home immediately, even though he could see I was upset.' Charlotte slumped down into the sofa, arms crossed.

Jane trained her features against the disgust she felt for Eddie. He was such a poor choice: weak of character, arrogant, supercilious and entirely controlled by his mother. He would bring disrepute to their good name, if Charlotte didn't ruin it altogether with this latest turn of events. 'Did you remind him that this baby couldn't have been made without his help?' she said, trying to be delicate. She picked up her cup. The tea had gone cold.

'He wants me to consider all options, so that we can go ahead with the wedding.'

'All options,' Jane repeated. 'And, Mother, you believe the best option is to ruin my life for the sake of Charlotte's reputation.'

'Believe me, Jane, if we can persuade Melba that Charlotte is simply being responsible, taking care of her sister in her time of need, then she will go along with rescheduling the wedding. She knows Charlotte is a good match for Eddie, and she doesn't have to know anything about this . . . this hiccough.'

Hiccough, Jane repeated silently, mocking her mother in her private despair.

'Our name, our connections, is what she's after, I'm no fool. If no harm has been done and both parties remain favourable, then there is no need for this child to ruin what is a perfectly good union of two families.'

'No harm done?' Jane repeated, appalled.

'We simply can't have a baby in the way, Jane,' Charlotte said, as though that was the final word on it.

'Then get rid of it!' Jane said, hating herself as she spoke the hideous thought aloud.

Charlotte and her mother looked equally shocked at the notion. They were horrors, both of them, but even they would not involve themselves in aborting a child. Jane knew her mother had struggled to become pregnant and had lost several precious, much-wanted lives in miscarriage, which had left its scars on her parents' marriage and showed itself in her mother's often embittered attitude.

'I don't mean that,' Jane added hastily, turning back towards her forgotten painting so they wouldn't see the gathering tears. The perfect paint colour had dried and hardened in the little dish she had mixed it in. It looked how she felt, she thought. She steeled her voice. 'But I don't want to be a mother. Not yet. I certainly don't want to have anything to do with this cruel plan. Are you even considering the child's situation in all of this?' She looked up again, meeting her mother's gaze.

'What do you mean?' Eugenie asked, looking dumbfounded.

'I mean this tiny boy or girl who arrives. They will feel unloved and unwanted from the moment they discover that their mother turned her back on them because of money.'

'The child won't be unloved or unwanted, Jane,' Charlotte said. 'You're always saving lost and abandoned things. You'll love my child as your own.'

Her sister's child, thrust into her care against her will? Unlikely. Jane scoffed. 'Such presumption. I am not ready to be a mother!'

'Neither am I,' her sister rounded on her. 'And I'd be useless at it. But it's up to me to save this family from destitution by marrying Edmund. Why can't you understand that?'

'Enough!' Eugenie commanded, rising from the sofa. 'We need to make a plan. I think Charlotte is perhaps six weeks gone.'

'How can you be sure?' Jane demanded.

'We can set our clocks by your sister's monthlies. She is never early, never late. What's more, she's been sickening, or have you been too lost in your drawings to notice? Her breasts are tender. I don't need a doctor to confirm what my instincts have been telling me, what I've stupidly tried to ignore. Besides, I can't call on any doctor here. Only the three of us and Eddie know, and I intend that it remain that way. If my experience is anything to go by, Charlotte, you will start showing in another six weeks, my girl,' she said, casting a wearied glance at her eldest daughter. 'We cannot have the London tongues wagging at the new tightness of your clothes or holding up their lorgnettes at the theatre and querying whether your breasts have enlarged. No! You will both

11

be gone before that occurs. I will make the arrangements, including for the betrothal to be formally announced. Both of you get packed.'

'Where are we going?' Jane asked, horrified to realise she was already resigning herself to accompanying Charlotte.

'My great-aunt in Wiltshire. You can go there.'

'Wiltshire!' the sisters said together in shared dismay. They each had unhappy memories of visiting their aunt, a spinster who was even more bitter than their mother.

'Hortense will keep our secret. She's as poor and hungry as a church mouse. I'm sure a little rent and food money will enable a swift decision. Anyway—' Eugenie looked around with resentment at the sound of a knock. 'What is it, Mrs Poole? Can't you see we're busy in here, clearly in need of privacy?'

'Forgive me, Mrs Saville,' Mrs Poole, their middle-aged housekeeper and only servant, said. 'A very important message has arrived from the palace.'

'The palace?' Charlotte repeated in a tight voice.

Jane watched her mother and sister shift their attention to Mrs Poole, who held out the silver tray her mother insisted all mail be delivered upon. The envelope was a rich cream with the royal crest. Jane didn't know whether to worry that the King had succumbed to his illness or to scream her frustration that her plight simply had no currency any more. Her mother had spoken her ghastly plan, her sister was happy and Jane would just have to cope until she could speak to her mother again. There was still time to change things. She swallowed her anger as she'd taught herself. There was no point to it, she'd learned. Only once the bluster was done could any decisions be made or action taken.

'Oh my stars!' Her mother's expression began to crumple as she took in the contents of the note.

'What is it?' Charlotte squealed, near breathless.

There was another long pause as Eugenie stared at the note and looked around. Jane presumed she was searching for the smelling salts again. Her mother could be so dramatic when she chose to be.

'Our King. He's . . . he's . . .'

Silence tucked itself around them, as though trying to soothe the shock. Even their housekeeper looked horrified.

'Thank you, Mrs Poole,' Jane said. 'Please do not discuss this with anyone.'

'Of course,' the woman said, with a small curtsy. She departed.

'May I?' Jane asked. Without waiting for her mother's response, she reached for the note and read it quickly. 'The King has suspected appendicitis and will be undergoing surgery.'

Charlotte gasped, hands to her mouth. 'Could he die?'

Jane blinked with frustration at the pointless question. 'Anyone could die during an operation, Charlotte, but I imagine the very top surgeon in the land will be consulted. No, I doubt he will die with the operation, but he certainly will if he doesn't undergo surgery.'

The women nodded sombrely in response; they might not have respected Jane, but they trusted her knowledge on such things.

'Come on, darling,' Eugenie said briskly to her eldest. 'We have some calls to make and arrangements to change . . .'

Charlotte stood and helped her mother to her feet.

'You can get back to your daubing, Jane. We shall see you for our evening meal,' her mother said over her shoulder. She leaned into Charlotte's helping hand.

Jane watched, her mouth ajar. Apparently her quandary had been overlooked by something more important in her family's eyes. She didn't much like Charlotte lately, but she was her sister and Jane did love her. But as much as she cared about her family's future, she couldn't do what they were asking of her. Surely she could argue her way out of this and make her mother see the cruel, ruinous nature of it. Besides, Charlotte would take one look at her child and fall in love, and then refuse to be parted from her son or daughter . . . wouldn't she?

2

There had never been a second conversation about her opposition to the vile plan, but Jane remained hopeful that Charlotte would change her mind as the pregnancy progressed and she began to feel her baby grow inside her.

Eugenie had moved her two daughters to Salisbury, Wiltshire, where they lived in a townhouse a few steps away from the main cobbled square. Hortense, as her mother had been convinced, was more than happy to accept rent and, with nothing interesting to say, kept herself to herself.

The girls lived 'in the gods', as they called it, at the very top of the three-storey house, which had been built in the eighteenth century. The proud cathedral city of Salisbury was just thirty miles south of the grand Regency city of Bath, which had once been the spa town and playground of those with eye-watering wealth and those who aspired to it. If they'd lived in the previous century, Jane imagined her sister would have gone shopping for a husband in Bath, where their family would have been welcomed due to their fine lineage. Bath no longer attracted the elite; it had fallen out of favour during Victoria's reign after the young princess discovered

15

that a local had commented on the thickness of her ankles when she opened the royal gardens, and, as punishment, she had never visited the city again.

Salisbury, Jane believed, was Bath's country cousin, famed for its magnificent cathedral and pious population. It sat on the edge of the vast Salisbury Plain, with its intriguing Stonehenge. Her father had brought her and Charlotte to marvel at the ancient structure that no one could fully explain, and Jane had been fascinated, discussing and posing ideas for what it might have been – a primitive burial ground to a sacrificial circle, or perhaps a place where divine inspiration might be found. Charlotte had simply leaned against one of the standing stones and complained that it was cold and damp, and when might they go home?

The city, neatly planned in a grid, had been divided into chequers, each with a unique name. Where they lived was in the Three Cups Chequer, which was known mostly for its brewery and cider house. Charlotte resented the roughness of the neighbourhood, but Jane was grateful for the roof over their heads and the distance from their mother and London. It didn't solve her dilemma, but life, if she was truthful, was blissfully peaceful here, and she spent much of it in the Cathedral Close, sketching, making studies of its plants and flowers, and trying to help prepare Charlotte for what was coming.

Their mother had visited briefly for Christmas, laughing delightedly in spite of herself at her eldest daughter's protruding belly. 'I was always much rounder for both of you,' was her only remark.

Jane had clung to the hope that as the pregnancy progressed, particularly when Charlotte felt the quickening, she might come to feel maternally protective and more determined to keep the child, no matter the consequences. Jane imagined how she would admire her elder sister – finally – for a brave decision that was also the right decision.

But the moment never came, and Jane's worst fears began to gather as she overheard her mother making plans for the early spring wedding, whose date was, in reality, still on the edge of winter. She tried to confront her but was told Christmas Day was not the time to discuss the matter. Jane kept the peace only to discover that Eugenie had stolen away in the early hours of the following day, no doubt to avoid further confrontation. No amount of hand-wringing or letter writing could change the fact that her mother considered this act to be Jane's duty. So now she had to rely on Charlotte's maternal instinct taking hold, if it even existed.

Sadly, as the birth of the child approached, Charlotte defied Jane's great hope, becoming less and less caring by the day.

'I can't wait to be gone from here without it,' she snapped after an apparently sleepless night, suffering indigestion.

'Charlotte, you need to eat less—' Jane tried but was cut off savagely.

'Why don't you try carrying around a hungry elephant in your belly, Jane? Maybe then you can make that sort of remark.'

'It's just an observation. I'm trying to be helpful.'

'Well, you're not! Keep your unhelpful observations to yourself.'

Jane had continued with trepidation – she had to keep trying. 'Charlotte, listen, I don't know much at all about motherhood, but I'm very doubtful that you can simply leave your newborn baby behind. And can we also just be very clear that I have not agreed to take on his or her mothering? I've been happy to be here for you throughout this pregnancy, but I plan to visit our mother this week and have this out once and for all.'

'Too late, Jane. Our mother is busy planning a wedding with the Cavendishes. It's all organised. I have to get this thing out of my belly, go home to London and get this body quickly back into some sort of figure for a spring wedding. She's used all our savings so you cannot back out now. You know the plan!'

'Charlotte, I never agreed to this!' Jane said, her voice high and breathless. This was all happening too quickly, out of her control.

'Well, the wedding is in March, so it's too late to change your mind. Perhaps I'll start a new trend in society by wearing white fur and heavy lace. Mother wants the ring on my finger before the days get warm, so I only have weeks to shed this baby blubber. Mother has employed someone to help with food and some special exercises. I've told her we'll never get a flat stomach, but she's got a girdle in mind that will tighten things up until I can achieve it naturally.'

Jane shook her head, aghast. 'It's all about you, Charlotte, isn't it? I'm stunned. Do you feel *anything* for this child?'

'Nothing. It's a total inconvenience.'

'*It*? This is your baby. A precious little person who belongs to you and Edmund – he or she was surely made with love and—'

Her sister made a scornful sound. 'Made with lust, Jane, not love. Very different. Not that you will ever experience it,' she added, her tone turning to pitying. 'But love will grow between me and Edmund. I know he will learn to love me, and I shall adore him. He loves my looks already – he says I make him look better, even success-ful. And his mother certainly loves our name and its connections.' She laughed cruelly. 'I certainly love their money. I won't know myself, and I shall look after you and Mother, don't fret on it.'

'I don't.' Jane paused, trying to summon an argument that might sway her sister's determined stance.

'Good,' Charlotte said with a sigh.

'Is that really enough for you? A potentially loveless union? Enough that you'd turn your back on a child?' Jane looked at her sister in genuine curiosity.

Charlotte's gaze narrowed. 'How many ways can I say this, Jane? I don't want this child. It's not helpful to my life in any way.

Eddie will learn to appreciate me, and I intend to make him happy. We will enjoy a life that is rich in every way. His mother can change my life, change *our* lives, Jane! The child is in the way of all that.'

'Melba won't affect my life. *You* are the one doing that! I don't wish to raise your child. I have my own plans, my own dreams—'

'Well, for our family's sake, it has to be this way,' Charlotte cut in. 'Father always spoke about duty and responsibility – this is yours. And I'll say that it's also your moment to shine in our mother's eyes. Perhaps I'll want another child later, when I'm married, but I don't feel anything right now except angry that it's inside me. I just feel anxious to get back to my life. Surely you can see that having this attitude will do a baby no good?'

Jane looked at her, lost for words, as her sister continued.

'I don't want to feed it, I don't want to care for it, I don't even want to look at it. It's just this thing that nearly ruined my life. But I know you take pity on all helpless creatures, so why is this any different? You can go ahead and take care of this one.'

In that moment Jane truly hated her sister and rightfully had nothing more to say. But tears stung her eyes as she thought of her niece or nephew; that they would be so unwanted was a shameful admission from their mother.

And that's when Jane committed herself to the baby.

Charlotte's waters broke one very icy morning in early January. The midwife was sent for. She arrived, brisk and slightly pinch-faced, although Jane allowed that her expression might be due to the cold. Mrs Palfrey looked strong but lean, with big hands that would surely make a baby look even tinier when she held them. It was her kind eyes, though, that reassured Jane. Right now, they rested on Jane and her labouring sister and, having seen the process dozens of times in her working life, she quickly declared that Charlotte's labour was moving at a tepid pace.

'I needn't stay. She'll be hours and hours yet. I think she'll be all of this day and the coming night at least,' Mrs Palfrey said.

Jane couldn't think of anything worse than Charlotte, now in labour, complaining twice as much as normal. 'Please stay. We will pay, of course. But with no experience to offer, I'd prefer that you waited with us.'

The woman gave a shrug. 'That will be double my fee.'

'Fine.'

'And my meals,' she added quickly.

'Of course,' Jane said.

Relying on Mrs Palfrey's judgement, Jane started preparing an easel for some painting. Considering her sister's labour had been glacial so far, with the midwife sighing each time she checked on its progress, shaking her head that the baby was not yet close to delivery, it was a shock when the situation changed. Suddenly Charlotte stopped her intermittent groaning and began giving loud, near hysterical shrieks.

'What's this?' Jane asked, bursting into Charlotte's room.

'Certainly unexpected,' Mrs Palfrey remarked.

'Do we send for the doctor?'

'No need, dear. Her body and that baby know exactly what to do. Besides,' she said, surprising Jane with a quick smile, 'so do I. The doctor will sign the birth certificate later.'

Aunt Hortense, who usually left them entirely alone, begged Charlotte to keep the noise down, claiming she had a headache, which Jane found amusing. Clearly her spinster aunt had no idea about what giving birth actually required of a woman.

Jane tried to at least soothe Charlotte, though she couldn't imagine there was much comfort to be found during the agony of childbirth.

'Take it slower on the vapours,' Mrs Palfrey warned, as Charlotte wrestled with the bronze facepiece that allowed her to inhale yet more chloroform.

'Be quiet, woman!' Charlotte snapped, sniffing hard on the tube that mixed water and chemicals to create the vapour. 'It was good enough for our former queen.'

Jane gave Mrs Palfrey a glance of apology, even though the midwife was surely used to snappish behaviour from labouring mothers.

'She needs to be alert to push. If she takes too much, she'll just pass out.'

'Charlotte?' Jane tried.

'What?' Her sister was testy, already sniffing again deeply.

'Just go a little easier on the chloroform. I don't want anything untoward to happen.'

'It won't,' Charlotte answered but her tone had become dreamy and faraway. 'Oh, please make it stop.'

'I can't believe it,' Mrs Palfrey whispered to Jane, 'but she's dilated to full width. The child is imminent.'

Jane squeezed her sister's hand. 'Soon, Charlotte,' she said, excitement coursing through her. 'Battle through, dearest,' she said softly, surprised that she sounded so kind. In fact, she couldn't fully let go of her rage at Charlotte's self-centredness.

Charlotte mumbled something unintelligible.

'What was that? I didn't hear you,' Jane said, moving closer to wipe her sister's forehead, which was beaded with little baubles of perspiration.

'I wonder who it will look like,' Charlotte murmured.

Mrs Palfrey gestured to Jane that she was just fetching something, and Jane watched her count out some fresh squares of linen and pour boiling water over a pair of ominous-looking scissors that had been freshly sharpened.

Jane turned back to Charlotte, resisting the urge to shudder. 'Well, sister, you're exceptionally pretty so I'm sure your good looks will shine through in your child.'

'No! You don't understand. He wouldn't accept it,' Charlotte said, shaking her head and becoming freshly agitated. The chloroform was working against her now.

'Calm, calm,' Jane said soothingly, stroking her hair. 'Talk to me through this pain. It will help. Just speak to me. Look at me.' She got her sister's attention. 'If we talk, you'll get through the pain. Tell me, why wouldn't he accept it?'

'John . . .' her sister murmured, drifting off for a moment.

'Charlotte? Charlotte?' Jane shook her sister. 'Are you all right?'

'Hopefully he'll never see it.'

'Oh, Charlotte, Eddie must. I hope you'll both soften to the idea of raising your child.'

'He mustn't know,' she whispered and then seemed to fall asleep momentarily.

Mrs Palfrey was at her side in a blink. 'No more chloroform. She's properly ready. We push on the next contraction and help this baby out,' she said sternly and removed the mask from Charlotte's grip.

Jane roused her sister. 'Charlotte?'

She seemed slightly more alert. 'What?'

'Is that the name you've chosen if it's a boy . . . John? What about if it's a girl? What pretty name do you like?'

'Oh, Jane, call it what you like. I couldn't care any less if I tried,' she growled, before crumpling into fresh agony.

'Mrs Palfrey, will Charlotte cope without this pain relief?'

The midwife shrugged. 'The curse of Eve,' she said, as though that were a complete answer. 'Your sister needs to be more stoic,' she added with a tutting sound. 'All mothers go through this. We don't want to harm the baby, do we?'

And with that question, Jane noted, she'd made Jane complicit if she insisted on more pain relief. 'Certainly not,' she murmured, biting her lip in frustration.

'Then she must push on ... *push* being the important activity now.' Mrs Palfrey's tone sounded so final and accusatory that Jane suspected she was withholding the helpful vapour as punishment for Charlotte's birthing a bastard.

Charlotte wailed as another contraction revived her – or perhaps at the loss of her inhaling equipment – but all was forgotten for the time being as Mrs Palfrey told her to push. 'Encourage her, Miss Saville. Make her push *now*!'

Everything else faded away while all focus went to the safe delivery of the child. He had slipped out quickly, much to Jane's surprise and relief, the midwife expertly catching him and smacking his bottom to elicit the wail of life, which thrilled Jane.

'It's a boy,' Jane murmured. She cut the umbilical cord with the fearsome scissors, as instructed by the midwife. All the while, Charlotte just lay there with her eyes closed.

'Oh, Charlotte, you have a beautiful son.' Jane wept, unable to help herself, tears of happiness coursing down her cheeks as she looked at the perfect child in her arms. All the anguish she had suffered these past months was momentarily forgotten at the sight of her nephew, perfect in every way: already pink, looking for his mother's breast, fine downy golden hair coating his sweet round head. She held him with nothing less than awe. 'Here, hold him close.'

'Let him smell you,' the midwife ordered Charlotte. She was brusque, but she'd brought the boy into this world safely, and Jane noted she was now attending to the third stage of labour. 'As soon as you hold him, you'll forget all about the agony of his birth.' She looked up from between Charlotte's legs. 'Get him onto your breast fast, my girl. Make the bond,' she encouraged Charlotte, not at all humbled by servicing a gentlewoman. Jane suspected that, with no father present or even spoken about, Mrs Palfrey had surmised just how far from 'gentle' Charlotte might have tiptoed.

Jane had to let this frustration go. Frankly, Charlotte deserved some pain for her behaviour, as well as her assumption that Jane would just accept being labelled as the mother, forever seen as a woman who had lost her innocence out of wedlock.

'Charlotte?' she murmured, kissing her sister's head, trying to comfort her. 'The afterbirth is coming. And then it's all over. Stay awake now. Get it done.'

Charlotte's eyelids fluttered open momentarily. 'A boy?' she moaned in enquiry.

Jane nodded and smiled. The baby was quiet in her arms for the moment, but she needed Charlotte to hold him close to her skin and feed him. 'Clever you. Charlotte, he is beautiful, strong. Ten fingers, ten toes and perfect in every way. I'm proud of you. He is heavenly,' she said gently. 'Here he is, meet your son.'

Charlotte actually raised a hand and Jane smiled, expecting her to take him, but she was wrong – Charlotte reached out with enough strength to push the child back and away. Jane's eyes widened in shock at the hostility.

'Keep him away from me,' Charlotte said, her tone icy. As she opened her eyes fully and groaned at a fresh contraction, she turned her attention to the midwife. 'Get everything that belongs to him out of me!'

Jane inhaled sharply. 'But Charlotte—'

'I hate him! I hate what he's done to me, to my body. I hate you for thinking he's special or important. Give him away for all I care. Smother him, even.'

Jane gasped again, retreating with the child in her arms. She met Mrs Palfrey's eye, and she could swear the midwife mouthed 'Cruel whore'.

The woman shook her head. 'Well, the least you can do is provide some milk for him. Your breasts will be heavy with it soon and you'll be glad for the relief when I show you how. But even now you might feed him with the first milk. It's called colostrum and will nourish your child no end.'

Charlotte shrieked again at a final contraction, and Jane watched the midwife deliver the afterbirth and study it carefully. 'All is well,' she said, looking up at Jane. 'This will need to be burned.' Conveniently it was a winter birth and fires were lit daily, so there was relief in that at least. 'I can help with finding a wet nurse.'

'You will?'

The midwife shrugged. 'If the mother refuses to feed, that's what happens. Cow's and goat's milk is sometimes used in the rural areas, and you can probably afford the new formula that some Swiss fellow has invented, but if you want my advice, he needs a mother's milk – his own or someone else's.'

'Where will you find a wet nurse?'

'I know a woman whose baby was stillborn yesterday. She'll likely help . . . for some coin.'

'Yes, please. Thank you.' The woman was blunt, but she was not unhelpful or unskilled, and she clearly wanted the best for the child . . . unlike his mother.

'Charlotte.' Jane turned back to her sister to try once more. She had to, for the boy's sake. 'He is the most important achievement of your life. He is perfect. Please, look at him.'

'Get him away from me,' Charlotte spat, turning her face away. 'I'll smother it myself if you don't get that thing away from me!'

Jane barely recognised her sister. It felt unbelievable, but she reasoned it must be the pain or just overwhelming emotion. She would feel better soon. 'Will you name him?' Jane pleaded.

'No!' Charlotte yelled as loudly as Jane had ever heard. 'I hate him. What don't you understand about that? Leave me and take that creature with you.'

Jane fled, clutching the silent newborn, running to the attic room she had set up herself, using her paltry savings, to make Charlotte feel comfortable. She'd bought a rocking chair and a new crib for her sister's child; everything else was old or borrowed. Her mother had deigned to send funds for the child's layette, but coming to visit anytime soon was clearly expecting too much, according to her recent letter.

I'll leave it to you, Jane, to get your sister through the hardest moments, and then she needs to focus on regaining her full strength and figure in order to secure her marriage to Edmund Cavendish on Saturday 7 March. I'm sure you will raise my grandchild to the best of your ability.

That was that! Her first grandchild! The note was heartless. No wonder Charlotte was so pitiless and cruel. She was their mother all over again.

3

To this day, close to age thirty, Guy Attwood sometimes felt dizzy when he looked up at the twisting circular staircase and remembered himself as a youngster, being dared to run up to the slim ledge that traced around the Great Hall of Blenheim Palace. He had gone high enough in those days to make even the most courageous feel daunted. But his efforts weren't born from courage so much as adoration. All he'd wanted to do at age seven was please the fellow grinning up at him from sixty feet below.

'Come on, squit! You can do it,' the teenager had yelled. Winston was only six or seven years older, but the age gap had felt like a chasm back then.

Guy could recall being close enough to see the brushstrokes of the painted ceiling, which depicted General John Churchill, 1st Duke of Marlborough, in Roman dress, kneeling to present his plan of the Battle of Blenheim to Britannia. Then he'd cast another nervous but determined glance down at Winston, who'd had the good fortune to be born here and to call it home.

Prince George, the Duke of York, grandchild of Queen Victoria, son of King Edward VII, and third in line to the British throne, had entered the Great Hall and followed Winston's upturned gaze to where Guy was steadying himself on the ledge, his arms outstretched, to follow through on the dare. 'You'll kill the fellow, Winston! One slip and he's splattered.'

'He's as steady as a rat on one of your ship's ropes, watch him. Go on, Guy. Look straight ahead and show His Majesty that you aren't nearly as scared as he is for you. The ball's up there somewhere.'

The ledge was so slim, it had felt like a tightrope. He didn't think Winston had ever had the stomach to come up and risk this balancing act. Finding the lost item was just an excuse for the dare but, once he was there, it was important to find where the white ball had lodged itself against the equally white stonework.

He'd found it, to the cheers of Winston and an impressed nod from the adult royal. And when the ball landed on the black and white marble tiles, Winston failing to stop its trajectory, it was the duke who caught it deftly before it bounced anywhere near the great vase balanced on a nearby pillar.

'Oh, good catch, your highness!' Winston said. 'Come on, Guy, get down the stairs. We're picnicking on the lawns, apparently. There're warm scones with jam and clotted cream, and I'm not missing those.'

The Duke of York had already gone by the time Guy had clambered down the winding staircase and won a grin from his friend.

'No more balls in here, my friend,' Winston warned.

'Only our own,' Guy remembered saying, winning an explosion of amusement.

That memory felt sharp and brightly etched in an endless summer of laughter. Now Guy stood here, two dozen summers later, contemplating King Edward's death. He'd travelled to Blenheim Palace after the news had broken. Feeling downcast about the man he'd admired for his wide appeal across all levels of society, he felt it right to come here, to where he'd met the King and his family on various occasions. Deep down this was also a place of great comfort for him: Blenheim had been a centre of school holidays, freedom and fun. Winston now lived in London but back then had regularly invited Guy here for school holidays, and invariably Guy accepted, preferring the company of his pal to going home.

Charles Spencer-Churchill, 9th Duke of Marlborough, happened to be at the palace when the despatches circulated throughout the nation that the King was gravely ill and Guy headed to Blenheim for the weekend to get away from all the gossip and anxiety in London.

'You don't mind me turning up, do you, Sunny?' Guy asked upon his arrival. The nickname came from Charles's earlier title, the Earl of Sunderland. Guy had been present when the King and Queen had invested him as a Knight of the Order of the Garter at Buckingham Palace. In fact, he'd been around the Spencer-Churchills for most of his life and considered them close friends.

'Not at all. I think you and Winston see more of Blenheim than your own homes.'

'Happy memories from our much younger days,' Guy admitted. 'A safe place.'

The Duke nodded, but Guy felt awkward: Charles had once admitted to him and Winston that as much as he loved Blenheim Palace, it held only bitter recollections for him. He was referring, of course, to his loveless marriage to the spectacularly wealthy and infamously adulterous Consuelo Vanderbilt, of American railroad money.

Winston scoffed when Guy had told him about the conversation. 'Don't feel too sorry for him. I know you're a bit of a prude—'

At least Winston no longer referred to him as 'squit' or 'little Guy'.

'I'm not a prude. I'm just black and white about some things.'

'Some things?' Winston laughed. 'You need to find the greys, my friend. Most of us see them and learn to live within them. It's easier. It's also kinder to others, as you'll discover. Anyway, I have it on good authority that Sunny told his new bride on their honeymoon that he had married her for the convenience of her large fortune and that he loved another. Given Consuelo had been forced to marry him by the two families, I think that's a fair indictment on Sunny. Don't get me wrong, I'm as fond of him as you, but I can't imagine marrying for anything other than pure worship.' He grinned, evidently thinking about his wife.

'You got very lucky with Clementine.'

'What about you, old chap? I hear it's bees around a honeypot.'

Guy took a slow breath at the same old enquiry, which he received from just about everyone these days. 'It must be me. I find the women my mother loves to line up so . . .'

'So what?' Winston asked, gruff and direct.

'Er . . . well, let's just say they're not like Clementine. Your wife's beauty aside, she has depth and drive. She's interesting and has a wit. She matches you.'

'You're right. I'm mad for her, and I wish the same madness to overtake you. I know it's only been two years since I proposed, but I can't imagine a day when I don't feel exactly how I feel about her now.'

Guy shrugged. 'I rest my case. I promise you, when I feel like that, I'll propose. Maybe I'll do it right here at Blenheim in the Temple of Diana, as you did.'

Winston chuckled. 'Don't leave it too long. Family and all that.'

Guy had been working in London at Kew Gardens when the shocking news of the King's death broke, and again it had felt easier to come here, where there was always a bed for him, than travel back to Merton Hall, the Attwoods' stately home in Warwickshire, up north. His parents had not been surprised when they learned he was going to Blenheim in this time of national grieving.

A dead sovereign had a rousing effect: it made everyone feel a keen desire to be home, or at least among familiar surrounds.

'Such a short reign,' his mother, Adele, had lamented when he'd called.

'But a good one,' Guy replied.

'Your reign is fast coming, Guy, when you'll need to be more present here,' his mother had counselled, seguing into a topic close to her heart. As always, her tone was compassionate. 'I suppose you're on one of your missions, are you?'

He gave a soft sigh. 'I was until news of the King's death. If only I could excite you and Father about my work for the Horticultural Society.'

'Darling, I wish your father could excite you about engineering and manufacturing. I know it's important to you and—'

'It's important for Britain, Mother. I know hunting apples seems like a hobby, but this work will save heritage apple trees up and down the country for future generations. Father laughs, I know he does, but if we let our fruit trees die away, what next? Our timber, our vegetables, our wheat, barley . . . What would happen to the single malt Dad enjoys if we lost our barley?' He sighed. 'I am gainfully employed by no less than Royal Kew, who consider my research vital. Please trust that.'

Before she could offer her expected advice, he spoke for her. 'And when I have to, Mother, I'll step up. Don't think I don't know my responsibilities to the business, but Father has all the right people in place. I've been learning about the family's different fingers in different pies since I was a boy, so I'm not that green.' The family business was in manufacturing: coal, steel and textiles.

'Your father is giving you a lot of rope.'

'I know. We've agreed that I'll relinquish this scientific pursuit when I'm thirty and commit myself fully to his empire.'

'You are almost thirty.'

'A few months yet,' he qualified, feeling petty for saying it.

'Need I remind you that we have only one heir and no spare? How many more apples do you plan to hunt, son?'

He'd nodded as he held the phone to his ear, feeling properly admonished. His parents had been understanding to a fault. It was indeed time to take his place and follow his duty. 'One,' he said, in a sudden blaze of inspiration.

'One?' she repeated. 'All right. And is it so important?'

'It is. Now that our King has passed away, it's probably the most special apple I shall ever use my sleuthing skills to find.'

He could all but hear the wheels in her mind turning. 'To mark a royal death?' she asked in a sombre tone.

'No, Mother. To mark a coronation of a new king: George, the Prince of Wales.'

'Oh, of course!' She chuckled softly and sheepishly. 'Gracious, how marvellous,' she said, sounding brighter. 'Would your friend George appreciate it?'

He laughed. 'Probably not, but the country will in terms of posterity, and Royal Kew certainly will. It shall be my final flourish . . . a farewell to my, er, youth.'

'So, what is this apple, Guy?'

The idea felt like a firework going off in his mind. He hadn't properly thought it through, but the idea was already gaining momentum. 'There's an old, old apple that's sweet and red, with bright shadings of yellow and orange. It dates back to the sixteenth century, but Kew and I believe it may just have survived – a couple of trees somewhere here in England.'

'And what do you call this apple?'

'Its old name is a Scarlet Henry.'

'Do you plan to rename it, then?'

'Yes. If I do find this . . . this treasure, then I shall formally name it the Rex – because it's for a new king.'

4

SALISBURY

September 1910

It had been four months since King Edward VII's death, in spring. The collective grieving had passed and summer had brought optimism for the reign of George V. Now, as they progressed into autumn, the coronation was on the minds of the British people.

Jane was staring at the great cedar trees in the cloister-garth; they were browning in places, losing a few of their needles to make way for new ones. She paused to check on Harry, who was walking, as instructed, around the great square of the cathedral with his wooden hoop, using a small stick to keep it rolling. He'd prefer to be running, she knew, but she'd forbidden him from making any sort of noise in rushed activity in this sacred, quiet space.

It was surprisingly peaceful today but only because it was so early. Soon the space would be busy with strollers on this early autumn day, still mild enough that the cool of the stone arches was a gift. She was grateful for the opportunity to enjoy this ancient cloister, which she cherished.

Young Henry Saville, who went by Harry, turned the corner and was headed her way.

'Come on, shall we start back?' she asked as he neared. 'I promised Aunt Hortense we'd visit this week.'

He pulled a face. 'She's always telling me off.'

'That's because you never sit still.'

'She smells funny.' He'd stopped the revolutions of the hoop with ease, without even needing to look at it.

'No, she doesn't. You just don't like her perfume.'

'She's ancient and she doesn't really like me.'

'She is old, yes, and probably finds the noise of children a bit wearying. She hasn't got long to go, Harry. She's ailing and will probably pass away soon. I can't imagine she'll see out the year, if I'm being honest, so it's important we visit. Let's be kind. And besides, she likes to see how you've grown.'

He nodded and sighed his agreement. 'Why do people stare at us, Mummy?'

Jane blinked; she hadn't anticipated the switch of topics.

'I try to be good, but I see them staring. Sometimes they point.' He was looking straight at her, with a puzzled expression as he awaited her answer.

How could she tell him the truth? No seven-year-old needed that sort of reality. A little boy needed security and praise to give him the best chance to grow up confident, even if they were living mostly off the kindness of another these days.

'Could it be that you're just such a handsome boy?' she said.

He gave her a sighing look but also a shy grin.

'I really believe it could be that. I have no other explanation,' she lied, giving a dramatic shrug to widen his grin. 'Ice cream?'

He gave a little jump of pleasure, locking his small arms around her waist, the query forgotten and slipping away as his hoop clattered to the flagstones. 'Ice cream,' he repeated, his voice filled with gleeful anticipation. 'Is the man here?'

Jane never tired of her son's hugs. She bent to kiss the top of his head and inhaled the aromatic fragrance of his gentle, homemade shampoo: the drops of rosemary oil she'd added to shavings of Castile soap and rainwater. Sometimes she used oil of rose for her own, but Mr Angus had said a boy smelling of roses gave the wrong idea. She'd listened. There was no other father figure in Harry's life and William Angus, for whom she kept house, seemed to be filling that role more and more, even though he was old enough to be Harry's grandfather. He had become a wonderful companion for her too.

'I suspect the ice-cream man might be right outside the Cathedral Close, yes. He gets good passing traffic on days like this. Come on. It might be a bit early, though, Harry.'

'What if he's not there?' Harry began to worry, taking her hand and hurrying alongside her.

'Then I promise we'll go back later.'

'Maybe we can get William an ice cream too.'

She laughed. 'Maybe, but it might melt down your arm before we could get it back to him.'

'Then I'd have to lick it . . .' Harry cast a glance up at her, a sly smile on his face.

She waggled a finger. 'I know what you're up to.'

The Wall's man was indeed there, his bike parked just outside the Cathedral Close at the main North Gate leading into High Street. The arch over the carriageway had been built in stone during the mid-1300s, she'd learned, with a room on one side and a staircase leading to an upper room on the opposite side, but it had been reconstructed several times. They approached it, Harry trying to speed her.

'I like walking under this arch,' he said. 'Do they really close these gates? They look so heavy.'

'Every night for hundreds of years. We're all locked in each evening and let out each morning.'

'Are we prisoners?'

She laughed. 'If we are, we're happy prisoners. No, we're extremely lucky to live in the Cathedral Close.'

'Does that mean we're posh?'

She didn't answer that, and he'd spotted the ice-cream man ahead, so this thought would melt away as fast as the creamy treat. She glanced up to the statue of Edward VII, a modern addition to the six-hundred-year-old gate, added only the previous year in honour of his visit. And now he had finished his reign and a new royal was awaiting his crowning. The King's death had cast a dreadful gloom over spring, although the timing was kind, the summer's sunshine helping to lift people's spirits. She knew most were looking forward to the crowning of his son next year.

As they passed through the gate into High Street, Jane was reminded of why she had lived in this city these last seven years, staying long after her mother had sent her and Charlotte there. Harry broke free of her grip, though, and took her memories with him. She didn't need those bad thoughts on a bright day like today.

He skipped up to the cart attached to the ice-cream man's bicycle.

'Morning, young sir, and what's your name?'

'I'm Henry Saville, but everyone calls me Harry.'

Jane strolled up behind her son, smiling. 'Good morning,' she said.

The man winked at her. 'Now, Harry's a fine name for a strong lad who will grow into a strong man and always look out for his pretty mother. I'm still getting set up, but I shan't be long, young Harry. You're obviously eager.'

'Yes, we're sorry to be so early,' Jane said.

'No need to be sorry. I love my customers lining up and looking forward to their ice creams. There,' he said, closing a lid. 'I'm ready. What can I get you, young man?'

'Can I have a cornet, please?'

'You certainly may,' the vendor said, expertly grabbing the new-fangled wafer cone and opening the refrigerator's lid to dig into the tin of ice cream. He fashioned an orb of the deliciously creamy frozen treat and pressed it into place before handing it over.

'Thank you,' Harry said, eyes wide as he took the cone, his tongue already reaching for the ball of ice cream.

'And madam? May I get you one too?'

'Er, those cornets look lovely, although I admit I'm haunted by the penny licks of my childhood. Those tiny glasses with a miserably small scoop of ice cream, re-used without being washed.' She shuddered. 'The lack of cleanliness and disea—'

'Long gone, madam,' he dared to interrupt. 'We don't sell those any longer. The cornets are our latest and they're generous, but how about an ice-cream sandwich – you know, it's a slab of ice cream wrapped in paper?'

'Oh, yes, please.'

He beamed, reaching in again, this time to retrieve a small oblong of ice cream that was, as promised, neatly enveloped in translucent paper. He handed her the treat. 'Happy to throw in some wafers, madam, but I imagine you'll tear away the paper and use it to keep your fingers clear of the ice cream.'

'I shall do just that, sir.' She grinned. 'How much do I owe you?'

'Ha'penny each,' he said.

'How much is that, Harry?' Jane asked her son.

'A penny,' he said, his lips covered with melted ice cream.

'Well done, lad. There, I knew you were a smart one. You can come and sell ice cream for us anytime.'

Jane found a copper penny in her purse and paid the man. 'Please come again to this spot,' she said, smiling.

He gave her a salute in response and she turned to leave, only now realising people had begun to queue behind them.

A woman looked her up and down and, covering her mouth, whispered something to a friend. The pair shot a glance at Harry, then back at Jane. Jane didn't need to hear them to know what was being exchanged. She gently pushed Harry's shoulder, urging him forward before he could see them. 'Come on, darling. Let's head back.'

They retraced their steps under the main gate and entered the grand close of the cathedral, the largest in all of Britain, at over eighty acres. Jane could believe it. It was like a hamlet within the city, with its sprawling Choristers Green in the centre, around which majestic buildings and houses clustered. Some of their origins could be traced back to the thirteenth century. Already a couple of people were beginning to lay out blankets for a morning picnic so their children could run around on the grass. Couples were out taking a stroll, arms linked, some with prams, some with dogs, enjoying the fresh air of this September morning. They were making the best of the dying summer.

She smiled away her exasperation at the women in the queue. They didn't matter.

Harry skipped along beside her, happily ignorant of the attention and somehow managing to keep his hoop moving and lick his ice cream at the same time, although she was sure the cornet would lose its delicious spherical sweet treat.

'Here, Harry, let's sit and finish our ice creams.'

'May I go and stroke that dog?'

'Yes, but you must ask those people seated nearby if you may first. Remember what I've told you about other people's dogs?'

He nodded gravely, recalling the rule, and hurried away, steadying his ice cream, the hoop left at her feet. She watched him ask and be given permission. The labrador couldn't have been happier to have someone give it attention, she saw, and Jane lifted a hand in thanks before settling on the grass. She raised her face to the sun as its thin warmth landed, and closed her eyes and let the moment carry her away. Although she didn't like to press on the memory in quiet minutes such as these, the peace always tended to take her back to her first months with Harry.

Harry really was such a dear little fellow; she had loved him on sight, in stark contrast to her sister's attitude towards the child. Jane recalled in vivid clarity the second she had been handed the squalling infant, his face almost purple with his loud cries. She'd cradled him in fresh linens and offered him to his mother.

But these memories did her no good. They were like a malignant tumour, which grew a little more each time she paid them any attention. Remembering all the fear and naivety of the Jane of seven years ago, she looked at her son now – yes, *her* son – and knew she'd done a good job. He was safe, healthy, bright. She'd educated him herself until recently, setting him up well, she felt, for his current life, which had improved immeasurably since his audition to be a cathedral chorister earlier this year.

He'd been selected immediately for his pure voice and pitch. Jane had watched on with pride as Harry was presented with his surplice in an old ritual. Every new chorister for centuries had had his head gently lowered and tapped against the Cathedral's 'bumping stone'.

'I'm not really sure how this tradition has come about,' the rector admitted, beaming at the parents of the three new choristers. 'But the boys seem to enjoy the fun of it.'

Jane had stared at the bumping stone on the south aisle of the cathedral and marvelled at the darkened surface in the marked dip of the stone. How many heads had bumped it over the centuries? She'd smiled at Harry's delight when it was his turn to be congratulated and welcomed as their young new recruit.

So now Harry was a cathedral schoolboy because he was a chorister, and to her mind he was the happiest, brightest little fellow. He returned to her side. 'The dog's called Harry too, and he licked my face.'

Harry couldn't have looked happier, she thought. 'That's because your face has ice cream on it. Come on, let's get you home and washed up.'

They both turned and waved farewell to the dog's owners. As they walked down towards the cathedral – Harry's second home, it felt like – and turned left into the North Walk, Jane made a stern promise to herself. *I swear a pact to myself that I shall never willingly remember that time of Harry's birth again.*

There! It was done. Harry belonged to no one but her. He had known only the warmth and smell of her skin close to his; *she* was his mother. The woman who had carried him in her womb was simply that: a carrier, a receptacle. Jane forced herself to accept that Charlotte's only moment of mercy was in her decision not to abort her pregnancy. For this small heartbeat of clarity and rare grace, Jane was grateful, for she couldn't imagine her life without her son.

Harry pushed the final triangle of his cornet wafer into his mouth and began to speed up, spinning his hoop faster.

'Be careful, Harry, you could choke,' she warned him.

He laughed, pausing at their gate and opening his mouth wide to show her. 'All gone.'

She laughed at his antics. 'Good. All right, let me just clean up your mouth. We don't want William tut-tutting. You know how tidy he is.'

Harry squirmed against her ministrations with a handkerchief until finally she let him loose to open the gate and skip down the gently sloping path that led to the house. She winced as he nearly ran into a woman who suddenly emerged from the front door.

'Look out, laddie,' Mr Angus said, appearing behind her with a smile in his voice. 'You don't want to run over Mrs Garnet, do you?'

Harry looked startled and Jane was at his side in a couple of hurried strides. 'Oh, I'm so sorry,' she said, only being polite; Harry had not actually got within a foot of the visitor.

'That boy needs some control,' the stranger snapped.

Jane was stunned. 'Yes, yes, he's always in a hurry. We'll be more careful.'

She was met with a soft sneer and tightly pursed lips that reminded her of sucking on a lemon, as she used to dare her friends to do when they were children. Except this woman's soured look gave off no hint of fun.

'Mind that you do!' Mrs Garnet said, walking around Jane as though she might catch a disease if their sleeves brushed. 'Good day to you, Mr Angus,' she said over her shoulder, making her way to the front garden gate. 'I'll thank you to consider our conversation carefully.'

'Oh, I will, Mrs Garnet,' he said, lifting a hand in farewell with a cheerful smile. Then he dropped his voice. 'Silly old goat.'

Harry exploded into gleeful laughter.

'William!' Jane said, a look of wide-eyed admonishment cast his way.

'Hello, Jane, my dear. Hello, old chap. Come on. I didn't offer the goat so much as a biscuit. Actually, that's an insult to goats – I like goats. She's more like a dried-up old prune.'

Together, Harry and William Angus walked into the house laughing. Jane looked back up the path, guessing now what the 'old prune' had been up to.

5

Guy was staring out at the fields, which slid away to the left as the train from London Waterloo made its merry, chugging way into Wiltshire. He'd taken this journey several times already and although this was, as his father had suggested, the last-gasp attempt at finding the elusive apple, he forced himself to remain optimistic.

The truth was, he was feeling privately mortified by his own behaviour; he knew he was running away from his responsibilities. Not just to his family, but to a woman who had cultivated a perfect life in her mind, which involved him as her husband. He had never deliberately given the impression that he considered marrying her, but women of a certain age – and their mothers – could do a very good job of convincing themselves that a bachelor of a particular age and status was 'the one'.

Since his school days his mother had told him that he would one day become the focus of speculation. 'It will begin with the mother, Guy.'

'What sort of speculation?' he'd asked at fourteen, frowning. 'I haven't done anything.'

'Nor do you have to do anything in this case, son. This is happening with or without your permission. Mothers who have daughters in a certain strata of society will begin to watch the social pages. This starts years out, Guy, my darling. In fact, it may have already begun for you. If there's a particularly wily mother out there who, perhaps, has only one daughter, she may be looking at her one chance to make the perfect marriage.'

'Marriage?'

'Yes, darling. That heinous thing that manacles you to one person.'

He remembered laughing at that. 'I'm not thinking of marriage, Mother, but if I was, it would be to that lovely barmaid we see coming out of the local—'

'Guy, really! I don't want to know about your boyish longings. Share that with your father. What I'm discussing with you now is really quite serious.'

He schooled his features to be attentive; his mother rarely took this tone. 'So what do I do?'

'Nothing you can do. These mothers will watch you from afar. They'll watch us as a family and take note of what we do, where we go, what we acquire, which events you start to be seen at and, particularly, who your friendship group is. The mere fact that you are so friendly with the Churchills and the Duke of York is just fuel to the fire. And your handsome looks will fan the flames.'

He scoffed again at the compliment, which every mother surely said to every son. 'But don't I have a say?'

Adele Attwood laughed. 'Of course you do, but all this spying is important for these mothers to decide if you are worth pursuing. I can tell you now, you are worth all that investment and more, because you are an only child. Every mother of every daughter who moves in our society will already have an eye on you.'

'That's horrible, Mother. I feel . . . invaded.'

'It's just how it is.'

'I'll choose my own wife when the time comes,' he assured her.

'Famous last words, darling. You're already on a list of eligible husbands and, mark my words, mothers will be surreptitiously watching you, everywhere from the theatre to dances.' She put up a hand. 'But don't despair, son, you've got me. I'll help you sort the wheat from the chaff, so to speak.'

He was as good as his word. He'd dodged, ducked and woven a path of bachelorhood ever since. He escorted countless young women to balls, parties, theatrical shows, concerts and official royal events, but he never lingered in their lives long enough for any of them – or their mothers – to get a firm grip on him. This was mostly thanks to his research and study, which took him roaming around England.

But even Guy knew the time would come. It had eventually arrived eighteen months ago, when a woman called Maud, wife of Arthur Clarence, owner of a steelworks in the north, met Adele at an art exhibition. Guy had since pieced together that it was not, in fact, a chance meeting but a concerted mission that had been worked out with military precision.

Maud and Arthur's only daughter, Eleanor, was two years Guy's junior and, in Maud's opinion, an ideal option for the Attwoods to consider for their only son. Adele had not told him of this meeting or any subsequent conversations – that intelligence was garnered from discussions with Eleanor – only that he was asked to attend a family day for one of his father's manufacturing businesses, where all the local workers were given a splendid picnic on the lawns of Merton Hall.

Then, seemingly by chance, the Clarences would be visiting that weekend to see some friends in Warwickshire and, what a coincidence, they could call in to visit the Attwoods on the very weekend that Guy would be up from the south. The family strolled the lawns and chatted to folk, were introduced as friends of the Attwoods, and were asked to judge the children's fancy dress contest and pick the winner for the hamper of goodies, which was the big prize of the day.

His mother had been right: women were clever creatures when they set their minds to a task. He was the task, of course. And, yes, Eleanor caught his attention. She was pretty and her conversation didn't bore him. She had travelled and liked to read. They were friendly at the picnic and, at their mothers' collective urging, agreed that Eleanor would accompany Guy to see *Tom Jones* at the Apollo in London's West End.

'Guy loves that story about the foundling,' his mother assured the younger woman.

'I've read Henry Fielding's book and admired it,' Eleanor said.

Guy was impressed that she'd read a favourite of his. 'Oh, yes? And why did it affect you?'

'I like the way the narrator talks directly to the reader. I was no longer an observer of the story but one of its characters, in a way. I was participating.'

That compelling argument, delivered with a gentle shrug and a smile, captivated him: here was a woman speaking his language. So he agreed to meet her in London and escort her to the show. They enjoyed their evening and later, over a supper, talked candidly.

'I'm afraid my mother is looking to lure you into our world, Guy. I thought it only fair to warn you.'

He liked her honesty and the way she lifted her shoulder in an embarrassed shrug, a similar gesture to one she'd given on the staff picnic day. 'How scary is the danger?' he quipped.

'Well, her web is sticky. She's a very determined hunter.'

'Am I her only prey?'

'I have to be truthful and say yes. She's made her decision.'

He actually laughed. 'Do you not have any say?'

'Oh, yes, absolutely. I'm their beloved only daughter. My brother is happily married, already giving them grandchildren. So there's just me now, and at six years past my twentieth birthday, by which time my mother believes all girls should be engaged, she's getting worried that I'm being picky.'

'As you should be, Eleanor.'

She looked down into her food. 'The thing is, Guy,' she said, returning her gaze to him, 'I have picked.'

'Eleanor . . .' he began hesitantly.

'I know it's fast. But I'm helpless in this. I love you, Guy.'

'This is our second meeting. You don't even know me!'

'Yes, I do. Don't laugh, but I think love is about the soul. My soul knows yours. It yearns to be with yours.'

He looked away and cleared his throat, embarrassed, and he knew she could tell he didn't know what to say – certainly that the words she wanted to hear were not rushing to his mouth. He tried a softer explanation. 'Eleanor, I'm nowhere near making that sort of decision.'

'Your mother thinks otherwise,' she said gently.

'Yes, Mother and Father are very ready for me to make an engagement announcement. They want heirs, they want the sound of children's laughter ringing out around Merton.'

'But?'

'Knowing my parents as I do, they'd want me to be happy in that engagement, and that happiness only arrives when it's *my* decision – without everyone else who thinks they should meddle.'

She nodded. 'I know. And believe me, Guy, if I didn't feel about you as I do, I too would be recoiling at being manoeuvred. But we're the perfect match!'

'You're lovely, Eleanor, but—'

'Wait. Before you say whatever kind placation you were about to, can we be friends? Can we perhaps be companions for a while, so that you can test the relationship and see if it grows on you? I agree, we have barely had time to learn about each other but, as I say, my heart has already spoken. I can be patient for yours to do the same.'

'And what if it doesn't?'

She shrugged again. 'I don't know. But I'm prepared to wait. Are you happy to be my companion and see if we share mutual feelings?'

'Er . . . this is unusual.'

'No, I think it's wise. And so long as you don't humiliate me, Guy, by publicly seeing other women and allowing gossipy tongues to embarrass me and my family, then I'm happy to remain patient. I will not press you.'

'How much tolerance do you have?' he asked, half-joking, half-serious.

'Plenty,' she replied with a smile to show she was joining in good-naturedly. 'Let me be clear, because I realise this is a decision that affects not only us but the lives and wellbeing of our families. I love you, and I would marry you tomorrow if you asked me to. I do not require a ring on my finger for the time being, but after tonight, if you allow me, I shall consider myself promised to you. I will not step out with any other man, and while I won't put the same restriction on you not to attend parties or events, I will ask you not to appear with another woman on your arm. Go to any gatherings you like as a bachelor.' She looked embarrassed suddenly. 'Of course what you do in private is your business.'

'Eleanor, you do need to get to know me because I don't go to many gatherings, as you put it. I'm really very reluctant to attend parties or crowded events. Search your heart, because that's what you're facing if we end up marrying. I am not social, and your family is.'

'I don't have to search my heart over you. I loathe parties, but they've been the most sensible way to meet others. No obligation but a chance to see what's on offer, you could say.'

That made him laugh and she seemed to enjoy his amusement.

He opened his palms. 'All right. If it pleases you, I will gladly accompany you if we have mutual events but, Eleanor, if I get wind that your mother is touting you as the soon-to-be Mrs Guy Attwood, I will retreat. I have made no such promise.'

'I understand. I will not permit her to do that. But we need some sort of time in which to frame a decision.'

'I can't set that now. Perhaps we can consider that in a few months' time.'

'Are we talking years, Guy, for an engagement? Because I am giving you my very best years as I wait for your decision.'

'Two years at the most.'

Now, in his memory of that day, Guy could still see her eyes widening. Then she nodded. 'Two years it is. Before I turn twenty-eight.'

His two years were close to being up.

He'd bought time for one more trip from his parents, but it had not come about without a few battle injuries. These had been inflicted during his recent visit to Merton Hall, not too far from Stratford-upon-Avon. The manor was set on more than one hundred acres of landscaped grounds, originally designed by Lancelot 'Capability' Brown, which included a Palladian bridge, perhaps Guy's favourite place on the property. From even a young age he'd appreciated its austere looks and lines, which adhered strictly to proportion, symmetry and classical form. His mother had confessed she was sure the manor had once been the home of a mistress to a medieval king. But the historical records hinted towards something else.

'You know, I'm still to find the proof,' Guy had told her, 'but I'm convinced it's more than possible that Sir John Vanbrugh, the architect of Blenheim, had a hand in designing Merton. We know the Oxford master mason Townesend, who worked at Blenheim Palace, was involved here.'

'Oh, is that why you love Blenheim so much?' his mother remarked, with a gentle look of disapproval.

'I go to Blenheim because Winston's usually there, and a lot of my work is in the west.'

'Not during your school years, though. I won't begin to tell you how hurt I used to be that you preferred going to his home rather than your own.' His mother had never complained and, although he'd managed to ignore any guilt as a child, he could now see the pain he had surely caused by what must have felt like indifference. He couldn't admit to his parents that it was lonely and boring in this enormous manor, with his father always busy and his mother lost to her creative pursuits. It was no place for a curious, active boy to find any fun. Meanwhile, Blenheim was all warmth, sport, fun and roguish behaviour in the company of Winston and his constant stream of visitors . . . including beautiful young women.

'You sure it's not to avoid your dear parents, who only want the best for you?'

He kissed his mother's cheek, sitting down to the breakfast table, crowded with a magnificent spread. 'No. I love you both very much.'

'And how about the ever-patient Eleanor? Do you love her?'

'Still being patient,' he admitted, not wishing to discuss her, because it led to angst all round.

'Oh, hurry up, Guy. We're all you have, darling, other than Cousin Hugh. You know he's constantly angling to get in on the business, but your father wants an Attwood at its head.'

'Hugh is an opportunist at the best of times,' Guy said, shrugging.

'Which is why it's time, old chap,' his father said, putting down his newspaper to finally join the conversation.

'I know,' Guy admitted.

'Look, I think your idea is intriguing, if a fraction curious. It will no doubt be greeted by fanfare in the right circles if you pull it off.'

'Thank you.'

'But it doesn't – as they say – pay the rent, my boy.'

Guy stayed quiet. These were such well-trodden tracks that he and his father had walked.

His mother left the table, muttering about checking on a fresh pot of coffee, but Guy imagined it was to leave her two men to thrash out a familiar subject.

'I'm not getting any younger . . . or healthier.' Arthur Attwood was still an imposing man, though he'd had some health concerns of late.

'I know that too.'

'I know you know, Guy, because we've spoken about this repeatedly. I've given you a lot of rope, haven't I? I don't think I've been unreasonable.'

'Not at all,' Guy answered truthfully – and miserably. His father had been incredibly generous and understanding towards his only son.

'I've promised your mother the grand tour and all that. I think in her mind she lives in another age – a golden age, perhaps. But I can afford to give her what she dreams of. She's never been one for being lavished with jewels, or parties. Even this enormous pile of a house can be very lonely for her without the sound of a child's laughter . . . or a grandchild's.' He gave Guy a meaningful stare, and when Guy rolled his eyes, he put his hands up in surrender. 'Well, it's time. Time for everything that you know is your duty and ultimate responsibility: marriage, family, the business, this house.'

Guy nodded. 'I can't promise marriage, Father, not until I find someone worthy.'

'Worthy? Good grief, Guy. I would say Eleanor Clarence is more than worthy, based just on her tolerance of your being so rarely in her company. And still she holds a blazing candle for you. What does "worthy" comprise in your mind?'

'Lots of things that Eleanor is but, Father, may I speak frankly?'

'I would hate for you to be anything but that in my company.'

'Well, I guess I'm looking for my equal, I suppose.'

Arthur frowned. 'I know you don't mean money.'

'Certainly not. I know this sounds quaint, but I want to marry someone who makes my breath turn shallow, someone I couldn't imagine living without.'

Arthur gave a faint smile. 'Not quaint, more like a fantasy.'

'Why is that wrong?'

'It's not wrong, Guy, but it's not realistic. Eleanor is a wonderful partner for you.'

'I worry that she only appears that way to all of you.'

'Explain what you mean.'

'Eleanor is so obliging. She never rubs me up the wrong way. She understands me well, and so I feel we've become very good friends – but that's where it stops.'

'And you haven't . . . um . . .?'

Guy blinked. 'No! I mean, that's the point. She feels like a sister, not a lover. She's not a woman I can see matching me year for year as we grow older together.'

'Oh dear. Well, sister isn't good.'

'Exactly. She's lovely, but I don't feel that fire in my belly for her.'

'Does she know this?'

Guy shook his head miserably. 'I've searched myself for answers, and then when I forced myself to be honest, I realised that, as nice as Eleanor is, I don't love her. I enjoy her friendship, but that's as far as it extends.'

Arthur looked at him stern-faced. 'You need to let her go, then. She's been keeping herself for you.'

'I know, I know,' Guy said, sounding despondent. 'But whenever I broach the subject, she doesn't want to have the conversation. She says things like "Give it more time, Guy." Or "You've been so preoccupied, Guy, no wonder you haven't had time for me." She's just too flexible, too generous, too understanding. It's . . . it's sort of dull. But I don't wish to hurt her.'

'And yet you'll hurt her by not being honest.'

Guy gave a long, slow sigh. 'I can't win.'

'No, but you'll end the pain for both of you if you're candid.'

'I'll have to be blunt, because trying to be diplomatic doesn't work. But I don't know how she'll react if I sound cruel.'

'That's her problem, not yours. I know you've been quite direct from the start, but you've allowed that to become a bit murky over time. I don't blame Eleanor for thinking she's on track for marriage. Her mother certainly believes it.'

Guy swallowed hard. He knew his father was right. 'We put a deadline on it.'

'And when does that expire?' his father asked, sounding bemused. 'Sounds very businesslike.'

'Yes, exactly. It's an arrangement . . . It doesn't please me at all and yet I don't wish her injury. It expires next month.'

'Why not tell her now or last week, or last year, then?'

'I've tried!'

'And there's no other woman involved?'

'Absolutely not. And the women I've met who can match our . . . let's say *standing*,' he said diplomatically. 'Well, I find them the opposite of my mother.'

'What do you mean?'

'Well, you've described her rather accurately. She does not covet possessions. She's more cerebral. She loves her art, her garden, her books, her few friends, travelling the world . . . and the two of us.'

'Indeed. We're lucky men.'

'So I think if I am fortunate to find a woman who loves me for who I am and not for what I own, and I find her hard to live without, then I'll know I've found the right person to share the rest of my years with.'

'Well, I shall have to hope alongside your mother that this woman exists and that your worlds collide somehow, because I need you to take on the business. And your mother wants another generation of Attwoods to grow up in this house.'

Guy nodded. 'How do you feel about taking off for months on end for this trip?'

He was surprised and delighted to hear his father chuckle.

'Oh, well, your mother's been such a good old stick about everything – my endless work and meetings, my grumpiness. I feel this is the least I can do. She's never complained and has always been there for me. We wish to leave shortly. Can I count on you, Guy?'

He'd not heard his father so plaintive before. A small, internal voice pleaded with him to give his father the right answer, but a selfish part of him wanted to have one final hurrah and leave his mark for the new king. He attempted to negotiate his position without letting his father down entirely. 'Yes, but—'

'No buts, Guy,' his father interrupted, cutting the air with his hand emphatically. 'This is it. This is the moment I need you. I don't want to wait much longer to give your mother what she longs for.'

All humour had fled the room.

Guy couldn't quite believe he was shaking his head, but he needed to say it. 'You can count on me, but please give me until the end of autumn. I'll be home for the start of November.'

'So you can head off on another one of your harebrained excursions to find a bloody apple?'

Guy flinched. His father had never once struck him; any look of disappointment on the older man's face was enough to punish Guy. And neither had his father ever had to raise his voice, other than in alarm. He could not recall him shouting even once in anger. This was new. His father was angry.

'Harebrained?' he repeated in shock.

'Grow up, Guy! Finding a rare piece of fruit is not going to leave your mark on the world or impress a king. I'll tell you what impresses people. Sadly, it's wealth. Don't you think I had dreams? Don't you think I would have liked to forge my own path?'

Guy desperately hoped his mother didn't return right now. 'Didn't you?'

'I did what my father expected of me. And, Guy, I was working under his rule from fourteen. You've had twice as many years than I did to have your fun in whichever way you chose. I gave you that time because I didn't have it. The fact that you've spent those years in the pursuit of apples and history is your choice. You could have become lazy and louche on my money, but you haven't. For that I'm grateful, but come on, son. Give it up now. Take the reins.' Arthur Attwood held out his hand to close the deal.

Guy could feel his fingers twitching in eagerness to please his father and to fulfil his role; he'd never lacked a sense of duty, but he also needed to fulfil this dream or he'd surely live to regret it – and blame his father. 'Just this last search?' he appealed, hearing how pathetic it sounded. 'This is not for personal glory but for Britain.'

His father gave a sound of disgust. 'Our business is for Britain! We employ thousands of hardworking people, feeding families, keeping the bloody lights on and the country turning . . . that's for king and country, not a stupid apple!'

'Father, this is for future generations. If we lose this apple, then—'

His father gave a choked laugh. 'Seriously, Guy? Who would care but you?'

And there it was. The bald truth.

Who indeed would care but him? And yet it stung like no other words that had ever hurt him. 'Well, I'm sorry to be so disappointing, Father,' Guy snarled, unable to help himself. He hated his petulance, especially now that his mother had entered in that moment, smiling, only to be drowned by his sour remark.

'Oh, Guy,' she breathed, her features crumpling. 'Arthur, how could you?'

Her husband stood, pushing back his chair in deep annoyance. 'Adele, I offered our son a hand. He has known this day was coming, but he continues to put his own hobby above our family.'

'That's not true,' Guy bleated, looking between his parents. He needed to take control. 'This is not a hobby. I get paid for what I do.'

'A pittance!' his father said. 'It is little more than a private passion, and while I understand that Royal Kew admires your endeavours, I would personally admire you far more if you stepped up and looked after all the families who rely on us.'

Oh, his father knew how to hit the mark. No wonder he'd made such a success of broadening his grandfather's empire.

'Father, Mother, I am leaving now. I will return in less than a month, and I promise you that I will commit myself entirely to running the business.'

She spoke for her husband. 'Then we shall start making arrangements. Your father and I will go to Paris after Christmas and start a slow journey into southern Europe and beyond from then. All right, Arthur?'

Guy's father took a long slow breath and nodded before silently leaving the room.

6

Staring out the train window, Guy felt a fresh wave of guilt. He'd tried to defend his position, reasoning privately that he'd worked hard as an only son to please his parents. He'd aced his exams and been good at sport, had learned at his father's heel about the business, and taken accounting lessons at night so he could understand cash flow, to cover wages and costs while generating profits. He'd kept his lifestyle modest, never boasted about his family's wealth and been an affectionate and interested son. Some of his peers were truly disappointing to their parents, but Guy's father couldn't summon a single episode during childhood where he'd let the family down, publicly or otherwise.

And still his father wanted more.

You're nearly thirty, on your way to middle age. It's not a lot to ask.

And that inner voice was right. When his father most needed his support, Guy, his only son, had let him down.

He sighed, his good mood on returning to Wiltshire evaporating. Maybe he needed to cut this trip short, just go home and get on with his life – and marry Eleanor.

Eleanor. Another problem. He'd begged leave from her too, leaving her puzzled but used to his ways. If only she'd fight back or question him! But again she allowed him to do as he pleased. While he wasn't carousing or gambling or drinking, he was still not with her. What was in her mind? Why didn't she make demands? Could he spend his life with someone who gave in without a fight?

The woman opposite, travelling with her mother, accidentally tapped his shin with her foot, bringing him out of his thoughts.

'Oh my gosh, I'm so sorry,' she said, sounding mortified.

'Please, no harm done. It didn't hurt.'

'Even so, forgive me for being so clumsy.'

'Please don't think on it again,' he reassured her.

'Er, my mother eats like a bird and I've brought enough sandwiches to feed the whole train, it feels like. Could we interest you in a small picnic?'

He didn't want to engage in chitchat, but Winston had accused him on more than a few occasions of having a slightly frosty exterior, and he didn't want to keep pressing the bruise of his dark thoughts. He decided to be sociable. Contriving a smile, he introduced himself. 'Only if you have spare. My name is Guy Attwood.'

She blinked. 'Of *the* Attwoods? Warwickshire?'

That was precisely why he didn't like to open up. 'Er, yes, actually.' He should have lied. Now a whole new conversation would open up.

'Oh, good grief, how wonderful. I'm Mrs Margaret Bridge, and I do believe my mother knows yours . . . er, her name is Mary Jameson.'

He shook his head, still smiling. 'Forgive me, I wouldn't know.'

'That's all right. Do remember her to your good mother when you next speak. Now here,' she said cheerfully. 'It's cold ham with homemade apple chutney.' She paused, momentarily anxious. 'I do hope you like apples?'

He laughed. 'More than you can imagine, Mrs Bridge.'

'Really? Why do you say that?'

Laying out his handkerchief on his lap, Guy took a small bite of the sandwich. 'Delicious, thank you.'

'You're so welcome. Eat as much as you can.'

'These two will do.'

'So, you were saying . . .?'

Margaret Bridge was clearly starved of conversation, because her mother sat quietly beside her, chewing, saying nothing. He now wondered whether his neighbour had kicked his shin on purpose in the hope of starting something.

He frowned, trying to pretend he'd already lost his train of thought.

'Apples,' she nudged, chuckling.

He sighed inwardly. 'Ah, yes. I have been known to study them.'

'Truly? That's rather splendid.'

'I think so.'

'In what capacity, may I enquire?' She saw his hesitation. 'Do forgive me for my questions. My mother is extremely hard of hearing, and it can become quite a trial for our fellow passengers to have a simple conversation with her. But this is a long journey and I've forgotten my book. I hope you don't mind indulging a bored woman with some conversation?'

'Not at all,' he said, 'although how can you be bored with this glorious landscape?'

She smiled. 'I make this journey regularly to visit my parents. I'm taking my mother back after a visit to London, but I plan to stay a couple of months.'

'Wiltshire is a splendid place to live.'

'Yes, they've been very happy there for decades.'

'In Salisbury?'

'Yes. Have you visited before?'

'I've been to Wiltshire but never spent any time in the city.'

'How odd,' she remarked but without rancour. 'Most people begin with the old city and its marvellous cathedral.'

'I suppose most aren't pomologists.' At her curious look, he added, 'I hunt apples.'

'Oh, now, Mr Attwood, you are going to have to explain yourself. You have me totally intrigued.'

'I wish my parents shared your intrigue,' he said, smiling back at her and finishing the first half of his sandwich. She waited patiently for him to swallow. 'There isn't as much to learn as you might imagine.'

'Indulge me,' she coaxed.

He took a sighing breath. 'All right. Ignoring biblical references to the fruit of paradise, the humble apple as we know it today has unprecise botanic origins. It's a complex fruit – a hybrid, do you understand what I mean by that?'

She frowned. 'You'd best explain.'

'In simple terms it is the offspring of two plants.'

'You mean an apple is not an apple?'

'Not quite. We believe the original fruit grew on the slopes of what's known as Tien Shan, or the Heavenly Mountains, which form the boundary between western China and Imperial Russia. A very remote area, walked only by shepherds. The story goes that they were aware of forests of wild fruit trees that included apples, quinces, pears and even nut groves.'

Mrs Bridge sighed. 'Oh, I knew talking to you was going to be fun,' she said, clasping her hands in pleasure. 'Please go on.'

It was the best diversion from his problems. Why not? 'Well, short of a history lesson, Mrs Bridge, apples have been cultivated for many centuries. We believe they first arrived on our shores courtesy of the Romans but then lost popularity after the fall of the Roman Empire. They found new favour during the Norman conquests, and the French have had a long appreciation for the apple, dating back to the Sun King's particular fondness for cultivated orchards and fresh fruit at his table.'

'I've always thought of the humble apple as something terribly British.'

He smiled. 'We came rather late to the party, you might say, but once we understood the full breadth of its versatility, we embraced the apple with vigour. We have been stewing it, pureeing it, baking it, jamming it and turning it into everything from cider to crystallised jellies for centuries. It's been used for alcohol, medicine . . . Our varieties run into the hundreds.'

'Is this where you come in, Mr Attwood?'

He gave a light shrug. 'I like to help our horticulturalists to keep a check on apple stocks, particularly the heritage ones that we might be losing sight of.' At her frown, he continued. 'Essentially, we lose track of our apples each year, and if we're not careful we might lose them completely.'

'You mean they become extinct?' she exclaimed.

'Indeed. And that's the mission that you find me on.'

'You're hunting a potentially extinct apple?' Now she sounded awed.

'I am. And I'm very hopeful of finding it in Salisbury.' He didn't fill her in on the background; she was looking far too interested in his work.

'Well, that is impressive. The fact that a man of your age and standing can make time for this detective work is marvellous. The country owes you a debt, I'm sure. Anyway, my mind is now racing to all the gardens I know in Salisbury that might have an old apple tree hiding in its depths.'

He smiled. He really hoped she wasn't going to offer to join him in his hunt. 'I have some leads,' he said, and then the heavens smiled on him as the horn sounded and they began to feel the train slowing. 'Ah, seems we're coming into Grateley. I might just stretch my legs before the final haul into Salisbury.'

He made his escape. When he returned, both women had slipped into a peaceful slumber and they remained that way until they drew into the cathedral city.

'I was more tired than I thought,' his companion remarked, helping her mother with her coat. 'But it was a pleasure to meet you, Mr Attwood.'

He shook her hand gently. 'The pleasure was mine.'

'Well, here's to you enjoying Salisbury. I do hope you find your elusive apple.'

'Thank you.'

'Perhaps our paths might cross.' She held out a small card that she'd pulled from her pocket. 'Please remember my mother to yours. Her name is—'

'Mrs Mary Jameson, yes,' he said, smiling.

'Oh, well done you, paying attention. And if you need somewhere to rest after a weary afternoon's hunting, with a cup of tea and slice of cake, do call in.'

He diverted the conversation by offering to help. 'Do you need any assistance with your mother on the platform?'

'No, no. We shall be fine, but thank you.'

He gave a small bow and made his departure from the carriage, with a skip in his step now that he was on fresh territory where a secretive apple, destined to be renamed for a new king, might still flourish.

7

SALISBURY

Jane arrived with a tray, bearing a bowl of soup she'd made from boiling a fowl.

William looked up from his book. 'What's this? An early meal?'

'Yes,' she said, setting down the tray and drawing back the curtains more. 'You promised me you'd get out into our glorious sunshine. Instead I know you've trapped yourself inside all day.'

'I'm getting over the hideous visit of that woman,' he tried.

Jane gave him a look of exasperation. 'Don't use her as your excuse. You're looking drawn and unhealthy. Let's get some fresh air into you. What did she have to say, anyway?'

'I'm sure you can guess.'

'I'm sure I can. But I'd like to hear it.'

'Why, Jane? I find it intolerable hearing it, let alone repeating it to you.'

She enjoyed the soft burr of his Scottish ancestry, which pushed through when he spoke.

'For Harry's sake. I need to know who in our community will not look kindly upon him. He's not so young that he doesn't sense their awful gossiping behind their hands. And he's going to face more of it now that he's one of the choirboys.'

William gave a small clap. 'I'm still inwardly cheering over that.'

Jane's eyes narrowed as she pushed away small towers of books and documents to make space for the soup on his desk. 'You didn't have anything to do with that, did you?'

'Certainly not!' the old man replied, sounding vexed. 'Harry earned his place fair and square with his pure voice.'

She smiled, then gave a sigh. 'I shouldn't think so little of him.'

'I'm sure you don't,' William said, tapping her hand. 'You're just so modest in everything you do or say, including how you talk about your fine little son. He's growing into a wonderful chap with an excellent future.'

'Oh, we shall see. I haven't exactly given him the best start, having him labelled as the son of a fallen woman, have I?'

'Jane, my dear, he could have been born into abject poverty. He could have been born and taken his mother's life with him. He could have been born as an orphan with a miserable future ahead. But instead, he has been born to a loving mother, and has both her and a ferocious guardian looking out for him,' he said, tapping his chest. 'Not to mention his wonderful voice, an excellent education ahead of him, and the fact that he lives next to the world's finest cathedral. Truly, what more could a boy wish for?'

Jane laughed. 'When you put it like that,' she said, bending to hug the old man, 'he's really very fortunate.'

'He is, I promise you. And I want you to stop worrying about what those empty-headed women say. They've nothing more important in their lives than gaggling about others, spreading rumours and lies. That woman got short shrift from me and if she thinks I'll be donating any money to her cause, she's got another think coming.'

'Is that how she got past your door?'

'Indeed. Came in here all but shaking her money box, pretending she was here for the ragged schools, but really she wanted to tick me off for having a woman of disrepute under my roof. She indicated that you really should be living and working at the House of Industry in Ann Street or some sort of poorhouse. She clearly has no idea of your background as a widow, essentially, but I was not going to tell her.'

Jane was relieved; even lovely, generous William Angus had no idea that her sister was Harry's mother, and she was grateful that he'd accepted her story without judgement. He believed she'd lost her sweetheart during the battles in Africa before they could marry but after she had become pregnant. Jane had paid the midwife handsomely and it seemed that so far she had kept their secret.

'So what do we have here?' William shook her out of her thoughts.

'Er, it's a simple chicken broth. I don't like that cough of yours. Another reason to get you out into the garden and get some sunshine on your back. It will help your lungs.'

'Thank you, child. I think the angels sent you to me.'

Jane smiled. She loved William as much as she had loved her father, she was sure. He'd filled the hole that her father's sudden death had left, and he protected her in the same manner her father always had. He and Harry were the true blessings of her life, and she counted them daily.

'I think it's the other way around, William. Harry and I would be lost, I think, without you. I had to get away from my aunt, and I thank all the stars in the universe that glittered on us the day Harry rode his scooter into your shin.'

They shared a giggle at the memory.

'Here,' William said, moving some papers off a nearby chair. 'Sit with me a while and then you can stop hovering, pretending you're not watching me drink my soup. No, the truth is, I'd be living in a pile of dust and misery if you and Harry weren't here. You've turned my life around, do you realise that?'

Jane shook her head.

'I had no idea how lonely I was. I thought I loved my own company and my privacy – and my books – but these last six years I cherish as arguably my best.'

Jane smiled; she was touched. 'Did you never think of marriage, William?' It was the first time she'd risked broaching such an intimate topic.

He shrugged as he sipped his soup from a large silver spoon. 'I did.'

She had not expected him to answer so fast, or in the positive, and certainly not to open up.

He continued. 'There was a girl – Emily. Gorgeous creature. But she died of a fever before we could be married. There was never another for me after Emily.'

'Oh.' Jane wished she hadn't spoiled their happy moment with the query. 'That's so sad.'

'It is,' he admitted. 'But that was fifty years ago, my dear. I disappointed my parents in not finding anyone after her death, and then the months lengthened to years and then to decades. It's all right. I feel lucky that I've known a love that transcends the desire to even look for something close again.'

'Sad and pragmatic.'

'Maybe. It's also the truth. Many never experience that sort of love, and I comfort myself that I have.' He paused for another spoonful, then nodded towards Jane. 'This seems to be a morning of admission. You lost your fiancé, but do you ever think about marrying another? Was it true love, like me and Emily?'

She swallowed as he waited expectantly. He'd shared something personal, and it was only right she let him in too. 'I can't believe we're having this conversation. We've lived alongside each other for so many years and we've never been tempted to ask these questions.'

'True. But you started it.' He grinned gently. 'I don't want you to suddenly feel uncomfortable around me though, Jane, I—'

'No, no. It's not that. William, there isn't an adult in this world I'm closer to than you. But there are truths I haven't spoken of to anyone.'

'I know, child. And yet I feel if you share them, it might release you into considering a larger life for yourself . . . and for Harry.'

'Larger?'

'Allowing someone else in to love you both.'

Jane looked away. 'We have you.'

'But not forever. I'm seventy—'

'Don't . . . please.'

He didn't finish, nodding with understanding, perhaps noting the glistening of tears erupting in her eyes.

'I . . . I do want to tell you, actually. I just don't know how. Or even how you'll react.'

'Well, there's only one way to find out.'

'You may hate me.'

He gave a snort. 'Impossible.'

'Harry's not my son,' she blurted out, standing quickly and walking to the window to look down the front garden towards the cathedral. She waited, holding her breath, momentarily stunned that she'd let the secret out. Now it was loose, at last, jumping around the room gleefully to wreak havoc, she presumed. But there was no response. She turned to see William with a spoonful of soup halfway between his bowl and his mouth, his eyes down.

Slowly he put the spoon back into the bowl and picked up the napkin she'd rolled into the engraved silver ring. He unfurled it and dabbed his mouth, making no sound. Finally he looked up at her. 'Where is Harry?'

'Upstairs, playing with his trains,' she said, grateful that he took as much care as she did to protect Harry.

'Not for all the tea in China would I have expected you to say what you've just told me.'

Jane lowered her eyes. 'I've shocked you.' She sank back into the seat next to William.

'You have, but not for the reason you think.'

'Which is?'

'Your secret about Harry. It's not as though I didn't sense you were keeping something close that you feared sharing.'

'So you've always suspected I had a secret?'

'Why else would you be hiding away here?' he asked. She blinked. 'You're a talented, gorgeous creature, still young and capable of attracting a husband, but you move in the shadows, Jane. And Harry, dear fellow . . . I presume he has no reason to think you are anyone but his mother?'

She shook her head, then put her face into her hands. 'I am cursed. I love him so much and yet I lie to him every day.'

'You have your reason,' he said with so much tact, she could weep.

'Thank you for not asking what that is.'

'I'm sure you'll tell me if you think sharing it might help.'

'It probably would,' she admitted. She sniffed, then seized on an idea. 'But only if you finish all that soup and then come out in the garden with me and get some sunshine.'

He chuckled. 'I promise.' He began ladling the soup into his mouth immediately. 'I don't mean to be inquisitive either, Jane. This is your business. But I want to look after you properly – if I can help, I want to.'

'You already are,' she assured him, smiling at his sudden energy. 'You do, every day.'

'I'm eating,' he prompted her. 'Go on, if you're ready.'

She smiled sadly and told him her tale of woe, aware that the tension she permanently carried in her chest was gradually easing as she did so. 'And I've never asked the world for anything more – simply to let Harry grow up safe in the knowledge of being loved, and as a happy, confident young man.'

William stared at her, and she could feel his pain reaching out to touch hers. 'I'm so sorry.'

'Don't be,' she said matter-of-factly. 'I wouldn't have chosen this for myself, but now I can't imagine life any other way.'

'You cannot imagine yourself married? A man at your side?'

Jane dropped her shoulders with a sigh. 'I have two men. Harry and you.'

'And I love you both as if you were my own. I could, of course, offer to marry you, but that would bring a whole new curse of gossip and—'

She shook her head slowly. 'I wouldn't hear of it. What you've done for us already is more than enough. And, William, I wouldn't change it now if I could. This is my life. I am content with it.'

He rubbed his brow. 'What a ghastly plan cooked up by your mother.'

'Yes. Seen in the right light she could be accused of pragmatism, I suppose.'

'It would need to be a very special light.'

Jane actually laughed, surprising herself. 'Yes, that's true. My mother saw no problem in asking me to sacrifice everything. At the time I was shaking with anger. But it's my sister I worry for now.'

'You do? You've forgiven her, found room in your heart to consider her feelings in this, even though she cared little for yours?'

'It's taken me a long time, but look at what she's missed out on, William.'

'Well, you're right about that. I can see why you see young Harry as a blessing. I have to say, I'm staggered your family has never visited – oh, that's right. Your mother came once. I just presumed you had no one else.'

'You didn't look into me? I find *that* staggering.'

'I didn't need to. I liked you from the moment you applied for the job. I liked Harry from the moment he banged into my shin. And I've loved you both within a month of us sharing this house together. If I'm honest, I've never cared about your story, your background, or whom you belong to. And now that I do know, I care even less for those people. They're not welcome here,' he ended with a sneer, which Jane thought quite unlike the genial William she had come to know so well.

'Well, there's been no sign of them in seven years, so I suspect there is very little threat of them showing up. They got what they wanted and simply moved on with their lives.'

It was his turn to sigh. 'Jane, thank you for telling me. I tried to hold up my end of the bargain, but I can't sip another spoonful.'

'You've done well. Come on, let's call Harry and we can have an hour in the sun. Then you've kept your promise to me, and I shall consider what to make for supper.' She looked at him pointedly.

He groaned. 'I feel like Hansel from the fairytale being fattened up.'

'Are you accusing me of being a witch?' she asked, to make them both laugh. 'Do you know, I haven't told Harry that one yet. He'll love it. Come on now, leave those dusty old books and documents. I want to show you what I plan to paint next.'

8

Guy learned the easy layout of the city of Salisbury within a couple of days, and he was now a week into his hunt for the apple that seemed to haunt his dreams. He knew exactly what he was looking for, but it hadn't been sighted in close to a century.

He was seated by the open fire in the main lounge of the Red Lion Hotel in Salisbury's old quarter. He'd read up about the city, learning that its grid as a market town, especially with its massive cathedral, had originally been broken into chequers. There were twenty, all named, and he was currently sipping an afternoon cider in the area known as the White Bear Chequer, named after this very inn, which had been renamed sometime during the seventeenth century. The inn's buildings clustered around a central cobbled courtyard dating back to the fourteenth century, and he had noted traces of original timbering when he entered. Most of it, he realised, was now covered up with nineteenth-century improvements, and he had no doubt this new century would add still more renovations. The publican had proudly explained to Guy that medieval roof tiles, clay pipes and pottery shards had been discovered with the last round of improvements.

'And the base of some sort of jug, which the history buffs tell me is definitely from the middle centuries. They think it was probably made at Laverstoke.' The publican pointed to a cabinet, where the remains of a fine old piece sat.

'Amazing. It probably was used to serve ale,' Guy said, 'in those days when you ordered a jug of ale.'

'More likely cider,' the man said. 'They certainly used to order jugs of that! You can see some sort of green glaze on it. Apple green, the historians tell me.'

Apple green. Was it a sign? Apples were important to this part of England, with the west famous for its ciders. Some were so prized that in days gone by they were spoken of with the same reverence as French wines. Britain's consumption of cider far outmuscled any other country's, and cider needed the more acidic apples, which tended to lean into bittersweet or bittersharp flavours. And with plenty of juice. But the fruit he was looking for was for eating, not crushing.

Records at Kew noted unreliable accounts of his apple being spotted at the famous Salisbury Market, which had been enough of a lead to search here.

'Where there's smoke there's fire,' he'd said to his fellow pomologist at Kew. 'If Wiltshire was its last sighting, then that's where I'll go.'

'This is madness, Guy. You don't even know where in Wiltshire.'

'I know where it's not.' He grinned. 'I've closed the circle of that county, leaving only the city's gardens to explore. And it's too important to give up on now. This is for a new king . . . a celebration. And if we rediscover one of our oldest fruits in the bargain, I'll be a happy man. You know it dates back to the fourteenth century.'

'So you say.'

'Six centuries ago, man! Isn't that worth some effort? What if I can save it from extinction?'

His colleague sighed. 'You're just lucky your father can fund your apple hunts.'

Guy let his colleague walk away without further comment, not revealing how much he resented the barb. Was it sour grapes that he was onto something exciting for the coronation? Or was the man just envious of his wealth? Guy had made it a personal mission never to trade on his family name or connections, and he sighed now into his cider with fresh offence that people in the know wouldn't let him forget his money.

Here in Wiltshire, however, he was a stranger. And he was so enjoying the anonymity, he'd chosen to go by a pseudonym. Mrs Bridge had sat up straighter in her train seat at the very mention of the Attwood name, but she alone knew the truth. The innkeeper at the Red Lion, where Guy was staying, believed him to be Guy Keaney, an academic working on a project in conjunction with the Studley Horticultural College in Warwickshire. It was vague but convincing, and Guy thought it might encourage women to talk to him about their gardens, given the college had been set up for women in horticulture and agriculture; it was the first of its kind.

He had even taken the precaution of having a pair of spectacles made up with clear glass lenses. The optician had blinked slowly at his request, and now that Guy thought about it, it was a little over the top, but he wanted to leave Guy Attwood behind, at Merton Hall. He'd have to return soon enough and give up his studies, his roaming, his desire to write a book about apples, and instead take on the challenge that had been set the day he was born, when his father smiled at his son . . . an heir.

His anonymity notwithstanding, he'd drawn only a blank so far on his hunt. Not even a whiff of potential had he struck, though he'd found lots of apples, a great deal of them emerging from the great Ribston Pippin heritage apple, which had begun its life from three pips sent from Normandy in the early 1700s.

The apple he sought was even older. Once again French, but probably brought to England by the Dutch trading ships during the seventeenth century. Just thinking about it fired his imagination.

He had drawn circles around the city and had spent the past three weeks closing them, drawing nearer to the cathedral.

'Any luck yet, Mr Keaney?' a member of staff asked as she passed. 'We do hope you find your hidden apple.'

'I'm afraid not,' he said with a light shrug. 'But I haven't given up hope.'

'I think the people who've met you at this hotel are all putting out the word for you, seeing if anyone knows anything.'

'That's very kind, thank you.'

'So you started out in the countryside at Devizes, Downton village, and those places?'

'I did,' Guy said, nodding. 'It seemed logical to look at orchards and garden orchards in the rural belt first, but I'm down to the city as a final push.'

The woman frowned. 'I doubt you'll find many fruit trees in the city.'

'Oh, you'd be surprised.' He winked, trying to keep his spirits up.

'Well, good luck, sir. Can I arrange a top-up of your cider?'

'No, I think I'll go out for an evening stroll. The light is beautiful at this time, especially around the cathedral.'

'Good evening, then, Mr Keaney,' she said with a smile, leaving him to swallow the remnants of the delicious cider before he stepped out into the dusk of late summer Wiltshire. He'd learned that Stonehenge felt the country's earliest summer rays, before five in the morning, but the evenings stretched on past nine before light failed here – even longer up north. It was a glorious evening, and plenty of people were out and about making the most of it.

He headed down Milford Street in the direction of New Canal, at the end of which loomed the tall building of Richardson Brothers, a wine and spirits merchant. Apparently its cellars housed some sixty thousand bottles of wine ready for delivery, which he considered astonishing. He paused to allow the delivery van for Robert Stokes to park outside a shop entrance and he smiled at the sign on its back: *Teas blended, coffees roasted to suit the waters of the neighbourhood.*

A coal truck rumbled past, and Guy caught the pleasant mineral scent of nature, as though a pile of earth had just been turned over. He'd always enjoyed the smell of coal, but his nanny had not approved of the mess he would become after a forbidden visit to the coal cellar. He watched dust lift from the truck and wondered where it might settle: hopefully not on his shoulders. He passed the building of John Halle, a wealthy wool merchant who'd built the hall – a splendid piece of fifteenth-century architecture, considered significant, and one of the finest in England; presently it was a china shop. Guy imagined his mother stopping to admire the exquisite painting on display in the window. Among her many artistic pursuits, she rather enjoyed china painting and imported dozens of pieces of delicate plain white porcelain, from Meissen in Germany, mostly, to create decorated cups and saucers, milk jugs and sugar bowls. She liked to use twenty-four-carat gold on their rims or handles, so it was an expensive hobby – especially as she gave away most of her works. She wasn't the very best at it, but she was better than she gave herself credit for and had turned out some pretty pieces.

Guy's long strides carried him quickly to the parting of the roads. If he continued on in this direction, he would pass through the old area of Fisherton, past the clock tower on the way to the railway station. He'd walked down that street on his arrival and noted Maundrel Hall, which had been built in the mid-1500s to honour the Protestant John Maundrel, who had been burned at the stake in this area. So much history in this city.

Guy shook his head; he'd become a walking encyclopaedia about Salisbury, mainly because it meant so much to him to find the apple he sought in this oldest of cities. He blamed his indefatigable memory, which could absorb a lot of facts and store them reliably. Winston used to have fun testing it, grumbling that it was an unfair advantage and likely why Guy aced all of his exams, while Winston was never regarded by family or schoolmasters as anything resembling a scholar.

Guy considered his friend's smart mind. Perhaps as a youngster he had not known the best way to channel his own cleverness – it was certainly not in study – but it soon began to show itself in far more practical, and indeed artful, ways. Politics suited Winston Churchill to the tee, and Guy suspected his old friend would go far, maybe one day lead this country.

He turned left into High Street and could now see the impressive North Gate, which would lead him into the famous Salisbury Cathedral Close. He wasn't expecting to find anything within the Close for his search, but it was time to enjoy this magnificent architecture and setting in its summery loveliness.

Plenty of people were out enjoying the twilight walk, and Guy was impressed that so many children were playing on Cloisters Green. He had been fortunate to have plenty of acres to play on in his childhood, but he had wished for a playmate in those early years with whom to bash a ball around or climb a rope tied to a tree branch. The sound of their laughter and fun somehow lifted his spirits and yet made him feel sad at the same time.

Enough self-pity!

Guy passed the College of Matrons and paused to admire the monolith that was Salisbury Cathedral, rearing up ahead of him.

'Spellbinding, isn't it?' an older man said as he drew level with him, a woman of a similar age on his arm. 'We've been here most of our married life, and I always feel a rush of pleasure when I come back through the North Gate.'

Guy smiled politely. 'You live here in the Close?'

'We do,' the woman said with a soft smile.

Guy watched the old man tip his hat, clearly not wishing to intrude. 'Enjoy your visit,' the older man said as he patted his wife's hand and they walked on.

It was indeed spellbinding. Guy looked around for a bench to sit on so he could admire it for a while without being an obstacle to the other strollers. He spotted two benches close to each other on the opposite side of the Close next to a low wall. If he sat at the far end of the empty one, he wouldn't interrupt the two women on the other or, more to the point, invite their conversation.

He strode over and quietly lowered himself to the bench, lifting his hat briefly, for it would have been rude not to acknowledge others. But then he averted his gaze and pulled out a pocketbook about the cathedral, even retrieving his fake spectacles from his breast pocket and placing them on his nose. He'd appear studious.

He looked up towards the incredible spire. It was four hundred and four feet high, he'd read, and he wondered if that measurement had been deliberate to ensure it was the highest monument of its kind in the world at the time. It still retained that title. Construction for the medieval cathedral had begun in the thirteenth century, when the masons had been well versed in the pointed gothic arch, and its greater strength. Older cathedrals favoured rounded arches. His memory was unlocking its filing cabinets and tumbling out facts. Winston accused him of being a bore, but the accusation was always levelled in good spirits, and Guy took the barb cheerfully. Winston might have a bright, quick mind – capable of delivering a devastating one liner in a heartbeat – but Guy was the one around the dinner table who had something to say, if asked, about most topics, and could back up his opinion with fact. It continued to annoy Winston that his old friend's skill had not lessened with adulthood.

'I'm also far better looking than you,' Guy had once quipped when Winston was having one of his many moments of fun at his expense.

'Hear, hear to that,' Clemmie had said, drawing a surprised look from her husband. 'Oh, come on, Winston. You can't deny Guy's dashing looks. You might already be prime minister if you looked like him, my darling, but I love you anyway . . . for your mind and for how much you love me.'

'I do.' Guy had never heard Winston sound so emotional. 'I'm helpless around you.'

Guy smiled at the memory and his sense that that was what love must look and feel like. As much as his parents wanted him to leave bachelorhood behind, it would have to be that good to tempt him, something akin to what Winston and Clementine had.

He sighed out a breath quietly, enjoying the chance to let go of thoughts about his role ahead, running the business, and the fact that his parents needed him to consider marriage and a family to keep the name going. He could also let go of pondering his pursuit of the elusive apple. He was simply lost in wonder at the colour of the local limestone that this outstanding church had been built in and how it shimmered in the early evening light.

It was because of this that he didn't see the boy or sense the ball being kicked in his direction, until it made a dramatic entrance into his awareness.

9

Jane was seated on a bench under one of the great lime trees that had spread its branches wide, as though in supplication, giving praise for the end of the summer warmth. Looking up through its old mottled limbs, she noticed the leaves were the colour of small unripe lemons; they looked almost luminous with the early evening light shining through. She was transfixed for a few heartbeats, imagining how she might mix the colour, from its brightest moment through to its shadows.

'Warm blue and warm yellow to begin,' she murmured to herself, barely aware she was not silently thinking.

Harry laughed nearby. 'You're doing it again, Mother.'

She blinked, then gave a laugh. 'Am I?'

He nodded. 'Warm blue and warm yellow,' he repeated.

'Well, actually Prussian blue and gamboge.'

'What is gamboge?'

'Here, come and sit a moment,' she said. 'Look up into that gorgeous tree. What colour do you see?'

They both tipped their chins to consider.

'Green,' the boy said.

'Yes, that's obvious, Harry. More specific, please.'

Harry was used to this, so he played along. 'Very bright green.'

'Good. So it's not grassy, is it, which tends to be a more bluey green around here?'

'No, it's more . . . yellowy.'

'I'll make an artist of you yet! Exactly. It's got a lot of yellow. So to achieve that kind of green, I have to add yellow to what?'

'Blue,' he said, letting her know by his slightly vexed tone that he knew this bit all too well.

'Ah, but it must be a warm blue, like ultramarine or Prussian, not a cold blue such as cerulean. If I was going to paint the sea on a stormy day I'd use a cooler blue. So Prussian blue it is. And then we add that funny-named paint called gamboge, which is a rich, warm yellow. Some believe it comes from the sap of a tree but it's actually a latex, which is a milky liquid from a plant. Am I boring you yet?'

'Almost,' Harry said, standing to flip the leather football on his feet.

She had noticed how much better at sport he was becoming since going to Wren Hall, where the cathedral school was based. With a chuckle, she said, 'All right, you carry on.'

'I don't want to be rude.'

'You're not. You're an extremely polite little boy who has listened to his mother talk about paint all of his life. But this is your playtime, so off you go. Be careful.'

'I wish I had someone to play with.' His voice was a little plaintive.

'Won't the others—'

He shook his head quickly.

'Oh, well, maybe some of the other choirboys will turn up.'

'If they're with their parents, they won't be allowed.'

She was sure the blood inside her was boiling, as though a big fire had been suddenly lit beneath her. To Harry, though, she presented calmly. 'It will change, Harry. There's going to be someone who will want to be your close friend, I promise. They won't be able to help it. And then you'll be inseparable.'

He nodded, looking unconvinced. 'I wish I had a father like the other boys.'

'I know.' What else could she say?

'How did he die? You said you'd tell me.'

This was the conversation she'd dreaded since he was born, and she wished Harry wasn't quite as mature as he was at age seven. It was probably due to the fact that his closest friends were adults. But she still had a tiny glimmer of time. 'We agreed we'd talk about it when you were ten.'

'Why, though? Is it a secret?'

She didn't want to lie. 'Ten is a grown-up age,' she answered. 'I'd rather we stick to our pact.'

'Pack?' he queried.

'Pac-t,' she said slowly, pronouncing the final letter clearly. 'It means a deal, or a promise between us.'

'Oh. I like learning new words.'

'I know you do, and this is why you're growing up much too fast for me,' she said, suddenly hugging him, allowing the tears that appeared to dry quickly in the soft breeze. 'Don't grow up, Harry.'

He giggled. 'I can't help it. One day I'm going to be bigger than you, Mummy.'

She let out a dramatic sigh to make him smile as she released him. 'And you'll have to tell me to remember to wash my hands and brush my teeth.'

He hugged her this time. 'Don't grow old, Mummy. Don't leave me.'

'Never,' she promised.

'Is that a pact?'

'It is. Not until I'm very, very old.'

He smiled sadly and she realised the conversation, which she'd begun with levity, had taken a darker turn. Surely he wasn't already thinking about her dying? She would see to it that her son would never be alone. 'Harry, go and kick your football around and then we can go home and do something fun,' she said, forcing a distraction.

He squinted at her. 'Like what?'

'We can play snakes and ladders, or maybe cards.'

He gasped before exclaiming, 'We can ask William to play with us.'

'Good luck persuading him, but we can certainly ask. Go on now. Fifteen minutes – that's all I'm giving you.'

He deftly flicked the ball up onto his toes again and dribbled it away from her, around a dog and a few small children making a daisy chain.

She sighed and then inhaled the evening air. She was furious that a seven-year-old was outcast for the circumstances of his birth and now having to contemplate loneliness. She looked up into the tree again, thinking of how she'd fallen in love with him in the same heartbeat that his biological mother had confirmed her hatred of him, when a commotion struck up. She snapped out of her sadness, frowning and following the sound with her gaze.

A seated man was holding his face, while two women were moving: one splitting away to help the man, the other to remonstrate with a boy who looked both stunned and sheepish.

That boy was Harry, and her anger, which hadn't cooled, was further stoked at the sight of the woman standing over him, yelling. Jane picked up her bag and her skirts and began to hurry across the green.

The ball broke the left lens of his glasses before knocking them off his head. Whether it was the laces of the football or the broken glass that had done the damage, Guy didn't know, but after the initial shock of contact he realised his cheeks were wet. Slightly dazed, he reached to his face and his fingers came away dripping scarlet; he looked down to see his white shirt stained with blood.

He didn't think he'd made a sound, it had happened so fast, and yet chaos had erupted around him. There were a couple of children screaming and pointing, their mothers arriving to grab them, and the two women from the nearby bench were up and fussing like mother hens. One was touching him and clucking, looking distressed, while the other, tall and hefty, was giving a small, sad-looking child a furious telling-off.

And then he caught sight of a new woman all but running across the grass. She was far younger than the others, and pretty in a long skirt that reminded him of the rich blue of Vermeer's famous painting, which he had seen on a trip to Holland with his mother. The newcomer's blouse was so crisply starched it gave an architectural quality to her slim frame, and she was clutching her straw bonnet to her head as she arrived. His vision was compromised by the blood dripping into his left eye, but she looked distraught and ran to put her hands protectively around the lad's shoulders.

But the boy didn't acknowledge her arrival; his stare was now firmly fixed on Guy's bloodied face. He looked traumatised. Above him the older woman was still arguing, while the woman who was the boy's mother, presumably, remained silent. Her seething expression could surely curdle custard at a glance.

The other middle-aged woman was fussing around him. 'Oh, my word, that dreadful child,' she said, whipping out a handkerchief. 'Here, sir, let me help.'

'Madam, thank you,' he said, gaining his wits and equilibrium. 'I shall be fine.'

'You are hardly fine, Mr . . .?'

'Keaney.'

'Mr Keaney, you are bleeding all over yourself from that wretched boy's behaviour. It's to be expected, I suppose, with a mother like that!'

A mother like what? he didn't want to ask. 'Just an accident, Mrs . . .?'

'I'm Mrs Potts, and the other lady over there is Mrs Chambers.'

'Thank you for your concern, both of you, but I shall be fine.'

'Please let me—'

He gently pushed her dabbing hand aside. 'Mrs Potts, I shall head back to my rooms and attend to myself. Thank you.'

It was firmly said, and she withdrew her ministrations. 'If you're sure.'

'I am.'

He watched the mother, still silent, absorb the accusations. Lots of finger-pointing accompanied the tirade until Mrs Chambers, and her twisted mouth, eventually seemed to peter out. The mother, whose hands had not yet left her son's shoulders, now turned away from the haranguing and levelled her attention at the boy, who broke away and ran up to Guy.

'I . . . I'm sorry, sir.'

'What were you thinking, you badly behaved child?' Mrs Potts began, clearly thinking it was her turn to berate him.

'May I ask what you are thinking, madam?' his mother asked firmly. 'He's a child. Please stop bullying him.'

'Bullying?' Mrs Potts began in disbelief. 'Women like you should be locked away – and your little bastards,' she hissed, forming the word in a whisper, 'should be taken from you and given to proper families to be raised well.'

The boy's mother gasped.

Guy needed to step in. 'Mrs Potts, if you don't mind! Thank you for your concern, and now I'd prefer to handle this without your involvement,' he said, standing and moving away from the bench and the older women. He led the boy with him. A moment later his mother joined them, having bent to pick up the broken glasses.

'Sir, I must—' she began but he knelt down so he was at eye level with her child.

'You were saying . . .' he said to the boy, ignoring the woman.

'I am very, very sorry,' the child said. Everything about the way he was holding himself and his shocked expression, even the earnest tone in his voice, assured Guy that the boy was entirely genuine, rather than simply going through the motions of an apology. 'I . . . lost control.'

'You certainly did,' his mother said, sounding appalled. 'I'm Jane Saville,' she said, her tone tight, her hand held out politely.

'Guy Keaney,' he said, giving her hand a brief, gentle shake. 'And you are?' he asked, returning his attention to her son.

'My name is Henry Saville. But Mummy calls me Harry. So does William.'

'Is William your father?'

'No, I don't have a father. William is my . . . er . . .' He looked to his mother.

'I keep house for Mr William Angus,' she said baldly, glancing over her shoulder at the two women who were watching the exchange, thankfully out of earshot. 'I'm afraid he's our only friend in this place,' she said quietly. 'As you can probably tell. But that doesn't excuse what's happened today, Mr Keaney. I don't know how to begin to apologise.'

'Your son has apologised very nicely, twice now. I'd say that's twice as much as is needed.'

She blinked, a smile looking as though it might break through in relief, but she seemed to banish it. 'Er, how can we make this up to you? Perhaps Harry can run some errands or do some work for you? He's good at collecting kindling, or he'll tidy the coal scuttle, or—'

'None of that is necessary, Mrs Saville. I'm a visitor to the city. What happened today was an accident. Let's not make it anything more than that.'

'But you're bleeding.'

'Head wounds always look worse than they are,' he said, giving her a brief smile.

Harry tugged on his sleeve. 'Come home with us and let Mummy clean up your face like she fixes my knees when I graze them.'

'Every other day, it seems,' Jane said and stroked the boy's head, returning her gaze to the stranger. 'I'm really so sorry. Please come back to our home. We only live a moment away. I can staunch that wound, and you can at least tidy up a little.'

'I'll come,' Guy said, standing. 'Not because I need you to fuss over me, but I don't like the way those old bats are staring at you, or how vicious they were to you, old chap. Unnecessary.'

Now she did smile. 'That's incredibly gracious of you, Mr Keaney.'

'Call me Guy. No harm done, eh, Harry,' he said, squeezing the boy's shoulder. He pointed to his face. 'I'll say it's a war wound.'

Harry's eyes widened. 'Were you in the war, sir?'

'No.' He smiled. 'I was too young, but I have a good friend who was in South Africa. He was captured and famously escaped,' he said, not wishing the drop the Home Secretary's name.

Guy was touched that the boy took his hand. His mother picked up the football and he didn't miss her triumphant sideways glance at the two women. He put his own handkerchief to his face, purely to stop any further staring, and walked hand in hand with Henry Saville towards their home.

10

Guy was led by Mrs Saville around Choristers Green and past the northern porch and transept of the great cathedral. Harry had begun to dribble his football again, skipping slightly ahead of them.

'You couldn't possibly get weary of living here,' he remarked, taking in the beauty of the surroundings as they walked.

'The happiest days of my life,' she replied with a soft smile.

'So you're not from here?'

She shook her head. 'Not originally, no.' She added no further information. He felt her evasion.

'What brings you here?'

'Family,' she said gently but as though there was nothing more to say, and he could tell she was closing down that line of conversation. To press further would be to pry.

He nodded. 'I'm from Warwickshire,' he said, moving the exchange on to let her know he wouldn't pursue it.

'I've never been there.'

'It's pretty, but I'm a bit of a fan of the north.'

'So am I. My father took me once, and I think I was in love with Yorkshire from the moment we arrived. And there's another place I adore – not so far away – called Godlingston Heath. He took me there too. So what brings you here, Mr Keaney?'

'Well, for starters, I was curious about Salisbury and its grand history,' he said, waving a hand towards the cathedral.

'We're here!' Harry said, pushing open a garden gate.

'Mr Angus, the owner, is not at home at present,' Jane said. 'He's visiting an old friend in a nearby town.'

'I shan't stay long,' Guy said.

'And I won't keep you, I promise,' she assured him. 'But I really must do something for that wound, or your walk home is going to be intolerable, with everyone staring.'

He nodded. She was right; the last thing he wanted to do was draw more attention to himself. He was already worrying that his plan to remain anonymous had imploded. 'What a beautiful magnolia,' he remarked, pausing to stare at it. A confetti of large pink and white petals, like feathers from flamingos, littered the grass and the path beneath the tree. Its leaves were glossy in the evening light.

Jane smiled. 'Oh, you should see it in spring when it first blooms. It's intoxicating. This one will keep flowering until the first nip of autumn.'

Guy allowed the woman to lead him, with Henry at the front, down the curving stone path that dipped gently through its journey to the two steps at the front door. Guy stood back to admire the fine Georgian house he'd arrived at. 'What colour is this?'

Harry groaned. 'Oh no,' he said dramatically.

His mother laughed, and Guy was delighted to hear the glee in it. So far she'd been so dignified and tightly contained that he felt any unexpected question might startle her. It was surprising to hear the abandon in her amusement.

'Have I said the wrong thing?' he wondered aloud, making Harry's eyes roll further.

'Now she's going to give you a very full answer, Mr Keaney, and we'll still be standing here past my bedtime.'

'Oh, and you're complaining about that, are you, Harry?' his mother asked in an arch tone, though obviously amused.

'No,' he said hurriedly, grinning, 'but I'd rather be playing with my trains.'

'Take the back door, then,' she said, and he skipped away.

'I have missed something,' Guy said, frowning.

'Not at all. This colour has no name, Mr Keaney. Mr Angus worked with a colourman from the local painters and decorators.'

'I see. But Harry seemed to think you had something to do with it, didn't he?'

She grinned. 'I like colour, Mr Keaney. It's to that he referred, believing that I become tedious when I go too deep into my passion. Please, this way,' she said, taking out a key and opening the door.

'Call me Guy, please,' he said, following her into the house and immediately smelling roses from the large vase of coloured blooms on the hall table. The vestibule doors were slightly ajar, giving him fractional vignettes of each room that flanked it.

'And I am Jane, then,' she insisted. 'Shall we go through to the kitchen?'

He gave an I'm-in-your-hands shrug and she continued walking. 'There are four floors. Harry and I have the whole top floor. William uses the two middle levels, and the basement rooms are not used for much at all, except Harry's toys, bicycle and storage, really.'

'Where has Harry gone?'

'Oh, he'll be upstairs playing with his train set. Here we are. Please have a seat and I'll just fetch some things.'

He waited patiently, looking around the neat kitchen. It had some open shelving and painted cabinets, which struck him as modern. The kitchen at Merton Hall was three times this size, but it was also more formal and dated, with all the storage in heavy, dark timber. The kitchen table here was a honey-coloured pine that had been recently scrubbed clean and smelled freshly waxed; he inhaled the faint smell of the beeswax being overridden by the turpentine. The evening light set the well-burnished copper implements aglow, and he decided he couldn't feel more comfortable – well, perhaps if he wasn't quite so blood-spattered.

Jane returned. 'Harry's so embarrassed about what he did to you, I don't think he can show his face.'

'I'll see him before I go, to reassure him. I'm not so old that I've forgotten what it is to be a boy.'

'That's nice of you to say so. I think too many people do forget what it is to be a child, living around adult rules, and now and then just being . . . young and irresponsible. I don't condone for a moment what happened, but it was a singular error and certainly one my boy won't make again.'

'I hit a tennis ball that slapped straight into the side of an onlooker's head and, like Harry, I felt appalled at myself. And I once famously bowled a cricket ball indoors that took out my mother's favourite vase.'

She gasped, then chuckled. 'Did she forgive you?'

'Instantly,' he said, smiling at the memory. 'She cried and was sad, but she held no grudge. Not even a raised voice or angry face. I think it was her forgiveness that hurt more than my own disgust at what I'd done.'

'Mother's love.' She sighed, filling a small pewter dish with warm water from the kettle. 'It has no bounds – except when it comes to my own mother's.' He frowned, but she didn't give him a chance to query her. 'Right, let's see the damage,' she said, wetting a clean rag.

He began to peel off the handkerchief and then laughed with soft alarm. 'Oops, it's stuck,' he admitted.

'Here, I can do it. Let me dampen it,' she said, leaning in. Now the smell of wax polish was replaced by the delicate smell of lavender, moss, rose, geranium and perhaps something minty, as though Jane Saville had been rummaging around in an overgrown English garden. As complex as the notes were, they combined in the no-nonsense scent of a practical woman, yet one that was entirely feminine. He was used to more overbearing perfumes of women determined to catch his attention, secure in their wealth and their desirability as a wife. Except they rarely interested him; one or two, perhaps, had shown promise, but ultimately they seemed to be under the control of dogged mothers who had flung them like well-fletched arrows in his direction. He had no desire to be part of those families.

'Ah,' they said together as the linen finally gave way. Its loosening from his skin also gave the blood permission to flow freely again as Jane inspected his forehead.

'Hmm, well, it's a cut and a graze. I think the ball's laces did the damage rather than your broken glasses.'

'Damn, I left those behind.'

'No, I picked them up. Don't forget to take them before you leave. Could you hold that there firmly, please? We need to stop the bleeding. I'll get some collodion.' She disappeared briefly again, then was back with a small brown bottle. 'May I put some of this on? It should staunch the flow.'

'Yes, of course.'

She busied herself cleaning up the blood around his face, her thighs pressing against him, but she was seemingly oblivious to the contact. He felt her step back to scrutinise the wound and, surprising himself, missed her touch immediately.

'Right, I'm going to paint on the collodian and pinch momentarily. Is that all right?'

'Do whatever you must. I'm grateful.'

He felt the cool of the liquid being dabbed on, a slight sting and then the sensation of his nurse blowing gently on the wound before she did as warned and gently held the skin together. 'Just a few moments for it to stick,' she said.

'Are you an artist, Jane?' Guy asked, to distract himself from the discomfort.

'Oh.' She sounded surprised. 'Why do you ask that?'

'Your knowledge of house paint colours, I suppose. And I'm looking at a very lovely still life painting. I've noted a couple of others in this room. Are they your work?'

'They are. Yes, I enjoy painting. I only hang my work up in the kitchen and in our own rooms.'

'Your work is exquisite.'

She made a face. 'I'm not sure you can see that well, Mr Keaney.'

'Guy,' he reminded her.

'I would have preferred Mr Angus to paint the house a more classic 1700s colour of buttermilk or magnolia. However, William assures me that, despite the age of this house, we are past the Victorian age and our short Edwardian era of more strictly adherent palettes. I believe he has become more flamboyant with age and thus demanded some colour.' She chuckled. 'I looked horrified at his mention of Garden Green. It's a very beautiful hue, but it was much too loud, and so I worked with the colourmaster to perfect this gentle green by mixing William's wild suggestion with creams and neutrals, even some grey, to complement the surrounding parkland of the cathedral.'

'Is it gooseberry, do you think?'

'That's a bit too lime to describe the house colour. Perhaps it's more a young pea, or, if I thought you knew what I was referring to, then I'd immediately reference an apple I once tasted called a Granny Smith.'

He felt flabbergasted. 'But I do know that apple.'

Jane blinked in surprise. 'Truly?' she said, leaning back to regard him. 'It's Australian.'

'I know. I've tasted it too.'

'Oh, my.' She looked impressed. 'Then perhaps you can appreciate the colour I mean. Of course, it needs to be pulled back in its power,' she said, looking over his head and turning an imaginary knob in the air. 'Right back to perhaps twenty per cent – perhaps even ten per cent – of its true colour.'

'Brilliant,' he said, able to picture it. 'How did you come to taste a Granny Smith?'

'Well, how can I shorten a tedious story? An Australian friend of William's came to stay and he brought a range of curiosities, one of which was this near luminously bright green apple. He was very proud of it and cut it open for us to eat. It had lost some of its juiciness due to the long sea journey, but nevertheless it was . . .' She paused to examine his brow. 'Still surprisingly crunchy and tart, yet it had a sweetness that was addictive.' She met his gaze again. 'The bleeding's stopped, I'm happy to say.'

'Thank you.'

'May I dress it? I'll cut it very small so it's not too noticeable.'

He pulled a face that suggested he didn't want any further fuss, but she continued.

'Just to keep it clean for a day or so.'

He gave a nod of deference. 'Do you know, I think I must have met this same gentleman at Kew Gardens. He brought several specimens of plants with him, if I'm not mistaken. I believe his name was Sherwood.'

'That's him!' Jane exclaimed and he could tell she was not used to being so animated, immediately tempering her tone. 'His name is John Sherwood, and I think it was a family member of his who grew the apple.'

'Yes. He said it came about by chance,' Guy continued, giving her the full story. 'It was a seed, probably carried on French crab-apple crates that a family member, a Maria Ann Smith, took home to her orchards. Apparently she noticed the small apple seedling growing in her compost heap, and a new variety was born! Although no one truly knows the parentage, I can tell you it won't grow here. It's too cold; it needs that southern hemisphere warmth, or certainly somewhere with reliable summers, more south of dear old England.'

Jane stuck on the tiny dressing, running a cool finger across his brow. 'There,' she said, standing back to admire her handiwork. 'Maybe wear a hat for a couple of days. How do you know all this wonderful history about the Granny Smith?'

'Er, well, I do some work for Kew Gardens.'

'Horticulture?'

'Yes, you could say. More academic than the fellows achieving greatness with the soil, so to speak.' He touched the wound. 'Thank you again. I'll be out of your hair.'

'What about that shirt of yours?'

He looked down and grimaced.

'It's stained terribly and will draw a great deal of attention on your way out of here. How about I fetch one of William's shirts? You can return it anytime, and I'll get that laundered.'

'You don't have to—'

'Please say yes. Dressing your wound, cleaning your shirt, these are small ways to let me show how sorry we are. You'll ease my heart.' Her smile was genuine.

'How can I refuse you, then?'

'Go through to the laundry, and I'll just find something suitable for you.'

He had unbuttoned his shirt absentmindedly in readiness, but not taken it off. Even so, Jane all but jumped with alarm when she returned. 'Oh, Mr Keaney, I'm so sorry.' She shielded her face.

He laughed. 'Now that you've seen me half-naked, you really must call me Guy,' he said, hoping to quell her shame.

Jane was sure her cheeks were aflame. 'Er, here we are. This should fit,' she said, stepping fully into the laundry, looking beyond him to the far wall, but her treacherous eyes kept snatching glances at his body. His chest was flat and hairless, his belly firm, and although he seemed relaxed about being half-naked, he was far from showy, reaching quickly for the shirt she awkwardly held out and whipping it about his shoulders, his arms expertly finding the sleeves.

She just had time to catch one more glimpse and then that lovely sight was covered. 'I'll put the water on to boil; a cup of tea before you go, perhaps?' she said, skipping away and not waiting for an answer. Her neck was burning too. What was wrong with her?

Then Harry arrived to notice as well. 'Why are you red, Mummy?'

'I don't know, darling. I just had the hot water on,' she lied.

'Where's Guy?'

'Mr Keaney to you.' She frowned at him, but not angrily.

Harry was unmoved. 'He told me to call him Guy.'

'I'm here,' Guy said, stepping back into the kitchen.

Harry laughed. 'Is that William's shirt?'

'Bit roomy, isn't it? I'll tuck it in; no one will know.'

'Can I see your wound?'

'Harry,' his mother began.

'It's all right,' Guy said, and she had to turn away. She couldn't feel comfortable looking at him until she had full control. Given she'd never been interested in a single man in her lifetime – not that she'd had the opportunity these past eight years – she couldn't believe he'd made her blush. He was not flirting, he was not holding her gaze longer than necessary, and he was not touching her deliberately or saying anything that should provoke her blush. And yet she found herself deeply attracted to him. It was as surprising as it was exasperating.

'Your mother has patched me up rather well, Harry, so there's not much to see, I don't think.'

Jane cleared her throat. 'I was going to make tea but I'm wondering if you'd like some chilled . . .?'

'Just some water would be perfect, thank you,' he said, glancing her way with a smile and then back to her son.

'Can I show Guy my train set?' Harry blurted out the words.

'I don't think—'

'Please?'

'Right, a quick look and then I think I shall have to go, Harry,' Guy said, cutting her another glance to ask her permission.

She nodded. 'Quickly then, Harry. I'll have the water waiting.'

Harry ran off and Guy lingered a moment longer. 'You don't mind? I just want him to know I hold no grudge.'

'That's very decent of you.'

'I was always getting into trouble, forever climbing into somewhere or something I shouldn't be. I was an only child, like Harry and . . . oh, he is an only child, am I right? I just assumed.'

'Yes, he is. Quite the handful but truly a good boy.'

'Well, my mother said the same of me. When you have no siblings, you have to make your own fun. We don't mean to get into trouble, but it seems we do.' He opened his palms out, giving a boyish shrug.

She chuckled. 'Thanks for being kind to him.'

He waved away her thanks. 'Two flights, you said?'

'That's right. We're on the top floor.'

'I'll be quick.' He too disappeared.

And there again, he'd done nothing that wasn't simply polite or conversational, and still she felt it: an immediate kinship, as though her heart had recognised his and only in this moment had it realised how lonely it had been for all of these years.

11

Harry proudly wound up one of his toy trains and set it moving merrily around the track.

'No steam?' Guy asked.

'No!' Harry replied, sounding slightly exasperated. 'I'm not allowed. Mummy says I'll set the house on fire because she's seen trains with little lamps burning to boil the water.'

Guy nodded sadly. He'd clearly been spoiled as a child, and although he hadn't looked in many years at the impressive network of tracks and landscape he and his father had built during his childhood, he recalled it taking up one vast room of the house. And steam was their preferred method of propulsion. He watched Harry race over to wind up the carriage again and felt a moment's sorrow for the youngster; Guy knew how it felt to play alone for much of the time. His father had willingly participated in playing with the train set, however, even if for the most part he was far too busy and distracted.

'Does your mother play with you?' Guy wondered hopefully, feeling it wasn't the sort of activity a woman might enjoy.

'Oh, yes, all the time,' Harry said, forcing Guy to rethink his presumption. 'She sits on the floor and makes funny chuff-chuffing sounds sometimes. And she chases my train with another one, or we link them and pretend we're carrying loads of goods up and down the country. We're in York right now, I think, and London's over there.' Harry pointed.

Guy smiled. 'Well, my mother wouldn't even know what my train set looked like, Harry, so you're a lucky chap to have a fun mummy like yours.' He glanced around the room, now noticing an exquisite array of botanical drawings. 'Is this your bedroom?'

'No, mine's across the hall. This is my playroom. I have to keep it tidy.'

'Well, I like your taste in art.'

Harry looked up. 'Those aren't mine.'

'Are they William's?'

The boy shook his head, engrossed in reattaching two train carriages to their tracks. 'They're Mummy's. She painted them.'

Guy looked at the child sprawled on the floor. He knew he looked astonished, flipping his gaze between Harry and the water-colours, but the boy didn't notice. The paintings were even better than the couple in the kitchen. 'Do you mind if I look a little closer?'

Harry wasn't listening. Guy stepped over the tracks to the wall and peered at a study of native heartsease, which was commonly called 'Viola', or 'Violaceae' in Latin. 'Pansy' was the colloquial title for the plant with flowers in a troupe of varying colours. Jane had captured it beautifully, and he was so engrossed he didn't hear Harry arrive to stand next to him.

'Do you like that painting?' the boy asked.

'It's exquisite. Yes, I like it very much.' Guy's gaze roamed along the wall to an iris, its petals showing the fragile network of veins that were not unlike the human body. Its tri-form configura-tion allowed its ready absorption into Christian symbolism, Guy thought, his mind ranging across knowledge he'd acquired of this plant. 'Adopted by King Louis VII as the fleur-de-lis,' he muttered.

'Are you talking to me or to yourself?' Harry giggled.

'A bit of both, Harry old chap. Your mother did all of these?' Guy asked.

'Yes,' Harry replied, sounding bored. 'She's always painting.'

'Not always.' Guy smiled. 'Sometimes she plays trains, I hear, or rescues men who've had a football kicked into their face.' They both grinned. 'I'd better go. It's getting on.'

'Will you come again?' Harry looked hopeful.

'We'll see,' Guy said, immediately regretting the generalised answer, invented by adults to frustrate every child ever born. He led Harry out onto the landing. 'So you and your mother live up here?'

The boy nodded. 'Here's my room,' he said, flinging open a door.

'Excellent,' Guy said, not knowing what to say, although he suspected Harry hoped he'd take a tour. 'Come on.'

As he was about to turn back towards the stairs he couldn't help but glance through another slightly opened door, where an easel stood with a half-finished canvas. He halted in his tracks.

Harry, sensing that he'd paused, turned on the stairs. 'I thought you had to go.'

Guy had never been someone to pry, yet here he was doing just that, inwardly wincing. 'What's that room?' He nodded towards the door.

'Mummy's painting studio.'

'May I look?'

Harry grinned. 'No. I'm never allowed in there.'

'Right. Er, Harry, I'll meet you downstairs. I'm just going to wash my hands. Is there a bathroom here?'

The boy pointed. 'See you downstairs. I'm hungry,' he said, jumping down the stairs two at a time.

In a blink, Guy had crossed the landing and opened the door just past the crack at which it had been left. He stared, his throat dry and his pulse making itself known behind his ear, at the incomplete study of an apple.

At this stage it was still a sketch, a colour study completed before the artist would begin to paint. Jane had likely put it on an easel so she could look at it; he'd watched botanical artists work at Kew and knew they preferred to make their studies at a desk. He could just glimpse a scattering of other sketches of the same apple in various formats at the desk she probably worked at. The one on the easel showed the fruit in its ripened glory and she had even painted little squares to signify a gauge of colours. The others were all in lead pencil and he could see one showed the apple halved, another its blossom. There were perhaps six in all.

But the subject of the sketches dared him to open the door fully. He boldly walked into the private room and touched the colour study on the easel, taking it off its pins and over to the window so he could marvel at it in the light.

You know it's me, it said.

And he did.

He had no doubt it was the apple once known as a Scarlet Henry, the apple he hunted in his dreams. It was the apple he was going to rediscover and turn into a gift for a king.

But someone else had found it first.

Jane had fully collected herself by the time Guy reappeared downstairs. In the time her son and his new friend had been upstairs, she'd reminded herself that the reason she'd had no man, not even a single romantic caller, in her life was that she'd been just nineteen when she was forced to leave her home and everything she knew, and coerced to take on enormous responsibility, alone. No wonder she didn't recognise the signs of being attracted to someone or know how to respond.

But now she was in control again and smiling at the object of her fascination. 'Did you find the train set enthralling?'

Guy grinned. 'I was an addict at Harry's age too. He tells me you play trains with him. That's impressive.'

She shrugged. 'Really? William's a bit old to get down on the carpet, but he does his best to be a good role model for Harry. Did your mother never—'

Guy laughed. 'No, never! Don't get me wrong, she's a lovely woman and I adore her, but her interests and mine don't collide much, other than in art.'

'Do you paint?'

'No, I sketch a bit – not nearly as well as you, though.'

She blinked at the compliment, not knowing what to say, but he continued. 'The paintings in Harry's playroom are incredibly attractive. Actually, that's a lie. They're not just attractive, they're rather masterful.'

'Oh, yes? I forget those are there.' She smiled, feeling suddenly bashful.

'Have you ever shown your work to anyone?' Guy looked earnest.

Jane shrugged. 'William likes them.'

'I mean someone professional . . . from the art world.'

'No,' she said immediately, as though needing him to stop that line of thought. 'I used to dream of turning professional when I was younger but, no, that's a ridiculous thought now.'

'Why is it ridiculous?'

'I sketch and paint what's around me for my pleasure, that's all. That's enough.' She searched for a new topic, uncomfortable being under his gaze. 'What about your mother, what does she paint?'

Jane sensed he was aware of being deliberately diverted but he didn't miss a beat, answering brightly. 'Everything! Canvases, fabric, china, garden gates.'

That made her laugh.

'My mother loves art in all of its forms and guises, and I have suffered her enthusiasm my whole life.' He lifted one hand, palm up. 'Perhaps it explains why when I see an intriguing colour, I am ignited.'

'Ignited?'

Guy told her how the colour of her skirt reminded him immediately of travels with his mother to Holland and seeing the famous Vermeer painting, 'Girl with a Pearl Earring'. 'It's true ultramarine,' he finished.

'I've only ever seen that painting in images,' she said, sighing. 'How fortunate you are.'

'The ultramarine Vermeer uses for the girl's headscarf is even brighter in real life. It's extraordinary, actually, and this is coming from an art luddite. My drawings – which I only do if something catches my attention – are very basic.'

'That you even sketch something that fires your imagination is to be applauded.'

'Well,' he said, taking a more pragmatic tone. 'I sketch to remind myself of what I've seen. Does some fruit blossom have golden stamens, or how many petals? What does the bud look like?'

She nodded, feeling an even keener bond to this man. 'I always seem to complicate my work by trying to re-create something – just a tiny part of nature – perfectly on the canvas.'

'Then you're no different to Vermeer! Capturing a moment in time was his specialty – something ordinary, usually domestic. He would focus the observer on that mundane activity but make it so real, so personal – intimate, even – that it inspires a sigh of pleasure.'

'I'd like to see that painting and your amazing ultramarine one day. Do you know how expensive it is? I can't even begin to imagine ordering it, let alone using it.'

'Tell me about it. I'd like to know.'

She handed him a glass of cool water, which contained a sprig of mint. He smiled at the fresh herbal taste.

'The most expensive pigment ever created. It's so romantic really,' she breathed, not meaning to become so dreamy over it. 'It's more expensive than gold – it's even referred to as blue gold, because of the gold flecks that often appear within it. But the romance comes from it being one of the rare instances of true blue being present in nature.'

'I hadn't thought about that day in years, not until I saw your skirt,' he admitted.

'You see? While my skirt is hardly romantic, its colour instantly transported you back in time to childhood . . . I presume a happy time with your mother?'

He nodded, and she could tell it was a fond memory. 'What part of nature does it come from?'

'The pigment is derived from the stone lapus lazuli,' she continued.

'Of course,' he breathed. 'Where is it found?'

'Persia,' she answered, 'and even that alone makes it mysterious and exotic, because it's so far away. Artists of centuries gone only used it sparingly – that's if they could afford it, which most couldn't – and usually on one object. The sky, a vase . . . or a headband on a girl's head.' She smiled.

'I can see you love the colour too.'

'Oh, I do. As an artist it's one of those colours to inspire because it's true.'

He raised his brows in query and she continued.

'By that I mean that ultramarine has no trace of reds, greens or any brown tones in its pigment. It is quite simply pure blue.'

Guy nodded with enthusiasm. 'I'm glad to have learned this. And the stone itself is precious, so that's why it's so expensive?'

'That and the fact that extracting the deep pigment was so difficult. I think the Benedictine monks of Europe were the first to do so, back in the twelfth century.'

He whistled his awe as Harry clattered back in.

'You know, it was the colour often used to depict the Virgin Mary – after the rise of the Christian painters – and why, before women began to wear white to weddings, they wore blue for purity. Ultramarine is sometimes referred to as Marian Blue for the Virgin Mary.'

Harry tapped Jane's shoulder. 'Not more colours. Mummy, can't you see Guy will get bored and never come back again?' he whined.

They both laughed.

'Harry, your mother's knowledge of colour and the fabulous history that goes with it is one of the reasons I certainly *will* return to share a pot of tea with you.' Guy ruffled the lad's hair, and pulled him towards his hip in a sort of hug.

Harry comfortably and without any shyness leaned into Guy's legs, and Jane had to swallow her emotion. To see Harry responding so easily and naturally to a man only made her feel guiltier that he lacked more male influence around him. He'd never known a father.

'Well, I'm warning you now,' Harry said with a look of theatrical caution. 'She can talk right through the night about colour.' Harry's tone was light, and Jane laughed.

Guy returned his gaze to Jane, and she blinked in surprise at how that simple gesture made it all the way through her armour, built over years, to her heart. 'How about we make a promise to see Vermeer's work together one day?' he asked. 'We'll take Harry . . . and even William.'

'Oh, wouldn't that be something,' she said softly. It felt fun to share such a wild and pleasant thought. 'You can bring your mother! Er, there's no Mrs Guy Keaney, is there?'

He shook his head. 'No. I mean it, we shall all go. Well, thank you for patching me up and I'd better be on my way.'

'Come on, Harry, let's see Mr Keaney out, shall we?'

'Can we show Guy the garden?' Harry asked.

'Maybe we can go out that way?' Guy sounded hopeful.

'No, it's the back garden, so we'd have to tramp through the orchard and you'd end up in a confusing part of the Close.'

'The orchard?' His voice seemed to lighten. 'I'd like to see that.'

But she had already begun walking back into the corridor. 'I'm sorry you missed William,' she said, opening the front door.

'Next time, perhaps?' he offered casually, smiling. 'Bye, Harry.'

And now she was moved to see her son jump and Guy adroitly catch her child in his arms as Harry hugged him hard. 'Please come back. We can play trains and football and eat ice cream.'

Guy set the boy down. 'Sure.'

She cleared her throat of the choking sensation as quietly as she could. 'Harry sings in the cathedral choir. He might be picked for a solo.'

'Good grief, Harry, what a talent you are. May I come and watch you sing?'

Jane saw her boy's eyes light up.

'Next Sunday?'

'You're on.' He looked at Jane and held out a hand. 'Goodbye.'

She did not trust her words but nodded graciously as she shook his hand. She shot him a smile as he walked out of their door and back up the pathway. Harry waited and waved, as Guy turned at the gate and lifted a hand in farewell.

And then he was gone, but the effect he left on her heart and her son was not.

12

It was three days later when William stared at the final sketch and nodded once. 'Utterly marvellous, Jane,' he remarked. 'Are you doing a series, then?'

'Well, I've sketched it over so many seasons now that it seemed a waste not to feature all the elements: the bud, the blossom, the petals, the cross-section, the arrangement of pips and so on. But then it would become a scientific study, and that's not really what I like to do.'

'I think you should, though. Maybe you can turn your hobby into work and do scientific illustration for Kew Gardens. I know someone there. Perhaps I can speak to them for you?'

'Why would they want this apple, William?' she asked, smiling in surprise.

'Well, not this apple especially – it's just our garden apple. But if they could see your work, I'm sure they would snap you up to do proper botanical scientific illustration for their curators. Would that interest you?'

She shrugged shyly. 'I think it would. I mean, I couldn't leave Harry—'

'Of course you could, my dear.' He tut-tutted as though she was speaking nonsense. 'Harry will be a young man in the blink of an eye. He's already spending more and more time at school or in the cathedral, so his life is getting busier and your role as a mother is becoming more of a support than having to be with him every minute. Now is the time to be planning for the future. Besides, I'm here. I can always look out for Harry if you need to go up to London.'

'I told you I met that gentleman, Mr Keaney, who has something to do with Kew Gardens. Maybe he would have some thoughts on this . . .'

'Well, there you are! Two people pushing your name forward. You could easily show this as an example of your fine work, Jane. Maybe we should find out more about this apple. It's been here since I was a young man, planted by my father when he moved here from Scotland. I'm sure I recall my mother saying it came from an apple pip that was on my great grandfather's farm. I could be making that up, of course.' He laughed.

She grinned. 'So it's old, then.'

'Very old, or at least its parent is. Must be sixty years at least. This might be one of the last harvests it gives us, and you've recorded its fine fruit for posterity.'

'I noticed the yield has been waning over the years. Do you know its name?'

'No idea. My academic interests lie elsewhere, I'm afraid. Your new friend from Kew might know, though?'

'I don't wish to bother him. He's only here for a short visit.'

'Harry says he's coming to the cathedral to watch him sing.' William was watching her face carefully, she saw.

She looked away. 'He may have just said that to be polite, William.'

William shrugged. 'Give him a chance, Jane. How do you know it's not you he's so interested in, rather than being friendly to your boy?' He gave an arch grin as she reddened. 'Oh ho! That's got your ire up. Well, my dear, I think you underestimate your own appeal.'

'Oh, stop, please!' Jane covered her cheeks with her hands.

William gave her a hug. 'Can't an old man have some fun with his favourite girl? You're like a daughter to me, Jane. I know you describe yourself as housekeeper, but I hope you know you are so much more to me than that.' She noticed his eyes misting as he pulled back. 'You and Harry are my family.'

She pretended to slap him. 'Now, don't get me going too, William.' His words meant more than he knew.

Guy studied the two pictures in his possession, yet again, of the apple once known as a Scarlet Henry. It was believed to have arrived in England during the Norman invasions, and he felt sure its parentage came from the Carentan apple of France, which was first recorded in England in the 1670s. Tasting notes from earlier centuries suggested that it was a crisp, sweet apple that was exceptionally juicy, with plenty of acidity and a distinctive flavour of strawberry. It was, according to early reckoning, uniformly red with a few pale stripes on a golden yellow background. Inside, the flesh was bright, with no hint of yellow but a tendency for the scarlet skin colour to bleed gently into the rim. The cut shape was symmetrical, with a firm dimple at its stalk. He knew the blossom was white but looked pale pink from a distance, because of the blush magenta of the back of the petals. Its leaves were richly veined and glossy green, with paler undersides. It was a medium-sized, round and altogether handsome dessert apple.

It was fit for a king.

He'd already missed the buds and spring flowering season this year. Even so, he needed to get a look at the tree that yielded this fruit and, hopefully, a look at the fruit itself. It would be maturing now and ripening for mid-October, in his estimation. He could feel his blood all but bubbling in anticipation.

Guy had finished his breakfast and ordered a pot of tea to give him time to think. How could he get to the tree that had yielded the apple he saw on Jane Saville's easel? He'd been so preoccupied with getting into the orchard at the home of William Angus that he'd overlooked other issues that were now beginning to rear in his mind.

There was Harry. A lovely young chap who was obviously craving the company and attention of male role models in his life. He didn't want to hurt the child. Who knew better than him how hard it was to be an only child, and a boy being raised almost entirely by a mother? But Guy hadn't had to suffer any of the outside pressures that Harry seemed to endure, including the cruelty of those who seemingly couldn't care less about his feelings. Their stares, finger-pointing and ready tempers towards an undeserving victim, who had simply had the poor fortune to be born into a home that was fatherless.

He wondered why Harry's father was absent. What a cad to have abandoned such a bright child. Or had he died? That was even sadder.

And then there was his mother. Jane was the true surprise. Her despair at her son's misadventure had come bubbling out of her and still she carried herself so rigidly, as though if she relaxed, she might break. There was secretiveness lurking. She deliberately gave no clue to her original home, she lived with an old man as his housekeeper and she was raising her son alone, far from family and friends.

But above all of this, he found her transfixing.

Jane Saville was his real problem.

It had been three days since they'd met and yet she was still wandering around his thoughts, her Vermeer-blue skirt, with striking eyes to match, unforgettable. Not a skerrick of vanity in her appearance: no rouge at her cheeks, no colour painted on her lips, her hair tied back and tucked into a plain hat, no jewellery – not even a brooch. She could barely hold his gaze. He couldn't tell if that was shyness or a withdrawn personality that didn't enjoy company – she certainly wasn't used to friendship, he could tell.

And yet there was defiance there. As though life wasn't treating her well, but she was not cowed.

This quality mesmerised him. For the first time in his life, he realised he was entirely intrigued by a woman. She wasn't trying to attract him, make friends with him or engage him in any way other than politeness, and yet her conversation in just that short time had been fascinating. He'd learned something from her and, more importantly, he had enjoyed being around her. That was a fresh experience.

Too many of the women he met seemed to focus on a few connected elements: marriage, possessions, children, succession. Jane was different. Eleanor was too, to a degree, and yet marriage, a house, family and making a good future for herself and her children were still driving her.

He didn't blame women for this apparent fixation. History had repeatedly forced women to be competitive, in order to find a husband who would give them the security they needed. Unfortunately, though, this made so many of them . . .

'Tedious,' he murmured to himself over his third cup of tea. That's how he felt being around most of the women he'd met socially. Their conversation was supposedly sparkling, but they mostly talked about property, decorating, fashion, theatre, husbands, children and riches. Some, granted, were involved in charity work, looking after the wellbeing of the less fortunate, but it seemed like a lot of them did that out of duty rather than as a calling. He knew and respected the work of a couple of women who were absolutely dedicated to ragged schools and orphanages, but they tended to be rather dour, never able to talk of anything else.

Jane Saville, however, was an enigma. She was happily getting on with life on her own and navigating the world without a man to guide her. He truly believed society had shaped women to be dependent. So many families held traditional and highly conservative views on women and what they should or shouldn't do, and even Eleanor, for whom he had a great esteem, didn't stray too far from these expectations.

Talking to Jane – such an independent woman – just about colour was like a journey into a new world . . . a world he had never fully appreciated. His mother had tried, but she hadn't been able to make the subject nearly as romantic as Jane had managed to. He was also sure that Jane was more knowledgeable than Adele Attwood, and more talented.

He didn't want to get involved with this family, though. There was a real danger that it would pull him from his duty up north, and, despite the argument he'd had with his father, he'd promised his mother he would be home within the month. It was not in the plan to be diverted in Salisbury, and he also didn't want anyone getting hurt, especially Harry. He'd seen enough pain in his short lifetime, it seemed.

Nevertheless, the apple overrode all of his reservations. He must try to see it, but that meant engaging with Jane and Harry again. He had to be careful not to give the wrong impression. Still, he couldn't wait until Sunday, when he had an innocent excuse to meet with them again. He set his shoulders and left the inn, walking with purpose towards the house in the Close with the magnolia tree out the front.

He tapped on the door-knocker and waited patiently. He was almost tempted to knock a second time, but good manners prevented him from being a slave to his eagerness. He was ready with an excuse for Jane. When she answered the door, he would say he'd left his glasses behind and had stopped by to retrieve them.

Clever him. It was the perfect excuse.

Except when the door opened he was confronted by an elderly man, looking dapper in a dark waistcoat and high collar, his loosely knotted silk tie the colour of a rich grenache.

Guy removed his grey fedora and gave a sharp nod. 'Good morning. Are you Mr William Angus?'

'I am. Who is asking?'

Guy smiled and introduced himself. 'Er, I met your housekeeper, Mrs Saville, and her son, Henry, a few days ago in the Close.'

'Ah yes, I heard about that. How's the war wound?'

'Head injuries always look worse than they are,' Guy said, reiterating what he'd said to Jane and Harry. 'They were very kind but far too concerned.'

'Well, you made quite an impression on the lad. Hasn't stopped talking about you since.'

Guy felt his gut twist with worry. 'He's a lovely fellow.'

'How can I help you, young man?' There was something about the twinkle in the fellow's eye that gave Guy pause – suddenly he was sure he was being toyed with, though he wasn't sure how or why, until the older man continued. 'I'm guessing it's not me you're hoping to visit?'

'Er . . .' Did he mean Jane? 'Um, actually I left my glasses behind and wondered if I could pick them up.'

'Oh.' The fellow frowned. 'I don't know about that. Why don't you come in? Jane's not here and Harry's at school, if you're wondering.'

Angus was one step ahead of him. Guy didn't know whether to say he wasn't wondering, which would make him sound callous, or that he was wondering, which would make him sound like he was here specifically to see them, as the old fellow guessed.

So he said only, 'Thank you,' and smiled, hoping he didn't look worried as he stepped inside.

'She's not Mrs Saville, by the way,' Angus said, closing the door behind Guy.

'Pardon me?'

'Jane,' Angus said. 'She's not Mrs. Never has been.'

Guy opened his mouth in surprise and closed it again.

'Hope you're not a stuffed shirt, Mr Keaney. Too many people judge Jane harshly without knowing the full story.'

'No, I'm far from a pedant, Mr Angus.'

'Call me William. She seemed to like you.'

'Please call me Guy, then. As far as I'm concerned I met a kind, polite woman who is herself very easy to like,' he said carefully.

'Aha . . . what a good response.' William nodded.

'Is it?'

The older man shrugged. 'Non-specific, neither here nor there. Not damning, not affirming. Are you in politics, sir?'

'No.'

'Right, then. These spectacles of yours . . . any ideas, old boy?'

'Er, I may have left them downstairs, but perhaps she picked them up.'

They checked. 'No sign here, I'm afraid,' William said,

Guy took his chance, with Jane away. 'Er . . . her studio, perhaps? I mean, if she did find them.'

'Oh, you know about it, do you?'

Suddenly Guy was on shaky ground. William Angus was not a befuddled old man but bright and sharp, ready to trip up anyone who thought themselves smarter than him. It wouldn't do to under-estimate the man.

Guy told the truth about being upstairs with Harry to admire his train set and that he'd caught sight of the easel on the way downstairs and mentioned it to Harry. But he let himself mislead

William about having entered the studio. 'Only saw the studio in passing. He was very proud to show me his room, but Harry said his mother's studio was off limits.'

'Yes, she's very private about her work. She shouldn't be – I've not seen finer.'

Guy agreed, mentioning the studies he'd already admired.

'Why do you think the studio, then?' William frowned.

Guy's mind whirred and found an excuse. 'It's just a thought, actually, that they could be there. I didn't see her put them down anywhere in the kitchen where she patched me up. And I imagine she might have found them in her pocket later, and put them there, away from Harry.'

'I see. Let's go check, shall we?'

Guy's hope flared. 'Er, shall I stay down . . .' He let his words trail off.

It worked.

'No, no, come on. It's two flights up – I could use the company because I'll take an age to get up there.' William chuckled.

———————

Jane had walked Harry to school that morning and as she said goodbye, he had pulled out some spectacles and put them on, pulling a funny face. They were broken. Guy's.

'Harry, did you take these from the parlour?'

He nodded, grinning. 'I hoped we'd see Guy on the way to school.'

'But he doesn't live in the Cathedral Close,' she said, her astonished tone making him laugh.

He shrugged. 'Here they are,' he said, handing them back. 'I hope he visits again, though.'

'Well, he'll need these if he's to see anything,' she replied, tucking them into her pocket. 'Let's hope an optician in the city can help him.'

'The funny thing is, Mummy, I can see through them.' He frowned. 'I see normally, I mean. But when I look through William's spectacles—'

'Which I've repeatedly asked you not to do,' she said sternly.

'It makes me laugh how they make everything bigger.'

'And it makes you dizzy,' she replied. 'It's not good for your eyes to trick them like that.'

He nodded. 'Well, Guy's glasses don't do that.'

'Probably a very low magnification,' she said. 'Some people don't need strong glasses like William does. Now, into school you go or you'll be late.'

He hugged her and was away. She forgot about the spectacles and made her way to the cathedral, where she was helping repair the choir's uniforms in readiness for Sunday's choral presentation. When she was readying to leave, she felt the glasses in her pocket and took them out, mindful of damaging them further. She peered through them. The broken lens was disconcerting, but Harry was right, there didn't seem to be any magnification. Frowning, she picked up a prayer book to read with them on. No change. How peculiar.

The lenses, if she and Harry were not mistaken, were clear glass. How very odd, she thought, but then she was distracted by the reverend, who caught her attention to ask her something, and the spectacles were forgotten.

As she was walking back up the nave of the cathedral to leave, a woman stopped her.

'Excuse me, will there be a service here on Sunday?'

'Yes,' Jane replied. 'It includes a special choral presentation by the cathedral choir.' She smiled, pride taking over. 'My son will be performing.'

'Oh, how marvellous for you both. Thank you.'

'Are you visiting?'

'I am. I'm Margaret Bridge.'

'Jane Saville.'

They shook hands.

The woman smiled. 'Actually, I saw you a few evenings ago when I was seated in the Close with my parents, enjoying the lovely sunset hour.'

'Oh?'

The women walked out of the great door of the cathedral, arriving into the mid-morning sunshine.

Mrs Bridge gave a sort of sympathetic shrug. 'Yes, I saw what occurred with your boy's wayward football kick.' She tittered. 'A very good right foot, my father thought.'

Jane took a slow breath. 'Yes, most unfortunate. I'm sorry you had to witness that – Harry is normally cautious.'

'No, my dear, please do not apologise. I'm deeply sorry that those women were so vitriolic. It was so unnecessary to make a scene, especially as it seemed Mr Attwood took it all in good cheer.'

'Mr Attwood?' Jane frowned.

'Yes, isn't he divine? Such a desperately handsome fellow. I noticed he was bleeding. I was going to come over, but I saw you were sorting things out. Nothing serious, I imagine?'

'Er, no. I was able to patch him up very quickly at home.'

'You live nearby?'

Jane pointed, her mind racing to grasp what was going on. Why had he said his name was Keaney? 'Yes, just down there actually.'

'Oh, you fortunate creature. How lovely to live beneath this grand spire. Don't you just sigh every time you step out of your front door?'

'I do,' Jane admitted. 'It is inspiring.'

Mrs Bridge thought she'd made a jest and tittered again with delight. 'Very clever . . . ahem. And what does your husband do?'

'My husband?' Jane panicked. 'He's dead. We, er . . . we live with an old family friend.'

The woman clasped Jane's hand. 'Oh, my dear, I'm so desperately sorry to hear this. I won't pry,' she said, sounding as though she'd be more than happy to hear the full story. 'Raising that boy alone cannot be easy. And you're still so young and attractive.'

Jane was lost. She hated lying, she hated being trapped like this, and she especially hated that during this conversation she'd learned that she and Harry had been duped somehow. Why would he lie about his name?

'How do you know Mr, um, Attwood?'

Mrs Bridge gave a knowing smile. 'Well, because he is most eligible, my dear. This is no ordinary gent. This is Guy Attwood of the Warwickshire Attwoods.'

Jane felt suddenly dizzy. She knew of the family, of course, with enough wealth to make people like her mother sit up and pay attention. She had never taken a particular interest in any of those names or connections, but as a daughter of Eugenie Saville, you didn't get through life without hearing some of the gossip.

Guy Attwood! She'd been so flustered over his wound – and, yes, him, if she was honest with herself – that she hadn't paid attention to the Warwickshire connection he'd mentioned. But then why would she, given he'd told them Keaney? Good grief, her mother would die and float to heaven right now if she knew one of her daughters hadn't just met, hadn't just engaged with, but had actually welcomed one of the most eligible bachelors in all of England to her home. She gave a manic inward laugh at what her mother might say if Jane admitted to touching him.

And then she found her wits. The cad! The lying hound! What was to be gained by his guile?

Mrs Bridge was still talking. 'We met on the train from London, you see. Well, we fell into conversation actually, and I was rather chuffed to have the journey pass most pleasantly, engaged in learning about his work and study.'

'I can imagine,' Jane said, noting her voice was unsteady. She cleared her throat.

Mrs Bridge heard it, though. 'Yes, my dear, quite the catch he would be. And why shouldn't you consider it? He seemed rather gentle and friendly to you both, I recall.'

'I think he was just being polite, Mrs Bridge. He didn't enjoy the fuss.'

'But he still walked home with the two of you, snubbing those dreadful scolds.'

Jane nodded, recalling all too well her private triumph at turning her back on the women. But pride comes before a fall, they said, and here she was, falling. She'd been tricked.

'I didn't get to hear about his area of study. How fascinating,' Jane replied, loading her voice with fresh interest, which Mrs Bridge was only too pleased to fuel.

'Well, he's what is called a pomologist. I looked it up.'

Something to do with apples, Jane thought, thinking of the French word *pomme*.

Mrs Bridge continued. 'He studies – and would you believe actually hunts – apples?'

'My gosh,' Jane said, trying to sound impressed. 'How curious.'

'Indeed. Actually, he's doing something rather magnificent for the country – donating his time to rediscovering apples from centuries ago that are believed lost.'

'To what end?' Jane asked, her tone light, curious.

'Well, for Royal Kew, of course. You know how they compile all their historical facts. I gather he's one of the people who document things such as when apples first arrived on our shores. As I told him, I can't imagine England without its apples and would have thought they always grew here.'

Jane knew better from her art and studies. 'No, the Far East, I believe, gave us that gift.'

'That's right, Mrs Saville! I can't even recall where – deepest Russia or Mongolia or something.'

'The Orient, probably,' Jane offered, her mind skidding from thought to thought. The football wound had been a genuine accident, so he couldn't have contrived to meet her and Harry. So why the lie? *Or is it lies?* she wondered, remembering now the spectacles of clear glass. What was his game?

'Oh, and he's so charming, I'm sure you noted,' Mrs Bridge continued, tapping the side of her nose, irritating Jane, not that she showed it. 'My mother actually knows his. They're not good friends but certainly are acquainted, and I asked him to remember my good mother to his.'

'I'm sure he will,' Jane remarked. Hardly a man who would lie, she thought, feeling savage.

'Anyway, he's hunting one particular apple in Wiltshire. He told me he firmly believes the tree he seeks is in Salisbury. He's been searching for some time, and now that he's turned up in the Close, perhaps he believes there's a tree close by.'

Jane blinked. The mists were clearing. 'Or just sightseeing, like the other visitors.'

'Yes, yes, of course, but I'm so intrigued by his work – and him, of course. A very dashing gentleman. Do give my regards if you see him again, Mrs Saville.'

Jane didn't correct her. 'I doubt I shall, Mrs Bridge, but I will certainly pass on your wishes if I do.' She smiled sweetly. 'Well, I'd better keep moving. It was lovely to meet you.'

'And you, my dear.'

Jane turned for home and she felt her old foe, anger, rising to her throat.

13

Guy followed William up the first flight of stairs. 'So what is Jane's story?' Guy asked.

'No, that's not for me to tell,' William said, sounding firm. 'It's hers alone. If she trusts you, she'll explain.'

'I may not be here long enough.'

William turned on the stairs. 'Your loss.' He kept climbing. 'Keaney. I don't know that name. From London, are you?'

'Er, no, sir. My family's in Warwickshire.' Guy blushed, furious now that he'd trapped himself in his own lie.

'Mmm. Lovely part of the country. Just don't know the name.'

'We're not that well known,' he said, wanting to leave his breakfast all over the stairs they were ascending. Lying was not his strong point – he was better at evasion. 'I hear Harry's singing in the cathedral choir this weekend. A solo, perhaps?' he remarked, changing the subject.

'Indeed. Making us all proud. He'll make something of himself too, that lad. His enquiring mind and empathetic ways will lead to something good.'

'Medicine, perhaps?'

'Mmm, yes, medicine or engineering, something scientific, I suspect.'

'The complete opposite of his mother,' Guy commented as they reached the top of the second flight.

William was breathing a little raggedly and he paused. His expression was odd; Guy thought it appeared torn, as though he were hesitating to answer. Maybe he was just out of breath.

'We'll see. The family's artistic nature might shine through.'

'Oh, I didn't know there was family.' Guy knew he sounded too curious, which flew in the face of all that he usually was. Nosiness and gossip were not his currency. 'What I mean is, Jane gave me the impression she was alone in the world, if not for Harry and yourself.'

'Just a figure of speech,' William said and straightened. 'Here we are. We shall be swift and not disturb anything.'

Holding his breath, Guy followed William into the studio with his gaze firmly fixed on the apple.

There it was. No doubting it. The Scarlet Henry. Half-finished but unmistakeable. The sketch was masterful; he couldn't imagine what the finished work in glorious watercolour might look like.

'Now, spectacles . . . spectacles,' William muttered, poking around the room without disturbing Jane's art materials.

'My word, this is special,' Guy said, dragging his host's attention away from the task at hand.

William came to stand next to Guy. 'Oh, yes, I am positively entranced by this work. Of course, this is just the colour study. The final piece is beyond exquisite.'

'You've seen it?' he almost shouted. *Too eager, Guy!* He tempered his tone as William's expression reflected his surprise. 'Er, I mean, this is yet to be finished, surely? I know artists usually spend some time on their study sketches before moving on to the actual painting.'

'She was confident. She'd captured what she needed and so moved on to the painting.'

'May I see it?' Guy asked. There. Out before he could even stop his treacherous eagerness. 'I mean, it's not here.' He looked around in an exaggerated fashion. 'I'd love to see the progression.'

'It's not here because it's downstairs. Now, I don't think your spectacles are here, so perhaps we should . . .'

'Good morning,' said a new voice.

Both men swung around to see Jane at her studio doorway, her glance moving between them in slight astonishment.

'Oh, Jane, my dear, there you are,' William said. 'Guy Keaney's back.'

'So I see.' She didn't smile.

'We were looking for Mr Keaney's glasses. Do you know where they are? I'll leave you two to it. It's time for my mid-morning walk and chess game with Alf.' William shook Guy's hand. 'Nice to meet you, young fellow. Do you play chess?'

'Er, I do. Thank you for helping today. I hope our paths cross again, sir.'

William smiled. 'Jane can sort you out now.' He moved to the doorway and kissed her cheek. 'I'll pick up a nice cut of something for our evening meal.'

Guy blinked, watching William squeeze her arm, and then they were left alone.

She frowned. 'Hello again.'

He was flustered. This didn't happen to him; he kept himself so neatly in control, his emotions especially but also where he went, what he did, whom he met . . . Feeling disconcerted simply wasn't in his regular experience, because he never permitted himself to be in a situation that might have him perturbed. And yet that enquiring look from Jane Saville, silent and clearly flushed at his unexpected presence, was indeed perturbing. *Don't lie*, he told himself.

'I, er, returned to find my spectacles,' he began, feeling an explanation was necessary. 'But you were not home and William . . . Mr Angus was trying to be helpful.'

'How curious that he thought I'd leave them in my studio.'

'Yes,' Guy said in a voice of uncertainty. Then he shrugged. He felt ridiculous. 'Look, forgive my intrusion. I'll take them, if I may, and I shall disturb you no more.'

'Of course. They're broken. I do hope you have another pair.'

'I don't, actually. That's all right.'

'Is your sight bad? Will you be able to cope without being able to see properly?'

'Oh, I can see . . . I just can't read without them.' Guy winced inwardly at the fresh lie.

She nodded, an unreadable expression creasing her features. 'Well, they're not in here.'

'Right. I must say I can't help but admire this work,' he said, pointing over his shoulder at the sketch. He might as well try to open the conversation about the Scarlet Henry, which was calling to him from behind, even through his embarrassment.

'Yes, I couldn't help hearing.'

He swallowed. 'It's exceptional. I do hope you'll allow others to experience it. I would be happy to make those introductions, as I said before.'

'We shall see,' she said, turning and closing off the conversation. 'Shall we head downstairs? I have your spectacles in the parlour.'

Back on the ground floor, he could see how rigidly she was holding herself. 'Are you all right, Jane?'

She frowned. 'Why do you ask?' Her voice was tight.

'You look a little pale,' he said, skirting the truth. Something was definitely wrong.

'I'm fine. Thank you. And your brow?' She peered more closely at him but didn't come any nearer.

'Nearly healed. It was not much more than a deep scratch.'

'I'm pleased to hear that.'

He nodded, giving her a smile in response, but she wasn't finished. 'Because hopefully that means we have no further business together.'

He stared, thinking he must have misheard her. 'Pardon me?'

'Harry and I have made our most sincere apologies and you waved away any further fuss, so I believe the chapter is closed, unless you have anything further you need from us?'

'Um, forgive me, I'm not entirely sure I understand.'

'No?'

He shook his head, frowning.

'Then let me spell it out, Mr Keaney, or should I say Mr Attwood?'

He blinked in shock. How did she know his name?

'I would like you to leave Harry, Mr Angus and me alone. I'm not sure what your intention was, but I'm very sure I don't need or want to find out. You've lied to us . . . It's your business as to why, but I have no intention of putting my quiet, balanced life at risk.'

Feeling exposed, he lashed out. 'Balanced? You think how you live is balanced?'

She took a step back. 'It's not perfect, but I don't see that I have to justify to—'

'You can't shield your son forever from whatever secret you're hiding, Jane. I know there's something you're holding back, but I also know Harry will find out. And the longer you leave it, the more profound the effect will be on him.'

He watched her suck in a breath of despair and knew he'd hit a terrible wound.

'How dare you. You don't know anything about me.'

'How dare I what? Speak as plainly as you? I did lie about my name – you have me there. I sincerely apologise for the duplicity with you and Harry, as you both deserve better. But you're jumping to a presumption that is wrong. I meant no harm.'

'Then why the lies?'

'One lie. My name.'

'Oh, really? How about these spectacles?' she said, pulling them from her pocket. 'They have clear glass in them, Mr Attwood. Tell me that's not guile. Harry discovered it. I'm pleased he finds it amusing, because I don't. To me it's sinister . . . threatening somehow. What kind of game are you playing?'

He shook his head. 'Jane, listen . . .'

'No, I . . .' She shook her head. 'I briefly allowed my guard to drop; something I never do. I thought maybe Harry had a new friend – not forever – but someone who might bring a very brief and positive influence into his life. He does nothing but talk about you, and I thought for the short time you're here you might see him a couple of times. It was wrong of me to even—'

Guy stepped forward. 'No, it wasn't wrong. I'd like to see him again,' he admitted, surprising himself. 'Will you let me explain?'

'About the apple?'

He opened his mouth in surprise and shut it again.

'So it *is* about the apple,' she said, releasing her breath in a way that sounded mirthless and disappointed. 'That was a blind stab, Guy. That woman said . . .' She shook her head. 'I'm embarrassed to find myself standing here in front of you, feeling betrayed, though over what, I don't really know. Heaven knows I should not have trusted my instinct that you were somehow special, someone I could trust. Your expression tells me everything I need to know. Just go, please.'

He felt only shame and was desperate to repair this somehow; he couldn't leave it like this. 'May I explain?'

She shook her head. 'No. Here you are.' She handed the frames to him.

'I don't need them. I don't wear spectacles,' he said, miserable.

'We guessed. I want you to leave.'

'I will. But just let me tell you what this is about, please.'

She wouldn't meet his eye. 'I realise the injury to your face was an accident, but it seems it suited your plans perfectly.'

He sighed audibly. 'Jane, until Harry kicked that football and forced us to speak to one another, I had no idea who you were, or anything about you. You know that.'

'Do I? So why do I feel used, like I am part of some plan of yours?'

She stared into his eyes and he felt the full weight of the Vermeer blue impaling him. He needed to quickly give some sort of account of his behaviour before she tossed him out onto the street and he never got the chance to see the apple or, just as disconcerting, to see her again. Incredibly, her fury was appealing in a strange way; he liked that she clearly didn't give a damn about him, his name, his status, his wealth. She didn't care if she offended him or what that meant in society. Jane moved in her own tiny world. Whether she was happy about it, he couldn't tell, but she loved her son and William and that was presumably enough for her. It was refreshing to encounter a woman who was so complete within herself. Was 'content' the word? Maybe it was resignation. But she was not allowing herself to be a victim of whatever set of circumstances had rounded on her. That *he* had rounded on her, he thought glumly.

Losing patience at his silence, she snapped. 'Right, well if you're not going to explain, then—'

He put both hands up in defence and quickly spoke. 'My name is Guy Attwood and I am from Warwickshire. I didn't lie about that. I simply used a different name to avoid drawing attention to myself . . . the Attwood name tends to distract people. I don't know how you know about my work as a pomologist—'

'Mrs Bridge couldn't stop telling me all about you.'

'Ah.' He sighed, remembering how he'd regretted ever making eye contact with the woman as soon as that conversation began.

'I know who you are and what you are and even what you're doing here in Wiltshire,' Jane added. 'What puzzles me is what you want with *us*. Why did you come back here? And don't say your glasses.' She glared at the wretched things still in his hand.

'I want to see your apple tree,' he said, deciding now was the time to be completely honest. Even he could hear how pathetic that sounded. 'I'm sorry.'

'But how do you even know . . . Oh, my sketch?' She nodded as if it was all becoming clear.

'Yes,' he said. 'I would never have known had Harry not kicked that football at my head – by accident,' he said quickly, not wanting her to think he thought ill of her son. 'Can we consider it fate, do you think? Could that be the middle ground you meet me at?' She gave a frustrated sigh but didn't argue. 'It's amazing work, Jane, I didn't lie about that either. But more than that . . . the apple you've drawn, well, it could be the one.'

'You really think this is the apple you seek? Of all the places in England?'

Again he nodded, taking a while to answer. 'My instincts tell me this is the apple I'm hunting.'

She swung her gaze away from him. 'So all the business with Harry was . . .'

'Genuine,' he said, aghast. 'I had no idea about you or Harry or your apple tree. But I caught a glimpse of the sketch when Harry and I were upstairs – and you know I didn't ask to go upstairs, I was invited by your son and given your permission. It was such a shock that I knew I had to come back to see it, to ask you about it.'

She remained silent and he took that as permission to continue his explanation.

'I've been searching for this apple on and off for so many years. It's one of an ancient variety that we lost track of in Britain, once popular, but now there might only be one or two trees remaining in the country. Maybe none. I don't know. Wherever you got the apple that you sketched upstairs may be the last remaining tree . . . It could be a very last harvest for all we know, and then it's gone. Extinct.'

She nodded, her gaze calmer now, as though he'd said something that mattered. 'Go on.'

At least she was allowing him to speak. 'It's been a project of mine for years, as I say, but my life was at a precipice when the King died.'

'How so?'

He shrugged. 'My parents have been extremely tolerant. They've given me years to pursue my pomology interests, without much complaint. My father's an industry beacon, for want of a better word. He's helped to bring valuable work and wealth to the Warwickshire region, but now it's time for me to take over the helm. He and my mother wish to travel, and they expect me to . . .' He sighed.

'To settle down? Marry, have a family, run the business?'

He nodded. 'As I told you, I'm an only child, with no brothers or sisters to take over instead. Just me.' He gave a sad smile.

'You have both parents.'

He nodded. 'That's true. Both slightly absent, though.' He looked up. 'I love them, don't get me wrong. I went without nothing, other than family time, perhaps, but they've not asked anything of me until now. I know I'm more fortunate than most.'

'Why are you telling me this?'

'Apart from wanting to be truthful, I probably need to say out loud that I've let them down. This guilt . . . I have no one to talk to about it, so your bad luck is to be in front of me as I feel moved to admit my failing as a son.'

She looked vaguely amused.

'There's more,' Guy said.

'Go on, I'll be your hairshirt.' She grinned. She seemed to be less angry now, listening properly to his story.

Her comment conjured such a vivid picture that he laughed, wanting to hug her for it. 'There's a woman,' he began.

Her features straightened, her smile dropping slightly.

Guy looked at his hands. 'I'm letting her down too.'

'You're married?' Her voice was quiet.

'No!' he said, and it must have sounded as though he meant *perish the thought*. 'Sorry, I don't mean to sound as though marriage is not something I want. It is.'

'Just not with her?'

He sighed, embarrassed. 'Exactly.'

'Are you engaged?'

He shook his head.

'Then . . .?' She waited for him to explain.

'She believes herself promised to me and me to her.'

'Why would she get that impression if you don't share it?' The question was fair.

He confessed, and while keeping it spare, he did not sweeten the truth in any way. 'It's my fault.'

'Yes, it is. You've been weak.'

'I have, I've been cowardly. She has this way of delaying the conversation we need to have, making it seem fine to just go on as we have. Eleanor is lovely, but her determination to be my wife has made her blind to the obvious. I think half the reason I'm here, apart from looking for the apple, is to escape poor Eleanor.' He swallowed hard at this admission.

Jane shrugged. 'The fault is not entirely yours. You said she was claiming to be in love with you on the second occasion you met her, is that right?'

He nodded. 'I didn't deliberately do anything to give her the impression that I felt the same. In fact, I've been careful not to make any promises. But she won't give up.'

'Some women can be enchanted simply by what they see and how it might fit their notions of life.'

'Some women? Not you?'

'I don't have that luxury, Mr Attwood. But no. For me to give entirely of myself, I would need so much more in a person than how they look or sound, or their station in life, because all of those qualities can be distractions from who they really are.'

'You sound like an oracle.' He chuckled.

'No, I've just had too much time to observe the world and the people who populate it. So much emphasis is placed on appearances and status. But to learn what motivates someone, what thrills them, how they think and how they behave towards others will make how someone looks – glorious or ugly – disappear and not seem nearly so important.'

'Wise words. But Eleanor is pretty, gentle, intelligent. I shouldn't be running away.' He shrugged.

'But you say nothing of wit, or strength, or how she matches you.' Jane knitted her fingers together. 'I like to think marriage should feel like this. A really neat fit that both man and woman can feel about every aspect of their lives. She sounds far too prepared to bend to your will. Some men may like that, but I suspect you would not.'

'You're right. The way she just waits . . . it frustrates me. If we're talking about families and all that social status stuff, then yes, we're a good match. Our mothers certainly think so. And there's no doubting Eleanor's . . . commitment. She's been so patient with me.'

'But you're still not feeling as she does?' Jane smiled sadly.

'Not a bit. I tried to explain to my father that Eleanor and I have become so comfortable around one another that I really do consider her a friend . . . but if I'm being honest, she feels like a sister.'

Jane's mouth twisted in mild dismay. 'Oh, no. That's awkward.'

'So awkward!' he agreed, making her chuckle. 'I cannot consider her a potential wife for that reason alone, and frankly I never did. But I shouldn't have let it get this far.'

Jane nodded. 'So why did you?'

He ran a hand through his hair in frustration. 'Oh . . . I don't know, family duty, I think. Have you ever felt so compelled by duty to do something against your will, Jane?'

She blinked rapidly. 'I have.'

'My parents believe her perfect,' he continued.

'But they're not marrying her,' Jane countered.

He gave another sad laugh. 'I love my family and I do feel a tremendous responsibility as an only child, but still I disappoint them by pursuing my selfish interests.'

'Well, I believe you are a good son. I can tell you something about family duty and the havoc it can wreak. But sometimes, Mr Attwood, there is a case to be made for defying a sense of duty when what is asked goes too far. To do anything other than tell Eleanor the truth is to ruin her chance at happiness, not to mention your own. Life is a long time for most of us, and what a waste of two lives to force you to be together when you could both be so much happier and build much better lives alongside different partners.'

He was reminded of his friend, the Duke of Marlborough, and his deeply unhappy marriage to the daughter of the Vanderbilts. Both loved others and still went through with the marriage out of a sense of duty, but they were miserable and ultimately lived separate, unhappy lives.

'I don't know how to tell her. I've tried so many times that I know I will have to be blunt. But it will wound her.'

'Wounds heal. You've been weak in this, Mr Attwood. She is a young woman with a plan for her life that surely involves family, and you're preventing other more suitable men from entering the picture. That said, Eleanor, too, is being weak-minded about you. She's been ignoring all the signs, all of your attempts to make it clear that you don't think you have a future together. I can't speak from experience, but surely a man in love would be lavishing a woman with his time and affection.'

She couldn't speak from experience? Had her relationship with Harry's father not been a happy one? 'Indeed. And I have done no such thing. And still she tolerates me. She simply refuses to see the truth, seemingly happy to live with a contrived notion about me. She's built this world around us in her imagination, but now the deadline is upon us.'

'Deadline?'

'We agreed she'd give me two years.'

Jane's mouth opened in surprise. 'How very convenient. You've been stringing her along for two years?' She sounded appalled.

Guy scratched his head. 'I wouldn't describe it that way.'

'How would you describe it?'

'Er . . .' He blinked. 'I've been busy studying and hunting apples – she understands I am away a great deal and that I also live in London a lot of the time, whereas she is in the north. Anyway, now my days as a pomologist are numbered too. Shortly I must give it all up to become the industrialist my father expects.'

'He doesn't take your study seriously?'

'It's complicated . . . And I've always known where I must end up.'

'You are in a tangle, Mr Attwood – more than one.' She smiled and he was glad to see it. 'You have decisions before you.'

He nodded. 'I do.'

'And the precipice you mentioned? When the King died?'

'Ah, yes. Well, when King Edward passed away and I knew a new king was coming, it was like my last gasp . . . one more hunt for the apple that has eluded me since I began this area of study. I became galvanised to find it so I could rename it and present it to the new king.'

Jane frowned. 'Why? I mean, it's a rather charming concept, but what is all the ambition for?'

'Now you sound like my father.' He said it lightly, but sighed nonetheless. 'King George and I, well, we're friends.' He shrugged, never comfortable explaining his closeness to the royal family. 'I spent school holidays at Blenheim Palace and we are close, despite the age gap. There's nothing I can give my friend as a coronation gift that is in any way meaningful – what could he want? He's always found my interest in apples a bit daft, as he describes it, but he also admits it's romantic and he does appreciate the importance of Kew's work and the preservation of all our plants. He understands that what I'm doing might seem silly to most but is in fact quietly important to the country, perhaps even the world.'

Before she could leap in and say more, he rushed to assure her that he wasn't some sort of boffin. 'Look, I know it's quirky. I've promised my parents – and Eleanor – that all this effort will end with this apple. But it occurred to me that to name an ancient apple for our new King . . . well, it has a marvellous whimsy to it, but it also delivers back into our nation the potential to regenerate a lost apple.'

She nodded. 'How old is this apple?'

'Dates back to Norman times, at a minimum,' he said. 'Brought over by the French when they invaded us. But before that it was probably cultivated by Imperial Rome and, prior to that, likely the ancient Persians or Egyptians in the fertile crescent of the Nile.'

She blinked at him, seemingly stunned. 'A very old apple, then,' she said in understatement, making him smile sadly.

'Yes, a very old apple that would bring me tremendous pleasure to rediscover, and perhaps bring new life to. It's known as a Scarlet Henry.'

'I like the name Henry, obviously.' She grinned. 'And I can tell you it's a tasty apple.'

He looked up from the pattern on the rug to the ghost of a smile that he just caught in her expression. He began to stammer and then collected himself. 'You've eaten it,' he said, feeling sick with envy.

She nodded. 'It's tart and juicy. Quite delicious, actually. I've made many an apple crumble over the years with it.'

He groaned. 'Bloody hell. Jane, please, let me see this painting. William said you've finished it.'

'Did he indeed?' She turned. 'Well, I suppose you might as well see it all,' she said.

14

Jane's ire had cooled listening to Guy explain himself. He had duped her – there was no escaping that – but as he laid out his reasoning, she realised that it was a tame attempt at duplicity and he hadn't caused any harm, other than bruising her pride, perhaps. The chance of sighting the apple was an irresistible opportunity, which most people would not throw away. She might even see herself doing something similar if she were desperate to see a flower she'd never encountered before and wanted to paint.

This thought reminded her of the *Drosera* plant from her youth. What a find that had been. She'd made the discovery with her father, one of those sparkling memories that stayed with her and could comfort her in times of sorrow. She could conjure up that wonderful day striding across the heath in Dorset, arm-in-arm, and listening to him explain about the fearsome little plant that ate tiny winged creatures – and then they'd been lucky enough to see it!

According to her father it was ruby in colour, belonging to the family of sundews, and glistened with promise for curious insects that roamed the bogs of Godlingston Heath. She'd wanted to paint it then and there, having learned this was the only place in England – probably in all of Europe – that it grew. But the weather that November day had been merciless, and while the cold did not scare her, torrential rain had driven them off the heath, running for cover. They laughed at the heaviness of the raindrops that pelted them, then dried off by the fire in the hotel her father had booked. She had sat, hair still damp, sipping cocoa with him, his with a nip of brandy in it, while the manager fussed around them. And it was in front of that fire, sitting on the floor between her father's knees, that she'd begun her first sketch of the elusive plant. The *Drosera* was not particularly attractive and yet it was beautiful to Jane because of the happy memory surrounding that journey.

It was the last time they had escaped alone on one of their missions to find her a special flower to draw and paint for him. He'd never stopped encouraging her in her art. 'One day, Jane, you'll be pursued for this talent of yours.'

She'd not really understood what that meant, or even trusted it, really, because it sounded simply like something a loving parent might say. On his death, however, while her mother and sister had cleared his private study of valuables, Jane had been allowed to take his precious Waterman ink pen, his journals and her painting of the *Drosera*, which had hung in his study, much to her delight.

With that memory burning, could she really blame Guy for at least wanting to see the apple tree after years of fruitless searching? No. He hadn't set out to hurt her, he simply hadn't offered information when he could have – *should* have.

It was true that fate had forced them together, for no one could have contrived the football accident or any of the events that unfolded after that. In this, Guy was blameless, but he was showing a habit of not being transparent, and she wondered about the patient Eleanor and her lack of spine in making demands of the man she considered herself promised to.

Jane was leading him to the back of the house. 'Why the fake spectacles?' she wondered aloud.

Guy gave an embarrassed laugh. 'Forgive me for how this sounds,' he said, 'but I've spent my entire adult life being the focus of women's attention . . . either for their daughters, or those daughters themselves, if they're forward enough. They try to engage with me with the very real purpose of potential marriage.'

Jane laughed. 'Why is that a surprise?'

Rather than take offence, Guy looked impressed with her candour, grinning. 'It's not,' he admitted, and scratched his head. 'But while I have to accept that this is the normal pattern of life, I find it intolerable that my nature, my interests, my personality, my suitability . . . even my character have zero bearing on the attention. All that matters is my name.'

She gave a light shrug. 'And don't forget money. It's how the wheel turns. How do you see yourself changing that with fake spectacles?'

She was risking his feeling pathetic with her sarcasm, but over the years she had realised she owed no one anything, especially not society people. Guy Attwood may not have set out to hurt her, but any deliberate, guileful behaviour set her teeth on edge; it reminded her too much of why her life had taken its odd turn.

Her barb landed, she saw, but he handled it well, with a resigned smile, as though admitting he deserved it. 'Well, in my imagination the spectacles somehow change my appearance and I might not be as readily recognised. But reality has taught me that I can't fully escape the busybodies like the chamberpots. In fact – and here's something I've never admitted even to myself – perhaps part of the reason for allowing Eleanor into my life was to throw others off the scent.'

'Well, that's just cruel. Please don't admit that to anyone else.'

'It wasn't meant to be cruel,' he protested. 'It just happened. I would never deliberately hurt anyone, least of all a woman.' He sounded desperate for her approval.

She needed to lighten their conversation. 'Chamberpots?' she repeated, frowning, and then the jest slotted into place and she actually erupted into laughter. It was an odd sound to hear. How long had it been since she'd laughed without caution, without reason, with simple abandon at finding something helplessly funny? She had laughed with Harry all of his life, but that was different – that was a mother's adoration. To laugh with another adult over a joke was a delight. 'You mean Mrs Chambers and Mrs Potts?'

'Yes, I've called them that in my mind since the moment they descended upon Harry. Those two shrivelled old busybodies with nothing better to do than pull sour faces, scold others and point the finger.'

Jane sighed. 'Oh, I'm used to it.'

'Why, though?'

'Why am I used to it, or why do they do that to me?'

'Both.'

He looked hopeful that she might explain, but she couldn't . . . not yet, anyway. She gave a sad smile. 'If I knew you better, I'd tell you, but . . .' Jane shook her head. 'I'm a private person, and I prefer to keep it that way. Anyway, here we are. Let me put you out of your misery.'

They entered a parlour, where light flooded in from the garden. Standing away from the window were two easels. One had a painting of a branch of an apple tree, as though it had just been cut away from its parent. The other was a perfect study of its blossom, its buds, the apple as a cross-section, its seeds, how the stalk fitted to the fruit and, of course, its leaves.

Both were masterful, and Guy sucked in a breath with what sounded like awe, though she couldn't be sure.

Silence drifted around them as he moved closer and she held back, giving him space to admire the artwork. He bent forward to scrutinise it, and then he stepped away to take in the whole visual.

'This is it,' he breathed.

She felt excited for him. 'Your apple? You're sure?'

He nodded, mute and stunned as she moved to stand next to him. She was close enough that she could feel the warmth of his body.

'No mistaking it,' he said, his voice almost gritty with emotion from seeing the apple he had hunted for so long. 'I've never seen it in the flesh, obviously, but I have seen many studies of it.' He pointed. 'The leaves – their shape, colour and so on – are a giveaway, but it's these striations of yellow and orange beneath the rich red of the apple that make it appear scarlet from a distance. An absence of russeting, and the symmetry of the section.' He pointed again. 'And then the blossom; I see those deceptive pink petals in my dreams.'

'Deceptive? How so?'

Guy nodded. 'Ahh, because when you confront them in the flesh, the flower is a bright white – I'm sure you'd agree.'

She gave a soft laugh. 'You're right. Achieving that colour felt impossible for a long time. I struggled with it. That blush of pink was there but not there. I don't know how else to explain it.'

'I understand completely.' He took a slow, audible breath. 'Here's my apple. An apple for a king.'

Jane risked touching his shoulder, turning him back towards the window, and pointed. 'The tree is out there.'

His head whipped around and she watched him swallow. 'In the orchard you mentioned?'

Jane smiled. 'You can't really see it from here, but yes, at the bottom of the garden is a small orchard. The tree is there . . . and Mr Attwood, you need to breathe, please.'

He laughed and just for a moment he sounded like a madman. 'I'm breathing,' he assured her.

'There are two trees,' she admitted, and enjoyed watching his expression shift from amused to almost frozen in shock.

Finally, he cleared his throat. 'Bearing fruit?'

She gave a grin. 'Laden.'

He seemed to slump, his hand against the window. 'I daren't believe it.'

'You can trust me.'

He looked at her and when their eyes met, she hoped he could tell that she would not hold a grudge. It was time to let him off the hook, because to see him so emotional was enormously endearing. She could believe that he never meant her or Harry harm, nor Eleanor or his parents.

He let out a sigh. 'Jane, will you forgive me?' He stepped closer and she realised his eyes were not brown but almost the colour of terre-verte, a paint developed to echo the predominant green of the earth, except in his eyes it was mixed with both malachite and charcoal. His eyes were the colour of a forest, she thought, if you stood back and gazed upon a thicket.

He was waiting for her answer.

'I will. Grudges are such hard work.' She smiled.

Guy gave a small shake of his head. 'A pragmatic woman . . . I admire you, and I'm grateful for that pragmatism.'

'I know you had no idea about us or our apple, and I suspect I can be overly sensitive towards a situation in which I feel I'm being used.' As he opened his mouth to reassure her once again, she added, 'Even if I'm not.'

'Thank you. Have you shown this study to anyone beyond Harry and William?'

'No.'

'Does anyone else even know you're an artist?'

She shook her head. 'No, they know me simply as that *fallen woman.*' She hadn't meant to admit that. But then she hadn't meant to allow Guy Attwood into her life at all.

Shock swept across his face. 'What?'

She shrugged; she should not have said that and now he'd definitely want an explanation.

'Jane, what do you mean by "fallen woman"?'

'I'm sure you understand the expression,' she said, and she heard the defensiveness in her tone.

He watched her, saying nothing. And as she didn't elaborate, he seemed obliged to fill the silence, but not as she might have expected, simply saying, 'I'm sorry.'

'Why? It's not your fault.'

'I'm sorry that anyone should treat you badly.'

She shook her head. 'I'm so used to it, it really doesn't trouble me the way it might have years ago. But I am overly protective of Harry when people like Mrs Chambers and Mrs Potts think it's acceptable to attack a child. He is innocent. But they don't have the grace to accept that he has no understanding of what he was born into.'

Guy nodded. 'What *was* he born into?'

'A strange place, no family, no father, no . . .' She didn't finish. It was too upsetting. She looked away instead.

'Does he ask about his father?'

'Regularly.'

'And what do you tell him?'

'That he died.' Jane looked down.

'Is that the truth?'

'No.'

'But Harry will surely want to know about his father—'

'Yes, and when he does, I shall deal with that then. I'm doing my best for him. I need no further judgement. Everyone out there judges me daily without any knowledge of my true situation.'

141

'True situation? What does that—'

'Guy, for someone who resents intrusion by busybodies, you're certainly displaying a vigorous curiosity of your own.' Her only defence now was attack, or she knew she'd tell him the whole sordid story.

'Forgive me.'

'Asking forgiveness twice in one day,' she remarked, clucking her tongue, trying to lighten the atmosphere clinging to them.

He almost smiled. 'You're very tough on me.'

'Maybe someone has to be. Sounds like you've had it all your own way for a while.'

Now he laughed. 'Perhaps I have. One more indulgence then?'

'I can guess. I said the trees are laden, but they're not quite ready.'

'I'll know them on sight,' he said.

'It's this way,' she said, pointing towards the French doors that led out of the parlour. But just as they began to move they were halted by a cacophony of voices out in the hall. Jane recognised William's voice pleading with a woman to wait in the front sitting room; he must have just returned from his walk and chess game.

She frowned. 'What now? Sorry, Guy, I need to see what this disturbance is about.'

'Listen, I'll go, but can we meet again before Sunday?'

The noise in the hallway was getting louder.

'Yes, I'll come to the Red Lion.'

'May I leave via the orchard?'

She nodded. 'You may. Though I'd have loved to share the moment with you.'

Guy smiled. 'Then I shall wait for you. What's another day or two?'

Tension seemed to leak out of Guy's frame as his shoulders loosened with relief, while hers tightened with tension she hadn't felt in years. Jane could have sworn that was her sister's voice she could hear. Could it really be Charlotte?

15

The visitor arrived rather rudely into the parlour before Guy could disappear. Reluctantly, he moved swiftly away from the entrance and melted into the shadows at the back of the room, hidden slightly by furniture, as the door burst open.

'Ah, there you are!' the woman said and then gave a laugh. 'With yet another painting of yet another plant. Truly, Jane, have the years not changed you at all?'

'I see they haven't changed *you*, sister.'

Sister? Guy thought, surprised. He hadn't thought Jane had any family. He could see little resemblance between the women. The newcomer was clearly an older sister, who wore rouge and lipstick to enhance handsome, if rather overly painted, looks. Her hair was golden and swept up dramatically beneath a coquettish hat. She was as loud as Jane was quiet.

William hurried in, slightly breathless. 'Madam, I'll ask you to not run rampant without permission.'

'This horrid old man refused me entry,' Charlotte said, scowling.

'Charlotte!' Jane sounded horrified. 'Please show some respect. This gentleman is Mr William Angus, and he owns this house. It is certainly his permission you must seek to walk around it.'

Charlotte scoffed. 'I'm not interested in a tour of the house, Jane.' She turned to face William. 'Sir, forgive my intrusion,' she said without a smidgeon of sincerity in her tone. 'Now,' she began dismissively, 'do you imagine my sister and I might have some privacy, please? I come with some . . . er . . . delicate family news.'

William looked flustered but began to withdraw. Guy wondered if it was best he made his escape now, as he was yet to be noticed. But before he could move, Jane held up her hand. 'William, do not take another step away. Charlotte, don't you dare order anyone around in this house, least of all William. You're not even a guest.'

Guy watched the sister sigh dramatically and begin to unpin her hat. 'I wasn't ordering anyone. It was a simple request, Mr Angus.'

William stood to his full height. 'Your sister has asked me to remain, Mrs . . .'

'Cavendish!' she said, sneering. 'I'm married . . . well, I was married to Edmund Cavendish of Bloomsbury.'

'Was?' Jane queried, shocked.

'He's dead, Jane. That's what I came here to share. May I sit, please? Perhaps a glass of water is not out of the question either?'

Guy watched the sister – who he'd already decided was ghastly – affect a sort of swoon, touching a shaking hand to her forehead and looking around for a seat to collapse into. He'd seen it time and again in different households, as women turned to this sort of emotional blackmail if they weren't receiving the attention and fawning over that they were accustomed to.

'William, do you mind?' Jane murmured.

'Not at all.' The spry old fellow moved away to fetch the water, while Guy still felt awkwardly rooted to the spot in the shadows.

Jane sat down opposite her sister, whose back was to Guy. 'Charlotte, what happened?'

'With Eddie?' The woman gave a bitter laugh. 'He drank, partied and whored himself to death, Jane, that's what happened. In the end it was a street accident with a hansom cab that took him – his fault entirely – but he was so intoxicated he probably felt nothing when the frightened horse reared and knocked him down. He hit his head on the cobbles and died within a day.'

Eddie Cavendish. Guy recalled him now. The man had an American mother with an endless supply of money and an incredible thirst for social acceptance. The father overreached with his business dealings, but her money had saved him repeatedly. Guy had come across Cavendish at various gatherings but had never liked his brash, vulgar ways or his arrogance. He was sure the man was a most unlucky gambler too, and treated his wife abominably the few times they'd shared company. Guy wouldn't have recognised her, but then he'd never paid much attention to her and neither had her husband, it seemed.

William arrived, his hand shaky as it held the water. Guy didn't think the older man looked terribly well.

'Thank you, William,' Jane said.

'Jane, if you're all right here, I'll excuse myself,' William said, handing Charlotte the glass with a worried frown. 'Good day, madam.'

Charlotte did not respond but reached for the water as though parched. She drank greedily as William retreated and Guy envied him. How on earth was he to get out of this tricky spot?

Jane continued her interrogation. 'What about your mother-in-law? Melba is surely—'

'Melba's gone too. Back to America. Nothing to stay for once her son was dead.'

'But you are—'

145

'I'm nothing!' her sister cut in rudely again, banging the water glass down on a side table. 'I couldn't give her the grandchildren she so desperately wanted, and she wearied of us and our bickering. Once he was gone, of course she had no reason to stay, with no grandchildren to call hers. She certainly has no love for me. She says she's gone home on an extended holiday to see family, but I can't imagine she'll be back.'

'What about the house? What about—'

Charlotte began to laugh again. Guy desperately wanted to escape, but even as he thought this, Jane seemed to be ahead of him. She caught his eye and shook her head just enough for him to realise she didn't want him announcing himself.

Then you'd better make some excuse so I can extricate myself, he thought.

'Charlotte, I'm sorry that you've been widowed, but what are you doing here? I didn't even think you knew where I lived.'

'I opened the letters you sent.'

'That you never replied to once,' Jane countered, sounding injured.

Her sister shrugged. 'I had nothing to say.'

Guy listened to the exchange with disbelief. These sisters really did not like one another. What had driven them apart?

'And Mother?'

'Oh, much the same. Don't whine, I gather she visited,' Charlotte said, standing now, evidently revived by the water. She began pacing, touching things at the mantelpiece. Guy felt sure he'd be noticed any moment. What would he say? He began to think of excuses but all felt weak.

'She came once. That was nearly six years ago.' Jane sounded resigned.

'Look, can we go and sit in one of the front rooms, please?' Charlotte said, her tone dismayed. 'I saw much finer furniture at the front. And it would make me feel more like a welcome visitor.'

Jane shook her head with exasperation. 'Except you're not one, Charlotte. Besides, I can't imagine you're staying long.'

'Just long enough,' Charlotte said. Guy thought that sounded cryptic.

Jane frowned. 'Oh, Charlotte, I wish you hadn't come.'

Her sister made a tsking sound. 'So rude, Jane. But I can see you haven't changed much. At least you've updated your wardrobe somewhat. I wouldn't call it fashionable but it's—'

'Charlotte!'

'What?'

'Why are you here?'

'Can I not visit my sister?'

'Some warning might have been nice. How long has it been since Eddie passed?'

'Nearly five months.'

Jane gasped. 'And this is the first I hear of it? Why didn't you write?'

Charlotte shrugged. 'We weren't exactly a loving couple, Jane.' She smiled. 'Besides, you should read the death notices, like Mother, and then you'd have known and would have made contact yourself, which would have been polite. Now, are you going to offer me tea?'

Jane closed her eyes. 'Yes,' she sighed. 'I've forgotten my manners. Come with me.'

As they left the room, Jane looked over her shoulder at Guy, who had remained as still as one of her paintings, and gave a small nod, indicating now was his chance. He nodded in response and tiptoed to the French doors again. Wincing, he turned the handle to open one side and let himself out. It was very tempting to run down to the orchard, but he'd promised Jane he'd wait to see the apple, and anyway, he would be spotted from the kitchen. Jane wouldn't take kindly to that. The apple tree felt so close and yet as far away as ever, but he gritted his teeth and walked away from it, skirting the house to get to the front garden via a pretty, laced ironwork gate.

William was there, standing near the magnolia, gazing out towards the cathedral and looking grumpy. 'Making your escape?' he asked sharply.

'Yes. I don't wish to intrude on their conversation.' Guy nodded over his shoulder. 'I thought it best I leave them to it.'

The old man sighed. 'She's here to make trouble for Jane, no doubt about it.'

Where was William getting that? 'From what I gather, her husband has died and she's come for some support from her sister.'

'Don't you believe a word of it. That woman hasn't bothered with Jane in eight years. Not a word, not even a note, and now she's here crying on her shoulder? She's up to something.'

Guy put his palms up. 'None of my business.'

'Coward,' William said. It wasn't said meanly, but it also wasn't cast with any amusement. 'Off you go.'

He began down the path but turned back. 'William, I barely know Jane.'

The man shrugged. 'You know her better than her sister does, and I suspect what Jane needs more than anything right now is a friend who'll stand by her.'

'If she needs anything, please let her know I'm staying at the Red Lion.'

William shook his head. 'She won't ask for help, but I'm telling you now that an ill wind has just blown into Jane's life and she's got everything to lose. And I do mean everything she cares about. Good day to you, sir.'

Guy was shocked that William strode back up the path, entered the house and closed the front door on him, as though disappointed. He stood there momentarily, frowning. What was he expected to do about Eddie Cavendish dying and his distraught wife returning to the bosom of her family? He shook his head and left, confused, but with the distinct feeling that he was letting Jane and Harry down somehow.

16

The sisters were back in the parlour with a pot of tea, and Jane was relieved to see that Guy had departed, especially as she didn't want Charlotte getting too comfortable in one of the guest rooms at the front of the house. She wanted her gone, if she were honest.

'This is a depressing little abode, isn't it,' Charlotte remarked. It wasn't a question.

'I don't agree. I love living here.'

'Of course you do, but that's because you're a drab little mouse. Is that how you spend your days?' she asked, cutting a look towards Jane's painting of Guy's lost apple.

Jane ignored the query. 'Tell me more about Eddie,' she said, shifting her sister back to their previous conversation. 'I thought you were happy in the marriage.'

Charlotte gave a long sigh. 'I don't like my tea strong; you can pour it,' she said, nodding at the pot. 'No sugar and a drop of milk.'

She was still giving her orders. *You certainly need sweetening, dear sister*, Jane thought. Nothing had changed in Charlotte: still sour, still pinched about the mouth and hollow-cheeked – a thin appearance achieved by starving herself, no doubt. That was another reason Charlotte had found to dislike Jane: she stayed lean no matter what she ate.

'We were not close,' Charlotte continued. 'Although we could have been. I did love Eddie and told him so repeatedly, but he didn't love me. I realise now that he likely never did.'

It was a rare moment of honesty, and Jane could tell by her sister's dreamy tone that she had daydreamed of a good life with Edmund.

'That's the truth of it, Jane. We were a loveless couple and couldn't find much common ground, although I tried. Eddie's interests were antisocial, unfortunately, no matter how social he actually believed himself to be.'

'What do you mean by that?' Jane asked, handing her sister a cup and saucer.

Charlotte took a sip and sighed. 'That's very refreshing, Jane, thank you. What I mean is that Eddie liked everything that polite society frowns upon. And on top of his favourite pastimes of gambling, drinking and women, he developed a taste for mescal. Do you know what that is?'

Jane shook her head dumbly.

'I'm surprised you don't, because it's a natural thing,' Charlotte said with contempt. 'The sort you paint.' She let out a short laugh.

'Not from England, I'm guessing,' Jane replied.

'No. I don't really know from where exactly; I have no idea what it is. Someone said it's a cactus.'

'South America, then.'

Her sister shrugged. 'Anyway, if you chew it – and don't ask me how – it can alter the mind. Eddie liked it dried, crushed and rolled with his tobacco.'

'A hallucinogen, you mean?'

'Yes, I suppose so. Sometimes he would combine his special tobacco mix with the cannabis plant for what he called "an enriched experience" and his ultimate escape.' She gave a choked laugh of disappointment.

Jane almost felt sorry for Charlotte. 'Did Melba know all this?'

'She had to, but it was never discussed openly in the early years of our marriage. You see, he was never drunk, dishevelled, out of his mind in his mother's company, only mine. He was always on his best behaviour around his mother because she bankrolled his habits without even knowing it. She also funded every aspect of our lives, which meant I was beholden to her in every way.'

'But that's no surprise, surely? You knew that going into the marriage.'

'But I didn't know she would be so careless with me. She didn't care a whit about my life, my state of mind, my loveless marriage or how badly I wished to please them both. The fact is, Melba Cavendish loved my surname and what it might do for their social standing. She had no affection for me as a person and, I might add, it turned out she was well aware of her son's affairs. In fact, I'd go so far as to say she encouraged him to seek satisfaction with other women. I was not enough. And then ultimately, when she began to see her son clearly and realise how far he had fallen, I think she blamed me.'

Jane gave a soft gasp. 'I'm so sorry, Charlotte.'

'Are you? Do you really care?' She looked vaguely amused.

'I care about your marriage.'

Now Charlotte smiled but all amusement had fled. 'He only married me because it's what his mother wanted – the dutiful son. I don't think he ever actually wanted marriage or knew what being a husband meant. He was so unkind to me, Jane. I stuck it out because I had to, and I kept hoping . . .' She trailed off, staring out the window.

'Hoping?' Jane prompted.

'For a family.'

'Oh,' Jane said, dipping her gaze. *You had your chance at a family*, she thought blindly. *And you gave it up.*

'I knew a child or two would bind Eddie to me, but also his mother to us. I knew she wanted grandchildren, not so much to dote over, but to carry on the family name, and maybe to bring a sense of . . . normalcy, I suppose, to Eddie's behaviour. A respectability. A child would protect me.'

'And?'

'Well, it never worked again. Pregnant when I didn't want it, and then I couldn't achieve another pregnancy no matter what. I think he lost interest in me very early on, so that didn't help the matter.' Charlotte didn't blush at the admission but continued. 'And when I couldn't produce the heir, his mother lost all interest. They argued a lot over money, though she had plenty to go around.'

'Yes. Mother used to say that Melba rescued the Cavendishes.'

'Well, her fortune certainly did. But Eddie had a knack for squandering a fortune.'

'Good grief. What are you saying?'

'That I'm penniless, Jane. I have nothing to my name.'

Jane opened her mouth in shock. 'How can that be?'

'He spent it all on his gambling, parties at his club, on women, on cars, on his wardrobe . . . on drugs. He made some very poor deals, too. His father he was not,' she said, her tone laced with biting sarcasm. 'And to add to my woes, I lived in fear of him.'

'Fear?' Jane swallowed. What was Charlotte saying?

'When he was drunk he'd hurt me. He'd use me like one of his whores, and often he'd take out his frustration on me with his fists.'

Jane put her hands to her mouth in horror. 'Then you are best rid of him. Where was Melba in all of this? Surely she could see your bruises and—'

Charlotte sipped her tea daintily and shook her head, her face neutral, as though she hadn't just shocked Jane. 'No, he might have been in his cups, but he was still aware enough to land his blows where they wouldn't be seen. He threatened me with worse if I bleated to his mother. *He* was scared of her. And in spite of her careless attitude to me, I doubt she would have approved of violence.' Charlotte put her cup and saucer down. 'It's irrelevant anyway, because by the time he died, she'd had enough of his ways too. She and I simply weren't close enough for me to ask for her help. Even before his death Melba began to talk of returning to America. My surname hadn't brought the warmth she'd hoped, and certainly not from the royals. And now she's gone – and my chance of any future happiness with her.'

'I don't know what to say.' Jane put down her cup. She'd never imagined Charlotte had been so unhappy all this time. If she was honest with herself, she hadn't spent a lot of time thinking about her, once the initial shock of her departure had worn off. She'd been too angry but also enamoured of Harry to give Charlotte any more of her time and energy.

Charlotte shook her head with a rueful smile. 'She wanted something that I failed to give her. And now I have nothing.'

'But why, Charlotte? Your name is still sound.'

'Mother says the society folk whom Melba wanted to be around had begun to withdraw because of Eddie. He owed some of them debts – large ones – and he was a liability, I suspect, in many ways. He's ruined my name too.'

'This is very sad.' It was, but Jane had to prevent herself from following the thought that it was no less than her selfish sister deserved. 'Are you back with Mother?'

'Don't be ridiculous. I live in the London house – for now, anyway – but there's also the country house in Kent and various other properties I am now learning about. There are assets.'

'So those are yours now? You said you have nothing . . .'

'A ridiculous suggestion, Jane. Nothing was yet in Eddie's

name, so I can't inherit it. Melba owns it all, and she couldn't give a damn about me.' Charlotte impersonated Melba, then, with a good attempt at mimicking an American accent. 'You know, Charlotte dear, if only you'd given us some children, I would provide for you all.' Charlotte scowled. 'When I asked her what she meant by that, she assured me she couldn't care less about the property in England . . . that she would gladly bequeath it all to her grandchildren, if she had any, but she would not be leaving anything to me. The useless wife, that's what she called me.' She sat up straighter. 'Do you know what she suggested, Jane?'

Jane shook her head miserably, the very first trills of alarm already beginning to sound in her mind.

'She said I should sell my jewellery if I needed money.' Again she adopted the voice of Melba. '"Sell all that fancy stuff and buy a little townhouse and learn to live frugally." This is how she spoke to me.'

'So why don't you?' Jane asked, beginning to feel flustered; her forehead, she was certain, was becoming clammy. Surely her sister wasn't here to buy in Salisbury.

'Why? I'm angry! I should be treated better as Eddie's widow. She owes me that! I stuck by him and his awful behaviour for seven years. I stood by him at events, having to face the very women he was carousing with. I ran his household for him and Melba, but they were always on the attack. It was a pretty miserable seven years.'

'Maybe you should have had a dalliance of your own,' Jane said, trying to move away from her greatest fear.

'Well, I did, actually. A woman needs affection – perhaps not you, Jane, but I do. And now that Eddie's gone, I do need to meet someone I like – someone I can make a life with – but I am not giving up my rights. I stood by Eddie for all that time, and I should have something to show for that.'

155

'Beyond your jewellery and wardrobe, and use of the London house.'

'Exactly.' Charlotte clearly hadn't heard Jane's ironic tone. 'And Mother agrees. She wants me to go after what I'm entitled to.'

'How?' Jane asked. 'There is no Cavendish line,' she added, wishing the words away the second they left her lips. She looked away, unable to meet Charlotte's suddenly feverish gaze.

'That they know of, anyway,' Charlotte said, her tone slippery.

Jane stood. She needed to get Charlotte out of the house so she could think, terrified of her sister's motive for being here. 'Right. Well, are you staying locally, or did you just come down for the day? Perhaps I can organise transport to the railway station . . .?'

'I thought I might stay with you, sister.'

Jane felt sick but kept her expression neutral as she shook her head. 'This is not my house, Charlotte, and I have to admit that William doesn't enjoy visitors, and house guests even less. I would ask you not to presume. He will unlikely agree, especially as you were so dismissive of him when you arrived.'

'Well, you can talk to him because I shall be staying upstairs, Jane. You surely have enough rooms in this miserable house.'

'No. You can't stay here.'

'Fix it, Jane. I'm heading upstairs now.' Charlotte stood up and began walking towards the door.

'Please, no,' Jane said, feeling desperate. Her sister needed to leave. 'If you insist on staying, let's organise a hotel.'

'Oh, that won't do. I have important business right here in this house.' Charlotte flicked a piece of lint from her shoulder and looked up. Jane's heartbeat intensified to a pounding in her throat. 'Now, tell me, what time does my son return from school?'

And there it was.

Seven years of dread coalescing into her single fear. Jane could cope with anything . . . anything! But not this.

Since the moment Charlotte Saville had ruthlessly walked away from her son and left him gurgling softly in Jane's arms, Jane had promised herself she would become the boy's mother.

And she had. She might not have given birth to him, but in every other way that might count she was Harry's mother.

She actually retched in the parlour and had to steady herself, winning back control before she lifted a gaze of blazing ire at her sister. '*Your* son?' she said, words falling like glass splinters.

'Indeed. What did we call him again? Mother didn't say.'

'*We* did not call him anything. Can I remind you of how you referred to that vulnerable infant . . . a *creature*, a *thing*, among other nasty terms. You refused to name him, Charlotte, even though I begged you to. I got on my knees once over those awful four days and I pleaded with you to reconsider. And you refused. You refused to hear me, you refused to even look at him. You have never once held the child you birthed. You actually shoved him away when I tried to place him in your arms. You offered to smother him yourself!'

Charlotte didn't even look cowed; not the slightest sign of embarrassment or even contrition could Jane read in her face. 'That was then. Things have changed.'

'What?' Jane all but shrieked. 'What sort of answer is that?'

'The only answer. The truthful one, dear sister. I was young, frightened, I had been snubbed by the man I loved, whom I expected to marry, and I had given birth to a child he didn't want. If only you'd tried harder, Jane, you might now have family of your own, a husband at your side. You don't need the boy. I do. I'm telling you, Eddie would have loved his son if he'd held him. But now we'll never know. Eddie is cold in his grave. His mother has abandoned her life in England. And she's left me to the dogs.'

'How does coming here and demanding to see your child – and I struggle to call him that – change anything?'

'Because, Jane – and you clearly haven't been listening – Melba Cavendish has said repeatedly that if I'd produced family, an heir, she would have provided for us. She is grieving over her son. If I produce the boy now, she'll have to change her mind and give me what I'm owed.'

Jane felt her throat tightening as effectively as if Charlotte and Melba Cavendish were squeezing their hands around her neck. She had to take a moment to clear it. 'So you believe if you suddenly produce a child, all will be well? Won't they wonder where he's been all these years?'

'All shall be well. It's the truth, after all. I'll say that we wanted him to grow up away from the city, safe with his *aunt*.' Charlotte leaned on the word. 'The boy is Eddie's son. No one can deny it.'

'And if I do? If I say he's mine?' Jane said, the words spilling out before she could think them through.

Charlotte laughed and it was ugly and demeaning. 'You've never told a lie in your life, Jane.'

Jane almost laughed at that. 'Sister, I have been living a lie for the past seven years. I *am* a lie. So don't try and bait me. I will fight you on this.'

'With what? Are you now claiming to be his mother?'

'I am his mother, in every possible way,' Jane growled. She'd never heard herself like this, with something bestial and primitive about it.

Charlotte did not appear threatened, though, because she simply laughed. 'Well, every success with that approach, Jane. He's mine. And I want him back.'

'Never!'

'I'm taking him with me.'

'I will fight you with my last breath. You don't even know him.'

'I plan to. I plan to get to know my son and spoil him. I shall lavish him with kisses, and we may even travel to America to see his family over there. But for now he is coming back to London with me, and I shall be sending a telegram to Melba to expect an important letter and photograph from me. He's my son, and he's how I'll get what I deserve.'

'She won't believe you,' Jane blurted out. This couldn't be happening.

Charlotte just shrugged. 'I'll tell her everything. She'll forgive me for the lie when she sees her precious grandson.'

'I won't back you up. I'll say you're lying.'

'Mother will tell the truth.'

'Both of you can go to hell!'

That made Charlotte gasp. She looked shocked, but then she laughed. 'My, my, Jane. I don't believe I've ever seen you this stirred up.'

Stirred up was understating the fury she felt right now. 'Get out!'

Charlotte tsked. 'I suppose that means I really cannot stay, then?'

'Get out, Charlotte, before I do something I may regret.'

'Oooh, I am liking the new Jane. So much spirit. Is this what it means to be a mother? I can't wait to feel the same way when I put my arms around my son. What's his name, by the way?'

Jane swallowed hard. 'His name is Hugo John Saville.'

'Hugo,' Charlotte repeated, testing it on her tongue. 'Wouldn't have been my choice.'

'You had your chance,' Jane said. 'To name him. To know him. No one will believe you.'

Charlotte smiled, seemingly untroubled. She walked over to the mantelpiece, where there was a photograph of a seated Jane with Harry next to her, his arm resting gently on her shoulder. They were looking directly at the camera with a hint of a smile on their faces. 'Nice uniform. That's the cathedral school, I'm gathering? I saw some of the boys walking around the Close. He's a handsome fellow, isn't he? And I swear that could be Eddie standing next to you there, looking so relaxed. No doubting whose son that boy is.' She tapped the photo.

'You're lying. I know what Eddie looked like, and my son looks nothing like him.'

Charlotte sighed. 'Even so. Melba can be convinced.'

She sounded so confident that Jane began to panic. There was no way out of this. How could she tell the boy she loved so much that she'd lied to him all of his life? She was the only mother he'd ever known. She couldn't allow him to meet Charlotte, not even as his aunt.

'Leave now, Charlotte,' Jane said. 'So help me . . .'

Charlotte merely raised her eyebrows, picking up her bag. 'I *will* leave, for now. But I shall be back, and I want to meet my son.'

'I won't give him to you, Charlotte. He's *my* son.'

'Then I suppose I shall have to get the authorities involved. Mother said it would likely come to this, though I had hoped for your good sense to prevail. But . . . so be it. Good day, sister. I shall see myself out.'

Charlotte walked out of the parlour. Jane, for the first time in many years, wept uncontrollably for several long minutes.

That was how William found her. 'Now, now, my child. Tears are not going to make this situation better. Am I guessing right that your snooty sister has come to reclaim our Harry?'

Jane nodded through her sniffs. 'I told her his name was Hugo.'

He actually laughed, although it sounded choked. 'Why ever would you do that?'

'I have to thwart at every turn, William. It was all I could think of in the moment. Somehow I have to prove that while Harry might have grown in her belly for forty weeks, since then, since the moment he gave his first cry upon entering the world, he has been my son. He *is* my son.'

She felt his long, thin arms wrap around her. 'We'll find a way.'

'And if we don't?' She could barely hold back another sob.

'If we don't, we do only what's best for Harry.'

'I *am* best for Harry.'

'And that's how we'll approach this problem. He knows no other mother than you. Plus, she has to prove that paternity. You're going to have to be prepared to call her bluff, Jane.'

'What does that mean?'

'Find a way to put doubt in the minds of those who may listen to her.' She nodded and swallowed. He was right: crying achieved nothing. She had to take action and shore up her defences.

17

Guy felt like the worst sort of cad, stealing away from Jane and her problems, with William's words about an ill wind blowing through his mind repeatedly. Guy didn't want to feel responsible but try as he might to shake off the guilt, it was there. And he didn't understand why. These were strangers. Friends would assure him he owed no debt here, and in fact he'd been pretty decent about the injury to his face.

And still his inner voice, which Guy knew to be his soul – perhaps the very essence of who he was – suggested that he had been involved in subterfuge. It didn't matter how he tried to ignore it, he and his soul both knew he'd taken advantage of the situation.

After leaving Jane's home, he took refuge in the cool of the cathedral's cloisters, walking to its furthest point to find a quiet seat against the stone. What situation? he argued with himself.

The inner voice sighed. *Your spectacles. They were fake. That was your first piece of beguilement. The second was returning to the house on the pretext of collecting them. It gave you the perfect excuse to get back into her studio somehow and the garden.*

It's just an apple.

Not any apple, though. Your apple. The prize. The one you've hunted for a long time.

He gazed back through the elegant, arcaded cloister, admiring what was the largest of its kind in England. It had been added to the cathedral in 1260 or thereabouts; maybe it was two centuries after his apple had been introduced into England. Maybe William the Conqueror's invading armies had brought the species with them . . . or perhaps his apple had come later, from Normandy. This cathedral had known plenty of history, and it overlooked the very orchard where he believed his apple to be. That was a mystery he longed to solve.

The mystery of his guilt had not been solved either, and he didn't think he could do so without Jane.

So, you can't involve yourself with Jane without involving yourself with whatever the ill wind has brought, the inner voice reminded him. *And William all but suggested you should get involved.*

In what, though? He turned it over in his mind. Jane's life seemed simple. A woman raising a child on minimal means but with a gentle benefactor who cared about both of them. Her life was not tough, though it looked lonely. But many were lonely. *He* was lonely, when it came down to it, but he chose not to press on it, or even admit it to anyone but himself.

You like Jane, his inner companion prompted.

Guy sighed quietly but the cloister heard it and seemed to echo the sad sound.

I do. She gives no quarter. I like that about her. I like that it doesn't matter to her who I am. I will go back.

That's what you should do. Knock on the door. Apologise for leaving the way you did. And ask if you can help.

Yes, that way she has the opportunity to stop my interference, but at least I've offered.

And then you can ask if you might see the apple.

With a clear conscience?

Precisely.

Right.

One more thing.

What's that?

Eleanor.

Yes. He had been a coward. Jane had quietly shocked him with that accusation, but he knew in his heart the moment she said it that it was true. He had been avoiding being honest, thinking he was being kind. But it was cruel. He would confront Eleanor with the truth.

He stood. Time to face Jane.

'How can I help you, Jane?' William asked, looking dismayed. They were sitting in his study, where he had found her collapsed in a chair, one hand over her eyes.

'You can't, but thank you. This is my problem to solve.'

She cried again, this time in his arms.

'Oh, my dear girl. This will not do. And we shall not let this happen.

'She's his mother,' Jane sobbed. 'I can't compete with that.'

'Maybe so, but you can prove you have been his mother for the past seven busy years – his whole life. You've been there every minute, looking after his needs. While she has been absent since near enough the day of his birth.'

'The courts favour mothers.'

'They do. We shall get you the best solicitor and the best barrister in the land, Jane. We will not give up our beloved Harry without a fight. Now, please stop weeping,' he said, smoothing back her hair. 'I hope never to see you so undone again. We will fight this, I promise. Where were you going?'

She looked dumbly at the hat she'd grabbed from the hallway lying next to her. 'I needed to get out. I was going to stomp around the city, I think, and I came in here to tell you something. But you weren't here.'

'No, I was in the garden. It's a better place for breathing and letting out the tension. Then none of the nosey people can witness you.'

She nodded. 'I wasn't thinking straight.'

There was a tap at the door.

She tensed. 'My sister is probably back with the police.'

'Nonsense!' William said. 'And if she is, I'm here and we shall deal with this. Wait here.'

He stepped out to answer the door and she heard a distant male voice. Definitely police.

William returned. 'Jane, dear, you have a visitor.'

Jane looked up, expecting someone in uniform, her sister with a smug smile behind them, but she was shocked when she saw it was Guy Attwood back in the house. 'Oh,' she said, quickly wiping away her tears. 'Forgive me, I wasn't expecting—'

'I know, and please forgive the intrusion,' he began politely, and she caught a sheepish look thrown William's way.

'Guy, I know I was going to show you the apple tree but—'

'Don't think on that now. I can see you're upset, and in fact I came back not about the tree but to admit how badly I feel about the way I departed not so long ago.'

'It's fine.' She swallowed. 'I'm sure you could tell I was trapped too. I didn't want you feeling the same way.'

Guy shook his head. 'Hiding in the shadows and tiptoeing is not my style, and I'm ashamed I let you and William think it might be.' He shot a glance at the older man.

William cleared his throat in response, not meeting Guy's gaze. Jane wondered what message was being passed between the two.

'I was actually feeling awkward to be sharing something personal between you and your sister, so I thought that I should leave, and yet there was no easy time to suddenly step into the conversation.'

'I understand. It's why I said nothing too. The way she spoke to William was bad enough, but I didn't want you to be caught in her clutches too . . .'

'No, it was cowardly not to introduce myself to your sister. Especially as we've met.'

'Met?' Jane's voice squeaked. 'When?'

'Not recently, and not that she'd recall. I knew her husband.'

'How well?' She sensed his hesitation. 'You can speak freely, Guy.' She scrubbed at her cheeks, the tears having subsided. She must look a mess.

'I knew him well enough to know he wasn't my sort of acquaintance.' Guy looked down.

William chuckled. 'You should go into politics, Guy. Jane, that's Mr Attwood's way of saying he didn't like the fellow.'

She nodded; she'd picked up that not-so-subtle message for herself.

'You're right. I didn't like him. That's the truth of it,' Guy said, looking embarrassed but remaining candid. 'He wasn't what I'd call an upstanding fellow. His habits were . . . well, vulgar, shall we say?'

'Why don't we,' William agreed, amusement in his eyes.

Guy sighed. 'His tastes ran to the extreme and unmannerly,' he tried again. 'And it would not have been easy being his wife. But I wouldn't wish him dead, so I'm sorry to hear of your sister's loss.'

Jane blew out a breath. 'The truth is Eddie Cavendish was a cad before Charlotte married him, and it sounds as though he didn't change much after she became his wife. I don't know why she ever thought he would. She loved him, I suppose. Love can make one capable of overlooking the obvious.'

Guy cleared his throat, perhaps taking that as a timely barb, but she hadn't meant it as a taunt to him. She was lost in her thoughts about her sister.

'It was a miserable existence by the sounds of things,' she said sadly.

Guy nodded. 'But you obviously cared enough to be upset over his passing.'

Jane shook her head. 'Not really. I knew Eddie only from the tittle-tattle of London society and how he treated my sister before their wedding. I haven't seen them in years, not since . . .' She trailed off, looking down at her hands.

'I'm sorry that I didn't make the connection that you were from the Savilles of Hanover Square.'

Jane looked up. 'Would it have made a difference?'

'I'm not sure I understand,' he said carefully.

'Would it have made a difference to how you might have treated us, me and Harry?'

Guy blinked. 'Not at all,' he blustered. 'I . . . Jane, if you knew me better, you'd know I don't set much store by name or status.'

'And yet you hid yours,' she said, unsure why she'd taken this sudden combative stance. 'Guy, it's my opinion that you're highly aware of name, status and wealth, and what that means to all who meet you. You've admitted as much yourself.'

She noticed William tiptoeing from the room, although whether Guy was aware, she couldn't tell. He looked as though she'd just slapped him in the face.

'I don't trade on my family name,' he said, sounding firm. 'I think I proved that much.'

'I wasn't suggesting that you do. I'm just saying that you do care about the judgements people make based on reputation.

I am no longer Jane Saville to you, but Jane Saville of Hanover Square, and now all the weight of my family connections sit alongside me, in your eyes. But if you know our name, then you likely also know that my father passed away and left only women, no heir. Our family may have a fine name, but we're impoverished, so while I have a poor relationship with my sister, it is not because of her determination to marry into money. I can even forgive my mother for encouraging her in all sorts of schemes'—Jane's voice broke slightly on the word—'to preserve exactly the right presentation for making an advantageous marriage. On paper, a wedding to Edmund Cavendish, with his extraordinarily wealthy mother, was a dream come true for my sister – and for my mother, especially.'

'But what about you, Jane?' he asked. 'Why did your mother not make the same demands of you?'

Jane hesitated. How much should she tell him? 'How do you know she didn't?' she said, trying to buy time to think.

'I don't. I'm asking.'

She swallowed. She didn't want to lie any more. The truth was that she loved that he'd come back, whether simply to apologise and make amends or to try to help in some way. She didn't want to admit to herself that she was captivated by this enigmatic man who hid his credentials behind false names and his looks behind false glasses. She had enjoyed making him feel uncomfortable about Eleanor – on behalf of all downtrodden women – and yet she did feel Eleanor had brought much of his distance upon herself by being so needy, even as she pretended to be the opposite. But Jane had not been in such a situation, so who was she to judge Eleanor?

'My mother did not believe I was well suited for marriage – can we put it that way?'

'I'd like to know why. You seem perfectly . . . suited.' He looked away, his cheeks slightly reddened.

Jane shook her head. 'I don't know you well enough to explain further.'

'You know me well enough to trust me around your son.'

'I wish he was.' It was as though someone else had said the words. Jane had to steady herself, hand against William's desk.

'You wish he was what? I don't understand,' Guy replied, his voice small, confused.

She turned back, eyes blazing, ready to vindicate herself. *Let's see how he handles the truth he seems to be after. Let's watch him run away as fast as he can from you, Jane,* she told herself. 'Harry is not my son,' she said. 'His father is dead, I now discover, but Harry is the illegitimate son of my sister.'

Guy's features slackened to the point that his face had no expression at all. She nearly laughed, but she knew if she did it would come out sounding like she was mad in the head. Perhaps she was. Living this lie, pretending to be someone she was not, falling in love with someone who was unattainable. *Get rid of him, Jane, or you'll be hurt all over again.*

'There,' she said, her voice like granite. 'Now you know my great secret. Just go, please. You should not be fraternising with—'

He looked around but there was no William, just a closed door. His whipped his gaze back to her. 'Let me get this right. *Charlotte* is Harry's mother, not you?'

'Correct. Ten out of ten for comprehension. Now, please leave.' She felt sick.

He took a stride forward and grabbed her arms, momentarily forgetting himself. He stopped just short of shaking her. 'Explain this to me. Please.' He must have realised he was holding her tightly, because he suddenly released his grip.

Guy sounded so distraught she felt a surge of pity, and regret for her deliberate nastiness. She'd wanted to hurt him and turn him against her ... why? Shame? Guilt at her lies? Or was it because she felt such a powerful attraction to him that her only hope was to drive him away?

'I can't let you in,' she whispered, again shocked that she'd spoken her thoughts aloud.

'Why, Jane? Maybe I can help.'

'Help? Why would you do that? This situation is all of my own making. I've chosen to be this person – a liar, a thief who took another's child, an abuser of love – absorbing all that child's love without giving him the truth.'

Now he did shake her gently. 'Stop it! I know so little about you, but my instincts tell me none of those accusations feel true. Please.' He dropped his hands to his side. 'Jane, you're the most baffling, frustrating, obstinate woman I think I've ever met. You strike me as big-hearted and gentle, yet your tongue can cut like no other, and you possess a strength I sense is almost unbreakable. I can't help myself. I find you intriguing, and as much as I want to run from you and your problems, here I am, drawn like a magnet to them.'

She gave a laugh, surprised she could feel levity right now. 'What does all that mean?'

'It means, in a very roundabout way, that I really like you.'

Could he possibly feel the same way she did? 'What about Eleanor?' she asked.

'I told you, it never really began, other than in her imagination. I will tell her immediately. I just want to know you better.'

Her head snapped up. 'After all I've just told you?'

'You've told me nothing, other than that you are caring for your sister's child.'

She shook her head slowly. 'No, Guy, I really haven't been clear. Charlotte gave birth to Harry, yes, but Harry is my son. I did not carry him inside me, and yet all my emotions towards him mean I might as well have. I feel his sorrows, his injuries, his insecurities.

I feel each as a deep, physical pain, as though we're bonded. He is my child.'

'Tell me this story. Here, sit down. I will not judge you.'

'Are you sure?'

He nodded gravely.

'I doubt you'll find me quite so captivating in a few minutes. I'm not proud of what I've done.'

'I'll be the judge of that.'

Jane told him everything, from the day Charlotte burst into the conservatory with her news to the moment Harry had let fly and his football had accidentally connected with a stranger. She left nothing to the imagination, and watched Guy's expression deepen with shadows as his forehead creased, his mouth lost the playful tick at each corner, and his lids drooped with a hooded sadness.

Guy listened with increasing sorrow to the sad story of Jane Saville; not that she felt sorry for herself, he could surmise. If anything, the more she explained, the more her eyes burned with a pride . . . or if not pride, certainly a sense of satisfaction with the life she'd built for herself against the odds.

When she finished, she watched him for his reaction. He was careful to keep his features netural. She had spared him no detail, but he noted there were no embellishments or dramatic emotional additions. He'd promised no judgement and yet his immediate instinct was to make an excuse and get as far away from this problem as possible. Every sensibility within told him this was a spider's web of problems, fanning out, and wasn't limited to Jane. To become involved was to ensnare himself in the problems of Harry, Charlotte and all of her drama, and Harry's maternal grandmother, who he knew to be a cunning woman. His life just days ago had been on a neat, carefully planned trajectory, about which he'd made peace within himself, and now? A wayward football had knocked him off that path, but there was still time to right himself. A few well-chosen words and he might extricate himself from this pit of problems.

The soon to be crowned King George V would be none the wiser if the apple never emerged. An engraved cigarette case, or a beautifully fashioned letter opener, would arrive instead and be appreciated and that would be that. Perhaps in the future he might still hunt down the Scarlet Henry, purely for his own interest, when Jane and her 'son' had moved on.

But something tugged at him. There was something about this woman . . . He found himself *not* wanting to run, even though it would be the logical thing to do. Torn, he decided to take his lead from Jane for the moment, remaining neutral in his tone and his approach.

'So this is about money?' he asked.

Jane nodded. 'The only way Charlotte can access what she thinks is rightfully hers – and, frankly, it *is* rightfully hers – is to show up with Eddie's heir.' She gave a mirthless grin. 'I knew one day this would come back and hurt me, and the saddest part is, I don't blame Charlotte for using her trump card.'

'Really?' he asked, astonished.

'Oh, I blame her over and over again for ignoring her magnificent child for all these years. For pushing away her responsibility and denying him the love of his mother. That I can't forgive. But I can see how desperate she is here.'

'But, Jane, you can't be sure she would ever have loved him.'

'True. But even the little you know of Harry should tell you he is hard not to love.'

Guy grinned. 'He certainly is.'

'But Harry has the burden – not that he knows it yet – of people around here regarding his mother as a wanton woman . . . a woman who has fallen from grace. It brings shame upon him, even though it couldn't be further from the truth – I admit I have never been with a man. But I have to bear that title to keep Harry safe.'

He was appalled but didn't show it. 'I am not a parent. But, Jane, I believe only a mother would make such a sacrifice.' He shrugged. 'You may not have grown Harry within, but every inch of you is his mother.'

She smiled and he was enthralled that he could bring that out in her. 'Thank you for saying that.'

'It's the truth. So what will you do?'

It was her turn to shrug. 'I am lost. I haven't had a chance to do much more than weep – as you can tell.' She laughed weakly, pointing at her face, slightly swollen from her tears. 'I imagine Charlotte will go to all lengths required to prove he is hers, or, far more importantly to her, that he belongs to Eddie, and that will be that. Harry will become a Cavendish, I will give up my life once again. So now you know my problem.' She shook her head as if to shake off the misery she felt, and stood up. 'Come on.'

'Where are we going?'

'To see the apple tree. I need some air and a diversion for my racing thoughts, so that I'm thinking more clearly and am calm when Harry gets home from school. Besides, I think you deserve to see your precious tree. After all, you came back and you've helped to ease my shock. That's always the hardest bit of grief, isn't it?'

He wanted to say he didn't know, but he nodded. 'I'm sure it is,' he said, hating himself for standing and rushing to the door to open it for her. He couldn't wait to get out into the orchard.

18

Guy followed Jane like an obedient animal. She couldn't know that he felt as though he wasn't breathing properly, and that Jane's problems had evaporated in his mind for the time being. He felt distantly ashamed about that, but his anticipation at coming face to face with the tree was suddenly overwhelming. He knew it shouldn't be this important, but something about finding this tree and its fruit felt pivotal; it was the end of an era for him and the start of a new era for a new king. It signalled a new beginning.

'Are you holding your breath, Guy?' She turned and was actually smiling.

He hadn't thought she could find that dry wit within herself, today of all days. 'I think you can read me too well.'

She chuckled. 'That must be disconcerting for a man who gives little away.'

'It is,' he said, adding a grin. 'But somehow reassuring.'

She smiled back at him. 'Why is that?'

'I have very few friends, even fewer who understand me.'

She paused at a small garden gate that led into the orchard. 'Few friends through choice?'

'I'm afraid so. I have no female friends—'

'Other than Eleanor.'

'Yes.' Jane was right.

'Too dangerous to have women as friends?'

He felt momentarily pained. 'Maybe. I don't know. As a man, to get close to a woman platonically has complications down the track. If you become close as friends and then you, the man, fall in love, your female friend might resent her presence, and I think there's always a risk that the platonic friend could feel somehow slighted – or, at the very least, shut out – when you marry. I don't think I could bear the tension,' he admitted, frowning, which made her laugh. 'I do have plenty of female acquaintances, though, and I can be good company, amusing even, at an event or gathering.'

'What does that mean? That you can pretend?'

'No, I would hate to think I was insincere. It's more that I can always think of other places I'd rather be than stuffed into a suit and stiff collar, making small talk, but sadly I can be rather good at it.'

'You'd rather be alone?'

'Not alone. Just . . . not on show. I have plenty of interests, but they just seem to be quieter pursuits.'

She laughed gently. 'I understand better than you can imagine. I feel you're describing me. Now, come on. I can all but feel you trembling with anticipation. It's just through here.'

It wasn't a crowded orchard. A few small trees – pears, plums, an apple tree he recognised as a classic pippin – and then he halted. Jane hadn't needed to point or say anything. His gaze fell upon a gnarled tree and yet it was of a most handsome shape. It would have been glorious, maybe thirty years earlier. It had grown near the warm bricks of the garden wall, and was truly majestic. If he was someone who cried readily, he could imagine himself tearing up, perhaps even weeping. He was choked, though. He didn't have to go closer; he didn't have to touch the branches or the fruit. There was no doubting it: he was in the presence of the Scarlet Henry, which had occupied his thoughts for so long he felt he must savour the moment.

A second tree had grown further back near the wall's end, he now saw. It was equally handsome but not as large. He let out a breath. Two trees. That was surely enough to bring this species back from the brink of extinction.

'Guy?' Jane's voice was soft, clearly not wanting to intrude on this moment.

'It's my apple,' he said. His voice was croaky with emotion.

'Oh, how wonderful!' Jane clapped with delight. 'I'm very happy for you. Here, come closer.'

They both moved forward, and as she reached up to cup one of the ripening apples, so did he and accidentally covered her hand. Neither pulled away. She wasn't startled and he didn't apologise, even though both might be considered natural responses to the unintended touch. Instead, she raised her serious gaze to his and looked him square in the face. She did not act in any way coquettish; she did not feign shyness. She simply waited for his next move.

And his next move was a shock. Time seemed to slow as he leaned in and kissed her gently. Hers were not lips that were used to being touched by other lips, he knew that much, and yet they were soft and welcoming. He pulled back immediately, and saw her eyes were still closed and now a small smile played at her mouth.

'Should I apologise?' he asked softly.

She shook her head, still not opening her eyes, as though treasuring the moment. 'Not to me, only to Eleanor.' When she did open her eyes, they looked at him even more intensely than before. 'I'd forgotten how nice a simple kiss can be.' He blinked, adoring her honesty. 'The last person who did that was a boy,' she said with a chuckle. 'I think I was fifteen and he stole a kiss, just like that. Spontaneous and sweet.'

'Except I would like to do it again,' Guy said, surprised by his own candour. 'Not so sweet this time,' he added with a grin.

'Guy, please don't feel sorry for me. And by the same token, don't feel grateful to me because of the apple.'

'Is that why you think I'd kiss you? Pity, or gratitude?'

'Why else would—'

He didn't let her finish, this time taking her in his arms and kissing her properly, the way he'd wanted to since he'd first seen her hurrying towards him, her hands lifting her Vermeer blue skirt and her straw hat threatening to lift off her head and scatter her loosely pinned hair.

He did kiss her to apologise for the way the world had treated her, and he deepened the kiss to thank her for finding his apple and giving it to him. But, most of all, he kissed Jane Saville because she was the most intriguing, self-contained, motivated and cerebral woman he'd ever met. He loved her art, he loved how she handled her pain, he loved her single-mindedness and he especially loved that she didn't seem to care a damn about status or polite society. She was living a quiet life her own way. It was obvious this was not the life she would choose for herself – no one would choose it – but she was getting on with it, filling it with love, finding all the parts of it that brought her joy and celebrating that happiness wherever she found it, rather than dwelling on how unfair life was.

He finally pulled away, and this time she opened her eyes immediately.

'Definitely not so sweet,' she said, almost embarrassed. 'Delicious.'

Guy smiled. 'That's because you're very . . .' He couldn't think of the right word. 'Kissable,' he offered. He released her from his embrace, regretting it immediately, and took her hand instead, threading his fingers through hers.

She smiled down at their entwined hands but shook her head. 'I don't understand how someone like you is interested in someone like me.'

'What does that mean? Why not?'

Jane sighed. 'Have you lost interest in your apple?'

'No. But I've waited years for it. It will wait for me.' He paused. 'I fear you'll run.'

'I won't. I just don't think I'm good for you.' She looked down.

'Not good for . . . Let me respond. Firstly, I find you compelling in every way, Jane. I've never met anyone like you. I could talk to you about colour all day, I think. And I feel sure you would let me talk about apples and not get bored.'

'I wouldn't.' She smiled. 'I think your hobby is fascinating.'

'And secondly,' he continued, 'I think, as a fully functioning adult, I should be the judge of what's good for me. And you're very good for me, in my opinion.'

'But why, Guy? I'm just a whole pile of problems.'

He shook his head. 'If I'm not careful, I'll end up being forced to spend my life with someone I like but don't love. Eleanor adores me so much but I know I'd begin to dislike her. Or I'll end up with someone like your sister. And I've watched people coerced into marriage and how they spend their years in misery or seeking solace in other arms. I refuse to become like that. The Duke of Marlborough, Charles Spencer-Churchill, was—'

'Oh, a friend of yours?'

He frowned. 'He is, actually.'

'You're not trying to impress me, are you, Guy?'

'No.' He watched her smile. 'There, you see, you're not at all ashamed to bait me. And you're not the slightest bit impressed either, not that I mentioned him for that reason.'

'You were saying?'

'Charles and his wife lived such lonely lives. Consuelo was fabulously wealthy in her own right – American, a child of the richest of the rich – and she could have married anyone in the world she wanted to for love alone. Yet her ambitious mother chose a somewhat foppish Englishman who desperately needed money or the banks would foreclose. The attraction, though, was an impressive title to give their daughter and a palace to set up home in. She was a teenager. But she was in love with someone else. So was he, but he married her all the same, because he needed that money. She was the only way he could save his beloved Blenheim Palace.' Guy made the sound of an explosion. 'Can you imagine a young, romantic, passionate, ridiculously wealthy woman being told that? For all her beauty and wealth, he took her on because she could save precious stone and mortar. They had nothing in common and were forced to be together in a loveless marriage. I refuse to live like that. I want a woman to love me for the person I am, with all of my flaws, and I want to choose her because I can't imagine life without her.'

Jane smiled. 'You're a romantic.'

'Indeed. Why not?'

'Some of us can't afford to be.'

This time she moved fully away from him, unthreading her fingers from his. He felt the letting-go keenly.

She looked back at him. 'So tell me about this tree and its fruit.'

Jane felt she was living through a series of shocks, each one as devastating as the next in its own way. Her sister's arrival was the proverbial sword of Damocles, which Jane had always felt hanging over her. She'd made it through all these years, falling deeper in love with being Harry's mother, now firmly thinking of him as her son, and the threat of him being taken away had withdrawn to the shadows. It had never left her, though. It sat there, silent, like the sword above her head, with the potential to slice her heart open at any moment.

Charlotte had given no warning; she'd simply dropped the sword with her blustering arrival, full of privilege and presumption about Harry, never mind the pain she was causing Jane.

But now another shock. Guy Attwood's attentions really were unexpected. Jane could not have anticipated his affection if she had been given the chance to list one hundred potential surprises in her life. *He* admired *her*?

Jane's list would also not include falling in love with a stranger – if indeed that was what was happening. She knew she was drawn to him, but these feelings were new. More importantly, she had never expected the kiss. It was addictive. She'd not been in a position to have attention of this nature and so had simply disregarded any potential for being in love, having a partner in life, making a larger family . . . even having a home of her own.

Guy had opened up a whole new world of possibility. She needed to think, divert him, get him talking about his apple so the focus was off her and that kiss, no matter how much more she wanted another one, or how long she wanted it to last . . .

Years. She heard the word echo in her mind and dismissed it as a pointless wish.

'So tell me about this tree and its fruit,' she'd said just seconds ago, deliberately disentangling herself from his touch, which was sending powerful waves of desire through her . . . something else she'd not thought she would experience. And, of course, there was poor Eleanor in the back of her mind, weeping in the dark. She needed a moment to collect herself, to make sense of this.

He seemed to sense her need to withdraw and didn't make it awkward, instead turning with a sigh back to the apple tree that clearly had him in its thrall. 'I might bore you.'

'As I might have done to you when I spoke about colour. Take the risk,' she encouraged him.

He began to talk and, as he did so, Jane watched him fall completely into the joy of finding the tree, moving around it slowly, stroking its leaves, gently touching the ripening fruit that would be ready soon. He told her all about the search, where the apple had first come from and why it was now in such danger, alongside many other varieties, of being lost forever.

'Hothouse fruit, which was all the rage in the second half of the nineteenth century, was finally pushed aside about forty years ago, when we allowed our apple to once again rise to prominence as the supreme English dessert fruit.'

'This history is fascinating,' Jane said, revelling in all the detail he was sharing with her. 'How did the apple reclaim its popularity?'

He shrugged. 'I suppose the novelty of such exotic fruit had begun to wear off. Besides, gardeners who had strived so hard to produce something tropical, like pineapples, and gained so much notoriety for it, were suddenly being pushed aside by imports from places like the Azores. Meanwhile, high-quality table grapes, once an eye-wateringly expensive delicacy from very determined cultivators, were no longer considered the same luxury because they were being commercially grown by the glasshouse industry and were more readily available, no longer so exclusive. And then it stopped being socially – and indeed economically – valid to maintain acres of glass pavilions of exotic fruits because of cheaper imports. He sighed. 'Jane, have you tasted a fig from the Near East, or a peach from Asia?'

She shook her head.

'Oh, they are glorious. The thing is, after all the initial surprise and glee at accessing and growing this type of exotic fruit – like a peach or fig – their lustre began to wane because people started to believe their flavour was forced. People who knew what a delicious, ripe and brilliantly red strawberry from northern Europe tasted like began to turn away from the flavour of strawberries grown in England – forced to grow outside their usual conditions and less flavoursome as a result. So there was a sort of nostalgic, kneejerk reaction back to the pleasurable, honest and true taste of rural England . . .'

'The humble apple,' she finished for him.

He smiled. 'Exactly. A combination of wholesome food, simple in its form, with versatility like no other, and that epicurean diversity not found in any other English fruit. It brought the esteem back to the apple.'

'And by then, no longer only gracing aristocratic tables, I presume?'

'Exactly! Apple trees were bobbing up in lots of middle-class gardens.' He pointed to the tree they stood alongside. 'But this one has been here a long time.'

'If you think about it, the apple is so quintessentially English,' Jane said, realising she'd never considered such a fact.

'And it's done its fair share of warfare with imports from French, Canadian, American . . . even Australian competitors. You yourself have tasted the Granny Smith, and there are so many others that we haven't grown here. Imports from across the Atlantic more than quadrupled in the four years from 1875 to 1879.'

'Why is that?'

Again he shrugged. 'Ours looked a bit crabby, for want of a better word. Suddenly, in came this bright, cherry-red, clean-skinned, well-proportioned fruit. A crusade, nothing short of it, was launched by landowners, orchardists, nurseries, market gardeners, even just apple lovers, to modernise old orchards and improve our fruit to kick out the "Yankies", as they were known. There was a National Apple Congress held in 1883 on this very topic, the idea being to select a good range of apples for our growers to focus their efforts on. They concentrated on appearance, yield, reliability and range.' He put his hands up in the air. 'Surely I'm boring you now!'

'You're not,' she reassured him. 'Listen, Guy, I want you to have the painting.'

'What? No!'

'I insist. To me it's just another watercolour of an apple that caught my fancy. To you, it's . . .'

'A life's work,' he finished. 'I know that sounds dramatic, but finding the apple is the completion of an era: the final tying-off of threads that have felt loose for so long.'

'See,' she said, grinning, 'all that emotion and time tied up with this apple. Let my painting be a gift to you. Please take it.'

'I couldn't—'

'You can, because if you don't, I shall be offended.'

'I can't have that,' he said, moving a wisp of hair from her face and then stroking her cheek.

She smiled. 'Then come. Let me take it off its easel and wrap it for you.'

Neither of them moved.

'My mother's convinced this is what I do, and it scares off the women.'

Jane was confused. 'Talk about apples, you mean?'

He nodded, embarrassed.

'Quite a parlour trick of yours, no doubt.' Jane chuckled. 'I don't think so, Guy. I think you have probably deliberately scared them off.'

'You're right.'

'Not Eleanor, though, it seems.'

'I suspect I was waiting until I found the right person to make me want to change things with her,' he said, his gaze landing with weight upon hers. 'Someone who excited me. Someone I didn't want to be apart from.'

She swallowed. She didn't know what to say. This felt so sudden. 'Anyway, I'm very happy for you to have found your apple.'

He nodded, looking back to the tree. 'It's dreamlike to be finally confronted with what has eluded me for so long, but somehow it's also frightening.'

She wasn't sure he was only speaking about the Scarlet Henry. 'And why's that?'

'It makes me realise I have decisions to make.'

She didn't know what to make of that remark, and so she deflected it, changing the subject. 'I want to give you that painting. Follow me.'

He did so, back into the house, where he watched her unclip the watercolour from her easel.

'I wish I could give this to you framed, so it's a proper gift.'

'Proper gift? Jane, *you* are my gift. I've found you. I've found the apple. I've found . . . love.'

She blushed but didn't look at all embarrassed. 'I never thought this might happen for me.'

'Love?'

She nodded.

'Why not?'

Jane gave a small shrug. 'My life has been so small and so involved with Harry, I've barely looked beyond him.'

He tipped her chin and leaned in to kiss her gently once again. 'Our life is ahead of us.'

A clock chimed in the distance and Jane gasped. 'I have to fetch Harry from school.'

'Do you normally meet him?'

She shook her head. 'He's more than happy to go to and from school alone – it's hardly far. But today I just want to be there.'

'In case she is?'

Jane's mouth opened in shock. She had not even considered that. 'Forgive me, Guy, I must go. You must talk to Eleanor or we cannot be . . . together. Will you see yourself out?'

She left him standing with the painting rolled up, tucked under his arm, surprised and clearly with unfinished business between them.

19

Guy tapped on the study door.

'Yes?'

He opened the door a crack. 'Sorry to disturb you.'

'Not at all.' William waited, watching him.

'Er, Jane has told me about herself – I mean why she's here and who Harry is.'

William nodded. 'Good. It wasn't for me to explain.'

'No. She's gone to meet Harry from school. I think she's concerned that her sister might also go there to meet him.'

The old man grunted. 'What a wretch that woman is. She means Jane no good, and that boy will only be harmed by her arrival.'

'Well, I shall be at the Red Lion if anyone needs me,' Guy said, unsure of what else he might say.

'Right. I presume Jane knows as much?'

Guy nodded.

'Well, then, good day, Guy.' William stood, walked around his desk and shook his hand warmly. 'I'm glad you came back. She needs a friend.'

'She, er, she insisted I have this painting of her apple.' Guy nodded towards the canvas under his arm.

'*Your* apple,' William corrected him. 'Well, Jane doesn't give her work to anyone, so you must have impressed her, young man.'

Guy took his leave and arrived back at the Red Lion, his mind moving in several directions. He'd decided he would write to Royal Kew to let his colleagues know his stunning news of finding the elusive apple. Just the sound of the pen scratching on the paper would centre his scrambled thoughts, allow him to calm his mind and order his feelings. He needed to work out how to speak to Eleanor and what to do about Jane . . . and Harry.

The man behind the desk greeted him. 'Ah, Mr Attwood, I'm glad you're back. I was thinking of sending out a lad to find you.'

'Why, what's wrong?'

'We've received a telegram for you, sir.' He handed over an envelope.

'When did this arrive?' Guy asked.

The man glanced at his fob watch. 'About twelve minutes ago, sir.'

'Thank you.' Guy ran up the stairs, two at a time, and let himself into his room, tearing open the envelope.

It was from his mother.

Your father taken gravely ill. Heart problem. Come home urgently. Mama.

It was as if he'd been plunged underwater. Normal sound disappeared. He was hearing everything from a distance. The rumbles of vehicles in the street dulled, the creaks and sighs he'd heard all over the hotel were silenced. The only thing he could hear was an insistent ringing . . . an alarm. He sat on the bed and read his mother's words again.

Concise and precise. No doubt allowed for him.

Your father is dying is what that telegram conveyed. *And you should be at home.*

He'd only experienced dizziness of this nature twice in his life before now: that time he was trying to impress his friend Winston by clambering around a thin ridge sixty feet in the air, and just under an hour ago, when he'd risked a kiss with an irresistible stranger.

But this dizziness brought nausea.

It also brought fear.

He moved to the desk and hurriedly scratched out a letter to Jane. He had to leave, but he needed to reassure her that he was not running out on her at a time when she needed support.

> *My darling Jane,*
>
> *I have never written to anyone in this way. I have never felt such a strong romantic attraction or a need to be with someone as I do you.*
>
> *The world is moving fast, it seems. You received traumatic news today, and sadly I've returned to the inn where I'm staying to receive news that my father is dying. I must rush to his side; there are things to be shared. Please forgive me for not saying farewell properly. Should my father pass away, then I will need to be with my mother for a while and help with arrangements. I am sure you understand.*
>
> *I do hope you will forgive my absence and below is how you might contact me at Merton Hall. Please telephone and let me know how you are. I know how privately you guard your life, so should you not contact me I will presume that you wish to be alone for a while. As soon as I can, I shall come south again to see you, for we too have personal matters to discuss. If you need help, however, do not hesitate to telegram or telephone and I will respond immediately.*

Jane . . . the world has shifted on its axis somehow for me.
Finally I have found someone who intrigues in every way. I am
entirely enamoured by you and, without wishing to scare you,
I feel an exciting connection to both you and Harry. I will hold
hope that we might continue the 'conversation' we shared in
the orchard. I hope with all of my heart you feel the same way.
I'll see you and Harry as soon as it's possible, and please know
I will help you in every way that I can with regard to your
sister's claim and plans.

Yours affectionately, G.

He leapt to his feet and gathered up his few belongings, including the painting, then hurried downstairs to the main counter.

'Leaving, sir?' the man looked concerned.

'Yes, I'm sorry. The telegram had business news that I must attend to,' he said, not wishing to get into any conversation about his father.

'Oh, we shall be sad to see you go.'

'I shall be back soon.'

The man's face lit up. 'That's good news.'

'May I settle up, please?'

'Yes, of course. Let me just . . .' He trailed off as he checked through his book.

Guy held out the letter. 'Can you possibly have this delivered immediately to the Close?'

The innkeeper looked over his spectacles. 'I can do that. Er, Sheila, where is Tilly?'

The woman whose attention he'd caught approached the counter. 'She's just about to go off, Ted.'

'Ask her to come and see me before she goes, please. I have an urgent errand and it's on her way home.'

'Thank you.' Guy smiled tightly at them.

He was out of the inn within ten minutes and found it faster to run to the station than wait for a hansom cab. Within forty minutes of receiving the telegram, he was stepping aboard a train heading north.

––––––––––

Harry's eyes lit up when he saw his mother waiting for him outside the school, and Jane was struck by his easy way and complete lack of any embarrassment at being met by an adult. The conflicting emotions of Guy's presence in her life and Charlotte's arrival – the antithesis of his warmth – dissipated at the sight of her son's bright grin.

'Why are you here?' he asked, happily giving her a hug.

'Bye, Harry,' another boy said. 'Don't forget practice tomorrow.'

'I won't,' Harry replied and, at Jane's query, he sighed. 'They've added another rehearsal for Sunday.'

'But you sound perfect.'

'It's not for me,' he said, without ego. 'We have to make sure we all get the timing right, so they're going through a full rehearsal once again.'

'Oh, no, so we'll need to rewash and iron your cassock.'

He shook his head. 'It's not a dress rehearsal, so I can stay in uniform. Who's that?' He was looking beyond her.

She turned and in that heartbeat the old adage of turning to stone felt appropriate. She might have added others: blood turning icy in her veins, her heart skipping a beat, her breathing halting, her throat turning dry, her feet leaden. Yes, every cliché she knew that described this feeling of dread. They were all true, though, because she was experiencing them . . . even down to the momentary tunnel vision that focused on Charlotte's self-satisfied expression, which was mixed with something else. Surprise? What was it? Charlotte interrupted her line of thought with a wave.

'Hello, Jane,' she said, approaching, her hungry gaze turning away. 'And you must be . . .'

'I'm Harry,' he said brightly, but glanced at Jane. 'Er, Henry Saville. I'm pleased to meet you,' he added, as he'd been taught, holding his hand out politely.

'Henry.' Charlotte sighed, cutting Jane a glance, as though impressed at her giving the wrong name. 'And what charming manners you have, young man, and so handsome, my my. I'm Charlotte. I'm your—'

'Aunt!' Jane interjected. 'Harry, this is Aunt Charlotte from London. She's my sister.'

'Oh,' he said, sounding delighted. 'Are you visiting us?'

Charlotte tittered a laugh. 'I am, darling boy. I can't wait to spend time with you.'

Jane was about to lead Harry away but she was distracted by the presence of a stranger lurking nearby.

Charlotte followed her gaze. 'Jane, I want you to meet Mrs Eloise Hurst. She's the local almoner from around here; she helps with charitable matters and women's needs.'

Mrs Hurst stepped forward. Jane, suspecting her presence was connected with taking Harry from his home, wanted to hate her, but the woman had kind eyes, which settled gently on her and smiled at Harry as he spoke.

'I'm a bit hungry,' he admitted.

'You run on home, Harry. We'll catch up,' Jane suggested.

'Goodbye.' He waved to the three women and hurried away, down the path that would lead him to the only home he'd ever known.

Jane felt the tug of a primeval pain in her body. She couldn't pinpoint it, but it was there. And she knew why it was there. It was heartbreak. Guy had filled her heart up and now Charlotte had broken it.

Tilly Jones was meeting her beau, Tom Giles, and she was absolutely sure that this afternoon he would be making a proposal of marriage to her. She couldn't be more excited and had to force herself not to go about her maid's work at the inn with a silly loon of a smile all day long. Tom was a local orchardist and had recently set up his own cider brewery; his prospects were bright. Her parents were so delighted by her choice and anxious for a ring on her finger that they were longing for the proposal as well. With two other sisters to marry in the family, Tilly being happily settled would put a big smile on her father's face after a difficult few months since being laid off. In fact, she felt sure that Tom would offer her father a job if she asked him to.

She pulled on her coat and was buttoning it up, thinking about running into Tom's arms and kissing him hello, when Sheila stepped around the cloakroom door.

'Tilly, Ted wants to see you before you leave.'

'I'm off, though.'

'Yes, but he has an errand for you. Before you squawk, it's on your way home.'

'I'm not going home, Sheila, I'm meeting Tom.'

'It's not far. I'd do it myself, but I've got some urgent tasks here. Come on.'

Tilly huffed a little but nodded. She went to the counter.

'Ah, Tilly, thank you.'

'Sheila said you have an errand.'

'Yes, a note from Mr Attwood. I promised we'd run this round to the Close. It's number eighteen. Don't put it through the letterbox, Tilly. Ring or knock and hand it over. It must reach this person – Miss Jane Saville.'

'What if she's not there?'

'Hand it to whoever answers, please.'

'And if no one is home?'

'Then bring it back . . . and I mean today, not tomorrow.'

She couldn't disguise her frustration.

'Tilly, it's just around the corner,' he said, with a slight tone of his own exasperation. 'Please do it now. I'd appreciate it.'

She took the note and headed off at a brisk trot. She didn't want to be late on this most auspicious day, and she fretted that Tom might change his plans.

She found herself following a lad who was half-skipping, half-dawdling in the Close. He belonged to the cathedral school – she could see that from his uniform. One of the privileged. His blazer told her he was also a chorister, lauded in this city.

At a gate ahead of her, he turned in, and it was only when she sped up, worried that time was getting away from her, that she realised this was the house she was headed to.

'Er, hey. I mean, excuse me.'

The boy was halfway down the path to the front door but he turned around. 'Yes?'

'Do you live here?'

He nodded.

'What's your name?'

He smiled. 'I'm Henry Saville.'

'Ah,' she said, her heart skipping with happiness. 'I'm Tilly.' She checked the envelope. 'Is, um, is Jane Saville your relative?'

'She's my mother.'

'Great! Can you give this note to her, please? It's from a Mr Attwood.'

'Guy?'

'I don't know his name but he's staying at the Red Lion, where I work, and he's sent this note. It's just that I'm in a bit of a hurry.'

'Yes, I can,' he said, skipping back up the path and taking the envelope. He pushed it into his satchel.

'Thanks,' she said.

'You're welcome, Tilly,' he replied, impressing her that he'd remembered her name.

What Tilly couldn't know was that Harry's attention, especially when he was tired and hungry after a day at school, only stretched so far. By the time he had let himself into the house, poured himself some milk, eaten some bread spread with butter and jam, and gone upstairs to search for William, he'd already forgotten about the note.

20

With Harry now safely out of Charlotte's reach for the time being, Jane sighed out a breath and returned her gaze to her sister, who had not watched Harry leave but had kept her stare fixed on Jane.

'Mrs Hurst is aware of our situation, Jane,' she said.

Mrs Hurst smiled. 'I can see you're very close to your nephew, Miss Saville.'

Jane's heart shattered. She swallowed a dry sob. 'He's my son.'

'I'm afraid that's a lie and you know it,' Charlotte said.

'Not here, Charlotte,' Jane said, shaking her head. She needed to find calm, to keep the situation from spiralling out of her control. 'Mrs Hurst, perhaps I can offer you a cool drink at my home?'

'That would be most welcome, thank you, Miss Saville. Shall we?'

The unhappy trio walked in a stilted silence back to 18 Cathedral Close.

After they removed their hats, Jane walked them past William's study, where she could hear him clearing his throat, probably nose-deep in a research tome. She was glad for that, although she wished for his reassurance right now.

'Through here,' she said, leading the women into the parlour.

Harry arrived and leaned against Jane. She put a protective arm around his shoulder. 'Hello again,' he said, traces of a milky moustache around his mouth.

'Oh, this is lovely, Miss Saville,' Mrs Hurst said, gazing through the French doors towards the orchard, where Jane's world had so recently brightened into spectacular colour. It felt almost cruel for that brightness to be tarnished by Charlotte, but then that was Charlotte's way. Only she mattered. 'This art is beautiful. Who painted these?'

'My mummy did those,' Harry said proudly, stepping into the room and away from Jane's gentle grip. She felt the loss instantly, wanting to draw him back towards her protection.

Charlotte tried – Jane would give her that – pasting on a smile for Harry. 'Come and show us, Harry.'

He obliged, pointing and giving his simple commentary, while Jane's shattered heart felt pulverised to hear his pride, and his innocence. He had no idea of what was happening around him.

'Where's the apple painting?' Harry wondered. 'It looks so real.'

'I gave it away as a present,' Jane answered, giving a wan smile.

'To Guy?'

She nodded.

'Good. He loved it. Guy knows all about apples,' Henry said.

'Really?' Charlotte said, sounding indifferent. 'And who is Guy?'

'Mummy's friend,' he said. 'He's my friend too, but he really likes Mummy.'

Charlotte slid a cunning gaze towards Jane that asked a wealth of questions. 'Is that so?'

Jane sighed, knowing she shouldn't react; it would only give the situation with Guy currency. 'He's just short of being a stranger, Charlotte. Don't jump to conclusions.'

'I'd like to meet him.'

'You will like him when you do,' Harry assured her. 'He's very tall and very handsome.'

'Really?'

'And very rich.'

'Harry, that's quite enough,' Jane admonished. 'I don't know how you've formed that opinion.'

'Tell me more, darling Harry,' Charlotte cooed.

Encouraged, Harry obliged. 'Well, his clothes look more expensive than William's, and he has his very own train set that stretches around rooms. He told me he lives in a big house. And he's friends with the King.'

Charlotte gasped theatrically. 'Friends with the King, no less. We all like to think of ourselves as friendly with the royals.'

'No, but he really is—'

'Harry, go and wash your face, please. You have choir practice soon.'

'Yes, Mummy.' He turned to the two guests. 'I have to go now,' he said more solemnly than was necessary.

Charlotte gave him a hug. 'It's been lovely to meet you, Harry. And, in fact, I've suggested to your mother that you be allowed to come for a visit. I live in London. Do you think you would like that?'

'Charlotte, I don't think you should—' Jane began, feeling the situation spinning beyond her.

'I would love to,' Harry said, and Jane could see his features shining with anticipation. 'I've wanted to visit London forever, but Mummy hasn't been able to take us.'

'Well, I shall, young man. You can leave your mother at home to do her little paintings, and we can go and do lots of lovely things together.'

'Like what?' Harry asked, already excited.

'Oh, well, how about Madame Tussauds?'

Harry gasped. 'Really? One of the boys at school has been there and I feel so jealous.'

'No need. We shall do the wax museum, and of course we cannot miss Regent's Park Zoo.'

'The zoo!' Harry looked towards his mother, his eyes sparkling with glee.

'And, Harry, while I shan't be doing it, I think we can try you at skating on rollers at one of the great parks. If it was winter I'd be taking you ice skating in Chelsea, but we can save that treat for another time.'

'And the British Museum?'

'Of course. I don't live far from it, in fact. We can do anything you want, young man. It would be my pleasure.'

'Oh, thank you,' he said, flinging himself again into Charlotte's arms. 'I'd better go, or Mummy will give me that look.'

'That steely look she has on her face right now, you mean? I think that's for my benefit, Harry. She's going to tell me I am spoiling you once you've left the room, but spoiling you is my new hobby, dear little fellow.'

Harry ran from the room, unable to contain himself, yelling for William. Jane guessed he was going to tell him all about what had been promised.

'You can't buy him, Charlotte,' Jane said, her voice low and threatening.

'I don't have to, sister dear. He's mine. He's my issue. He came from my body.'

'You will have to prove it.'

Charlotte's laughter pierced her composure. 'Oh, Jane, you poor, sad creature. Of course I can prove it. I have photos of Eddie.'

'I'm afraid that's not enough, Mrs Cavendish,' her companion advised. 'That would be open to opinion.'

'He doesn't look like Eddie anyway,' Jane observed. 'He is keener in looks to our father, surely?' She hoped she sounded convincing, but even she knew she was reaching. Harry had fair hair like most in their family, but that was about it in terms of likeness.

'Our aunt, then. She was there,' came the convincing statement.

'Aunt Hortense is dead, Charlotte,' Jane snapped. 'It shows how far your interest goes for family. She's been gone for five years now. I attended the funeral, but neither you nor mother did.'

Charlotte gave Jane a dismissive look, turning to the almoner. 'Mrs Hurst, that child is mine. We have the doctor's note, or have you forgotten?'

Jane blinked. 'Doctor's note?'

'Yes, Jane. Perhaps you've forgotten Dr Furlough? He left his card and a note.'

'May I see it?'

'Whatever for? Don't you trust me?'

'Not an inch,' she said, helplessly truthful now.

Pinch-lipped, Charlotte dug in her bag and retrieved an envelope that had slightly yellowed over the years. 'Here.' She stopped short of throwing it at her sister.

Jane read it. She now remembered seeing this and wished she'd taken it at the time. How awkward that the only memento of Harry that Charlotte had kept was this damning note. Addressed to Charlotte, it stated that the doctor would leave the labouring hours to the midwife, and that he was to be called in the event of imminent birth or emergency.

'I don't wish to bring the police in on this matter, Jane,' Charlotte continued.

Mrs Hurst cut Charlotte a terse look. 'There is no need to involve the police, truly. I am here to help guide this conversation. Miss Saville,' she said, 'I can only imagine the emotional toll this is taking on you, but—'

Jane was hardly listening. One last desperate thrust, then. 'This letter,' she said, shaking it before them, 'addresses a Miss Saville only.'

Her words were met with a tense silence before Charlotte gusted a mirthless laugh. 'Oh, you jest, surely? You're going to say it belongs to you?'

Jane contrived a frown, surprised she could act so well. 'Why, Charlotte? Why would I jest about the single most important thing in my life?'

'Because he's not yours and you know it!'

'Then prove it,' Jane said, her tone matter of fact. 'Prove to Mrs Hurst beyond all doubt.'

'Miss Saville . . . Jane,' Mrs Hurst said, her tone no longer brooking defiance. 'If we return with proof, will you accept that? Hand the boy over to his mother?'

'I shall have to, for I shall have no choice. But I can't imagine from where you'll find it.'

The older woman turned to Charlotte. 'You can provide the proof your sister demands?'

Charlotte's stormy expression turned vicious. 'Don't you worry, Mrs Hurst, I shall find it.'

Mrs Hurst nodded. 'Then I think we're all agreed. We shall be back, Miss Saville. Thank you for your time. We can show ourselves out.' As she passed, she squeezed Jane's arm. Although her presence, her tone, even her words said otherwise, Jane had to swallow hard at the gesture of compassion. It told her that this woman was not without great sympathy for her plight and probably hated being in the middle of this tussle. It was some-thing; it did not make her grief any easier, but at least she knew the woman did not possess a heart of stone, and she would demand full and clear proof before she made any sort of authoritative decision.

They moved past Jane, but at the door of the parlour Charlotte turned. 'Oh, and Jane, I suggest you get Harry's suitcase packed. He'll be leaving with me before the end of the week.'

Guy strode into the sitting room at his family home to find Adele Attwood drawn and pale, dressed in black, looking like a tiny bird who'd been scooped up, having fallen from a nest. She appeared frail, her normally smiling face suddenly hollowed, and she was curled up beneath a blanket when, in haste, he'd opened the door without knocking.

She didn't seem to mind his arrival, which must have seemed like a gust of wind had blown into her private space.

'Mother?' he said tenderly.

'He's gone, Guy. I'm so sorry.'

'Gone?' he repeated, horrified. He had been hoping with all of his heart that his father had hung on long enough for them to have a conversation.

She nodded. 'It doesn't seem real. I thought he'd live forever, but his heart gave up.'

Guy could barely think straight. Still, he knew he had to hold himself intact for his mother's sake; she looked as broken as he felt.

'Guy, you look lost.'

'I . . . I don't know what to say. May I sit?'

'Of course.' She sighed, and he joined her, putting an arm around her. She leaned into him. 'I'm sorry you couldn't see him to say farewell. It was all so sudden.'

He broke then, unable to hold back the pain. His features crumpled momentarily.

'Oh, Guy, darling, be strong now.'

'Yes, I shall. I just have the worst regret.'

'I know. I wish with all my heart that your father and you had not shared harsh final words.'

'*I* was harsh, he wasn't. He was never harsh, Mother. He was tough in his expectations – which he also had of himself – but he was never cruel, never unreasonable. I was the wretched one. I can't bear what I said to him.'

She nodded. 'I want you to know he did not hold it against you.'

Guy searched her face. 'How can you know that?'

'Because we spoke about it.'

'My behaviour was uncalled for and immature. I expect better from myself than going on the attack with someone I love.'

She rubbed his arm. 'He pushed you.'

'Not without cause,' Guy said, shaking his head.

'You're determined to be hard on yourself, Guy.'

'I wanted to apologise to him. I thought . . .'

'Then why didn't you?' She had this way, his mother, of being ever supportive, ever loving, but with the power to reduce him with a few words. There was no sharpness, no trace of bitterness in her tone, only query, and yet the accusation was there, gentle and firm. *You should have* was what she was really saying.

'I realised today that I have led the most selfish of lives. I've enjoyed the single-minded love and affections of both my parents, the blessings their success bestowed, the freedoms they granted, and wealth . . . I have pursued my own interests and, without any intention to hurt anyone, I have nevertheless let people down.'

'Good grief, Guy, what's come over you?'

He looked at her miserably. 'A mirror was held up to me, I suppose you could say. Mother, I am going to tell Eleanor that the two of us can never be. We are not suited. I know this will let her down, but she deserves better.'

She remained silent, forcing him to fill that yawning gap.

'The fault is mine,' he said, looking at her. 'I know that. I've tried to see us together as a couple, growing older together as you and father did, but searching my heart, I see only an empty marriage for us. I do not love her.'

'No. That's obvious,' she said, taking his hand and smiling gently. 'I think all the parents wished it could be . . . and Eleanor, of course. Have you told her yet?'

'I was planning to write today and arrange to meet, then I received the telegram.'

'Telephone her to make an arrangement to meet as soon as possible.'

'Right. I'll call today.'

She blinked. 'Why this sudden decision?'

He shrugged.

'Have you met someone, Guy?'

He squeezed her hand. 'Can you tell me about my father first and foremost? What happened?'

'He was here one minute, talking about our grand European tour.' She gave a choked laugh before letting his hand go, putting hers just below her throat. 'And then he clutched his chest and groaned. I had no idea what had happened. But he was struggling to breathe, and he seemed to have short waves of pain. Doctor Connor did all in his power, and the staff at the hospital were very caring, but your darling father never fully came back to me. I am grateful that he recognised me, but he couldn't say much. He slipped away from me just before five o'clock this morning.' She sobbed. 'He heard the first tremulous notes of a robin welcoming the dawn chorus and he smiled at me, for those few seconds fully cognisant, Guy. It was so magnificent in that moment to feel so connected, and he said, "Kiss our boy for me. Tell him I'm proud of him."'

Guy hadn't cried properly since infancy. But he wept now with his mother, arm in arm, for the man he used to play trains with and whose very big shoes he would now need to fill.

21

It was Harry's solo that day in the cathedral, and Jane could see Charlotte already seated close to the front, as though she were a regular Sunday parishioner. She was like a contented cat preening herself vainly and already laying claim to today's soloist, who was in truth a stranger to her.

Harry had needed to rise above the singing skills of eight other boys being considered for the role of lead soprano for the cathedral choir. It was a task that not only carried a heavy weight of responsibility and endless practice, but also decorated him with a lustre that might glitter for years beyond that boyhood voice. Concerts, appearances, even some special considerations at school were now his.

But Charlotte had come back to ruin everything that their small trio – Jane, Harry and William – had worked towards.

Jane had to quell her despair as she pointed William towards some chairs on the opposite side of the nave to her sister and slightly further back, her small attempt to stay out of reach of Charlotte's contempt. She had to keep reminding herself that this was Harry's big day – hers too, if she could only find the right mindset to celebrate his achievement and feel pride for him, rather than shame and fear about what might soon happen.

William had not missed Charlotte. Once seated, he gave Jane's hand a squeeze. 'All will be well.'

'How can you know that?' she whispered, anguished.

'Because, Jane, your sister clearly doesn't know the first thing about raising a child.'

Jane shrugged, feeling hopeless. 'She can learn. I did.'

He continued as though she hadn't made the remark. 'And because she didn't want him then and she doesn't really want him now, she hasn't factored in what Harry wants or needs. She needs him, keep that in mind – not the other way around. Wanting and needing are very different.'

'How does that help us, though?'

'Because Harry is not a baby any longer, and certainly not helpless or without voice. Do you think he would just go and stay with her without any sort of objection?'

Jane shook her head. 'You heard what she's planning for him, the museum visits, the roller skating. What child wouldn't fall under her spell?'

'That will pass. Besides, you're underestimating Harry and how much he loves his mother'—he prodded her knee gently—'and I mean his real one – you!'

'Shh,' someone hissed softly in the row in front of them.

William pulled a face at the woman as soon as she turned back around, and that made Jane smile despite her mood. He was right. Harry might enjoy a holiday, but she didn't really know whether he'd want to leave his school, his home, his new status and the only family he'd known on a permanent basis. Surely that would prompt some sort of objection. She would have to count on that. And even that thought made her feel guilty: relying on a seven-year-old to cause a stir was unfair, but it was all she had for the time being.

William nudged her. 'Where's your Mr Charming, anyway?'
She cut William a silent, slit-eyed gaze of reprimand. 'Well?'

'How should I know?'

'When you didn't throw him out on his heel, I figured the, er,
conversation took a different turn.'

She hesitated, blinking. 'Whatever do you mean?'

He chuckled softly. 'Your blushing is enough of an answer.'

Jane gave him a small slap on his arm, astonished that she
could be playful given her mood. But then William always had a
way of lifting her spirits, helping her to see a situation from different angles, in the same way that she might study a plant in various
seasons to give it fresh illumination.

'I thought Mr Attwood was coming to watch Harry,' William
said.

'Hmm, yes, so did I.'

'Maybe he's running late.'

'Maybe,' she remarked and then the first soft strains of the
organ began. Harry had told her it had been built and completed
over three decades earlier. She smiled at William. 'You'd have been
a young man when this organ was installed.'

'I remember it well,' he whispered. 'Some four thousand pipes,
and some of them, which I had to crane my neck to see, stood
around thirty-two feet, we were told.'

The woman who had shooshed them now turned and
glared and they closed their mouths firmly in response, staring
forward.

To her right, Jane saw the clergy and their trailing choir begin
the long walk. She nudged William, giving the woman a look
of apology. It didn't matter. She was one of the people who had
labelled Jane as a fallen woman. Jane sighed. She would never win
Harry back if it came down to her reputation in the town.

In that moment, Charlotte turned and trapped Jane's gaze.

Her face shone with a look of pure smugness, but then a soprano choirboy began his solo. The sound was chillingly beautiful.

Jane looked away from Charlotte. This was not her moment; she would not give it to her. This was about Harry, and Jane intended to savour his performance, especially as a string quintet had come to the cathedral for this choral event.

She glanced at William, whose eyes were closed, no doubt to focus on Harry, and so she did the same, letting all other distractions disappear as Harry's pure, angelic notes began to lift to the glorious stone vaulted ceiling. His voice was absorbed by the special lightweight tufa stone at its crown, but it was echoed by the Purbeck marble columns and the limestone flagging and walls.

His soprano matched the soaring beauty of the surrounds. Jane opened her eyes to let her vision share in the experience; she noted that the stone sombreness was dissipated by the soft light through the grisaille windows, turning the cathedral's interior golden, which was surely intentional.

The effect of this illumination on her senses was always uplifting and for someone who saw life through the lens of its colours, just for a moment, the gentleness of the sun through the cathedral felt transcendent.

The clergy and choristers had made their way around to the nave and Harry's fellow choirboys sounded rich beneath his searing Latin for 'Miserere' by Allegri. Jane closed her eyes again to hear his voice as it reached higher and higher towards that yearning top note.

A single tear escaped.

Jane didn't know if it was due to her grief at possibly losing this precious child or due to an otherworldly joy in playing a part in him realising his potential with his heavenly voice. William reached into his pocket for a handkerchief, which she thought he planned to give her, but he put it to his own eyes and she knew he was experiencing the same gamut of emotion.

Wildly, improbably, her thoughts went to Guy and she silently whispered in her mind: *I wish you were here to share this.*

She had no business thinking this.

She had no hold over Guy Attwood.

But they had kissed, and something of an understanding had passed between them. While it came as a shock, it felt curiously natural and comfortable to Jane, as though two lost halves were reunited. It was hard to explain, even to herself, but she felt as though she had been waiting for him all of her life and the whole painful business of Charlotte's pregnancy and raising Harry alone in Salisbury had been in service of bringing Jane to that moment beneath the apple tree. And Jane enjoyed the fanciful thought that while Guy thought he was hunting the Scarlet Henry, his years of searching had always been bringing him towards the orchard, where they would each find not only a kindred spirit but potentially a love like no other.

There! She'd allowed the thought to roam free as Harry's solo drew to its final crescendo.

Yes, indeed. She had fallen in love. An impossible match between the wealthy heir and the impoverished woman raising a child out of wedlock. And yet she wished he was here, holding her hand, sighing with awe at Harry and this place, and sharing this moment of enlightenment.

Jane opened her eyes once again and her uplifted, serene state was deflated by the sight of Charlotte waving to Harry as he brought the dignified song to a close. It was beyond beautiful in its slow and dramatic tempo, sounding almost funereal in its moving notes.

She saw Charlotte had managed to catch Harry's eye and a small smile from him in return filled Jane with a raging jealousy;

that smile should have been hers. Normally he would look to her and William, but not this time. Charlotte had managed to divert him, and now her plan was to captivate him.

Capture him, Jane corrected in her mind. How was she going to compete with what Charlotte had to offer?

Guy was being briefed by a steady stream of people on the business for which he was now entirely responsible. He was taking a quick lunchbreak now, sitting with his mother in the parlour.

The funeral would take place in a couple of days, but soon after he'd be expected to visit all the major plants and the shipyard and begin the rounds of meetings with accountants, managers, forecasters, partners . . . And that was only the beginning. His mind was dazed, but somehow it was easier to be so distracted, because then there was insufficient room in his mind for guilt.

Guilt over losing his father before important words could be exchanged.

Guilt over leaving Jane so suddenly and for the same reason: important words needed to be said. He hadn't heard anything from her, so he had to presume the note had arrived and she was choosing to keep to herself for now. He had no choice but to respect that wish. He was the last person she needed pushing from right now, so he would do as William asked and remain supportive. And the best support was her knowing he was here whenever she needed, and a simple telephone call would have his voice in her ear and his love conveyed in person. For now, though, he would stay patient and wait for her to make the first move.

Today, he realised, Harry would be making his debut as a soloist for the choristers of the cathedral. He wished he could be there, and aired the thought aloud.

'Why does this little boy matter?' his mother asked. She

210

sounded callous, but he could forgive this; it was his fault that she knew too little. But now wasn't the time.

'I gave him a promise.'

'Well, it can't be helped,' she said. 'You're needed here, not just out of duty, Guy, but it means everything to me that I can lean on you at this time.'

'I know. But, Mother, I fear that when you break a promise to a child, it's somehow a much greater betrayal than with an adult.' And before she could ask, he added, 'A child sets store by an adult when they give their word. And this boy is an only child. He was determined that I be there.' He sighed. 'I, more than most, know how that feels.'

'And why is this child so important to you, darling? I don't understand. You can't possibly know him that well, given you've only recently become acquainted. He lives in Salisbury?'

Guy explained their chance meeting, leaving out Jane for the time being. 'He's important because he has so few people around him, and somehow I was important to him. It felt nice to really matter to someone.'

She looked at him, baffled. 'You matter to me. You mattered to your father. You certainly matter to Eleanor, poor thing. Have you spoken to her yet?'

Guy shook his head miserably. 'I called. She was out. I left a message that I wanted to see her. I said I would call again this evening.'

She looked at him sternly. 'And it matters to all of us in this household that you are here where you belong.'

'I know. I'm sorry,' he said, looking admonished. He stood and put an arm around her.

'I'm lost, Guy,' she admitted. 'Lost without him. What shall I do?'

'You'll mourn him. Then you'll turn that grieving inwards and cope. And at some point in the future you'll give up wearing black and start noticing the seasons again and enjoying being invited to events. It won't be the same. It will never be the same,' he said gently, pulling her closer. 'But you will invent a new life and learn how to enjoy it.'

She smiled. 'When did you get so wise?'

'The day my father died,' he said sadly. 'I am only now understanding the breadth of the work he did, the importance he placed on those who worked for him, and how he took their care so seriously. Big boots to fill, Mother.' He sighed.

'You'll manage. Arthur employed good people. Honest, loyal – they'd do anything for him and now for you. They'll make sure everything continues to happen on time, but you have to *be* there. If you're absent, they will lose faith in you.'

She was unwittingly tearing him in half.

'I shall not be absent.'

'Really?' She turned to him. 'You're absent now.'

'How so?'

She tapped her temple. 'Where is your mind taking you, Guy? And please don't say apples.'

He smiled. 'I forgot to tell you. I found my apple.'

'You didn't! The King's apple?' She gave a genuinely delighted grin.

He actually chuckled, liking that he could bring a smile to her face during this dark time. 'Yes. In Wiltshire, as I suspected, and in the Salisbury Cathedral Close, of all places.'

'A divine discovery,' she quipped. 'And has this anything to do with the cathedral choirboy you're apparently letting down?'

'Sort of.'

'I see.'

Her gaze was piercing, and he avoided her eye, moving to the window.

'Mother, I know my responsibilities.'

'Good. Because you cannot leave again, not right now, not in the near future, and—'

'Not ever?' he said, smiling to let her know he held no grudge.

'Guy. You have to be your father now. Do better than he did, son. This house was too quiet through our lives. It needs voices. It needs a big family and the thrill of children scampering around the grounds.'

He nodded. He wanted that too.

'Your father has left you set up, Guy. You will never have to worry about money, and he knew you're not a wastrel, but you have to make all the wealth he's left behind work for you, in order for those future generations to benefit.' She frowned at his faraway expression 'What happened, Guy, while you were away? And don't say nothing. I know you too well. Let me in.'

He sighed. 'Something did happen in Wiltshire.'

'A woman?' She stood, walking over to touch his cheek. 'Guy, tell me you've met someone.' A small smile threatened his lips but he wrested back control. 'You have!'

Guy nodded as he took in an audible breath. 'I have. I adore her, but I'm not ready to discuss it, Mother, so please don't push. I need to make a little sense of it . . . it's like a sort of madness.'

She actually giggled, but her eyes watered and she squeezed his arm, looking like she was fighting the urge to cry.

'I need to stay focused right now.' He took her hand in his. 'I will tell you everything soon, but please trust me. I need to talk to Eleanor, and sort out my thoughts, and the funeral . . .'

Adele let out a soft breath. 'I couldn't have imagined this morning, when I woke up feeling so dark and rudderless, that you would give me something so precious to lift my aching spirits.'

'Let's get through the next few days.'

'What's her name?'

'Her name is Jane,' he said, knowing his mother wanted her surname more than her first. 'But I have to be here, to think about what's immediately ahead. She understands that.'

'What's immediately ahead after the funeral is the reading of your father's will. I don't expect any surprises – everything is yours, Guy. You are an extraordinarily wealthy man, but you're going to be a very lonely one trapped up here with just your old mother for company. I lived with your father long enough to know that taking time away from his business interests felt near impossible. I can't imagine much will change for you. But if you love this woman . . .'

'Stop worrying, Mother.' He smiled to soften the words. 'I have every intention of formalising my relationship with Jane . . . if she'll have me.'

'If she'll have you?'

He nodded. 'It's . . . complicated. I will explain more about her soon.'

'Good. Shall we take a walk? Perhaps strolling on this mild day with my son at my side might help my gloom.'

'You don't have to be stoic.'

'He'd expect it of me.'

'No, he wouldn't. I don't mean that disrespectfully, but Father loved everything about you, including your temperament and ability to show emotion. You don't have to change because he's gone.'

'Gone,' she repeated, her eyes watering again. 'Every time that thought arrives, I want to curl into a tiny ball and pull the covers over my head.'

'Would it help if I admitted to feeling much the same?'

'Really?'

He nodded. 'A pillar of my life gone far too early.'

'It does help.' She smiled wanly. 'Come. Distract me from my grief. Tell me something about this woman you're feeling guilty for thinking about while grieving. The one you're not ready to talk about because you think I'm going to make a judgement.' She gave him a look as if to say, *Are you going to deny any of that?*

He stared at her with awe.

'Tell me I'm wrong.'

'You're not.'

She found a small, sad smile. 'Walk with me. Tell me about her and this boy.'

22

After the performance, Mrs Hurst and Charlotte were to return to the Cathedral Close, but this time William would be at Jane's side. Jane set up a table in the garden because it was probably one of the last few bright days of autumn, before the early winter chill, and she'd been planning for weeks to celebrate with Harry.

As she laid out the spread, his eyes shone with wonder.

'We've never done this,' he said, face shining with a smile she didn't think would leave for the rest of the day . . . or maybe it would, she thought sadly, knowing what was imminent.

'I told you I'd make it special.'

Harry flung his arms around her waist and she noticed how tall he suddenly was. How had that tiny child grown up so fast?

'You were brilliant, Harry. William and I are so proud of you.'

'I know, you've told me a few times now,' he said, grinning up at her. 'I thought Guy might come, though.'

She nodded and sighed, smoothing his hair. 'Yes, so did I. He probably had business to attend to.'

'Has he left Salisbury, then?'

Jane shrugged. Maybe, she thought. Found his apple and left. *Don't think like that*, she berated herself, although deep down she didn't know what else to think about his sudden absence. 'I don't know, darling. Can you fetch the jug of Vimto I've made for you?'

His mouth opened wide in happy surprise. 'Vimto! I've always wanted to taste it.'

She laughed. 'Well, now you can. A special treat.' Harry made everything, even the smallest of kind gestures, worthy of joy. She worried that Charlotte would change that lovely quality in him.

William stepped through the French doors of the parlour with their guests. *Be brave, Jane*, she told herself. *Be civil for Harry's sake.*

'Your sister and Mrs Hurst are here, Jane,' William said, unnecessarily announcing their arrival. He was scowling slightly.

'Welcome,' she said, trying to smile and failing, wanting to weep instead.

'Oh, wasn't Harry absolutely marvellous today,' Charlotte gushed, hurrying towards Jane and hugging her as though they were the closest of loving sisters. 'I'm so proud of him.'

Jane swallowed and dug up a smile, hoping it didn't convey how she was feeling. 'Yes, I was just telling him that.' She nodded at Mrs Hurst in welcome.

'And here he is,' Charlotte cooed. 'The wonderful soprano.'

Jane watched as her sister lavished Harry with insincere kisses and told him repeatedly how much she'd enjoyed his performance. They spent the next hour making small talk, laughing with Harry, Jane feeling tense all the while as she served her guests the midday spread of sandwiches and tiny cakes she'd gone to some trouble to bake.

'Mmm, Miss Saville, these fancies are very delicious.'

'Thank you, Mrs Hurst.'

'You were always painting, Jane, I never thought of you as a cook,' her sister remarked.

'No? I cooked most of our meals, Charlotte. But you were busy when we were in our teens and even busier when we'd come of age.'

Charlotte tittered a pretend laugh. 'I've never had a good memory, I'll be honest. I think I love to live in the moment,' she said, giving herself the perfect segue. 'Which is why, Harry, I have organised to take you home with me.'

Harry's face couldn't have shown more surprise if he'd tried. 'Really?' He cut a glance at his mother.

'Well, I told you I want to show you London and take you places and let you live in my big home. Would you like that?'

'I would like that very much,' Harry said, using his best manners, looking between Jane and William. 'Er, if my mother says it is all right to do so.'

'Oh, she has already said it's fine. It's organised, Harry, so why don't you hurry upstairs now and pack. We have a train to catch.'

'Pack? Today, you mean?'

'Yes, today,' Charlotte said, her tone oily and full of a fun she didn't, to Jane's knowledge, possess. *It must be exhausting Charlotte to keep up this pretence*, she thought.

Harry turned to his mother. 'But what about school?'

Before she could answer, Charlotte answered on her behalf. 'It's all right, Harry. I visited the school last Friday, and I've had a special discussion with the headmaster. He has given his permission.'

'Harry, why don't you go upstairs and work out what you'd like to take?' Jane said. 'I'll be up soon to help.'

Harry needed no further encouragement and ran off, making whooping sounds of delight.

'There you are, Jane, Harry's excited,' Charlotte said, as if this covered all that needed to be considered.

'Because he thinks he's going on a holiday. He's a child. He is not thinking beyond that. And I won't lie to him.'

'Good. Then tell him the truth that I'm his mother and he's coming to live with me.'

'I asked you to come with proof, Charlotte.'

Jane watched with increasing anxiety as Charlotte made a big show of picking up her bag, slowly digging around in it to retrieve an envelope.

'In here is a letter written by a Mrs Palfrey. Remember her?'

Jane's world stopped.

Mrs Palfrey. The midwife.

She'd completely forgotten about her.

Mrs Hurst cleared her throat awkwardly. 'Miss Saville, I, uh, was able to interview Mrs Palfrey, who was the midwife to your sister, and she has confirmed that Charlotte Saville gave birth to a baby boy . . .'

Mrs Hurst kept talking, but Jane was no longer listening. Mrs Palfrey! Of course. She'd thought the death of Aunt Hortense and the old doctor, who hadn't even been present at the birth, might be the end of Charlotte's ability to prove anything. After all, Jane had written her own name as the mother when the doctor wrote out the birth details, barely noticing the name. Given what she had been asked to do – to raise Charlotte's child as her own – it seemed the right thing to do.

Someone else was talking now – Charlotte, who had moved in front of her and was snapping her fingers in Jane's face.

'Jane? Jane!'

William arrived at her side.

'Please stop that, Mrs Cavendish,' he cautioned tersely. 'Jane will be fine.'

'Do we need smelling salts?' Charlotte sneered.

'We've never needed them before,' William replied, 'and

I doubt we need them now.' He looked away from Charlotte with disgust. 'Jane, my dear, are you all right?'

'Yes, thank you.' Jane covered William's hand, which was on her shoulder, to reassure him.

'Miss Saville,' Mrs Hurst tried again. 'I know this is very difficult for you, but—'

'Do you, Mrs Hurst? Have you had a child forcibly taken from you?'

'No, but—'

'Then how can you possibly know what I am going through?'

The woman looked abashed. 'What I mean is, I realise how hard this must be for you.'

'I don't believe you can even begin to fathom how hard this is for me, Mrs Hurst. I have been the only mother Harry has known for seven years. Charlotte didn't even know his name on the day she arrived here to take him away from me! She physically pushed him away as a newborn, and wanted nothing to do with him from the moment he left her body. She is not his mother in any way other than biology.'

'And that's what qualifies me to claim my child, Jane. As you pointed out, I gave birth to him, so he is mine. Thank you for looking after him. Thank you for raising him as well as you have. Now it's my turn.'

'Charlotte, you don't know the first thing about parenting.'

'I can learn.'

'You know nothing about Harry.'

'I can learn!'

'Charlotte. Please. Sister to sister, tell the truth. You cannot love him as I do.'

Charlotte shrugged; it was a careless gesture. 'I can learn to love him as you do, Jane. I know I am enchanted by him. I know I want to be his mother. I know I want to give him so much more than what he has with you, and I am going to be in a position to give him a wonderful life. I'll make sure of it.'

'Wonderful lives aren't about money, Charlotte!'

She gave Jane a look of disdain. 'Aren't they? Tell that to the poor.'

'Good grief,' William muttered.

'Miss Saville, Mr Angus, there is no way around the fact that Charlotte Cavendish has proof from a valid witness that Henry Saville—'

'Henry Cavendish,' Charlotte corrected.

'That the child in question,' Mrs Hurst continued, clearly not wishing to risk further heated words, 'is hers. This fact is inescapable, Jane,' she said, softening her tone, clearly hoping the familiarity might help. 'I am here to prevent this situation turning legal, involving the police and other authorities. Miss Saville, all you will do if you persist in denying your sister her right is delay the inevitable and ensure the situation turns uglier. I beg you to do what's right.'

To do what's right.

Jane nearly laughed. Hadn't she always done what was right? She was here right now, facing this trauma, because she had done what was right when her sister had rejected her own child.

The tears arrived. She hated looking weak in front of Charlotte and quickly dried them with her handkerchief and a fast hand. As she pressed the linen square to her cheeks, she took the moment to steel herself. There was no way around it; she could see that now. Not until she found another way. And using delaying tactics was not in anyone's interests, especially Harry's. Somehow she found the strength to consider what was actually best for Harry. How could she make this easier for him?

'May I make a suggestion?' she began.

Charlotte opened her mouth to shout her down, but Mrs Hurst held up a hand. 'Go ahead, Miss Saville.'

'As much pain as I know I shall suffer without him, I do want what's best for Harry.'

If Charlotte could have got away with a cackle of glee she would have, Jane was sure, but she made do with a look of deep self-satisfaction. 'I knew you'd see it my way in the end, Jane. He should be with his mother.'

'I agree, he should be with his mother – the only one he knows. Except you're forcing him to love a stranger. And he won't. Remember, you're no one to him. Harry is old enough to resent being effectively kidnapped.'

Charlotte blinked, unfazed by the remark. 'I'll make his life so wonderful he won't have time to think about the past.'

'That's quite enough, madam. I think you've done your damage, and there is no need to rub salt into a wound,' William growled, his disgust evident. 'Mrs Hurst, how do you suggest this unbelievably sad exchange occurs? What indeed do you think Jane should say to Harry?'

Charlotte looked ready to jump in and answer, but Mrs Hurst again forbade her with a look. 'I have to consider the child,' the older woman said.

'Well, I'm glad we both agree on that, Mrs Hurst,' Jane said with bitterness.

'It needs to be a gentle transition. He is not an infant incapable of decision, as you note, or unable to grasp something complex. The first steps should be to let this happen slowly, in my opinion. If both sisters would present it to Harry as an extended holiday, that might be a softer way of introducing a new life for him.'

'You mean I don't tell him I'm his mother?' Charlotte said, bristling.

'Not for the time being. It would be a massive shock, Mrs Cavendish, and not only would he feel betrayed by Miss Saville, who he believes to be his mother, but you might like to consider how he will regard you, as the woman who abandoned him at birth.'

That landed heavily, and Jane saw it strike Charlotte like a blow. She blinked fast. Her tone turned haughty. 'Very well. I'll be guided by you, Mrs Hurst.'

'Good. What I am suggesting is you take the next two or maybe three weeks to win his trust and to discover that you enjoy one another and living together. When he feels safe, we might all meet again and consider our next step.'

'For the truth, you mean?' Charlotte asked.

Mrs Hurst nodded. 'It will hurt, come what may, but I'm hoping by then that Harry will be far more invested in you, in his life and surrounds in London, and that any yearning for the home he knows might have lessened.'

Jane felt a deep wound open at those words.

'Mrs Cavendish,' Mrs Hurst continued, 'I would also counsel you against preventing your sister from seeing Harry. I would consider that cruelty – towards both of them.'

'Hear, hear!' William grumbled in the background.

'So,' Mrs Hurst continued, giving William a look of admonishment, 'let's begin this delicate journey with a holiday for Harry and a return meeting in, shall we say, a maximum of four weeks, here?'

Jane nodded. 'Right.' She didn't know what else to say. Nothing was under her control, anyway. Her tone turned hard. 'The cathedral choir is not going to be thrilled at losing their star soprano.'

'Oh, that's the least of my concerns, Jane,' Charlotte said. 'I have far bigger problems with securing the Cavendish estate.'

And there it is, Jane thought, *the portal into your soul. How to get your hands on property and money. Harry's just a means to an end.* She wished she had the courage to say it aloud, but to do so would make her want to fly at Charlotte with her fists, and that in itself was a thought too far.

A window opened upstairs. 'Are you coming, Mummy?'

Charlotte looked up. 'Coming, darling Harry.'

Jane felt sickened that, in his excitement, her precious child didn't seem to notice the wrong mother had answered.

23

'Guy, I'm so sorry. We've received the terrible news of your father's passing. I don't know what to say,' Eleanor gushed down the telephone line.

'There are no words. It was sudden.' Guy sighed. These were not the circumstances under which he wished to speak to Eleanor, but they were the only ones he had.

'How is your mother doing? We will, of course, come for the funeral.'

'Eleanor, you don't have to.'

'Don't be absurd. We must pay our respects.'

'Listen . . . Eleanor, I need to see you. Can we meet?'

'How romantic. But can't it wait until after the funeral? It doesn't seem like the right time . . .'

Guy closed his eyes in frustration. How could he put this? 'No, Eleanor, this can't wait. It's about us.'

'Oh.' Her tone changed. 'Well, you should tell me now, then.'

'I really do think it's best we speak face to face . . . It's about our future.'

'Guy, I can't bear this. I shall not wait. Please just spit it out.'

225

He took a deep breath. There was no choice but to confront and speak the truth. 'It is not easy to say this to someone I like so very much, but the fact is I have decided that we shall not marry.' He heard her shocked intake of breath but continued. 'I know you'll find it hard to forgive me and I won't ask for your understanding, but I think you deserve an explanation.'

There was a pause, and then Eleanor spoke, sounding as rational as ever. 'Guy, you're upset,' she said soothingly, annoying him. 'This is not a time to be making rash decisions.'

'It's not rash. It's been coming for an age, Eleanor. I should never have agreed to our arrangement. It was unfair on you, because I never did feel how you did.'

'That's hard to hear,' she admitted, her tone brittle.

'I wish I'd been more direct with you before now. But every time I have tried to broach this, you've fobbed me off or changed the subject, or made light of the gravity of what I needed to say. You are very good at deflection, Eleanor. And I think deep down it's because you know this is how I feel and you're hoping that by not hearing it, you can dodge it. But I cannot allow you to avoid the inevitable . . . the truth. I do love you, dearest Eleanor, let me be plain about that.'

'Then—' Her tone was plaintive and confused.

'But not in the way you want me to. I don't love you romantically, and I never will. Any marriage between us would be under false pretences, to keep two families happy.'

There was a frigid silence down the telephone line.

Finally she spoke. '*I* would be happy,' she said.

'And I would be miserable,' he said firmly.

'Oh, Guy.' Her voice faltered and became tremulous. 'How beastly of you to say such a thing.'

'I have shied away from honesty with you because it felt cruel. Now, I'm risking cruelty in order to release you, so that you can find someone who can love you in the way you should be loved. Eleanor, I love you as a friend. Dare I say I feel almost brotherly around you.' She gave a sound of disgust. 'But marriage? I would make you miserable.'

'You don't know that. You make me very happy, Guy.'

'No. All you do is bend to my happiness. And once married and forced to live under the same roof, Eleanor, I'd be even more absent, and I refuse to hurt you knowingly.'

'You're hurting me now,' she pleaded.

'This hurt will pass, though. It's better to bear it now before there's a wedding, or a child, before your reputation is compromised and the pain becomes constant.'

'Does your mother know?'

'Yes. She's not happy with me, but she agrees that in the long run I am probably doing you a favour by letting you find the right man to marry.'

'I've spent two years waiting on the one I want to marry.'

'I did warn you of this, and it's why we set that deadline. You know I never promised you anything. This way, if you can permit it somehow, we can retain a friendship – we will always look after one another.'

'There's someone else,' she suddenly said, catching him off guard. 'On my life, there's someone else, isn't there?' she demanded, realising he wasn't denying it.

'I have met someone, yes.' He hated to admit it; he'd wanted a clean break, and Jane was not the reason he did not want to marry Eleanor.

Now she began to weep. He could hear other voices arriving and asking what was wrong.

'It's Guy. He's with another woman!'

Eleanor disappeared and he waited. Her mother must have taken the receiver.

'Guy, what is all this? I'm deeply sorry about your father and we probably shouldn't be having this conversation now, but I have to ask. What is making my daughter weep so?'

This was why he'd wanted to do this in person. He really did care about Eleanor and hated the idea of her being so distraught.

'Mrs Clarence . . . Maud. I am not *with* another woman, as Eleanor claims. But I have made a decision for us not to marry. I don't believe I will be the match for her that you believe I will. I think I would make her life intolerable and lonely. You must accept my decision, which I am making in both of our interests.'

'But, Guy, this doesn't make sense. You two are so well suited . . .'

'I don't think we are. But we are well suited as friends. I love her as my friend, but I don't love her in any other way. I've tried to explain that. What's between us . . . well, it's not the same—'

'So there is someone else? Is that what you mean? Have you met another woman?'

'I have,' he admitted, finding it easier than fielding the questions, which were feeling suddenly relentless. 'Our relationship, I hasten to admit, has not progressed beyond an accidental meeting and a subsequent hour in each other's company, but, Maud, the way I feel about someone who is not much more than a stranger should set off alarm bells for you and your daughter. I have never felt about Eleanor the way I felt about Jane before I even knew her name. We met by chance, and I was enamoured. Now, please, understand that Eleanor is my friend and I will always be that for her if she would like me in her life, but I cannot be her husband. I'm sorry. She refused to listen to me when I tried to explain this countless times, so I'm afraid it's come as a shock.'

'Right. Well, this is very disappointing – a most unhappy situation – as you can imagine, but I suspect you have other sad business on your mind and we should not intrude. You'll understand if we don't attend the funeral of your good father?'

Guy felt relieved. 'I do understand.'

'I shall write to your mother. She knows, I presume?'

'Yes.'

'I will not disturb her in her mourning. Please remember us to your mother during her bereavement.'

'I shall.'

When the phone receiver was finally placed back on the cradle, Guy sat down heavily in his father's chair and gave a long, slow sigh. It seemed all he could do was disappoint people.

───────────

The funeral was over, and the last mourner had paid their respects. Guy and Adele were finally alone, back in their enormous and handsome home, which suddenly felt much bigger without the man who had filled it with the hustle and bustle of business, visitors and entertaining. The absence of his loud voice and contagious laugh was keenly felt.

Guy watched his mother remove her dark veil and carelessly place it and her hat, with its flash of white ribbing, on a side table as they walked into a drawing room. It was one of the home's many formal rooms, most of which they didn't use, other than on special occasions. But he wasn't sure there would be many such occasions now as they were both much quieter people who didn't often feel the need to surround themselves with guests, as Arthur had.

This room had become his mother's private sanctuary; it spoke clearly of her artistic nature and love of light. She had decluttered the stuffiness of the Victorian room the moment she'd decided to take it over as her own. Guy remembered from childhood how this room had once been heavily draped and overfilled with decorative pieces and embellishment.

His mother understood fashion, but like all artists – Jane came to mind readily – she understood the beauty of light and how it might change a room over seasons, over a day even. The joy of this room seemed at odds with the dark gown she was wearing. It, like her room, had few embellishments, apart from deep cuffs, a collar in snow-white organdie and three pearl buttons, which matched the jewellery she had opted for.

'I do like this room,' he said as he watched her collapse into a comfortable sofa and place her head in her hands with a sigh. 'Deceptively simple,' he observed.

'Simple . . . but surprisingly expensive,' she replied, her voice muffled. She looked up and he was pleased to see slight amusement in her eyes.

'Father didn't care a whit about what you spent.'

'No, I know he didn't, darling. He just went through the motions of complaining.'

'You've really opened it up,' he said, trying to avoid too much discussion of his father, with the coffin so newly placed in the family mausoleum.

'Pale colours will always do that.'

'I'm glad those velvet curtains are gone. I used to cough whenever we were in here.'

She chuckled. 'Your father loved them. He liked to be cosy. I've actually kept a lot of the Georgian pieces because they're so elegant . . . almost whimsical.'

'It all works marvellously. And now your walls are display-ing your art, and your china is in the cabinets. Looks very special, Mother.'

'Guy, you've never been in the slightest bit interested in my art. What is going on? Is this that woman having an effect?' At his almost sarcastic glance, she prodded him. 'The woman you refuse to speak about. Is she an artist or something?'

Guy's insides felt as though they'd somersaulted. His father had always warned him against what he called women's intuition:

'Never ignore it or think it doesn't exist, son, because it will come up and bite you. Your mother's especially good at crystal-ball gazing, it seems!'

He smiled at the memory.

'What's amusing, Guy?'

'Something Dad said to me a few times.'

'Oh, yes, do share.'

He told her, realising it was pointless to try to avoid mentioning his father. She clearly wanted to keep talking about him. It wasn't upsetting her. If anything, it was keeping her from crumbling.

'Gosh, I miss him desperately,' she said, laughing at the remark but also dabbing at her red-rimmed eyes to catch the tears that welled.

'You were so composed today. I felt only admiration for how you carried yourself.'

'Really, darling?' she asked, sniffing, looking surprised. 'Well, that's because you were at my side and keeping me strong.'

He took her hand. 'I won't leave you.'

'Ever?' she said, finding a sad smile. 'No, don't answer that. I fear you'll say yes, and I refuse to be a burden.'

'You're not, I promise.'

She found a smile. 'Guy? Lift my spirits, would you, please? Stop avoiding it, tell me about her – your artist. I've had to put up with Maud Clarence's whining letter disguised as condolences. Apparently, Eleanor is inconsolable.'

'I can't help that. I never lied to her.'

'Yes, but you never told her what was in your heart.'

'I tried to.'

'That's not good enough. Have you told this new woman how you feel?'

He shook his head. 'I never got the chance to.'

'Well, I'm all ears, darling. Now is the moment to tell me about her.'

He sighed. There was no escaping it. Where was the weakness in his armour that she could look right through and see to his heart? He sat down opposite her, flicking out his frock coat, undoing his collar and loosening the silk tie that had been looped into a bow. He despised all of this formality; he'd worn this same suit for the funeral of King Edward VII and now hoped this ensemble would be well out of date by the time he needed funeral attire again. *Years and years out of date*, he wished with earnestness.

'You look very handsome. Has she told you that?'

Guy smiled. 'No. She's not one for those compliments.'

Adele's face lit. 'Good! Your ego doesn't need it. But I want to assure you that she thought you were terribly handsome from the moment she saw you. Tell me how you met.'

Might as well tell the truth. All of it, get the shocks all out of the way now.

'Well, it was when her son accidentally kicked his football at my head.' He hurried on. 'That's how I got the cut,' he said, pointing to the fading scar.

'You said it was from the branch of an apple tree,' she said, filled with indignation and accusation.

'It so easily could have been. I didn't explain because I wasn't ready to tell this story. I don't know that I'm ready now.' He looked at his hands.

'Come on, spill.'

He took a deep breath and met her gaze. 'I know that the shock I'm feeling is not entirely about my father. I believe I'm in love for the first time in my life.'

He wasn't ready to watch his mother weep again and he jumped to her side, but she flapped her hands.

'No, no, Guy darling, these are happy tears. I can't believe that on this day I have something that makes me weep with joy and yet here I am, with news to lighten my heart. I want to walk straight back to your father's newly laid coffin and tell him.'

'Maybe tomorrow,' Guy said gently, putting an arm around her. She suddenly seemed small and frail.

'He would be so thrilled to hear this news.'

'I know. But this is not a day for congratulations or happy talk. At least I've told you. I already feel easier for saying it out loud; now perhaps I'll believe it myself.'

'Wait!'

Here it comes, he thought. *Brace yourself.*

'You said her son kicked his football and wounded you.' She frowned.

'He did.'

'Oh, Guy, are you in love with a widow? It all gets so complic—'

'Erm, not exactly, no.'

Her frown deepened and she became very still as he watched her make all the necessary connections. 'Unmarried . . . with a son?'

'Yes, but if you let me—'

She stood. 'Absolutely not. No, no, Guy! This is not happening.'

'Nothing's happening, Mother.'

She began to pace. 'A disgraced woman, a fallen woman, in our family? Over his and my dead body.' She groaned.

'Mother, don't get further upset when there's no need.'

'No need? Guy, you're our only son. You're the heir to this entire empire that your father has built and left for you. This house, the businesses . . . No, Guy, no. Please don't muddy our name and everything we've achieved by bringing in disrepute.'

Disrepute. If only she understood. He wanted to defend Jane to his mother, to rail against the accusation that she was somehow unclean or unworthy. But both he and Adele were in a state of high emotion, and this was not the time to discuss Jane Saville.

He sighed out his frustration. 'Mother, I want you to calm down. Let's not discuss this now. I am here with you, and you alone. The woman I speak of is far away.' He had to swallow his guilt at that admission but his father's passing had to take precedence. Out of duty, loyalty and love he was here in Warwickshire and not in Wiltshire. 'Let's wake up tomorrow and face a new day without Father, without rancour, without anxiety. We are grieving. Let's just focus on all that we must sort out. Truly, I have plenty to keep my head spinning. Finding time for myself to grieve will be quite the circus act.'

That did seem to calm her down. 'You will not steal away?'

Guy had to stifle his disdain at how that sounded. 'No, Mother. I shall not steal away. I shall be here. Now, I do think you should rest. Come on. We can talk about Jane another day.'

She allowed him to guide her out of the room and upstairs to her private wing.

'Send up Helen, would you, please? I do suddenly feel as though I've had all the stuffing kicked out of me.' She sounded newly fragile.

'Right away. She might bring you a brandy too. Drink it, Mother, and rest. I'll see you a little later,' he said and kissed her cheek.

As he closed the door, he realised there would not be any swift answer to his dilemma. He'd always thought his parents forward-thinking, his mother especially very modern in her approach. But when it came to him, it seemed his mother regressed into the most conservative of parents. Well, she was going to have to accept that his heart was not so conservative. It simply was not capable of shifting the direction of Cupid's arrow. A direct hit had been made, and Guy was now bonded to Jane Saville. He wished she would call. Should *he* call?

Best not. He needed to stay true to his word and give her the time she needed right now. He had written his affectionate letter, so she would be in no doubt about how he felt. Importantly, he had assuaged his guilty conscience over Eleanor and could now pursue Jane's hand without any shame.

24

SALISBURY

Since Harry's departure 'on holiday', William's health had worsened. They'd sat on the cold Salisbury train platform for what had to be an hour after Harry's train had pulled out, Jane sobbing, and William doing his best to comfort her. Finally she heard his urgings to move and they helped each other home. There were no hansom cabs at this time and William moved slowly from the train station, down the small incline onto Fisherton Street and the walk that should have taken ten minutes but took twice as long, through to the North Gate entrance and into the Close.

By the time they'd arrived at number eighteen, William was struggling to breathe and Jane had to snap out of her misery to get him tucked into bed. She'd warmed it with a clay bottle filled with hot water and covered him with extra blankets. He didn't leave that bed for days, concerning Jane enough to call for the doctor, who visited immediately.

When the doctor reappeared in the parlour, to Jane wringing her hands, he smiled sadly. 'He's comfortable now.'

'Will he recover?'

'To a point.'

'What's ailing him? He's not that old.'

'He is terminally ill, Miss Saville. Perhaps he might tell you more himself . . . It's not my place and I am bound by privacy.'

'My apologies, of course. I understand.'

'What I can tell you is that he will likely not recover fully from this setback. He's sliding backwards now, for want of a better term, and it would be wise for your own emotional health that you make peace with that.'

Jane shook her head and swallowed a gasp, which might have been a sob; she wasn't sure.

'Where's the lad?' the doctor asked.

'Er, he's gone to stay with family in London for a while.' She was surprised at how easily and efficiently she could explain Harry's absence.

'That's probably a good thing. I thought he was tremendous at the service last Sunday, by the way. Just magnificent. I know William's very proud, so I can only imagine how you feel as his mother.'

'Thank you, Doctor. Yes, William and I can't believe that tiny baby is now singing to the heavens so sweetly in the cathedral.' She knew he was now making polite conversation to reassure her, to keep her calm and pave his way to extracting himself. She should show him she was not a woman who displayed histrionics. 'What can I do for William?'

He nodded, as if pleased with her composure. 'Exactly what you are doing. Keep him warm, keep him resting, keep him eating as best you can, lots of fluids.'

'Will he leave his bed?'

He nodded. 'Knowing William, I suspect in a day or so, he will try.' He gave a tight smile. 'He'll be weak and, between us, it will likely be a false rally, so to speak. Each of these attacks weakens him further, and you know how bad he was earlier this year.'

She nodded; she had been very concerned about the older man when he'd struggled to breathe and was generally weak.

'Nothing wrong with William's mind,' the doctor said, sounding as though he wished it were otherwise. 'He's talking about his will and tidying his affairs. This suggests he's accepting what's to come, and that's a great milestone to reach.'

'I am not so accepting,' Jane admitted.

'I understand. There is, however, nothing more we can do. It would help him, I'm sure, if you were able to remain composed and assist with any of the arrangements he might wish to make.'

'I'll do my best.'

He shook her hand. 'I can see myself out, Miss Saville. You've been a marvellous tonic for William. I'm sure that you and Harry have extended his life by simply being in it.'

'That's kind of you to say,' she said.

He nodded, then gave his tight smile again. 'Call me when . . . er, when the time comes.'

She couldn't bear it. 'Thank you,' she managed to say before turning away, tears already falling.

———————

Later, having helped William to sip weakly on some beef broth, she decided to clear her head momentarily of its crushing sorrow and take a walk around the Close while he dozed. If she could just think outside the sadness of her life and get some perspective, then she might be able to make a loose plan for her future.

She had a vision of setting up regular visits with Harry that did not involve her arguing with Charlotte, instead negotiating calmly and rationally in a way that didn't engage with Charlotte's natural propensity to be cruel. Where had that leaning come from? Jane had had the same upbringing, the same support and love of her parents . . . *Except that's not true, is it?* a small voice whispered from within.

Though it remained unacknowledged, it was understood by both girls that Charlotte was favoured by their mother, while Jane had been favoured by their father. It perhaps wasn't so noticeable to others, but the girls had grasped it from a young age, and Jane thought they'd both accepted it. Although Jane had been a traditionally pretty child, she had not turned into the beauty her mother had hoped for. Her nose was narrow, and her face had matured into sharper angles through her second decade, as the dimpled fullness of youth had receded. Even her body shape had changed from a rounded, sweetish appearance into a hollow frame. It was not deliberate. Her father had been the same, and he had always said his mother was tall, lean and angular.

Charlotte, meanwhile, had an hourglass figure truly suited to the corseted shape of the Edwardian era, a curvier look she shared with her mother. Age had turned her mother into a squatter, more solid version of herself but Charlotte was exquisite in the latest fabulous 'S'-shaped fashion. In contrast, Jane's chest was flat enough not to take any pronounced form beneath her clothes and her movements were lithe and measured, like a dancer's.

'You're like a starved bird,' her mother used to say, except Jane never starved herself, not like her sister, who deliberately went without to ensure she could achieve a tiny-waisted look. Being hungry all the time made Charlotte cantankerous and her mood at odds with the natural beauty she possessed. No narrow nose for Charlotte – hers was a perfect button within a sweet, heart-shaped face. While they shared an eye colour, Jane somehow felt Charlotte's eyes dazzled when she wanted them to.

Her sister had all the tools to be popular, envied and pursued, and yet she found time to be churlish, often cruel, to Jane. It seemed what she most wanted – the approval of her father, when he was alive – had not come easily. Father and daughter had found it difficult to find any common interests, which frustrated Charlotte, who possessed a personality, in Jane's opinion, that craved constant adoration.

'You try too hard to get his attention,' she'd once said to her sister.

'And you do nothing to earn it, and yet he takes you away with him.'

'Charlotte, we have similar interests, Papa and I. Are you going to spend a day roaming across a heath with him looking for a rare flower? Are you interested in the latest steam engine and the speed it can reach?'

'Why are *you* interested in that?' Charlotte had shot back.

'I don't know.' Jane laughed. 'I find the world fascinating. You're more interested in fashion than art, and the right restaurant to be seen in rather than the food itself. You don't go to the ballet to appreciate the incredible beauty of it, you go there to be noticed and spend most of your time looking through opera glasses at who is in the audience. Mother is like that, but he is not. It's not a criticism, Charlotte, merely an observation.'

'Well, I think he should take more interest in me,' Charlotte had huffed.

'Then tell him. Stop blaming me. Better still, take more interest in him and his pursuits.'

'I am not going to learn the rules of cricket, Jane!'

Jane shrugged. 'It's quite an interesting and strategic sport if you pay attention.'

And so, as they'd matured, Charlotte's complaints had turned inward to make her bitter, Jane surmised. And she'd angled that bitterness at Jane, an easy target – easier to blame than their father or herself. Jane had been on the receiving end of Charlotte's anger since before their teens. She'd learned how to deflect it, how to absorb it when necessary and how to defuse it when she could.

But now this was about Harry.

This was a new cruelty, beyond Charlotte's track record. It certainly wasn't about trying to build a relationship with Harry or make amends for her past conduct. It was about money. Money and status, the two elements that ruled Charlotte's existence.

Jane shook her thoughts free of that sourness. She had to think about Harry's education; maybe the school could work out some sort of transfer to a London choir. She would have to insist that Charlotte find an excellent school for Harry to match the level of education he was currently enjoying. Even now, in her darkest hour, she was looking ahead to maybe having Harry for the school holidays, and if Charlotte needed to be away, she would be the first to step in and offer to take care of Harry's needs.

She was still doing up her coat, having just closed the front door behind her to head out on her walk, her mind lost to the conversation with Charlotte about Harry spending school holidays here in Salisbury, when a woman's voice sounded.

'Miss Saville?'

Jane blinked, jolted from her worrisome thoughts. 'Yes?'

'I'm sorry to interrupt you. I can see you were stepping out.'

'Nothing urgent. I was simply going for a stroll,' Jane said, frowning, as the woman moved elegantly down the path towards her. She was dressed in a soft charcoal suit of fine wool. The skirt hung in a fitted shape to the knee, with neat box pleats to the ankle. A matching jacket was tailored to fit the woman's lovely figure to perfection. Its three large tortoiseshell buttons cinched her waist beneath her breasts, which sat proudly beneath a caramel-coloured silk blouse edged with lace. Her shoes were heeled, dark grey leather that looked like fresh coal catching the sun. Her bag was a polished crocodile skin in brown, and her toque, the final flourish to her ensemble, was poised atop her immaculately pinned strawberry-red hair. It had a single feather winging coquettishly upwards, its flecks and stripes of brown matching her buttons. None of this expensive styling was lost on Jane, but the woman wore her garments without any extravagant jewellery or affectation. Here was someone who was used to the very best of textiles, fashionable accoutrements and tailoring.

'May I join you on your stroll?' the woman asked in a pleasant tone.

'Um . . . may I ask who you are, please? This is actually not a good time—'

The woman, who had to be in her mid-twenties, had a heart-shaped face not unlike Charlotte's, and warmth in her smile that touched her blue-grey eyes, which, if Jane had to paint, she might begin with Egyptian or perhaps Prussian blue and then pull it back towards the cool greyish hue of this woman's eyes.

'I am Miss Clarence,' the woman said, dragging Jane from her reassuring ruminations on paint. 'Eleanor Clarence.'

Jane swallowed. 'Eleanor.' *Guy's* Eleanor? What was she doing here?

The woman must have noted the recognition in Jane's tone. 'Ah, he has spoken of me, then.'

It was so direct, so determined not to waste time on explanation or hedging via polite conversation, that Jane was caught off-guard. She had no words, only a damning sort of stammer. 'I . . . I . . .'

Eleanor smiled. 'It's not your fault.'

Jane found herself blinking in an attempt to regain her equilibrium. 'Um, what's not my fault?'

'Trying to form a relationship with him. I don't blame you. Jane . . . may I call you Jane? I blame Guy. He can't see what he does with his effortless charm. You are simply a victim of it.' She tittered and Jane heard the confidence, which Eleanor had been working hard to promote, begin to falter.

How on earth had this woman even found her? 'Would you like to come inside?' Jane thought she owed it to her to be polite at least.

Eleanor glanced around; she looked suddenly trapped.

'Or the garden?' Jane offered.

'Yes, thank you.'

'Follow me, please, Miss Clarence.'

'Call me Eleanor; we seem to share a bond.'

Jane showed her through the side gate and down the path that led to the back of the house. This was where Guy had kissed her. This was where her sister had stolen Harry from her. It might as well be the scene for another unnerving confrontation, she thought.

'Please sit,' Jane said, gesturing towards the garden bench. 'Can I fetch you something, Eleanor? A drink or . . .?'

'Nothing, thank you.' Eleanor brushed imaginary leaves or dust from the bench and sat on its edge. Jane seated herself on the single outdoor chair that William normally favoured to look out on the garden, through the arbour and past a glorious statue of a woman, which had come from some important manor. There had been a pair, William explained, but he had only been able to acquire one.

'This is charming. I see that leads to an orchard. Apples?' Eleanor mused.

'Among a pear and plum, yes.'

'He would have loved the apple tree, no doubt.'

More than you could ever imagine, Jane thought. 'Eleanor, why are you here?'

The woman looked at her earnestly, those grey eyes wide. 'You can't take him from me. You simply can't.'

Jane hesitated. 'I suspect Guy will do as he chooses,' she tried.

'Guy and I have been seeing one another for two years.'

'Just under, I gather.'

Eleanor looked rattled. 'I see. So he's told you about . . .'

'Your arrangement, yes, he did. Eleanor, it's obvious you care about him.'

'That word doesn't quite touch it, Jane.'

Jane nodded, understanding and feeling suddenly sorry for the woman. They were only a couple of years apart in age, but Jane felt ancient by comparison. This girl had seen little hardship, perhaps no adversity in her life. 'You love him,' she corrected.

'So much so that I am prepared to humiliate myself by visiting you here today and begging you to not pursue your relationship with him.'

'No woman should beg over a man,' Jane said, dismayed.

'Guy is my life,' Eleanor continued, ignoring Jane's comment. 'He has been since he first walked into it. He is my sun and moon. When he's around it's midsummer. When he's away I am in my winter.'

Jane wanted to laugh. It was heartless, but this young woman was far too romantic for her own good. 'He's just a man, Eleanor, and men can be deeply disappointing. As disappointing as women, I hasten to add. I don't think the frailty belongs only to the male community. We disappoint each other all the time.'

Eleanor looked confused. 'What are you saying?'

'I'm saying that Guy is not perfect.' Jane smiled gently; she did not want to be harsh.

'He is to me.'

'Then he will disappoint you. And surely already has.'

Eleanor frowned. 'Has he disappointed you?'

'Yes, as a matter of fact. A couple of times, the most recent right now with no word from him. He was here and then he was gone. No call, no note, just silence.'

'His father died.'

'Indeed.' She said no more but inside she was reeling. Wouldn't he have told her something so huge?

'You see, I'm already so forgiving. With all that goes on in his life, I would not expect anything of him – as you surely do.'

'I expect nothing of him. In fact, I am not thinking about him,' Jane lied. 'I have an important situation that I am navigating right now. I'm afraid it's taking all my thoughts and space in here,' she said, tapping her temple.

Eleanor smiled, as though she was happy to hear it. 'He just doesn't realise I am the right woman for him.'

'Hasn't he had nearly two years to make that decision?'

'You were not in the frame, Jane. And now I need you to step out of it,' Eleanor said bluntly.

She made it sound so reasonable. Jane took a breath. 'He's not here, if you came looking for him.'

'I know where he is. I came to see you only. I think he'd hate me if he knew.'

'I don't believe Guy could ever hate you. But may I be honest?' Jane didn't wait for the woman's answer because she suspected Eleanor would not want to hear what she was going to say. 'I think to love someone so hard and so blindly is to smother them. Don't you want Guy to love you without you holding on so tight?'

'I give him so much freedom. He can do as he wishes, as long as—'

'And still, it seems, he must feel cornered,' Jane cut in.

Eleanor shook her head as though Jane was speaking in riddles. 'I have to fight for him. It's why I'm here.'

'You don't have to fight with me. I do not see him as mine to fight for, or even give back.' That was something of a half-truth. Jane did not want to lose Guy, but what choice did she have? He had said a lot of pretty words, but a man like him could not truly be with a woman like her. It was time to let go of all hope for Guy and her.

He wasn't here. His disappearance and silence spoke volumes, even if his father had passed. He could have sent word, surely, and would have, if he really cared.

'He loves you,' Eleanor insisted.

'I doubt that. He has not said as much to me. And Eleanor, Guy and I hardly know one another.'

The woman frowned in such deep dismay that Jane felt compelled to explain how she and Guy had met.

'You've seen him only twice?' she finally said, sounding bewildered.

'That's all.' Jane shrugged. 'And on both occasions with someone else in our midst.' That too was a half-truth, she thought, remembering the kiss, which, frankly, she couldn't forget. But it would ease Eleanor's heart, especially as Jane made the decision to remove herself from Guy Attwood's life as of this moment, tamping down the pain this idea brought. It simply wasn't to be.

'And this was about his apple?'

Jane nodded. 'Our meeting was quite by chance – a complete accident. But the apple was what brought him back the second time.'

'Not you, then. So why is he leaving me for you?'

'Are you sure you're not jumping to a conclusion? I have not heard from Guy. We were supposed to meet last Sunday,' she said, keeping it vague, 'but he didn't turn up.'

'Guy said he would not be marrying me.'

'I can't speak to that, Eleanor.'

'Yes, but he told his mother about you. You are the reason he would not be marrying me, he said. And his mother told my mother. And my mother believes where there's smoke there's fire. What did he say about me?'

Eleanor really was still a child, Jane thought, as she listened to her rationalise and admit how much control she handed to others.

But Jane didn't blame her. It wasn't that long ago that Eugenie Saville had forced her daughter to do something that would change the course of her entire life.

'Guy did tell me about you,' Jane admitted.

'And?'

'I don't think it's my place to—'

'This is my life!'

Jane sighed. 'He said he had his reservations. I don't believe he's ready to make the commitment you want.'

Eleanor stood and paced. 'That's obvious. Jane, of course you're the complication. I have to ask: do you love him?'

'I don't think that's a fair question.'

'Why?'

'I hardly know him.'

'That's irrelevant as an answer to me. Unlike you, I *do* know him, and I *do* love him. If you're undecided or he's simply a casual interest, then please, would you let him go?'

She made it sound so reasonable. Jane stayed silent as Eleanor continued.

'Guy really doesn't know what he wants, but I am good for him; everyone thinks so.'

Except him, Jane resisted saying.

'I don't put any pressure on his life, and I will be the very best wife. Dutiful, loyal, ever willing and a good mother to his children.'

If you think that's what he's looking for, Eleanor, you really don't know him.

'Our parents adore us together. We are good for each other.'

Jane sighed audibly, but that didn't seem to slow Eleanor's earnest words.

'Jane, have you never felt the need to fight for someone because you knew they needed someone to fight for them?'

Harry, who had been wandering around the edge of her mind, suddenly ran into full focus. Had she fought hard enough for Harry? Or had she capitulated because she was scared of the consequences? She had acquiesced, she now assured herself, in this moment of awakening, simply because she didn't want him hurt.

Not good enough! she heard in the dying voice of William. *He's going to be hurt anyway. It might as well be the person who loves him so very much who delivers that pain, because you'll be there to soothe him. Charlotte will not. She will bludgeon him with the truth, and then leave him to heal alone.*

So she should fight back?

Of course! she heard not only William but now her father too.

'Are you listening, Jane?'

'Yes, of course,' she fibbed. 'Eleanor, can I lay your concerns to rest by assuring you that I am not intending to see Guy again?'

'You're not?' The younger woman looked shocked.

'No. As I explained, our meeting was pure coincidence.'

'But he told me, he told his mother—'

'Well, he hasn't uttered anything of the kind to me. May I speak my thoughts?'

Eleanor didn't look sure. Her eyes were glittering – with the knowledge that Jane was no longer her rival, Jane suspected – but she seemed uncertain about whether she wanted the candour.

Jane softened the blow but landed it all the same. 'Perhaps you need to ask yourself why he would say these things. Guy might be feeling unsure about the approaching deadline. He may not be ready to commit in the way you wish, and so he's trying to throw reasons in the way.'

'Why wouldn't he just say that he's not ready?'

'I can't speak for Guy, but the man I met was reticent and private. I doubt he finds it easy to speak the truth to someone he cares about so much. But I assure you, I am not in your way. If you want my advice, give him more time.'

Now Eleanor's eyes shone. 'Oh, thank you!' She actually hugged Jane. 'I can do that. I can be patient.'

Jane extricated herself. 'One more piece of advice? Don't compromise all your hopes or your time over a man. It seems to me that you could have anything you could want in this world, so—'

'There's only one thing I want in the world. Guy is my world.'

'Then he's all yours.' Jane shrugged. She was baffled by women like Eleanor and her sister and horrified that Eleanor, who could have anything she wanted, was choosing to let her whole life rest on the affections of a single man. A man who didn't want her, according to him. This was surely how Charlotte had felt about Eddie. Jane would not tolerate such a situation. Better to live frugally and on her own terms.

She saw Eleanor back to the garden gate and into the Close. 'There are cabs to the station from North Gate,' she said, pointing, and then waited to wave, sensing that Eleanor would look back with a smile of private smugness that she had come and won her prize. 'Good luck, Eleanor,' she murmured. *And good luck, Guy,* she thought.

———

When Jane went inside to check on him, William looked up from his pillow, his pallor grey against its starched whiteness.

'Comfy?' Jane asked.

He nodded once. 'I'm proud of you.'

'I don't know how I'm going to do this yet.'

'You'll find a way. I know you will. At least you'll go down fighting.'

She smiled back at him sadly.

'Listen, Jane, I want you to leave.'

She frowned. 'Leave?'

'Yes. I don't want you here when I die.'

'William, you're not—'

'Come on now,' he croaked. 'You and I don't lie to each other. I am dying. I am days away, if that.'

'Then I shall stay until—'

'No, you won't. I don't want that.' He paused to cough and she waited, feeling dismayed by his attitude. 'I don't want you to remember me croaking to my final breath. Call the doctor, organise a nurse who can take care of immediate needs and leave me.'

'William, please.'

'No. This is my dying wish. I want to remember you, my beautiful girl, like this, strong and determined, not bleating and teary over me. I want you to go somewhere away from this house, away from Salisbury even, with its memories, where you can think clearly and work out how to get Harry back. No, Jane.' He raised a weak hand as she attempted to speak. 'I'm leaving the house, my savings and all my chattels to you and Harry. It's yours. I want you to remember me in this home fondly and not have to share in me dying here. I'm doing you a kindness, I promise. Now, would you please do me the kindness of doing what I'm asking of you?'

'But to leave you now is surely cruel,' she protested.

'To stay hurts me more. Please, Jane. Please.'

She swallowed, crying, and nodded.

William squeezed her hand. 'Thank you, my darling girl. Now go and ring the doctor and make haste to leave.'

She wiped her eyes. 'I don't know where to go.'

'I've left money in an envelope on my desk for this reason. Go anywhere you choose, somewhere you can think through your situation carefully. Your next move with your sister is critical.'

'My mind is empty of what might tip the scales back in my favour. I have nothing.'

'That's because your head is full of sorrow . . . over me, over that cad, Attwood, and over the loss of your son. Go somewhere that fills you with inspiration and let your thoughts roam free. You will think of something, Jane.'

'And if not?'

'Then you've left no stone unturned. Right now, you've capitulated to threat and the fear of injury to Harry. I say you stare that beast down, Jane. Confront it. Risk everything to win everything that matters to you. I know you can do it.'

She nodded. 'I do love you, William. Thank you for being my guardian angel.'

'I think it's the other way around. You need to know the last seven years of my life have been the very best ones. You and Harry gave me a new lease on that life; I think I would have died much sooner if not for the two of you. I've known laughter and joy . . . and love.'

They stared at one another.

'I don't want to leave you,' she said, wiping away fresh tears.

'I know. But I want you to leave me,' he insisted. 'Go today. Just get on a train and go somewhere far away from all of this.'

She packed a few items, found the envelope on William's desk, marked with her name, and spoke with the doctor, who agreed to make all the necessary arrangements. Jane took a wander around Harry's room, touching his toys, his precious finds and his drawings, and momentarily lay on his bed, her head touching the pillow that so recently had touched his. Then she took a few final minutes to walk around her painting study, using that brief time to take down the sketch of the apple. She couldn't look at it. She never wanted to see that apple again and hoped this was indeed the last year those two trees bore fruit. Guy had let her down. She'd risked herself by falling for him, and now she needed to put him in her past. He was a mistake. A moment of madness in which she'd envisaged another life for herself.

No. Her life needed to be about Harry. And she was going to find a way to get him back. She blew a teary kiss to William before she left and then had to look away when he too let out a sob, which he tried to disguise as a cough. She went downstairs, closed the front door on the haven that had kept her and Harry safe all these years, and walked away without looking back.

25

WARWICKSHIRE

It was two weeks before Guy could consider returning to Wiltshire. He had needed to observe a week of mourning alongside his mother, but he'd felt better for sending a long letter to Jane, pouring out his heart. He had explained that following the note he'd sent her on the day he'd had to rush off, his father had passed away. He told her how she had been in his thoughts each day and that he couldn't wait to be reunited with her. He apologised again for missing Harry's solo and promised he would make it up to him, before asking carefully what had occurred with Charlotte. He even suggested a holiday at Merton Hall.

> Harry will love all of the nature around him and he can run wild; we'll teach him to fish, to ride, to visit my childhood hide to perhaps see the great grey shrike if it winters here on its annual migration.

Another week had flown by as he sorted out business interests and made sure the various managers were moving ahead smoothly under his guidance. In that time he'd reluctantly retired his father's secretary and confidant, Reg, an older man who was glad to hand over the reins.

'It won't work, Guy,' he'd said gently. 'I'll keep referring to the way your father and I did things, and you'll keep railing against them. Ultimately you'll find me a barrier, potentially a burden.'

'But I need someone to steady the ship. You're that person.'

'No, Guy, you are. You must lead. Appoint your own people. I want us to remain friends. I've known you since you were born, so I'd rather that relationship remain intact. But I'll be at home in the garden, probably wrestling with weeds and glad for any distraction. Visit, ask questions, for advice even. But with you a new era begins, and a fresh broom needs to sweep through.'

Reg was probably right, Guy realised. 'Well, if it's all about the new age, then I suspect I shall appoint a woman.'

Reg raised his eyebrows. 'Are you sure, Guy? They can get awfully emotional.'

Guy laughed. 'Reg, thirty years ago, most secretaries were men. Do you know how many are now?'

'I wouldn't have a clue. I have lived in a bubble working alongside your father for decades.'

'Would it surprise you that three quarters of the country's secretaries are now women?'

'Good grief!'

Again, Guy laughed. 'That's the modern age, so I shall be appointing a woman as my right-hand man, so to speak.'

Reg chuckled. 'There, you see, I'm already outdated. Let me speak to an agency I know. We might be able to find you just the right person.'

Guy spent most of that week interviewing potential private secretaries and he was beginning to doubt he'd find the right person until Miss Alice Farmer walked through his office door. He immediately sensed he was in the presence of someone who was comfortable in her skin. After speaking with her for a short while, he was confident she would be capable of handling a lot of tasks and managing others – including him – and she clearly had flawless stenographic skills.

'Miss Farmer, I suspect this job is a big one. I'd rather not pretend it's anything else. I have large shoes to fill and I'm learning as I go, so I'm going to need a lot of help.'

'Which I shall be pleased to provide, Mr Attwood. I'm not daunted.'

'I wish I could say the same.' He smiled.

'Mr Attwood, I want to address something that might be at the back of your mind, which is whether I have a personal life that may get in the way of this demanding position. I realise you're much too polite to press, so let me put any fears to rest.'

He cleared his throat – here was another woman who could read his mind. How did she know that's what he'd been thinking?

'It doesn't say in my paperwork, but I am a widow.' She paused and he filled the gap with the expected moue of sympathy.

'I'm very sorry,' he began. 'You don't need to—'

'Forgive me interrupting, Mr Attwood. But John died five years ago, and I have found my peace with my grief. I hope you don't mind me being candid?'

'I prefer it, Miss Farmer.'

'Well, John was my other half in every way. I have felt like half a person since he passed.'

Guy must have looked suddenly awkward at just how honest she was being, because she smiled.

'That's not easy to hear, I realise, and I don't mean to discomfort you. I'm sharing this so you know I have known my great love and I am not in search of it again. I miss him every day and I've come to the conclusion that no matter what others think – including that at thirty, I am still young enough and capable enough to attract another husband – I am not the slightest bit interested in having anyone take his place. I am comfortable in my loneliness, you could say. I've worked at an accountant's office for the last two years, as you know, but I'm now ready to fill my life with something more challenging, more . . .' She frowned as she found the right word. 'Satisfying,' she settled on. 'I am amazed at the breadth of business that your father established. It's exciting and I know it could easily keep me busy for twenty-five hours of any day.'

'Nine to five will do me just fine, Miss Farmer,' he hurried to remark.

'And I will fill those hours with busyness on your behalf. I'll keep you on the straight and narrow, Mr Attwood. I'm sure that's what you're looking for – someone to put out fires for you, and to brief you as needed, and to run the office in your absence, fielding calls, generally thinking how you might when you're not at your desk. Don't get me wrong, I have no intention of running any business, but I see you have two young secretaries. They're going to need reliable managing so their work flows at a reasonable and steady rate. These are all tasks I'm suited to.'

'Miss Farmer, I think you're perfect for the job, and I'd like you to begin as soon as you can.'

'I can start in a few days, Mr Attwood. I have scouted a bedsit I can rent.'

'Oh, our head office is at Warwick, as you know, and we have our own accommodations. I'm sure I can arrange for a roomy flat, or a cottage if you prefer.'

She looked astonished. 'I'm not sure I can afford to cover the cost of something more spacious on my single wage.'

'You won't need to. I shall make it part of your condition of employment. I want this to be a long-term appointment, Miss Farmer, so let me make it as attractive as possible. The accommodation will come with the job. You already know the wage.'

'But that's rather extravagant, surely?'

He laughed. 'I like your modesty. I don't see it as extravagant, but as essential. If my new private secretary is comfortable, happy and secure, it means my working life is all of those things too. I shall be away more than I'm here. You shall have to learn to be me. That responsibility deserves equal reward.'

'I don't know what to say.'

'Say yes!' He stood and held out his hand.

She stood too, looking pleased.

'Why don't we put you up in a local hotel for the first few days while you sort out the new place to your requirements? They're all furnished, but if something is lacking or you'd prefer to install your own furniture, that's fine. I'll have the outgoing Mr Reg Bank sort out everything for you. Er, I shall be away when you arrive, but I'll write out some early instructions.'

'How long will you be away, Mr Attwood?'

He frowned. 'I'm not sure. Perhaps a week.'

'All right. I'm sure we can manage just fine in that time.'

He smiled. 'I shall keep you fully informed.'

'Thank you for everything. I look forward to working with you, Mr Attwood.'

'And you, Miss Farmer. Shall I show you your office? And you can meet the two secretaries, both lovely girls.' He gestured for her to go first, far more relieved than Miss Farmer might have imagined that he could now turn his attention away from the office.

Guy sat with his mother in her conservatory, which had been built to her specifications as a new bride with a wealthy husband, eager to please. It was, in his opinion, a glorious blending of artistic sensibility with nature, but it also spoke of ego and wealth. There was no doubting its enormous expense: light spilled onto large tiles past gilded arched windows, themselves works of art, giving the space a golden hue that made Guy feel as though he were floating in the verdant garden of Merton. It was here that his mother liked to read, paint, listen to music and entertain her friends on fine spring and summer days. The conservatory offered just the theatre she needed, sitting high and looking down over rolling meadows. It was impossible not to be impressed, but he'd always found this space comforting. Except right now it felt like his old headmaster's study. It would host a conversation that would be uncomfortable, he knew, but it could not be avoided.

'Guy!' Adele welcomed him with such pleasure in her voice, he immediately felt guilty. 'Reg rang yesterday and told me how busy you've been.'

He kissed her cheek. 'You smell lovely,' he said, memories of childhood prompted by the scent of violets.

'Your father's wedding gift on our first night together.' She took a breath to say more and Guy raised his hands and his eyebrows in horror.

'Say no more.'

She chuckled, amused despite her obvious sorrow. 'You're easy to tease, Guy. How are you coping?'

'Better now that I've appointed Miss Farmer.'

She looked at him in query and he explained how impressive the woman had been.

'She sounds brilliant, darling.'

'Oh, I think she will keep us all in check. More to the point, how have you been? I hope you'll forgive my absence.'

'Of course. I know where you've been, and in fact the few days of solitude have probably been wise. I've cried a lot of tears, and then it was as though your father visited and told me to pull myself together and not be needy.'

'That sounds like something he'd say,' Guy remarked.

'I shall try harder.'

He gave a soft sigh. 'Early days, Mother. Don't be too tough on yourself.'

'Shall I order some coffee? I've had some, but . . .'

'No, I'm fine actually.'

'How is Eleanor?'

He sighed. 'I haven't spoken to her again.'

'How did she take it?'

'As you'd expect.'

'And you haven't heard any more?'

He shook his head. 'Silence. It's a surprise, I'll admit.'

'I think that's wishful, Guy. A woman as in love as Eleanor doesn't bounce back so fast from this news, if she bounces back at all.'

'You'd rather histrionic calls and visits?'

'No, but it would be reassuring somehow. I think the silence is a little . . . odd.'

Guy shrugged. 'Maybe she's giving herself time to come to some understanding.'

She laughed a little unkindly. 'Again, wishful. Oh, you men can be so dim sometimes. Eleanor has interminable patience, I'll give her that, but it won't be to reach a level of understanding, Guy. The quiet you're experiencing will be her planning to launch a new attack.'

At this he laughed. 'There's nothing to fight for, or win.'

'Only in your mind, darling. Not in hers, I suspect. Her parents are feeling bitter, so they'll be helping to ward Eleanor off, no doubt, but she's got spine where you don't see it. I don't think she will be dissuaded as easily as you think.'

'What do you think she doesn't understand about "I don't love you and I don't wish to marry you"?' He felt frustrated; he could not have been any clearer with her.

'All of it. She's madly in love with you. She feels she's earned you through her patience and now has every right to expect you to honour the arrangement, which I'm sure she sees as some sort of old-fashioned betrothal.'

'Well, she's going to be disappointed, because while I am a man in love, it's not with her. In fact, I'm leaving tomorrow.'

Her gaze became hooded. He knew his mother well enough to know she would not make this easy for him. 'Leaving?'

'I have to go back to Wiltshire.'

'To *her*.'

'She has a name. Jane.'

'So you said.'

'I'm glad you recall.' He hated the way he sounded but he felt defensive of Jane; she didn't deserve his mother's disdain.

'She's a woman of disrepute, Guy. This is dangerous. For you, and for the family name.'

'Mother, she's no such thing!'

'She has a son. She's no widow. She's not even married.'

'It's not her son!'

There! It was out. He felt only relief, even though he knew this detail was private. He trusted his mother to keep this to herself, and thought Jane would understand.

His words brought silence to the room and a stillness as they regarded each other in separate shock, him at his raised voice and his mother at the revelation, no doubt. Guy could hear a bird warbling somewhere nearby and even more distantly he thought someone might have dropped a pan in the kitchen, but it could have been his ears playing tricks.

'What on earth does that mean?' his mother demanded, breaking the tension.

'If you'd lose that tone of disgust, I'd like to explain.'

'Guy, how do you expect me to feel? We haven't asked much

of you, but we have had simple expectations that shouldn't need to be said.'

'I know them.'

'Then why defy them? Why risk offending your greatest supporter?'

'Because I love her, that's why.'

'You barely know her.'

'That's true,' he admitted. Adele had been so happy when she'd first heard of Guy's feelings, but hearing of Jane's son had changed everything, it seemed. 'But I love the little I know.'

'This will tarnish your name, Guy. We've managed to keep the Attwood name clean and tidy for generations.'

'I'm sure we don't know the half of it over generations but, even so, I can assure you that Jane brings no stain to our name. Firstly, she is a Saville.'

Adele's nostrils flared as she took in a silent breath. He knew that name meant something to her. It was the name of a good family that still moved in royal circles. 'Didn't they fall on hard times?' she asked.

'The father died, leaving a wife and two daughters to fend for themselves,' Guy said. 'They've managed well enough. A London house, I gather.'

'Well, that can't last. How many years has it been?'

'I don't know. Probably a dozen.'

'And it doesn't occur to you that Guy Attwood walking into her life is just about the best thing that could happen to a Saville daughter? The mother is an opportunist, I know that much.'

'Can you blame her?'

'Yes. When she targets my son, I do.'

Guy shook his head. 'She doesn't even know about me.'

'How can you possibly say that?'

'Because Jane barely speaks with her family.'

'Why? I'll tell you why. Because she's brought shame.'

Guy gave a loud and frustrated groan. 'Stop it, Mother. I say that with all the respect I can muster. I love you dearly, but I hate it when you fall into the trap of every other society-conscious woman protecting her own.'

'That's my job.'

'No, you're so much better than that. And you should not concern yourself with social matters other than injustice. And Jane has seen her share of injustice.'

'Am I supposed to reply to that?'

'I just want you to listen, without interruption, for a few minutes.'

She gave a theatrical sigh. 'Nothing you say will improve my opinion, but go ahead, Guy.'

'Thank you.' He told his mother all that he knew about Jane and the Savilles and was aware of her expression changing from distaste to enquiry and then a hint of shock. He brought his explanation to a close. 'She did not give birth to Harry, but she might as well have. Her heart is big, her sense of family duty intact, and her love for this child is enormous. Unlimited. She is a good woman.'

Adele looked momentarily flustered. 'Well, I don't know what to say to all that.'

He shrugged. 'Admit you feel sympathy for her situation.'

'Well, I do, but love can't be based on sympathy, Guy.'

He smiled. 'This is not sympathy I'm feeling, Mother. No, that's for you to feel, and all the other detractors who leap to a conclusion about her. What I feel is something I can't even explain – I've never felt it before. I want to protect her. I want to fight for her. I want to give her the security she deserves. Only the old man she keeps house for supports her, cares about her. And yet she's selfless.'

'Oh my,' Adele breathed, sounding dismayed. 'You're really smitten. How has this woman got her claws into you?'

Guy looked at her in a way he had never needed to; she was usually so encouraging of his pursuits. 'She's not like that at all, Mother. She did nothing to pursue me, but I have fallen for her anyway. You have wealth, respect, status . . . why you'd give a flying fig about what the gossipy social climbers might say about me or the woman I love, I don't know. Aren't artists meant to be liberal in their approach to life?'

'To my life, yes. But to yours? You have very big footsteps to follow.'

'Can you let me worry about that? Otherwise I'll give up before I begin.'

'Don't be ridiculous!'

Guy sighed. He couldn't remember the last time a conversation between the two of them had become this heated. 'You're being ridiculous if you think that I can turn away from this drive to be with Jane. Mother, if I can't be with her, I think I'll spend my life as a bachelor or a monk – now, wouldn't that be a shame for your plans of succession?' He was needling her now, he knew, but he couldn't help it.

She ignored him. 'But, Guy, think this through. This boy of hers. How does he fit in to your plans?'

'I have a plan. You need to trust me as you have before. I need you to give her a chance. She's a spinster from a good family, and had that family not put such outrageous demands on her, I suspect you'd be more than willing to see us married and starting a family.'

'I would be,' she admitted. 'I'd be deliriously happy.'

'Then break out the champagne, Mother, because I intend to marry Jane Saville. The only blight on her name is your prejudice and others who share it. For my sake, get past it, because it's all in here,' he said, tapping his temple. 'Jane is single, eligible and simply taking care of someone else's child because that child was unwanted. And, frankly, she owns my heart even if she doesn't know that yet. I think you'll like Jane enormously when you meet her. And you'll adore Harry Saville – he's a charmer.'

His mother was searching his face, her eyes glistening with tears. He wasn't sure whether the emotion was disappointment, regret or simple sadness, but it made no difference to his own feelings. He was relieved when she lifted a hand to stroke his cheek.

'It's amazing that you could have had any dazzling woman in the world, and you choose the broken one.' She sighed softly.

'The broken one will leave all the others you wish for me in her wake through her composure, intelligence, creativity and wit. I promise you, she is dazzling but she's just never been allowed to shine.'

Adele kissed her son's cheek, then nodded. 'Then bring her to me. Let me meet this woman who holds my son's heart ransom.'

26

Guy's smile died on his lips when William opened the door, leaning heavily on a walking stick. A concerned-looking nurse stood behind him. William looked as though he'd aged years since they'd last seen each other.

'You're back,' the older man said without much expression.

'William, what's happened?' Guy frowned, taken aback. He didn't move across the threshold even though William had turned and limped slowly away, leaving the door open. 'Is he all right?' he asked the nurse.

'Dying, not deaf or demented,' William said sharply. He turned back to face Guy and gave a slow blink. Whether it was a gesture of disappointment or even disgust, Guy couldn't tell. 'I don't have long, it seems, so you'd better hurry up and say what you've come here to say.'

'May I join you?'

'Please yourself,' William said. This time he kept walking.

Disconcerted, Guy dutifully followed him into the house. There were no fresh flowers in the hallway, which Guy had appreciated on his previous visits. He sighed, wondering whether to call out for Jane, but he followed William into his study.

'William . . . er, sir, what has gone wrong?'

'Yes, Mr Attwood, something is very wrong. Very wrong indeed.'

'How can I help?'

'You can't. Besides, you're too late,' the older man said, sounding glum. He leaned his thin elbows on his desk and allowed his head to droop into his palms momentarily. 'And I don't mean for me. I am not long for this earth. I'm talking about Jane and Harry. You're too late.'

Guy frowned. 'Too late for what?'

'To help them.'

Guy swallowed, shocked, as this was not what he'd expected to hear. 'What are you talking about? Where are they?'

'Not here, I can tell you that much,' William growled with an accusatory stare. He tossed an envelope across the desk and Guy recognised it immediately. 'This arrived too late as well.'

Guy picked up his letter to Jane. 'Why wasn't it opened?'

'It's surely private?' William glared.

'Yes, but—'

'She's gone, Attwood. Fled. Quite rightly too. That girl's had so much cruelty in her life, and you're just another of the thankless people who use her and abuse her.'

Guy's mouth opened but nothing came out. The old man seemed to enjoy the awkward pause, still scowling in Guy's direction.

Guy found his wits. 'All right, William, I feel we're speaking in riddles. Can you tell me what it is that I have apparently done wrong and why Jane is not here? Do you mean she's out or no longer in Wiltshire?'

'I mean both!' William snapped. 'She's gone and I'm happy

about it.' He pointed a finger. 'I warned you about the ill wind blowing in with her wretch of a sister. If you were half the man we thought you might be, you'd have been here to lend some support. Where were you on the Sunday you promised to watch that boy sing his heart out for you?'

Now Guy was shocked into a stunned silence. William's accusatory words echoed around him. The edges of his vision blurred, as though his lenses had been smeared with grease, so all he could see was William's stormy glare. The older man seemed to be speaking from far away. And yet Guy could smell the base note of turpentine in the furniture wax from the man's desk and chairs, as though his other senses had switched to keen alert. Randomly, he imagined Jane dusting in here. Did she dust? For some reason he didn't think so. He was convinced the old man kept her here for company rather than from a true need for housekeeping, so perhaps someone else had been in to clean. No doubt the fellow adored Harry. He seemingly had no family, so perhaps Jane and Harry had filled that emptiness and now he was angry . . . That would explain why he was blaming Guy.

Guy's consciousness returned loudly, as though he were an old wireless tuning back in. He could hear laughter outside, he could hear birdsong, he could certainly hear William, who was now waggling a crooked finger in Guy's direction and speaking with a tone of disgust.

'Lothario!'

Guy blinked. 'What?'

'You heard me.'

'How dare you, sir!'

'How dare I?' William's voice grew louder. 'How dare I accuse you of entering her life under dubious circumstances, you mean? Or how dare I accuse you of currying favour with her son as a means of getting to her painting? How dare I accuse you of romancing Jane in the garden so you could get time with your precious apple tree? Is that what you mean? Or how dare I look at you as a heartless cad who won her affection, got what he needed and then disappeared right at her most vulnerable moment?'

'I don't know what to say,' Guy said, genuinely lost for words and stinging from the rebuke. He could admit much of it was true.

'How about goodbye? We've had enough of you.'

'William . . .'

'Angus to you, Attwood.'

Guy drew in a low breath to calm himself. 'Sir,' he tried again. 'May I explain?'

'Why? Does it help Jane or Harry?'

Guy didn't wait for permission, telling the older man what had occurred. 'My father died on the day Jane's sister arrived. There was a telegram waiting for me when I returned to the hotel after I left here. I was duty- and honour-bound to get home as fast as possible. I was trying to be with him before he took his last breath; I had something really important I needed to say to him. I also needed to be with my mother, who was losing her best friend, her most beloved person.' Guy's voice was cracking and then it gave way with his next words. 'I had to get to my father; I needed to tell him that I loved him and I was sorry. But I was too late.'

He felt for a nearby chair and sat, half-angry, half-stunned.

The silence that followed his admission was heavy. And then he felt William's hand squeezing his shoulder. 'I'm sorry you didn't get that opportunity.'

Guy cleared his throat. 'Yes. Too much left unsaid.'

'Often the way. Forgive my ranting.'

Guy shook his head. 'I don't know what to say other than that I have not romanced Jane under any pretence.' He looked up at the older man. 'William, I love Jane with all my heart.'

William nodded. 'But, Guy, you've been gone so long and with no word.'

'I wrote. I had it delivered . . .'

William tapped the envelope on the desk. 'I know. Here it is, but she'd left by then. She never saw this.'

'No, I sent a letter on the day I left. It was brief, but it explained everything.'

'What letter? She received no word from you. She has lived with only silence, waiting daily for something that might reassure her, I could tell.'

'No, no, that's not right. The innkeeper was having it delivered before I even caught the train.'

William shrugged. 'Nothing arrived.'

Guy looked back at him in horrified disbelief. 'But that means she has no idea why I've been gone so long.'

His companion nodded. 'That's what I'm saying. She's deeply hurt. She also had a visit from your fiancée.'

It was explosion after explosion. 'I beg your pardon?' It had to be Eleanor, Guy realised, but how had she even known to come here? And calling herself his fiancée?

'I don't have the whole story, but some very pretty woman paid a visit. She didn't come inside or I'd have met her, nor did she stay long. They talked in the garden. Jane told me it was your fiancée asking her to step aside.'

Guy's shock was complete. That explained Eleanor's silence; she had been busy shoring up her position. 'William, sir,' he began, 'I have no fiancée. I have never had one; Jane knows this. I told her everything about this woman, and how we're just friends, but our mothers—'

'With all due respect, Guy, I don't have time for this. Anyway, Jane made it clear to your friend, I gather, that she could have you. And Jane left soon after.'

Guy tasted a sourness in his throat. How had things got so out of control? 'Tell me everything, please.'

William sighed. 'Not on an empty stomach. Come on. The Ox Row Inn calls. It's probably the last meal outdoors I'll eat. I may even die at my plate, but it will be worth it,' he admitted, with a grim smile.

Not long after, Guy found himself sitting in a pub that dated back to the sixteenth century. The Ox Row was only a brief walk away, but William had needed a cab and it had taken all his strength to get into it.

'Takes the name from a place where the out-of-town butchers would come to slaughter their cattle for the main Salisbury market. It was called the meat "shambles". But there's Oatmeal Row and Corn Row, too.'

'Yes, I read about this – it once had a huge, thriving medieval market selling just about everything.'

'Still does. Tuesdays and Saturdays. Goes back to the twelfth century. We'll have the roast chicken, shall we?'

Guy shrugged. He wasn't hungry, but he didn't want to disrupt the mood now that William was calm and prepared to talk. He waited while William ordered for both of them. 'And a couple of pints of Arkell's,' he said, 'Thanks, Verna.' He returned his attention to Guy. 'I hope you like a pale ale?'

Guy couldn't wait any longer. 'William, tell me about you. You said this might be your last meal outside. What's happened?'

The older man shrugged. 'I thought I'd be gone by now, to tell the truth. But I've had a late rally. Maybe just enough to enjoy my roast and ale within it. I've been sick for a long time. I wish the doctor would let me go, but he keeps attending to me and I wake up to face another day.' He gave a genial grin. 'It's just teasing me.

I don't have an appetite. I'm eating simply to thumb my nose at death, which comes for me.'

Guy didn't know how to respond, so he moved the conversation on. 'Please, tell me everything. Where's Harry?'

William's features immediately drooped back into their former maudlin appearance. 'The boy's gone. Into the clutches of that woman.'

'Jane's sister? Without a fight?'

William nodded. 'Charlotte could prove he was hers by birth. And if you know just a fraction of Jane, you'll know she would not get involved in any fight that might be to the detriment of the boy. She considers him her own son and so, for Harry's sake, she felt she needed to let it happen. I can assure you I urged her to fight. I offered to employ London's best law firm, but she wouldn't hear a word of it. Fought me instead! "William, that will just put Harry in the middle of bitterness and anger. And it won't change the fact that the boy I consider my son – and love as my son – is *not* my son." It broke my heart, I readily admit, to see that child carted away by a stranger.'

Guy couldn't believe what he was hearing. 'How was he?'

'Oh, all smiles and joy because he thought he was going off with his aunt for a holiday in London. He's like any other excited youngster who's offered the sights of the city. That was Jane's idea – to soften the blow by pretending it's just for now, and they'll explain later once he gets used to that woman.'

Their luncheons arrived, along with the fragrance of roasted chicken, which momentarily lifted Guy's spirits.

'When did Jane leave?' Guy asked. He took a bite of the food; he hadn't thought he was hungry, but his stomach responded immediately. 'Please eat.' He nodded towards William's plate.

William picked up his knife and fork and obediently began pushing food around his plate, though Guy noted he wasn't really eating.

'She left soon after Harry was taken away, and within hours of your fiancée's visit.' At Guy's glare, William corrected himself. 'The woman who thinks she's your fiancée. Jane kept up the pretence of a holiday to Harry – don't ask me how – and then all that stoicism collapsed the moment we waved them goodbye at the railway station. We sat on the platform for more than an hour while her tears subsided. I have to admit I felt stunned that the little fellow I'd known since he was months old, like a little grandson to me, had been taken away – forcibly removed from all the love and family he'd ever known.'

'This is reprehensible,' Guy said. 'Surely she can't actually believe—'

'Charlotte Saville has the law on her side,' William said, shaking his head, 'and she also has a burning desire to squeeze every last bit of money and property she can from her husband's estate – and by that I mean his mother's wealth. It turns out she owned everything. So Charlotte is effectively beggared, save the clothes on her back and the jewellery she might pawn. Her only hope is proving to that American woman that her useless son fathered an heir – Harry.'

'I came here to ask Jane to marry me and allow me to take Harry on as my own.'

'Too little, too late, Attwood. Why didn't you ask her before you deserted her and the boy?'

Guy glared at William again. 'I hardly had the chance. I've explained what was going on.'

William appeared unmoved. 'I'm near to death. I don't have to care about anyone's fragile feelings any longer. I won't apologise – I'm furious with the world, and that includes you.'

Guy actually spluttered a laugh into his pale ale and, surprisingly, William joined in. 'I don't know why I'm laughing,' Guy admitted.

'Because otherwise we will cry,' the older man said gently, his humour dissipating as fast as it had arrived. 'That girl is all alone in the world.' He shrugged. 'She didn't want to leave. I sent her away.'

'Are you mad? Is *she* mad?'

William laughed bitterly. 'Yes. We've both been overtaken by a madness of grief. Jane might be quiet, but her imagination lives in a world of light and colour. Nothing I said could ease her despair. I decided the only way forward was to push her out of the door and force her to confront her loss.'

'By making it worse?' Guy asked, aghast.

'It's a matter of perspective. She would have set all her pain aside to fuss around me until I died. And look at me, still here. I would still be holding her back.'

'From what?'

'From what? Heavens you're dim, Guy.'

'So I'm told,' he replied.

'From fighting back and retrieving Harry from that awful woman's grasp.'

'How?'

William shrugged unhelpfully. 'I don't know. But that's what Jane is now going to find out because she has the time and she has the space up here.' He tapped his temple. 'Not bothering about me.'

'So she knows . . . I mean, about you?'

'Of course. I had to be blunt to force her hand, but Jane knows my time is up. She's watched me deteriorate over the years. We hid my bad days and my even worse nights from the boy, but she was more than aware of my frailty.' William dug in his pocket and retrieved a letter. 'Here, read this.'

Guy withdrew a single sheet from the envelope.

My dearest William,

I have known only kindness and generosity since the day we met in the Close. You have been a father to me at a time when I desperately needed family, and you have been that important grandfatherly figure in Harry's life, teaching him so much and helping me to raise him in a way that makes us both proud of the boy he is and the man he will be.

But now Harry is gone. I never asked for him, but he became mine and I have viewed him as such since the day of his birth. To have him taken away so ruthlessly has left me an empty vessel. There have been two desperately unhappy moments in my life. The first was when my father died suddenly and my life changed irrevocably as a result. He was my everything. The second was the day I was told by my mother of her plan to make me Charlotte's scapegoat, and I spent the next months in private mourning and disbelief that my life could sour so swiftly. Of course, I didn't know the baby developing in Charlotte's belly would become my everything.

Even though I dreaded it for all of his life, nothing could prepare me for losing Harry, made worse by the fact that I am losing you too. I have enjoyed the very best years of my life with you and him as a strange but wonderful little family. Our home has been full of love, laughter and constant blessing. You taught me to enjoy life again, you encouraged me to paint again, you took care of us. For this I give you all my love and gratitude, William.

I thought, just for a blissful moment, that I'd found the other half of my heart in Guy Attwood. I didn't know romantic love could strike so hard, so fast, so alarmingly intensely, but Cupid's arrow found me and I toppled helplessly into the arms of the person he chose. I thought for those shining couple of days that life had taken a new and ridiculously happy turn.

But it was a lie . . . an aberration. Guy left me as suddenly as he'd come. He left no word, only my regret that I'd trusted him and my pain for loving him. It seems I allowed my infatuation to misguide me. It was the apple and not me that he fell for. And now that he has found his precious apple tree, I am no longer important or surely I would have heard why he left and hasn't returned, or even written. Meeting the woman who intended to marry him only hardened me further.

And then there is darling Harry, ripped away against all our wishes. He is an innocent in this, and I dare not face him with the truth. How can I explain that the mother he knows has been lying to him all of his life? How do I explain that his true mother never wanted him? And why she does want him now? To tell him the truth of her need for money is just heartless.

All of this is to say that you're right and that it is time for me to leave for various reasons. I need to be entirely alone with my pain, to work out that I'm strong enough to face it or if there is a simpler way to accept it. That we had nearly eight years of family joy together will travel with me and comfort me; please know this.

I want to be at your side but I know you prefer otherwise and I respect those wishes. Is it cowardly to admit that I am relieved I shall not be forced to watch you die? By the same token, you should not bear witness to my slow death either, which is what is happening to me, I'm sure.

Deepest love always. May your spirit travel onwards, William, and yet always be able to find us and smile upon us even if Harry and I cannot be together. Watch over him.

Jane

Guy folded the letter back into its envelope. 'And she just left?'

'Indeed. We knew we wouldn't see each other again. The house is hers when she's ready. But I need her to take control or that wretch of a sister will.' He shook his head.

'Where did she go?'

'I have no idea.'

Guy frowned. 'I want to know where that note ended up rather than in Jane's hands. She would be here now if she'd received it, I'm sure of it.'

'She could only read into that silence precisely what she did. I do not blame Jane for feeling betrayed, just as I do not blame myself for thinking you are an opportunist.' William spoke slowly and deliberately in between shallow breaths to ensure he made his point.

Guy stood, throwing the letter onto the table. 'I'm going to find her.'

'To do what?'

'To help!'

'How can you?'

'I have resources, contacts . . . If it takes everything I have, I will find her, and I will help her get Harry back.'

'That sister is not giving up the boy.'

'We'll see about that. Do you know of any favourite place Jane has around here?'

William considered the question, then shook his head. 'She likes Salisbury Plain, but I told her to get away from the region. Honestly, I can't imagine where she might head.'

'To London to see her mother?'

'Definitely not.'

'Maybe to catch a glimpse of Harry?'

William sighed. 'No, she is going somewhere for a clear head. And she wouldn't risk upsetting these early days that he believes is a holiday.' He dissolved into a fit of coughing, and pushed his luncheon away. 'Gah, I can't even swallow properly any more.'

Guy nodded. 'Let me settle the account and I'll help you get a cab back to the house.'

'No, it was my idea. And I can walk. What's your plan?'

'Find her and marry her, if she'll have me. I shall make us a family.'

William gave a firm nod. 'That's what I needed to hear. I liked you, Guy, but you dismayed me with your disappearing act.' He held up a hand before Guy could jump in. 'I've heard you out, and it's not me you need to convince – it's Jane.'

Guy slowly walked William home, feeling the man at his side weakening with each painful step. By the time they entered the house, he made no fuss when Guy picked him up like a child and carried him upstairs to his room. After getting the old man into a nightshirt and safely under the covers, Guy assured him that he would be calling the doctor.

'The nurse will be in shortly,' William replied.

'I don't care; I shall have the doctor call in,' Guy said, taking his hand; it felt like holding a bird of prey's claw. He had done so once, and knew the feel. It was a fine peregrine falcon, like the ones that nested on the spire of Salisbury Cathedral.

'I only have a few words left, Guy, and I don't want to spend them on fury or accusation. Accept my apology. I am an angry old man feeling hopeless, and I had no business taking it out on you. The fact that you're here means you will try to find her.' He shook their linked hands for emphasis. 'Find her, Guy. Marry her! You have my blessing. Make that boy yours. For some reason he already idolises you – can't see why myself,' he said and actually chuckled, making Guy's eyes sting with tears.

Guy was not prone to weeping, but he could feel a surge of guilt that he hadn't been there to hold his father's hand as he had reached his final breaths, but he was doing so for a near enough stranger. Curiously, it felt comforting. He was glad he could be here now for William.

———————

At the Red Lion, only just keeping his frustration under control, Guy learned that the note he'd written to Jane, explaining why he had to leave, had been taken immediately by one of the maids when he'd left two and a half weeks ago.

A young woman called Tilly was summoned to stand before him and the owner of the hotel. She arrived wide-eyed, and Guy could see she was trembling.

'Tilly, this is Mr Attwood.'

She curtsied. 'Good afternoon, sir.'

'Tilly, do you remember the letter you were supposed to deliver to number eighteen of the Close a few weeks ago?'

'I do, sir,' Tilly said, nodding at her manager, her voice sounding stretched thin with worry. 'I took it immediately.'

'Are you sure?' Guy pressed.

'Yes, sir. It was the same day that my Tom asked me to marry him,' she said, anxiously twirling a small ring on her wedding finger. 'I was running late to meet Tom, and so I had to hurry around to the house.'

'How do you know it was the right house?' Guy asked.

'I checked with someone who lived there. It was a boy, actually. He was coming home from the cathedral school – I knew by his uniform – and I asked him if the lady whose name was on the envelope lived there. I'm sorry, I'm so nervous I can't remember the name.'

'Jane Saville,' Guy said.

'Ah, yes, that's it.'

'Don't be nervous, Tilly,' her boss said kindly. 'This is important.'

She nodded, still looking terrified. 'I asked the boy if Jane Saville lived at the address, and he said she did and that he was her son.'

Guy closed his eyes momentarily, already guessing what had happened next. 'He took the note, did he?'

She nodded again warily. 'Yes, sir.'

Guy didn't want to ask whether Harry had offered or she had asked him to take it, because if it was the latter he thought he might regret the anger that would follow. 'Thank you,' he said to Tilly, only just managing to feign gratitude.

Tilly looked between the two men before another quick curtsy and then she fled.

The man turned to Guy. 'Mr Attwood, I'm so sorry, it seems—'

'Yes, I think we can both imagine what occurred. The child's mother is none the wiser as to the letter's contents.'

'What would you like me to do, sir?'

'There's nothing to be done,' Guy said and sighed, realising the truth of that statement. 'Tilly did as she was instructed, although maybe handing it to an adult would have been a wiser move. Please don't think on it further.'

He left, allowing his fury to slowly dissipate as he stomped his way through Fisherton to the railway station. Anger was useless now; only action would solve his crisis.

27

Harry sat on the stairs and watched his aunt's contorted face wrinkle even deeper in consternation.

'What do you mean, Melba? I have him here.' There was a pause as she listened. 'I am not lying!' Another pause. 'How dare you. I was faithful to your faithless son for seven long years . . . No, you listen to me, Melba. You have a grandson. His name is Henry and—'

Aunt Charlotte looked like she was fuming; the woman on the other end had obviously interjected.

'But he refused to let me tell you I was pregnant, that's why!'

Harry blinked. She had promised him so much, but her affections had begun to feel false, mostly lavished upon him when others, such as the housekeeper or maid, were around. He didn't really like this place, but she'd promised to take him to see the wax museum and the zoo.

'Melba,' Charlotte said, her tone sharp and cold. 'You said if there was an heir, then you would grant me property and an income. Your heir is sitting right here.' She listened. 'Why does it make any difference whether he was born before or after our marriage?

280

Eddie is Harry's father. I can prove this; I have the midwife who delivered him from my body and—'

Harry considered what he was hearing. It was hard to make sense of it, but William had taught him to never jump to one conclusion. *Think about a problem from various angles. The right answer will show itself.*

Harry would think on this when he was alone.

'Yes, maybe it was straight into the arms of my sister, Melba, but Eddie insisted I could not have a child out of wedlock, even if it was his. Harry is your grandson. Do the right thing.' There was a final pause. 'You can't do this to me. What do you mean you've already found a buyer? This is my house!'

Harry watched his aunt stare at the receiver and then hold it to her ear again. 'Melba? Melba!' She crashed the earpiece back onto its cradle. 'Damn that woman!' She spun around, her face filled with fury. 'And damn you, Eddie. I hope you're in hell, where you deserve to be.'

Harry called out to her. 'Aunt Charlotte?'

She looked up and saw him on the stairs. 'Oh, don't bother me now, Harry,' she said, her tone dismissive. 'And don't creep about and listen in on other people's conversations.'

'I didn't mean to.'

'Well, you're sitting there, aren't you? Did you not mean to sit down and eavesdrop? Wicked boy!'

He was shocked. 'I . . . I promise I just came downstairs to ask a question and then I sat down because it looked like you were busy. I was wondering about our visit to Madame Tussauds,' he tried.

'You're like your father, do you know that? Take, take and then take some more. Well, he's dead and you're no use to me any more, it seems.'

'Aunt Charlotte, I don't know what you mean. I don't even know who you've been talking to or why.'

She approached him; her body language felt threatening. He shuffled back up a step away from her. 'I was talking to your American grandmother, as a matter of fact, who is a lying dog-bitch of the highest order.'

Harry gasped at her hostility. He'd never heard someone speak so rudely.

'She promised me money and a roof over my head if she had a grandson or granddaughter. I told her about you, Harry. You might as well learn it now, if you haven't already worked it out: I am your mother. The woman you call Mummy'—she said the final word with a grimace—'is in fact your aunt. You are my pointless, inconvenient son who might, a few weeks ago, have actually been of some use. Now, I'm afraid, you're as redundant as the day you were born.'

Harry backed up another step, standing now.

'Do you know what redundant means, Harry?'

He shook his head, holding his breath at the naked aggression.

'It means unnecessary, unrequired, unwanted. You are all those things to me, Harry, as of this moment.' Her eyes sparkled with rage.

He didn't know what she was talking about. Why was she so angry with him? 'Then let me go home.'

'Home?' She laughed but he could tell it wasn't genuine. 'To your aunt?'

'To my mother,' he said weakly.

'*I* made you, not her.'

'But I love her. I don't love you. Please, can't I—'

'No one loves me, Harry, you're simply joining the queue.'

'I think my mother might love you if you're her sister.'

Charlotte gave a tortured groan of a laugh. 'And that's the truth. She probably does, the poor wretch.'

Harry began to put it together in his mind. 'So my father was Edmund Cavendish, who you've told me about?'

She sneered. 'It won't help you. He was a bastard, just like you. Except he was a different sort of bastard. He was the mean, selfish, despicable kind. Whereas you . . .' She smiled with sugary sweetness that had not a mote of sincerity in it. 'You're just a bastard in the biblical sense. You were conceived out of wedlock, Harry. That means your horrible father took me for his pleasures and you were the result, but neither he nor I wanted anything to do with you. You offended him for simply existing, and you offended me because I never wanted you. You would have ruined everything then, and now you're still ruining everything!'

Harry felt tears coming and squeezed his eyes shut hard against them. He'd promised himself when he won the choir scholarship that he would never cry again; he was a big boy now, so William had counselled.

But he couldn't hear William's reassuring words right now or imagine his mother's gentle, encouraging touch. All he could see was the woman in front of him who seemed to be blaming him for everything that had gone wrong in her life. And she was claiming to be his mother and telling him his father was a terrible man and that he was just like him. How could that be true?

Harry fled upstairs to the sound of her berating mockery.

'That's it, turn your back on me and run like your father. You're as treacherous as he was!'

———

Harry hid under his bed, which was conveniently near a wall, and he could back himself into the shadows like a dog in a cave, knowing it was safe from behind.

Except he wasn't safe. Suddenly the world felt dangerous and frightening. He had never known the world to be like this. He'd known it to be challenging; he'd known bullies at school and severe schoolmasters who threatened to cane backsides and knuckles for small misdemeanours, and he'd known stares of disapproval from adults when he was with his mother.

But he'd never been uncertain of himself or his place in the world, because he'd always had her.

Her smiles, her tender voice, her hugs, her stories about colour and art, which he loved even though sometimes he teased her. She used to make up stories about flowers and trees, he remembered, giving them names and building grand tales of the world of plants they lived within. He could make her laugh and he knew she thought he was the most important thing in the world.

Where was she? Why would she let him come here? What had she been thinking when she had agreed to send him away with his scary aunt? Surely his mother had known what she was like, but then she had seemed so lovely and kind, and she'd sounded so fond of him almost immediately. He had no family besides his mother, and William, in a way, so it had been thrilling to learn of an aunt.

Or was Charlotte actually his mother?

That was a confusing and frightening idea. He'd never met her before, at least not that he could recall, and he had a good memory. How could it be true? And why would his real mother allow her to say that?

Unless Charlotte wasn't lying.

She seemed to know his father.

Edmund Cavendish. Eddie, she called him. And she didn't seem to like him. She didn't seem to like anyone . . . not her husband, not her sister, not him, and definitely not the person she had been speaking to on the telephone – Melba someone. He wished he knew how to use that contraption, but who would he speak with? William! Maybe the headmaster at the school?

School. He actually missed it right now and would have preferred to be back there in his daily routine, which he enjoyed. He missed the choir and his singing practice. He missed home. His room here was nice enough, but it wasn't the same, he thought, still hiding beneath his bed.

Charlotte hadn't bothered to follow him upstairs. She really didn't seem to care about him, even though she had made out that she was so pleased to bring him into her life. It had been fine for a while, but then he noticed she kept making telephone calls and getting angrier with the operator by the day. It seemed that the person on the other end was not answering. Charlotte had begun to take out her frustration on him.

Finally, this morning, the telephone had rung loudly, its jangling chime harsh on the marble hall table. He was sorely tempted to pick up the heavy receiver and listen, maybe even whisper a hello to hear a voice from far away talking back. What magic it was. But Charlotte had snatched the receiver and yelled at the person she called the telephone operator to put through the call immediately. And then it had clearly all gone wrong for her.

What was he to do about this? He couldn't fix her problem. He couldn't make Aunt Charlotte happy again. And he couldn't stay here for much longer. It felt scary and lonely now. She was no longer interested in him as anything other than someone to yell at and complain to. It was best he left, but how would he do that?

Walk out of the back door, go through the back garden gate and just leave, said a voice from within himself. *She won't even know you've gone. Go on, move!*

Propelled by an overwhelming fuel of fear and homesickness, Harry crawled out from under the bed and listened. He could hear nothing in the house – not even a creak. He stood, tiptoeing over to his bedroom door. He opened it a crack and listened again. Nothing.

With trepidation, but also new motivation, he stepped out onto the landing. A floorboard did creak then and he winced, waiting. There was no sound. It was the housekeeper's day off and the maid would likely be busy downstairs. His aunt was probably fuming in one of the reception rooms. Harry sighed and continued to wait for any sign of movement.

There was none. Maybe she was resting – perhaps even asleep, having raged so much.

He noted that the day was bright outside as he cast his glance towards the landing window, and it was then that his eyes fell on a small door. He'd been warned by his aunt not to go out there when he'd first arrived and he'd promised he wouldn't. In his life there had always been a good reason for rules, so he hadn't thought to disobey Charlotte . . . until now.

'That door, Harry, leads out onto a small porch on the roof and to the fire escape, which winds down to the ground floor. The door is always locked and the only time it can be used is if a fire should occur and someone up here needs to escape.' She'd pointed. 'You see, dear Harry, there's the key. Now, do I need to remove it? Because I know little boys are curious.' She had chortled.

'No, Aunt Charlotte. I promise I won't go out there.'

It was clearly his best route outside, though. Otherwise he'd have to try to tiptoe down flights of stairs and possibly encounter the maid or, worse, his aunt. And even if no one happened upon him in that fraught moment of stealing across the vast hallway at the bottom of the stairs to the grand front door, having to get that door open without causing any noise or disruption felt like a mountain to scale. Instead, he could just quietly sneak out through the fire escape. He wasn't scared of heights. He'd already climbed to the spire of Salisbury Cathedral and looked out over Wiltshire. He'd even seen the peregrines that traditionally nested around the top of the cathedral.

He'd have to travel light. In fact, he'd have to leave most of his stuff behind if he was going out the fire escape. Decision made, Harry moved back into his room and looked around it. The new toys

Aunt Charlotte had bought him were overwhelming: toy soldiers, an expensive German teddy bear, magnificent glass marbles – far more impressive than the ordinary marbles he had at home. He'd got the sense that she was giving him too much – it didn't feel right, like maybe she had some sort of expectation of him in return. He just didn't know what. He had toys at home, but most were practical sports equipment or birthday and Christmas presents, usually items to add to his train collection.

Charlotte had expected him to play with his toys most days; he was used to playing alone, but he'd thought this holiday was for him to spend time with his aunt. They didn't eat together either, as he and his mother and William did most evenings. There was always laughter around their little table, but there was no laughter in this house. He wouldn't miss it, he decided.

So if he was leaving, what did he need? He looked around his bedroom. He had been making an effort to keep it extra neat so his aunt would think well of him. He wouldn't take clothes, because his satchel couldn't hold very much and his small suitcase would be too cumbersome. He put a couple of toy soldiers into his pocket, along with the coins his mother had tied into his handkerchief: six farthings, a threepence and two sixpences, along with a new florin that William had pressed into his hand. He hadn't had a chance to spend it yet; the few times Charlotte had taken him out, she'd insisted on 'treating' him.

Altogether he knew he was shy of four shillings. Even so, it was more than enough to get home, he was sure; it felt like a fortune. He decided to tie most of the coins back into his handkerchief so they wouldn't rattle around in his pocket and tempt a would-be pickpocket. He felt alone and unsafe enough already without becoming a target for a thief.

He left a couple of farthings and pennies loose in his pocket. And that was it – he needed nothing else but to find his way home somehow. It was tempting to tiptoe into the kitchen for some food to eat so he left on a really full belly, perhaps with a couple of biscuits in his pocket, but he did not want to risk it.

Harry wanted to be gone.

He pulled on his coat, because it was easier to wear than carry, and tiptoed to the door that he'd promised he would not open. He winced as the key squealed slightly in the lock, and when he twisted the handle he realised the door was stuck. It clearly hadn't been opened in a long time. He would have to risk the noise of pulling it open.

He looked down over the banister to the floors below and saw no movement. He took a deep breath, reached for the handle, twisted and, with all of his strength, yanked the door. It opened, and the soft voile curtains on the small window of the landing· immediately flapped, and his bedroom door slammed open with the air rushing in.

He gasped. Waited. Nothing.

Move!

He closed the door behind him, without looking back or down, then clambered onto the iron steps. Aware that if he hurried they might shudder and make a noise, he forced himself to step carefully down the twisting column. He hoped with all of his heart that no one noticed his movement through a window, but he couldn't let that break his rhythm. He kept going, not thinking, not counting, just descending, knowing that the ground would eventually find him if he didn't stop.

Finally he hit the last step and almost leapt with terrified joy onto the pavers, leaning back against the brick of the house to catch his breath. He could see the back gate, whose lock was mercifully at a height he could reach. With a cursory look around to check there was no one immediately visible, he made a dash for it.

Once through, he realised he couldn't close it from the outside. While he felt bad for leaving the back garden exposed, he shook it off; this was the only chance he was going to get. Without looking over his shoulder, he began running down a small alley that ran behind the houses of his aunt's posh street, his hurrying footsteps echoing on the cobblestones.

28

South England

When Jane left William, feeling distraught but determined, she didn't know where she would go but she'd packed so lightly it didn't matter. She had money enough, and that would do.

Never before in her life had she known such freedom. Never before in her life had she felt so imprisoned by her emotions. Never before in her life had she felt so out of control – not even when her mother had cornered her, using family duty as the post to chain Jane to and guilt as her whip, forcing her to accept a ruined reputation and a child who was not hers.

And yet, what wouldn't she give to return to that life of just a few weeks ago?

Before Charlotte had returned.

Before William had taken his final turn towards death.

Before she'd met Guy Attwood.

All of them had conspired, wittingly or otherwise, to ensure that while happiness might be glimpsed on the horizon, it would always be taken away from her.

Victim, victim, victim! The word played over and over in her mind for the whole journey to who knew where.

She travelled first to Berkshire with no plan, arriving at Reading and then catching a train to Windsor. Here, as she wandered with no true aim, she revisited some of the places she'd been with her father. She recalled with tremendous fondness the times, during her childhood, that she'd travelled with him on his business visits. It had been a treat for her, but as an adult she could now see it was her father's way of protecting her from her mother's critical tongue and her sister's jeering. She and her father got on very well and made good company for each other, so he never seemed to mind taking her along if it was appropriate. Sometimes he'd make her wait in the hotel, reading, and at other times, if it did not offend anyone, he would permit her to sit quietly while he carried out his meetings. She was like a mouse, barely making a sound, other than the turning of the page of her book. Afterwards he would smile and take her somewhere historic or interesting before they returned home. These trips had been few and far between, but they lived vividly in her mind as days of great joy, to be alone with the person she loved most in the world.

She wasn't surprised to find herself looking up at Windsor Castle. Her father had brought her here when she was just nine.

'William the Conqueror built this, Jane,' he had explained. 'Over eight hundred years ago.'

'Was it his palace?'

'Well, it was his fortress to guard the western approach into London. He also enjoyed a good hunt, and all the forest around here gave him everything he wanted when outside of the capital.'

Jane could remember their conversation word for word. Lost in the past, she barely noticed the people pushing by her, casting vexed glances over their shoulder or signalling that she should step to the side or move on. She shook her head. Getting lost in her thoughts helped about as much as getting lost physically. But no one knew where she was, and she intended to keep it that way for a while until she felt strong enough to face her new reality of being entirely alone in the world, with no one to love and no one to love her back.

How tragic she sounded. She didn't enjoy feeling this cowed; it didn't suit her. Her mother and sister had always accused her of being contrary, prickly, argumentative and many other adjectives that described her tendency to object to their wishes – usually things that required Jane to bend or accede to something she found unreasonable. She'd had to learn to stand up for herself, because her father was gone and he had been all she'd had against them.

Jane sighed. This was getting her nowhere. She should move on. She returned to the train station and bought a ticket to Southampton. This was another destination she had travelled to with her father, and it felt far enough away that she could be alone with her thoughts.

During the journey she reached a decision that felt right in her mind. If this was to be a time of reflection, visiting places that evoked happy memories of her childhood, then there was one place that stood out as her fondest recollection.

Out of politeness, Jane fell into conversation with the woman sitting across from her, who had a restless child of about four and a baby in tow. Jane rummaged about in her bag, pretty sure she had some licorice allsorts; she found a few tied in a handkerchief. 'Here, can I divert your son with some sweeties?' she asked quietly.

The woman's shoulders slumped in relief. 'Thank you,' she breathed. 'Divert him however you wish.'

Jane smiled sympathetically. 'What's your name?' she asked the child.

'Richard,' he answered, suddenly shy.

'Well, Richard, would you like a sweet? I do hope you like licorice?'

His eyes widened in delight as she opened the fabric to reveal the brightly coloured treats.

'Are you sure?' his mother asked.

Jane nodded. 'I always keep a supply for my son.' It felt soothing to talk aloud about Harry.

'Oh, is he at home? In Windsor?'

'No,' Jane said. 'He's gone to his aunt's for a holiday in London. I'm taking the opportunity to visit some places I haven't seen in a long time.'

The woman smiled. 'How lovely. I envy you.'

'Well, Harry's turning eight, and I promise you, life gets a lot easier once they're school age. You'll get more time with the little one.'

'She's a handful, but Dickie is very helpful, really. He's just tired of the long journeying. We got on in London.'

Dickie was busy staring at the sweets. 'You can have them all,' Jane offered, 'but you ask your mother how many you can eat right now.'

'Choose two, Dickie, and I'll hold the rest for you.'

Jane and the woman shared a smile at the complete concentration Dickie was showing as he chose which of the six allsorts he would savour first.

'Where are you off to now?' her companion asked. 'My name is Anne, by the way.'

'Jane. I was getting off at Southampton to stay a day or so, but I've just decided in the last few minutes, actually, that I think I'll go to Dorset. I can make it there today; I noted a good connection when I was looking up train times earlier.'

Anne looked interested. 'I've never been to Dorset.'

'Oh, it's wonderful.' Jane smiled.

'What's there for you?'

Jane sighed as the memory came gladly and happily. 'My father took me there as a child to see a strange flower.'

'Really?'

'I think I'll take the pink one with the black dot in the middle,' Dickie piped up, sounding earnest. 'And the square with three layers of yellow, black and white.'

'Why don't you throw a licorice twist in there too?' Jane winked at him. 'Your mummy won't see,' she whispered as they glanced at Anne, who was busy fixing the baby's bonnet.

Dickie grinned and greedily picked out the three sweets.

'I'll give the rest to your mummy,' Jane said, handing them across to Anne, who gratefully took the small bundle.

'You were saying about the flower?'

Jane nodded, falling back into her memory. 'There's a place called Godlingston Heath in Purbeck, Dorset, where a curious flower grows.'

'Curious how?'

'It's carnivorous.'

Anne gave a soft gasp. 'Truly? I didn't think England possessed carnivorous plants.'

'I won't say for certain, but at the time my father took me, I recall him saying that the only place on the whole of the earth to find this particular species growing wild was on Godlingston Heath. In the boggy parts, he said.'

'And what does it eat?'

'Oh, bugs and small gnats. It's not very big. And it's not very attractive from a distance, but close up, under a magnifier, it is delicate and exquisitely beautiful. It's a deep crimson, but from far away with the surrounding bog it looks rusted and uninteresting. Maybe that's how it catches its prey – by appearing colourless among its surrounds, and therefore harmless.' Jane laughed at the image.

'Tell me, Jane, why the interest in a flower? You seem to know a lot about it.'

'I paint flowers, so I study them often. Watercolours.'

Anne looked delighted. 'An artist?'

Jane nodded, slightly embarrassed. 'I like to do botanical studies most of all.'

'Oh, how wonderful. My grandmother was friends with Marianne North. Do you know of her?'

Jane gasped. 'Of course. She broke the mould, defying social norms and travelling the world for her art. Such a fiercely independent spirit.'

'Indeed. I'm no expert like you, but her vivid paintings bring the world of the plant to life.'

'I've seen her work at Kew Gardens.'

They talked a while about painting, and Jane was sorry to wave goodbye to the small family as they reached Southampton.

When Jane alighted in Dorset and all the steam had dissipated around her, she found herself standing on the platform at Swanage on the Isle of Purbeck. The peninsula was rimmed by the English Channel to its south, and by marshland created by the River Frome and Poole Harbour. She recalled from her father's conversation that the area was known for its famous marble. 'Since the dark ages, its marble has been mined and shipped by sea to its destinations,' he'd told her.

'What sort of destinations?' she recalled asking.

Her father had lifted his shoulders in a half-shrug. 'Ooh, places like Salisbury, which needed its marvellous sombre colour for those soaring columns in its cathedral. Do you remember them in the nave and transept?'

Her twelve-year-old self, full of curiosity and intelligence, remembered that family visit to the cathedral so well. She and her father had walked around with their eyes raised, marvelling at the ceiling, the clear light, the walls of Chilmark stone, which gave the cathedral its soft grey, and the columns of dark Purbeck stone, which, when polished, came up almost black. The Purbeck was also used for some of the flooring, and her father had pointed out fossils trapped for millennia in the stone. Jane's jaw had dropped open and she had taken her father's magnifying glass to study them. Charlotte, meanwhile, had yawned and grumbled that she was bored, and had gone to find her mother, who under the guise of saying a prayer was taking a rest in the pews.

'Purbeck is limestone, if I'm not mistaken,' her father had muttered. Jane had marvelled at its beauty and age.

She wondered if she would see any of the rock this time. Someone coughed nearby and she turned around. 'Miss, are you all right?' the stationmaster asked.

'Er, yes, sorry, lost in my thoughts.'

'It's just this is the last train for—'

She dredged up a smile. 'It's fine, thank you.' She walked away, unsure where she was headed. She would probably need to take a room in Swanage, but she could easily walk into the town.

She passed the ruins of Corfe Castle, which she'd gone to with her father on that same trip. It didn't look any different now, still as mysterious and romantic as back then. On a visit to see Aunt Hortense, the family had taken a daytrip into Dorset, ostensibly to see the white sands of Swanage, but Jane's father, being interested in history, had tried to talk to his daughters about the town and nearby castle. Charlotte had left in a huff of tedium, muttering that she thought they had been going to the beach, but Jane, as always, had listened and learned.

In fact, their very last father and daughter trip had been to Swanage because he'd had business to do in Poole. Jane had asked to accompany him. She had been fifteen then. He'd readily agreed and afterwards decided to take a couple of days with Jane to walk the heath.

'Do you mind, Jane?' he'd asked. 'London can be so stuffy and grimy, I love these opportunities to be out in our lovely countryside.'

'Not at all,' she'd replied, as enamoured as he was by nature. 'There's something I want to try and find.'

'A place?'

He smiled secretively. 'No, a flower . . . a plant, actually. A rather clever one.'

Now he had her completely intrigued. 'What is it?'

'It's called *Drosera*. That's not its full name, of course, but that's the genus. I thought you'd like to see it too.'

'I would. Why is it special?'

'It's carnivorous,' he said, sounding almost gleeful.

She looked at him with amazement. 'In England?'

He nodded. 'Clever little thing, it is. And listen to this, Jane.' She leaned in as though he was going to share a secret. 'I believe Godlingston Heath is the only place in the world right now that this curious little insect-eating plant lives.'

She gasped.

'Apparently. Let's try to see it for ourselves.'

They had walked for a full day on the heath together and had indeed found their secretive plant. It belonged to a genus commonly known as sundews, he explained as they walked, and it was not especially attractive unless one admired the profusion of leaves that grew close and tangled. Its overall colour was ruby, which would attract humans as much as its prey: insects.

'They come in all sorts of shapes and sizes, but this one belongs entirely to Godlingston Heath. Apparently some people take sundew as a tea, because it has some very good medicinal properties, including for breathing difficulties.'

'How clever,' she said, staring at the glistening damp tendrils that extended from the plant. 'And how do they trap their prey?'

'It's sticky, so an unsuspecting little winged creature gets trapped. I've read it can kill its prey in about fifteen minutes, and then takes weeks to digest it.'

She stared at her father. 'Oh. Not a very nice plant, then.'

'Well, lions kill too, and we admire them for their beauty.'

She laughed. 'This isn't a very beautiful creature, Papa.'

'I suspect you may change your mind up close. If we put it under our microscope, I think you'll find it is splendid.'

Was he the only businessman in London who also had a portable microscope in his study? Perhaps. He was right, though. Scrutinising the plant specimens they had brought home showed the *Drosera* to indeed be beautiful in the abstract.

As Jane walked into the main town, she decided she'd been sent here by some guiding hand in the back of her mind, which must have been paying attention to William's advice to get away somewhere that she could think clearly. While it felt a little strange here and she didn't necessarily know her way around – it had changed considerably since her last visit – it still felt achingly familiar. It was prompting memories of laughter and discovery, but most of all it prompted thoughts of a time of great happiness, when she felt secure with her father and loved by him. It was a place of comfort.

She returned to the hotel where her father had brought her. The man behind the reception desk was polite and welcoming. She booked a room for three nights, not knowing how long she needed. Here she could rest and think.

All she knew was that she needed to find a way to beat Charlotte at her own game. The stakes were too high to worry about family or duty. Harry was hers, and she intended to get him back by any means.

29

LONDON

'Mr Attwood,' a voice exclaimed, elevated in pitch and laced with oiliness.

Guy was startled. He swung around to see Charlotte Cavendish walking towards him across her long, spacious reception room. 'What a pleasant surprise. I think we've met before at some party or other, haven't we?'

'We have,' he said, giving a tight smile and touching her outstretched hand momentarily. 'I knew your husband.'

Charlotte was an undeniably attractive woman with symmetrical, even features, and her noticeable height lent her an air of authority – perhaps even superiority – that she clearly revelled in, being the height of most men. Not Guy, though; he stood several inches taller than most of his peers, and so, as she drew closer, he deliberately stood to his full height to force her to pause further away than she'd perhaps intended.

'Ah, well, everyone knew Eddie. I do hope he didn't owe you money,' she tittered. When he didn't smile, she backtracked. 'Forgive me, a poor jest for a grieving woman.'

She didn't look to be grieving, dressed in a mid-blue day dress the colour of her large eyes.

She seemed to read his thoughts. 'Eddie would not approve of me garbed in black. He said grief should reflect joy that a person had walked this earth, had lived a life.' She smiled. 'I doubt he meant himself, because I think Eddie planned to live long and heartily. Even so, I respect his joie de vivre and refuse to mope around in black for a whole year.'

'There's always lilac,' Guy offered.

'I detest lilac. That's an old lady's colour. And mourning for months on end is for old women who have nothing else to do.'

'But you have things to do, Mrs Cavendish?'

'Certainly. I have to carve a new life for myself. I don't think a man like Eddie, or even you, could imagine what it's like for me. I had all sorts of plans for the future, only to have them cut short. Now I am facing poverty.'

There was nothing to say to that, so Guy remained silent and waited for her to continue.

'I've had to sit down and think about how to move forwards, Mr Attwood.'

'And Harry sprang to mind?'

Her gaze turned narrow. 'Oh, so you know my son? Which means you know my sister,' she said, making it sound accusatory.

'We met recently in Salisbury.' He didn't elaborate.

Charlotte didn't seem interested and certainly wasn't embarrassed by what she said next. 'He may look like leverage to others, Mr Attwood, but no one can deny he is my son. Look at his colour and build – he's just like my father, and certainly our family,' she said, picking at invisible lint on her dress before she turned a defiant gaze on him.

Guy desperately wanted to say how curious it was that she only recognised Harry's status seven years after his birth, but he kept his own counsel on that for now.

Charlotte relaxed slightly back on her heel, her gaze not

leaving his. He found himself wanting to look away but fought the inclination.

'You really are the handsome fellow that I've heard women mention.'

'I wouldn't know about that, Mrs Cavendish.'

She gave a laugh. 'Such false modesty, Mr Attwood.'

He shook his head. 'Not at all. I don't set much store by how someone looks, myself included. I consider behaviour a far more vital essence of a person,' he said evenly, but it still sounded pointed.

He won the hesitation he wanted from her. 'Is that so?'

He nodded. 'Yes. We're all born with our looks, but we can all improve how we behave and how we approach life each day. We can become better people if we choose to.'

'I wonder what better means, though. Wealthier, perhaps?' She tinkled another laugh.

He shook his head gently. 'Kinder. More generous. Empathetic.'

'You live in a different world to me, Mr Attwood. I suspect you're a romantic, but I think only rich people can take that sort of heavenly attitude. The rest of us have to biff it out in the real world.'

He made a point of looking around. 'You don't appear to be struggling, Mrs Cavendish.'

'I'm a fine actress. Eddie has left me just short of a beggar.'

'I'm very sorry to hear that.'

She shrugged. 'I like to shock people when I tell them that, but you don't sound shocked.'

'I told you, I knew your husband.'

Charlotte must have realised they'd reached an impasse, because she abruptly moved on. 'Anyway, as delighted as I am to entertain you, Mr Attwood, should I have been expecting you? Or perhaps this is business of my husband's?' She smiled; it might have been pretty if only it were genuine. 'If so, may I point you to—'

'No, I came to see you, Mrs Cavendish. So thank you for agreeing to meet.'

She gestured to a seat. 'I was hardly going to turn away Guy Attwood of Merton Hall,' she said. 'May I offer you something, Guy . . . May I call you Guy?'

He heard her flirtatious manner easing through. 'Yes, you may. And, no, I require nothing other than your ear for a short while.' He sat down.

'Oh, how intriguing. It's all yours. Forever if you like it.' Now she laughed, highly amused, and then settled, clearing her throat. 'Please call me Charlotte. You make this visit sound so mysterious. I'm captivated in every way. Now, did my father know yours?'

'Quite possibly,' Guy said. 'They moved in the same circles and, if I'm not entirely mistaken, I think they might have attended the same club in London.'

'White's?'

He nodded. 'Indeed.'

'Eddie preferred the Garrick; he said it was more bohemian and he liked the theatrical folk it attracted.'

Guy blinked. They really had reached the end of the period for small talk. 'May I tell you why I'm here, Charlotte?'

'Do, please.'

'I'm here because of your sister.'

'Because of Jane?' She couldn't have sounded more surprised if he'd said, 'I'm visiting from the moon,' he was sure. 'I'm intrigued how your paths could have crossed . . . how you even know her name.'

He took a moment to give a small chuckle of his own. He was going to enjoy this. 'Charlotte, I intend to marry her.'

It was several glorious seconds as he watched the shock arrive, be somehow understood, and then truly sink in and register across her face. Her complexion blanched and her smooth forehead began to ripple into deep furrows of consternation, her brows hooding, her mouth drooping. Even her bright eyes seemed to cloud with a sort of furious puzzlement.

He waited for her astonishment to subside.

'Jane?' she began with a tone of incredulity. 'Are we truly talking about the same mousey, plain creature? Jane Saville, my sister?' She couldn't have sounded more sceptical.

'I believe so.'

'Wait! You're the friend Harry referred to. Handsome, rich . . . with a train set.'

Guy grinned. 'Where is Harry?'

She ignored his question. 'This can't be right, Guy.'

'Why not?'

'You want to marry Jane?' Charlotte said her name as though asking the universe an impossible question. Then she laughed. 'I know Jane, and I can't imagine how she could possibly even know you or, more astoundingly, how she could possibly interest you. She's never interested any other man.'

He shrugged. 'Perhaps she'd never met someone of her equal.'

Charlotte gave a fresh laugh. 'It would be hard to find someone that boring.'

'Then I must be a dreadful bore.'

'No, I don't believe this. Look at you! You and my sister are no match. Are you sure we're speaking of the same person?'

'I can tell you how we came to meet, if that might reassure you. We met by chance in Salisbury. It was young Harry who introduced us, over a game of football, actually. As to the interest, I think she's the most intriguing woman I've met in my life.'

Charlotte was shaking her head as if denying all that he was saying. 'But you were seeing Eleanor Clarence, if I'm not mistaken.'

'We were very good friends,' he said, surprised she knew as much.

'More than that, surely? The last time I saw her, Eleanor told me she was deadly serious about you.'

'Well, Charlotte, as you can guess, I didn't feel the same way.'

'She was talking about an engagement!'

'Maybe to her friends and acquaintances. She and I never made any promises to each other. I would make her miserable.'

'Not according to Eleanor, you wouldn't.'

Guy shrugged. 'That's because she was talking about the polite person who accompanied her to the theatre, escorted her to parties and dined at her home a few times – along with a group of other guests. I think you'll find our mothers were far more interested in the union.'

Charlotte looked shocked. 'But Eleanor's one of the most beautiful and eligible women in England.'

'Our mothers are a better match for each other than I am for Eleanor, trust me.'

She gasped, a splayed hand to her chest. 'I shan't tell Eleanor you said that.'

He wondered how many others she would share it with, though. 'Best not. I really don't wish to hurt her feelings any more than I have already. Believe me, she would have quickly become glum spending more than a few days alone in my company. Eleanor needs entertainment and engagement. She'll be much happier now.'

Charlotte nodded. 'John Curtess will be relieved if you're out of the race. He's had his eye on Eleanor for a year or more.'

'That's none of my business.'

'So why have I become your business?' Charlotte again changed the direction of the conversation abruptly, but Guy was grateful he could finally get to the point.

'Where is Harry?' he repeated, keeping his tone light.

'Upstairs in his room.'

'May I see him?'

'Can we finish our conversation first, Guy? I feel you came here with something to say.'

He got straight to the point. 'I did. I would like to make you a proposition.'

'Really? How very intriguing. What if I told you I have a proposition for you?'

Guy sensed her tone was returning to flirtatious, perhaps even calculating after their detour into Guy's relationship with Eleanor. He blinked. For the first time since stepping into this house, he felt uncertain of himself. 'And what might that be?'

She smiled – ah, there was the scheming, creasing across her features – and stood. He guessed it was partly to take control of their discussion, but mostly so that he could admire her fine figure. She moved to the fireplace, where the light from the tall sitting room windows streamed in to dance across her perfect complexion and glint against her golden hair. 'In spite of whatever my sister has told you, you do understand that Harry is my child.' It was not a question.

'So I gather, but he could just as easily be hers.'

She shook a finger. 'I have proof. Can you also understand that I have been badly let down by Eddie and the Cavendish family?'

'Charlotte, I'm not wishing to speak ill of the dead, but I can't say I'm surprised that Eddie disappointed you.'

'He made so many promises,' she said, sounding momentarily wistful.

'Eddie was always . . . ambitious,' Guy said as diplomatically as he could. 'But I think you are too,' he added, surprising himself.

She intensified her gaze to a stare of accusation, and he felt obliged to justify his comment.

'I mean, why else would you take on someone like Eddie? You surely knew what he was like before you married him . . . or did you think he would change?'

'A bit of both, I suppose. I liked his single-minded attitude.'

'And his wealth.' *Guy, what's wrong with you?* He wished he could take that back, and yet she didn't seem offended.

'Of course I liked his wealth,' she replied without hesitation or shame. 'I have no intention of ending up impoverished, Guy. I've seen it up close, and it's not something I'm prepared to suffer again. And that's why I'd like to propose . . .' She left her sentence hanging.

'Propose what?' He frowned.

'I'd like to propose to you.'

He stared back at her, dumbfounded. Had he heard correctly?

'Let's *us* get married,' she said. She sounded so confident, her gaze open and hopeful.

He opened his mouth to speak but she cut across him.

'No, before you jump to deny me, listen.' She took a breath and a moment to organise her thoughts. 'Jane is no good for you, Guy. She sees herself as an artist, and that apparently permits her to be temperamental, lost in the ether of creativity. She does not live in the real world where we do and where we face real-world problems.'

He really wanted to say something now but she continued.

'Jane is probably frigid,' she began again, matter-of-factly, and he nearly choked on his own breath at her daring. 'I can't imagine she's ever kissed someone, let alone been intimate. And she's so old now at twenty-six that I doubt anything is going to change that; she's probably incapable of having a family. You are encouraged by Jane because . . .' Here, she began to raise a finger with each important point she wanted to make. 'First, she's a Saville. And that name counts for something despite our lack of resources. I think

306

your family would be very happy for you to marry one of the Saville girls. Both our families are used to the royal court. Frankly, I think your family might appreciate you marrying at all.' That was the second finger in the air.

Up went the third finger. 'Given my life's experience, I think I can make you a far better wife – a perfect one, in fact, because I have no expectations of you. I have no romantic views of marriage. You can lead the life you want, and I will make no demands upon you other than us giving the impression of a solid marriage. A charade it might be, but it needn't be fractious; I think friendship and companionship can be just as enjoyable as romantic love in the right pairing. If I make no demands upon you, you might extend the same courtesy to me. We should dine together maybe twice a week and we should be seen at some social events together, smiling at one another – what's hard about that?' She didn't pause long enough for an answer. 'Of course, we would set up home together. Beyond that, you can do as you please, so long as you are discreet. I want to live the life I got used to, but without the shame and humiliation that Eddie seemed to relish bringing my way. He was cruel and so is his mother, but I don't sense that cruelty in you, Guy. We're perfect for each other.'

She finished abruptly and waited. He was still working through her astounding proposition – it scared him far more than not finding Jane, he decided. He allowed his response to be the first words that came into his mind, which was unfortunate.

'It's curious you say that, because I do sense that cruelty in you, Charlotte.'

'Pardon?' She fluttered her eyelids in astonishment.

Too late now; it was said. 'You're awful,' he said.

Her quizzical look began to rearrange itself into a scowl. Here was the real Charlotte, without the layers of well-practised guile, and she was not at all attractive.

'I would sooner go through life alone, unloved, and yearning for company than be shackled to you, Charlotte. You have no empathy, no moral compass, and your selfish disregard for anyone but yourself is on display to all. You are transparently vulgar. I may not know your sister well, but just a few hours in her company taught me all I needed to know about her capacity to love, to put others before herself, to not covet or interest herself in what she doesn't have. Jane celebrates what she does have, and the few people who love her do so for exactly who she is. I fear no one could love you for exactly who you are. Eddie, I suspect, could see right through to your greed, your desire for wealth, status and power over others, and your heartlessness. And once you were denied what you wanted, what you did was even more heinous than abandoning your child within the hour of his birth. You demanded that child's return from the woman who had raised him, loved him, given him a home and every comfort a child needs. You are despicable, and your proposal makes my flesh crawl with dismay that I even had to hear it.'

Enough. He forced himself to stop. Revealing all of that was probably a mistake, but she'd pushed him to his edge. Would she back down, or had he just made things worse?

Charlotte was shaking with fresh rage, and she wasn't going to let him leave until she'd unleashed it. 'How dare you come into my home and speak such disgusting accusations at me?'

Guy shook his head. 'None of this needed to be said. You have brought it on yourself with your maniacal idea. What possesses you to think I would consider marrying you? I told you, I love—'

'I was not speaking about love. I was speaking of a union that would help us both.'

'What you're missing is that I don't need help, as you put it. You seem to believe that I suffer the complex that you do of how society views me, Charlotte. I couldn't give a damn, whereas you probably spend most of your days in angst, plotting how to ensnare a man who can provide what you think society expects of you. You tried that and it backfired miserably. It will again. And I respect myself too much to be that man. I don't need a strategy for marriage. You called me a romantic. I believe I am exactly that. My whole notion of marriage rests on loving the person I want to give my name to, give my life to, give everything I own to. And I have chosen Jane . . . if she'll have me.'

'If she'll have you . . .' Charlotte repeated in wonder, then cackled an almost hysterical laugh. 'If she'll have you,' she repeated in a choked voice of fury. 'Guy, why the hell are you here?'

30

Apart from his strong soprano voice, Harry had learned through his schooldays that he had two other reliable skills, and he knew he'd be drawing on both of them from here on to get home to Wiltshire.

The first was his ability to navigate. They'd learned about maps and how to follow them, and he'd proved himself to be one of the better students at finding his way when set a task to get from A to B. The masters considered this an important skill, and although it hadn't meant much during the lessons they called 'Life Skills', which included other practicalities such as pitching a tent or rowing a boat, Harry realised now what a boon it was.

Working out how to walk from Russell Square to Waterloo Station using a map and then setting that course in his mind was where his second skill came in. His memory was considered exemplary. A couple of the schoolmasters had muttered words like 'astonishing' or 'extraordinary' when they'd discovered that he could memorise information so convincingly – and accurately. Right now, he had the route between the house at Russell Square and the big railway station firmly in his mind.

It was a straight enough line of approximately two miles, which did not daunt him, but his plan was to avoid the most obvious path in case his aunt came looking for him. Instead, he would track away from somewhere called Lincoln's Inn and towards the Seven Dials at Covent Garden. This meant he would pass the Royal Opera House, which they'd strolled by, and use Bow Street to connect him into the Strand before moving on to Waterloo Bridge. He would then cross the great River Thames and keep following his nose to Waterloo Station.

What he hadn't fully taken into account was that he would skirt the British Museum, and that was a temptation too great. Like a puppy being led down Great Russell Street, he turned towards the grand building and entered its majestic gates. At school they'd heard about the new northern wing construction. He wondered if it was built yet, but his great hope was to get into the Great Reading Room that William had spoken about. In fact, William had promised to take him there. 'The envy of the world,' he'd said.

Harry had taken care to dress neatly that morning, hopeful that his aunt would take him out. While she'd proved to be a disappointment in that regard, he was glad no one would consider him a scallywag as he approached one of the museum guards. 'Good morning, sir.'

'Morning, young fellow. Are you lost?'

'No, sir.' Harry pointed over his shoulder. 'I'm here with my, er . . . uncle,' he said, hoping he'd be forgiven for the lie.

'Oh, righto. How can I help?' the guard said.

'Um, I was wondering, sir, as my uncle is busy, um, studying something, may I look at the Great Reading Room?'

'Ooh, no, young man,' the man tut-tutted, looking momentarily bewildered at the query. 'I'm sorry. You need what's called a Reader's Ticket from the Principal Librarian, and that must be applied for in writing. You need to qualify, you see. Does that make sense?'

Harry was disappointed. 'It does, sir, but it doesn't help me.'

The man smiled kindly. 'I can see that. Why would you want to see the Great Reading Room, then?'

Harry explained that he was on a special holiday to London visiting relatives, where there were no other children and the grown-ups were not interested to bring him to the amazing British Museum for any length of time and that this visit was a mere coincidence and he would not be here long. He explained how much the British Museum, and particularly the Reading Room, meant to him. He was no stranger to over-egging the facts a little. 'I only have this morning before I shall be taken to Waterloo Station and put on a train for Salisbury, sir. I would consider it very special to be able to tell my school headmaster that I visited the Great Reading Room of the British Museum while I was in London.'

The man nodded. 'So you should. I'm rather surprised, young man, that you have not been brought to the museum during your stay.'

'That's because I'm only in London because my aunt is grieving,' he said, shocking himself at his ability to keep embellishing his story.

'Oh, forgive me. I'm sorry to hear this. You're here for the funeral.'

'Well, I didn't go,' Harry said, the only truth he'd told. 'But it seems such a pity to be here in the capital and not . . .' He trailed off, sighing. 'Anyway, thank you, sir. I'll be on my way.' He began to turn away.

'No, wait, hold up, lad.'

'Sir?' He looked up hopefully.

'You're a polite youngster, and manners can open doors, you remember that. I'm always telling my son to mind his manners and people will respond in kind.'

Harry waited, sensing the shift in the guard's intention.

'Look, I'm the senior guard here. My name is Stan,' he explained, and Harry blinked to cover his desire to cheer. His luck seemed to be holding. 'So, if you promise to remain as quiet as a mouse, I shall escort you upstairs and allow you to peep in.'

'You can do that?' Harry said, genuinely breathless.

The man shrugged, taking off his uniform hat and smoothing his hair before he replaced it. 'I'm due a tea-break. We can do it during changeover. Wait here, will you do that?'

'Yes, I will, Stan, thank you,' Harry said and watched the senior guard move over to the area called the Room of Inscriptions, where he whispered to another guard.

He returned. 'Right, lad, what's your name?'

'Henry Saville, but people call me Harry.'

'Well, Master Saville, come with me. We shall have to be swift.'

Guy remained calm, but he stood. 'I was about to explain that to you when you decided you had your own proposal. I'm sorry to have been so blunt, Charlotte.'

She gave him a measured look. 'I don't think you are sorry. I think you are someone who always speaks his mind.'

'That may be so, but I don't enjoy hurting someone's feelings.'

Charlotte shrugged. 'I have no feelings. Didn't Jane tell you that?' Her eyes glittered with tears and he thought she might use them to cajole him, but instead she looked away, withdrew a handkerchief from a pocket and dabbed her eyes. He waited until she turned back, composed. 'Forgive those tears. I have no space in my life to be weak. I have an evil mother-in-law who is about to turf me out onto the streets.'

He frowned. It couldn't be that bad, surely. He opened his mouth to say so, but she spoke again.

'She says the house is already sold, but even if that's a lie she will sell it knowing I came into this marriage with nothing but my care for her son. And he abused that while she turned a blind eye to his behaviour. I think she encouraged him to have his affairs. I can't imagine why. I ran this house for them perfectly. I organised everything every single day so that our lives ran smoothly, and while I wasn't expecting any thanks, I did expect to be considered an equal. But that never happened. I was always poverty-stricken Charlotte Saville who would sooner bow to the Cavendish money than find her grace. But what good is grace when you can't feed or clothe yourself? My own mother is getting older and will soon enough need help, and the house she's living in is our cousin's now. He is kindly allowing her to continue living in it, but soon she will be my problem because Jane has nothing to do with her.'

'Your mother has nothing to do with Jane,' Guy countered.

'But Jane is still her daughter.'

'And she is still Jane's mother and hasn't done right by her.'

Charlotte scowled. 'Jane looks quite well set up, if the truth be told. And now you've come along. She clearly has the goddess of good luck watching over her.'

Guy was unmoved by this play for sympathy. 'Do you really think so? I don't think her life has been lucky at all.'

'Seems to be looking up, though,' she said, sneering. 'What do you see in her, Guy?'

'I see myself. I see my equal. I see the twin of my soul.'

She gave a fresh grimace.

'Too romantic for you?' He smiled. 'I see a woman whom I trust for her honesty, respect for her determination, admire for her artistry, and adore for how she looks at me.'

Charlotte looked disbelieving. 'How she looks at you?'

'Yes. She doesn't see houses, land, wealth . . . nor jewellery, fine clothes, servants and all the society events. Jane sees me, the odd fellow who hunts apples and doesn't really fit anywhere. I suspect Jane would like me if I pushed a barrow around and sold apples for a living.'

'Do you really think so?'

'I do.'

Charlotte's shoulders slumped, as though in defeat. 'You really do love my sister?'

'With all my heart. And I need to find her.'

'What do you mean?'

'She left Salisbury soon after you took Harry to London.'

'To go where?'

Guy shook his head. 'If I knew that, I wouldn't be here. Did she come to London?'

'To see me?' She sounded incredulous.

'Maybe to see Harry,' he tried, knowing it wasn't true.

'No. Not unless she's skulking around corners to catch a glimpse of him.'

'She needs him.'

'*I* need him.'

'No, you don't. Charlotte, let's be truthful with each other. You have no interest in Harry, other than his potential to keep a roof over your head and an income from the Cavendishes.'

She blinked.

'It's only us here,' he said, waving his hands in an arc. 'Whatever you say, you can deny because there are no witnesses.'

'All right.'

'All right?'

'Yes, the boy is my leverage.'

'Do you care for him at all?'

'I hoped I might, but I suppose I should be candid. No. He is a stranger, and while I find his affections flattering, I think he's quite tiresome and needy.'

'That's because he's a child with needs.'

'You asked me to be honest!'

'Indeed. So if Harry were to disappear but you could somehow still achieve your ends, you would not be unhappy?'

She laughed. 'Only in my best dream.' She gave a dramatic sigh. 'Melba Cavendish has made it very clear to me only an hour ago how little she cares about my ends, as you put it. I thought Harry was the ace up my sleeve, but she refuses to recognise him because he was born out of wedlock. Eddie left behind a lot of debt and she is now making arrangements to sell this house because she has no intention of returning to London to live.'

'So your plan has been thwarted?'

Charlotte nodded. 'I'm left with no home and a bastard child, although she has at least agreed to settle her son's debts because they reflect on the family name. Beyond that, she told me to make the best second marriage I can and hope my new husband will take on the child. That was all she offered.'

'I see.' Guy looked at her carefully. 'What if I could make your life feel whole again?'

———

After leaving her few things in her sparse but comfortable guest room, Jane went out for a long walk, returning to the Swanage Pier, which had so delighted her when she had visited with her father.

The old pier alongside it had been built for loading the Purbeck stone onto ships bound for London, but apparently the local stone merchants didn't like paying the toll and continued to load from the beach as they always had. And so the old pier had been left to rot.

The pier Jane stood on had just been opened when she and her father visited, and she remembered being excited to run down its long arm, which zigged and zagged into Swanage Bay. Through its boards, which sounded dull beneath her feet, she could see the sparkling waters of the bay. She recalled running to the edge and leaning over the iron railings to stare into the depths. At night the lamps were lit, and on one summer evening, she and her father had strolled the full length of the pier and up the steps to sit on the benches beneath the canopied kiosk to eat hokey-pokey ice creams, the new seaside craze, even in the winter months. She'd never seen her father eating ice cream before; come to think of it, she'd never seen her father wear the content and satisfied smile he had as they sat, hand in hand, enjoying their frozen treats and staring out into the dusk.

'You see those white columns, Jane?' he'd asked.

She had followed his gaze, licking her ice cream. 'Yes. They've broken from the white cliffs.'

'Indeed. Those are called Old Harry Rocks.'

She chuckled. 'I like that. Are they made of chalk?'

'Well done. Yes, and old Harry himself is that column standing alone. There, next to him, is Old Harry's Wife.'

Jane laughed again as he continued.

'And once upon a time, Old Harry and his wife were linked to the Needles – you know, those other chalk formations we saw when we visited the Isle of Wight? – by a chain of chalk hills.'

'Did they fall into the sea?'

'They did.'

'So we could have once walked to the Isle of Wight instead of taking a steamer?'

This had made her father chuckle. 'I suppose,' he said in a dreamy voice that she would never forget. He had seemed so happy on that short trip.

The pier had been built as a landing point for passenger steamers coming in from Poole and Bournemouth as the holiday market had begun to increase for daytrippers looking to relax at the seaside. But now it was servicing thousands of people per day.

One of the steamers was approaching now and Jane smiled as she remembered being on board with her father. It had been a magical few days, so memorable that she could almost smell the coal being burned in the bowels of the vessel and conjure the taste of salt on her lips and the sweets her father bought her almost as soon as they stepped off the pier.

She could remember their conversation vividly; her father never failed to make discussions interesting or enriching. He knew she possessed a curious mind and he wanted to ensure she was always using it.

'This orange pastille is delicious,' he'd said.

She'd giggled. 'I wanted the blackcurrant one, so I took it before you could,' she admitted.

'Rowntree's introduced these in 1881, and in just over five years, their humble sweeties were accounting for twenty-five per cent of the company's tonnage. Do you understand what that means?'

'Erm,' she said, pushing the blackcurrant pastille into her cheek with her tongue so she could speak. 'It means that one quarter of the company's work was going into making these fruit pastilles.'

'Very good. Almost right. It means that one quarter of the company's production of sweets was focused on fruit pastilles, so a lot of sugar, machinery and staff efforts were focused on producing these little sweets,' he said with a grin.

'How do you know these things, Papa?'

'Oh, it's my job to be across all sorts of interesting facts about interesting companies like Rowntree's.'

'Well, I hope they never stop making them, because I could eat the whole tube,' she said.

'Save some for later,' he said. 'We'll need them on the heath.'

That's when they'd found the *Drosera* plant.

'I'd like to see you record this using your artistic skills,' her father had said.

And she had. She painted it as best she could and presented it to him as a gift a few weeks later. She'd taken care to memorise details from her first impression, scrutinising its sly, prey-enticing stalks, which covered its leaf surfaces. Her father had told her that Charles Darwin, the famous English naturalist and biologist who had died in the year of her birth, had studied the *Drosera* at length.

'He was quite fascinated by this plant, more than any other for a while,' her father explained, beaming at her rendition. 'Jane, I feel like you've captured a moment in time here – in our time, just the two of us.' He smiled.

And that's how she thought about that painting: it was theirs. No one else could share its meaning or its emotional importance in her life. That had been their last trip together and the discovery of the British *Drosera*, though not important in anyone else's life, represented something very special for Jane, especially as her father had hung her painting on his study wall. It was one of the few items she carried with her after his death, like a time capsule of her love, affection, laughter and joy in her father's company.

Jane wasn't trying to recreate that moment, here at Swanage, but it was a comforting walk back through her memories to a time of happiness and security. William had been right to tell her to get away from Salisbury, which held so much memory, all of it suddenly painful to recall.

She took a slow walk down the timbered boards, watching all the activity on board as the steamer prepared for arrival, and allowing her mind to wander. What could she offer Charlotte to change her mind? The wind was cutting through her warm clothes, driving her back into the town, where she stepped into a tearoom with steamy windows and a happy, cosy atmosphere, thanks to plenty of customers. Was she the only person who wasn't happy? She felt her eyes begin to water.

'Can you fit one more in?' Jane asked a waitress. She hated that she felt so teary.

The woman looked around with a sigh. 'First,' she said, and Jane enjoyed her rounding into the rhotic 'r' that was distinctive of people from this part of England, 'we have to find one that may be emptying. Ah, there's a couple about to depart,' she said, beaming at Jane, and then her expression fell. 'Oh, my darling, why do you weep?'

Jane forced a smile. 'Sorry, no, the wind blew a piece of grit into my eye and it's making my eye water,' she said, quickly dabbing a handkerchief to her face.

'Here we go, I'll just clear the table,' the waitress said. *I'll* came out as *oil*, and Jane felt sure she could listen to the woman speak all day. 'Do you want me to look in your eye, my lovely?' the waitress offered, peering closely at Jane.

Jane grinned. 'No, I shall be fine. Just a pot of black tea with milk, please. Thank you so much.' She dabbed once more at her eyes and banished the tears. They were of no use to her or Harry, or their situation. What she needed was either leverage or something that Charlotte wanted. But where was she going to find either of those?

Could she offer her time, perhaps? Become Charlotte's live-in maid? That would at least keep her close to Harry. Perhaps a deal could be negotiated whereby she became responsible for Harry's needs and Charlotte wouldn't have to be troubled by the day-to-day tasks of raising a child?

She'd need to think on all of this, work out which was the best approach. Deep down she didn't think Charlotte would allow them both to mother Harry. She'd need another position that took a more aggressive stance and met Charlotte head-on.

31

LONDON

Facing Charlotte, Guy could feel himself becoming angry even though he forced his tone not to betray it. 'Answer me. Will you consider me taking Harry back to Jane? Will you consider relinquishing all claim on Harry and permit her to formally adopt the child she has raised as her son for his entire life?'

Charlotte scowled. 'How does that make my life whole again?'

'Well, if you agree to that, I shall see about you remaining in this house.'

'But how?'

Guy shrugged. 'I'll talk to Melba Cavendish.'

Her eyes fluttered with puzzlement. 'I don't understand.'

'Our family knows her family in the United States.'

'Of course it does,' she said, unable to hide her emotions quite as well as him. Her sarcasm shone through. 'How well?'

'Well enough to have that sort of conversation.'

'Why would you do this for me?'

'It is not for you. This is purely business – I am negotiating a bargain with you.'

Charlotte impressed him with how she shrugged off – no, ignored – the insult. 'This is all very well,' she said. She was clearly trying to sound nonchalant, but he could detect the greedy note underneath, along with a touch of disbelief. He could understand how she might not be able to believe her luck right now. 'But how do you propose I should live? It's fine to have this roof over my head, but what about maintenance and food and, oh, everything that is involved in the running of this house and indeed getting on with my life?'

'Getting on with your life is your own problem. You'll have to learn to live within your means until you can find someone to share your life and provide properly for you. I will organise a conservative amount to be provided in a one-off payment to quell your fear of the bailiff knocking on the door.'

She shook her head, baffled. 'I don't understand.'

'Yes, you do, Charlotte, because you're more worldly than your husband ever was. You can rest assured that there will be enough – if you use it wisely, you will not want for food or the means to heat this house or transport yourself in the short term. Beyond that, it's up to you.'

'What about my staff? I must have a maid.'

'She can be retained if you cut back on your extravagant lifestyle. I shall do my best to negotiate that you keep this roof over your head. You may have to pay a small rent, but what I give you will cover that. I don't know Melba Cavendish personally to guess at her response.' He shrugged.

'All right, so what happens now?'

'There's no give without take,' Guy said, his features straightening to a sombre countenance. 'Let's be clear here, Charlotte. I don't like you. I have so little respect for you it's negligible.' He was amazed she didn't so much as wince at the insult. Her hide was tough, but then she'd endured years of Eddie Cavendish; any woman would become hardened. In this he could feel a smidge of sympathy for her. 'Don't expect that this offer extends beyond today. This is a once-only proposition awaiting a decision now as I stand here. You allow Jane to adopt Harry, or I walk away and you can take your chances by selling your jewellery.'

She regarded him. Guy felt like a bullfighter waiting for the beast to charge and try to hurt him. And hurt him she would if she denied his proposal. He didn't believe she would be so bull-headed, though, to turn away from the security he offered.

'So this house would be mine?'

'No. Let me repeat: if I can negotiate a deal with Melba, then I expect it would be yours to live in, but I can't see her transferring ownership to you, not with the debts she's having to pay off in Eddie's name. And if you remarry or bring anyone else into the home, I suspect the deal would be broken.'

She ignored his threat. 'What will you negotiate, then?'

'Perhaps that Harry will inherit this home on the day you leave it.'

She gasped.

'It's best we're clear,' he said. 'If Melba agrees, then I shall put this in writing and have it signed by a solicitor so there is no mis-understanding about this arrangement. If you remarry, then you become the responsibility of your new husband and he can accom-modate and look after you. None of us will be supporting another man. Do you understand?'

She nodded. 'Any other conditions?'

'Yes, one. You will return Harry to your sister *today*, and not tell her of our arrangement. Let her think you have thought long and hard about what you did, and that Melba also reconsidered her position.'

'He's my child, Guy.'

'Only by the letter of the law. In every other way, he is Jane's son, and you know it. Besides, Charlotte, if you loved Harry as much as Jane does, he would be here with you now. He's meant to be on holiday. I would have thought you'd want to spend every minute with him.'

He watched her blush. 'I'm not sure Harry and I are suited to one another.' She shifted awkwardly.

'No? Why am I not surprised?'

'I find children . . . well, I become impatient with their needs.'

'Well, at least you're being honest now.'

'So all I have to do is agree to give up Harry and you'll represent me to Melba?'

He sighed. 'I will try very hard and if she refuses, then I will look at new accommodations for you.' He hadn't meant to offer so much, but he wanted her to agree.

'Well, I shall not be giving Harry up until I have a firm decision from all parties, in writing.'

'But you don't even want him here!'

She shook her head. 'No, I don't want him, but he's the only bargaining chip I seem to have. It appears that everyone else wants Harry and is prepared to pay in kind for him. In fact, I need money right now to feed him, pay the servants, and—'

He opened his wallet and took out a note. 'Here. That should cover this week's wages.'

Charlotte blinked at the money in front of her. Clearly she was not used to cash being at her disposal. She gave an audible gasp and then quickly covered her shock. 'Could my mother move in here?'

'Of course. Family is important. And if you'd only grasp that you might actually have a relationship with Jane and Harry that is both affectionate and reliable, you could have a happier family life.'

'And what about you?'

'Obviously there's self-interest here, Charlotte. I want to marry Jane, and if she agrees, I shall give Harry the name of Attwood.

You will never, ever have him back as a Cavendish, do you understand? He never was one – the Cavendishes have not wanted him.
And the only Saville who wanted him is Jane. But the Attwoods
will make him their own. You will agree to this in writing and in
the presence of a solicitor that I will formally adopt Harry, on
Jane's say so.'

They looked at each other in tense silence. He could see she
wanted to agree because everything suited her, but still her strategic
side won through.

'Not until you confirm this roof over my head,' Charlotte
finally said.

He sighed. 'I'll put everything in motion. Now, I want to see
Harry.'

'All right. But he stays here with me for the time being. Are we
agreed?'

'I have no choice but to agree.'

After carefully folding and pocketing the money she had
been given, Charlotte held out a hand. 'Thank you, Guy. I hope in
coming years you might think better of me.'

'I hope I shall too.' He held her hand this time and gave a small
bow over it.

She let go. 'I shall just be a moment or two.'

He waited, inwardly giving a long sigh of relief that the first
part of his plan had worked. This wasn't the hard part – he'd
always thought security was the way to persuade Charlotte to
relinquish Harry, and he'd been right. The harder part would be
convincing Melba. But he had a vague idea of how to do that. It
would mean—

'Guy!'

Charlotte was back in the room, looking mortified and frightened at once.

'What is it?'

'Harry's gone!'

'Gone?'

'I think he's used the old fire escape and left the house without being noticed. Guy, he's run away!'

32

Harry followed Stan further into the Great Court of the British Museum and his jaw gaped when he was allowed to tiptoe briefly into the glorious Reading Room beneath its great dome.

'Impressed, young Harry?' Stan asked in a whisper.

Harry nodded, though he suspected the guard already knew what he thought. 'All those books,' he breathed, stunned.

'If we laid those bookshelves out, they'd cover around twenty-five miles,' his companion continued in a whisper. 'Look at that ceiling – breathtaking, isn't it?'

Harry nodded again, enraptured.

'It's made of papier-mâché. Can you believe it?'

Harry gave Stan a sideways look of disbelief.

'I kid you not,' his companion assured him. 'I know it looks so solid, especially with all the iron that holds it up, but the clever designer – Mr Sydney Smirke was his name – realised they needed something that was lighter in substance. It's not exactly weightless, but blimey, it's a fraction of what it might have been with traditional materials.'

'The light in here is like a cathedral,' Harry said, admiring it.

'A cathedral to knowledge and culture,' Stan whispered with a grin. He squeezed Harry's shoulder. 'We'd better go.'

Harry took one last look around. 'When I grow up, I'm coming back here and I'm going to get one of those tickets.'

'Good for you. I hope I'm still here to welcome you, Harry Saville.'

———

Harry couldn't know that at that moment Guy Attwood was running on a direct path towards the British Museum, his mind scrambling.

He'd left Charlotte at the house.

'But shouldn't I come with you?'

'No. You need to wait here in case someone brings him home or the police try to contact you.'

'Harry won't give this address,' she said, as though it was obvious.

'Why ever not?'

She turned sheepish. 'We had a bit of a row this morning.'

'What happened?'

She told him. 'Look, Guy, I was completely rattled by Melba's call and the way she dismissed me so cruelly.'

'So you took it out on a child?'

'Not exactly. I thought he needed to know the truth.'

'What did you say?' he asked, looking at his watch. He needed to go, but maybe this would give him a clue as to where the boy had gone.

She shrugged. 'What could I say but the truth? The boy needs some reality in his life.'

He rolled his eyes in genuine despair. 'Really, Charlotte? You don't think Harry lives a real life back in Salisbury with little or no money and a scholarship the only way for him to get the education he deserves?'

'I don't mean it that way!'

'How do you mean it?'

'I thought he should know who his true parents are.'

'What, so you could really hurt him? That could have waited, Charlotte, until a better time. What did you say to him?'

She blinked as if stung. 'I told him who his good-for-nothing father is . . . was,' she corrected. 'And I told him I am his mother.'

Guy could hardly believe she would be so cruel. 'No wonder he ran away.'

'So I'm to blame?'

'Of course you are. Who would want you as a mother, especially as you make it so clear you cannot bear him around you? He's a child!' Guy snapped. 'You broke his world. He wasn't prepared to hear any of that, and certainly not delivered so bluntly. He's running away from the pain you've caused. This was not the time.'

'Oh, really? When would have been the right time?'

'Not now, that's clear,' he growled. 'Right, I'm going to look for him. Stay here. Wait for word.'

'Where are you going? You don't even know in which direction he's gone.'

'Of course I do. Harry will be making his way to Waterloo Station, so he can get to the only home he knows and the person he knows truly loves him. But if he's stopped by adults, he may be forced to give this London address so, please, Charlotte, stay by the phone and make sure your staff know to answer the door to any caller.'

She looked peeved as he turned to leave. 'Shouldn't I call you a cab?'

'Harry's on foot. I stand a better chance of catching up to him if I run.'

Guy didn't wave or look back, taking the steps to the front door two at a time. He ran, skirting the gardens that Russell Square was built around, in the direction he presumed Harry might have headed, and then hesitated, asking himself what Harry might do at this point.

He wouldn't have moved towards a road with a lot of people, Guy thought, but then again, London had a lot of people everywhere. Particularly in this area of Bloomsbury, although in fairness it was an elegant part of the city and quieter. So where? Would Harry have risked using the Underground? The Russell Street station had only opened a couple of years ago. Guy had arrived from Waterloo Railway Station himself using this Underground line, emerging onto Great Russell Street.

His eye caught the flap of an old poster outside the station promoting the British Museum. He looked away, pondering which way a lad might go. There were four stations in close proximity to the museum that he knew of. It occurred to him that Harry might fear taking the wrong line, but Guy corrected himself as quickly as the thought arrived, remembering the medals of recognition for Harry's navigational skills at William's house. Harry wouldn't struggle. Still, Guy decided, he *would* ignore the Underground to avoid anyone, particularly policemen, asking questions of a boy travelling alone there.

'No, he'd stay on foot,' he murmured to himself. He noticed the wind flapping at the poster again. Guy blinked. 'Of course!' Guy realised that if he continued down this route he'd pass the British Museum. Harry would probably know that, and he didn't think the boy would be able to resist the opportunity to at least sight it. And he would still be headed in a relatively straight line towards Waterloo Bridge and onwards to the railway station that would get him back to Salisbury.

Guy didn't hesitate a moment longer. He set off with a long stride, apologising to other pedestrians as he dodged them. He couldn't know, as he arrived anxiously at the entrance to the museum, that he'd missed Harry by mere moments. But he knew in his gut that no youngster of Harry's natural curiosity and intelligence could walk past this magnificent place of enlightenment and deny himself a few minutes of exploration.

Guy hurried inside and began asking every guard he could find if they'd seen a boy walking around the museum on his own. For the most part he was met with puzzled expressions and shakes of heads.

He breathed out, exasperated. At least he was familiar with this building, which he liked to stroll through each time he visited London. He moved swiftly through some of the halls, craning his neck around the presentation cabinets and tables to see if he could spot a boy in awe at one of the exhibits.

After fifteen minutes of fruitless searching, keenly aware that each second ticking by took Harry further from him, Guy returned, dejected, to the cloakroom for one final try. A man who seemed to be just going on a break turned back, having overheard his query.

'A lad, you say? We did have a boy in here a bit earlier.'

'About so big?' Guy asked eagerly, his hand hovering around his waist. 'Fair-haired, neat parting,' he said, gesturing a line down the left side of his own hair. 'Polite, on his own?'

'I'd say. We thought it was odd he was alone. But then we found out he wasn't.'

Guy blinked. 'Did you speak to him?'

'No, it was Mr Simpkin who was talking to him – er, he's one of the senior guards.'

'Is he around?'

'Should be, he's just come off a tea-break, I think. Hold on, sir, I'll check.' He disappeared for minutes that felt achingly long, and then returned alongside a steely-haired man with a military-trimmed moustache.

'Stanley Simpkin, senior guard, sir,' he said, offering a hand, which Guy gladly shook. 'How can I help?'

Guy gave his name and explained he was looking for a boy called Harry Saville.

'Ah, yes, did you mislay him, sir?' he grinned. 'He did tell me he was with someone in the museum.'

'He did?'

'Yes, Mr Attwood. Said he was with his uncle, although to be honest I didn't sight him. That must have been you, sir.'

'I'm afraid not, Mr Simpkin. He was alone, as far as I know. He seems to have . . .' He looked at the three men watching him. 'Well, it seems he's run away.'

'Good heavens!' Stan exclaimed. 'He struck me as a confident young fellow, didn't seem anxious or confused. In fact, he was very keen to see the Reading Room.'

Guy gave a sad grin. 'That sounds like Harry.'

'He said his uncle, who you now tell me doesn't exist, was doing some study before taking him to Waterloo Station to go home to Salisbury.' He frowned.

'That would be right, except he's on his own, trying to escape London and get back to his family in Salisbury.'

'Well, you'd better hurry, sir, and get yourself to London Waterloo, because the lad's got about twenty minutes on you now.'

'Thank you,' Guy said, taking them all in with a glance. He began to run.

———

At the ticket counter, a friendly man looked over the rim of his glasses at Harry. 'One way?'

'Yes, please.'

'A child single to Salisbury . . . that will be one shilling.'

Harry counted out his money and put the silver florin into the bronze cup.

The ticket seller scooped it up. 'Two bob,' he said. 'Ah, one of the new ones.' At Harry's frown, he showed him the image of the windswept Britannia on the face. 'Most have a shield or emblems of Britain's constituent nations.'

Harry nodded with a smile.

'Are you travelling alone, young man?'

'No, sir. I'm, er, with an uncle. But he's fetching some things from left luggage. He gave me the money to buy my ticket.'

'So he already has his?'

'Yes,' Harry said, amazed at his ability to fib so confidently. 'He has a return, which he bought a few days ago.'

'Shouldn't you be in school?'

'Yes,' Harry said, 'but I have to attend my aunt's funeral in Salisbury.' He felt a little guilty at invoking such a sad reason, but he needed to be convincing.

'I see. I'm sorry to hear that, lad.'

'It's all right. I didn't know her, but my uncle insists I attend to pay my respects.'

'Ah, well, it's the right thing to do. Here you go. That's your ticket and two tanners for your change.'

'Thank you.' Harry smiled again and pocketed his pair of sixpences. He was set to travel, just as his mother had taught him, but she really wouldn't be so proud of him at this moment. She might admire his resolve and even his bravery, but she would not be impressed by his lies. She was a stickler for honesty, although that seemed an awkward thought if she really wasn't his mother. He was so confused. 'Um, when is the next train to Salisbury, please, sir? Er, my uncle is feeling a bit flustered over the funeral and all that,' he explained.

'The boards will tell you. But platform five, I think, for the next one. That leaves at ten minutes past noon. Do check it with a guard, in case the platform has changed. They do from time to time.'

'We will. Thank you.'

Harry walked into the main concourse of the station, busy with passengers arriving and departing or standing and waiting for their trains. The big station clock told him he had just under half an hour to wait, so he strolled the length of the station, passing platform five, which was near the newspaper kiosk, where lots of people crowded to buy papers and magazines. He loved the metal smell of the tracks, the ironwork ceiling and decoration and, of course, the trains themselves, wheezing in with a majestic puff of steam. He returned to the newsagent via the enquiries counter, dodging porters and guards looking at their fob watches. He looked at the sixpence he had put in his pocket not so long ago and decided he was famished. He chose a Fry's Chocolate Cream, a treat he shared with his mother every now and then, plus a small bag of Maynards Wine Gums.

He tucked the penny change away and looked around for a vacant seat. Most had gone but he saw an older man look up, check his watch, close his paper and suddenly lurch to his feet. Harry wasted no time taking his place, then ate three pieces of the Fry's Chocolate Cream in quick succession, the delicious crack of the dark chocolate pleasing him. The simple fondant centre oozed like toothpaste but it tasted so much better, the rich vanilla in perfect harmony with the silky chocolate. He'd heard this was England's favourite chocolate bar and thought he understood why. One of his schoolmates, whose father was somehow loosely connected to the confectionery industry, had told him that they made hundreds of thousands of Fry's Chocolate Creams every day. Harry wondered how many people might be eating a bar at the same time as he was. This amused him briefly before he turned his attention to the wine gums, deciding to save the rest of the bar for the train journey.

'You'll ruin your teeth,' someone said.

He looked up to see a girl, close to his own age, leaning against a pillar. He grinned. 'Says who?'

'My father is a dentist,' she said in answer.

Harry feigned a shudder. 'I don't like dentists.'

'He's a nice one.'

Harry wanted to say none of them were nice, but wisely said nothing.

'Are you travelling alone?'

He nodded. 'I often do.'

'You fibber.'

'I'm not fibbing,' he lied.

'Children aren't allowed. You have to be registered or something.'

He shrugged. 'Then I probably am.'

'Do you go to boarding school?' the girl asked.

'No.'

'Why aren't you in school, then?'

'Why aren't *you*?'

'We're going with my father to Devon.' The girl pointed over her shoulder at a man standing nearby, studying the board.

'Why?'

It was her turn to shrug. 'Not sure. There's some big gathering of dentists or something. He's taking all of us for a bit of a holiday after.'

'How many of you?'

'Mummy, me, and my two brothers.'

'Where are your brothers?'

She pointed again to where a boy sat in a small upright pram and an infant was being bounced gently on a woman's lap.

'Oh, I see. Are you going to the seaside?'

She nodded. 'We're going to Cornwall.'

Harry wished Aunt Charlotte had taken him to the seaside instead of staying in her boring house. 'My name's Harry. Actually it's Henry Saville, but people call me Harry.'

'I'm Lily.' She leaned forward, balancing on one leg, and offered him her hand, which he shook politely.

'That's a pretty name.'

'Thank you.'

'Actually you suit it.'

She smiled. 'Are you saying I'm pretty, Harry?'

'I suppose so.'

Lily gave him a grin. 'Where are you going?'

'Home. In Salisbury.'

'Where's that?'

Harry moved his head from side to side. 'On the way to Cornwall.'

'So will we be on the same train?'

Harry glanced towards the board. 'Maybe. I leave at just after midday.'

'Hang on,' Lily said, raising a finger, then running back to her mother. He watched the mother turn and look his way and ask her daughter a question before nodding. He didn't want any trouble, but she just smiled and said something, and then Lily returned.

'We're on the next one. Daddy has a meeting somewhere in the station rooms, Mummy says, but she asked if you'd like to join us for some sandwiches and a cup of tea in the station dining room?'

'Thank you, but I've eaten,' he lied, preferring not to answer any more awkward questions from adults. He just wanted to get on the train and get home to his mother and William. London had promised excitement, but it had not been kind to him.

'How old are you?' she demanded.

'Nearly eight.'

'I'm already eight,' she said, sounding triumphant. 'It was my birthday a few days ago.' She gave a little twirl.

He smiled. 'Happy birthday.'

'So, as your elder, I'm telling you that you should eat with us.'

He laughed. 'I can't. I need to get my train, which is leaving soon.'

She stared at him. 'Have you heard of pen friends?'

He nodded.

'Well, maybe you can write to me. If your letter is interesting, then I might write back to you.'

Harry didn't know what to make of Lily, but he liked how direct she was. He also liked the shape of her mouth and the way she'd suddenly dance like a ballerina while she spoke, as if it was the most natural thing in the world. 'Are you learning ballet?'

'No, why would you ask that?' she said, pirouetting and then laughing. 'Yes. One day I will be a famous ballerina.'

'I believe you.'

'And what will you be?'

'I don't know. I sing in the cathedral. I'm the lead soprano.' He shrugged.

'Well, maybe one day you'll be a famous opera singer.'

'I'd rather be an adventurer.'

'That does sound exciting. Do you have a notebook with you?'

'No. Normally I would, but I didn't bring much.'

'I'll be back.' She grinned and danced away from him like a pretty bird, returning with a calling card. 'This is my father's card, but the address in London is ours. You can write to me there if you feel like it.'

'All right,' he said, taking the card. 'Thank you.'

'Keep it safe. You don't ever want to lose me, Harry Saville.' He felt transfixed by her eyes, as large and pale as the dawn sky. 'Mummy says we must go. My brothers are restless.'

He nodded, and held out a hand. 'Well, it was very nice to meet you. I hope you enjoy your holiday.'

'Thanks, Harry.' She surprised him by not taking his hand but instead kissing his cheek. 'Travel safely home.'

'Bye, Lily,' he said, touching his cheek. No girl had ever kissed him before.

He watched her spin away again, light on her feet, and join her family, who were moving as one. He waved and grinned, and then the family was swallowed up by the river of people moving through the station.

He looked at the card and read the details. Her full name was Lily Mason, and her home was in Kensington. No, he wouldn't lose or forget Lily, he thought, tucking her father's calling card safely into his shirt pocket near his heart.

Guy arrived, breathless, into London Waterloo, all but skidding onto the main concourse. He had run most of the way from the British Museum but had slowed to a fast stride through the busier streets, realising how out of shape he'd become. He needed to address his fitness; as a teen he could run one of the fastest miles in his school. His gaze scanned the station.

He moved through the space doggedly, calming his breathing. Stopping at the kiosk, he called out over busy people grabbing their newspapers and tossing coppers towards the woman behind the counter.

'No, love,' she said, 'I've only just taken over and Alf's gone for the day. Can't help yer there.'

He gave a silent salute of disappointed thanks and continued on, carefully moving through the station, leaving no part of it skipped over by his watchful gaze. He visited the bathrooms and the enquiries counter, then moved over to the timetables, which hung in great sheets from wooden rollers. He even went down the steps from the middle of the station, which led to the city trains and out onto Waterloo Road. Nothing.

He returned to the station concourse with a sinking feeling; his only hope now was that Harry had successfully got himself onto a Salisbury train. Harry was a smart boy, and a cautious one too. He wouldn't take any unnecessary risks. Although running away flew in the face of that cautious nature – not that he blamed him under the circumstances.

Guy returned to the main board between platforms six and seven to check when the next Salisbury train was. It went all the way into Devon and Cornwall, a journey he'd like to take. It was leaving soon, and he swung around to check the passengers, just in case Harry had emerged or even attached himself to any of them. Everyone was ready, gathering near platform five to wait for the announcement that their train was readying to depart.

Guy could hear the train puffing and wheezing. He began asking people whether they'd seen Harry. Some answered quickly and negatively, some looked at him as if he were irresponsible and others just shook their head, clearly wishing he would leave. He wondered if he had developed some sort of wild look in his eye.

His last option was a family nearby. The father was holding a toddler, the mother an infant, and a young girl with long legs like a newborn giraffe's was dancing around them. She was making her toddler brother smile at her efforts, but her father was casting an eye of warning towards her.

'Lily, please, be still!'

'I'm just practising.'

'Not in the station, darling.'

'Er, excuse me, sir,' Guy said, catching the man's attention. 'Guy Attwood,' he introduced himself. 'I'm looking for a young lad. Er, I seem to have lost him.'

The man looked baffled. 'I've seen at least a dozen boys of varying ages this morning,' he offered unhelpfully.

Guy described him. The man shook his head. 'Sorry, I haven't really been paying much attention,' he said, shooting a look across his family in explanation.

'Do you mean Harry?' the girl danced up to ask.

'Harry . . . yes!' Guy said, his voice excited. 'That's exactly who I mean.'

'Harry's gone,' she answered. 'He took the earlier train.'

'You let your son travel without you, Mr Attwood?' the mother asked, stopping just short of tutting.

'Not exactly, madam. He's not my son. I am trying to find him for his family.'

She looked even more perplexed, but the sound of the tannoy saved him further conversation by loudly announcing that the train from platform five would be leaving shortly.

'Come on,' the father said. 'That's our train. Good day, Mr Attwood, and I hope you find the lad.'

The family began to move, but Lily hung back. 'Harry will be fine, Mr Attwood. I offered for him to travel with us, but he was keen to get on the first train home to Salisbury. He seemed very sensible to me.'

He smiled at this alarmingly confident child. 'Thank you—'

'Lily, please!' her mother remonstrated over her shoulder.

'You'd better hurry,' Guy said.

'Tell Harry not to forget to write,' she said, and then she was gone.

33

SALISBURY

Guy knocked wearily on the door at number eighteen in the Cathedral Close and felt his shoulders slump with relief when Harry answered the door, eating an apple of all things.

It was not a Scarlet Henry, Guy thought, smiling inwardly. If he were to guess, he would say a local apple to Wiltshire known rather appropriately as 'Chorister Boy', yellow flushed with red and a juicy white flesh. He recalled from his mental file that the apple was first grown twenty or so years earlier, and now here it was being enjoyed by a schoolboy, no longer lost, with juice dripping down his wrist.

'Guy!' Harry exclaimed and flung his arms around Guy's waist.

Guy had to admit Harry's affection was touching. Relief continued to flood through him as he tipped up the boy's chin and checked him for any scars from his journey. 'Are you all right, not hurt or . . .'

'I'm fine. How did you know?'

'That you'd run away?'

Harry nodded sheepishly.

'Word moves fast, Harry,' Guy said cryptically, not wishing to share what he'd negotiated with Charlotte.

'I'm sorry,' Harry said. 'William's already given me a right telling-off.'

William was still alive! Another wave of relief surged through Guy. 'Where is he?'

'In bed. He's not well. The nurse is up there.'

'And your mother?' Guy asked, using the lightest tone he could summon, filled with hope that she might have returned.

'I don't know.'

'How long have you been home?'

Harry shrugged. 'A couple of hours or so.'

'How did you get in?'

'I know where the spare key is kept,' he said with a glint in his eye. Then he pointed upstairs. 'He asked for me not to disturb him.'

'Right, you finish your apple and wait for me. Perhaps you can write to Lily,' Guy said, cutting the surprised boy a grin. 'She asked me to remind you to do so. I'll be with you soon.'

Harry blushed, much to Guy's amusement.

Guy climbed the stairs and tapped on the door of William's bedroom, which Harry had pointed out on his first visit, then waited. The nurse greeted him and he introduced himself as a close family friend.

'Please wait a moment,' she said.

He stood at the door, listening to whispered tones, and then she was back, opening the door wider. 'Please come in,' she said.

Guy tiptoed into the room, where the curtains had been half-drawn. It was at the back of the house, so the space was already dim, and it smelt musty. He was immediately keen to fling open the windows and let some fresh air in.

He turned his gaze to the older man. 'William?' he said gently, shocked by how ghostly the man appeared in his bed. His nose poked out over the top of the coverlet, and his hair was lank and long against the pillow. He looked like a corpse already. 'It's me, Guy.'

He'd only been gone a day.

'Have you found her?' the older man asked, his voice weak.

'Not yet. But I've taken care of something important for her. Her sister won't trouble her any more.'

'Now you must take care of the boy,' William croaked.

'I promise.'

'Then go. Get him away from here. And send for the doctor. My time is here.'

———————

Guy found Harry in the parlour, looking fidgety.

'Is William all right?' he asked.

'Not really,' Guy said. This was the best he could say that wasn't a lie but wouldn't frighten the child too much. 'He's old and he's sick, Harry.'

'Can Doctor Bramley help him?'

'He can certainly make him comfortable.' Guy tried to smile.

Harry paused. 'Is William dying?'

There it was. A child's directness. Guy forced himself not to mince his words. 'I think he is, yes.'

Harry blinked and Guy watched him fight the urge to weep. *Brave boy*, he thought. *Keep fighting.*

'Does my mother know?' Harry asked.

'She likely does.'

'Then where is she?'

'I don't know, but I promise I'll find her for you.'

'I'm not going back to Aunt Charlotte's.'

'No. And I wouldn't send you there either. I have another idea.'

Harry looked worried. 'I left my clothes behind in London.'

'That's all right. We can organise some new things if you need them. But first, do you know where Doctor Bramley lives?'

'Yes, he's in the Close.'

'Go and fetch him, Harry. I think he should be with William.'

Harry did as he was asked, and Guy took the time to return upstairs to Jane's painting room. He hoped there might be a clue in there as to where she might have gone. Quietly, he rifled through papers in her desk, feeling embarrassed and guilty poking around her things. There wasn't much to glean. His eye caught on a letter from Jane's mother, and he made a mental note of the address. The other paperwork here was mostly receipts and orders for art supplies, with glorious names for paint colours such as cinnabar green – he liked the sound of that – or scarlet lake, which he saw was made up of equal parts cochineal lake and vermillion, and then alumina sulfate. How extraordinary, he thought.

He reached for a book about the history of colour and got lost momentarily in the section on the old Dutch Masters, who, in the early 1700s, were adding resins to their traditional paint recipes to intensify the colour. The mixed paint was poured into pig's bladders and sold to the buyer. He gave a soft snort of glee and then realised where he was and that time was against him. He looked around once again at her desk; there was nothing here that would help him.

Above the desk was a painting of a strange-looking flower. Not a botanical study like his apple, but a simple, lifelike rendition of a curious plant he did not recognise. The painting looked old, certainly not as sophisticated in its approach as the works he had seen hung around the house. Perhaps this one had been done in her youth? It showed her talent in all of its potential, and yet was raw in its honest presentation of that single ruby bloom, almost alien-looking.

It was an oil, an impression of a flower that one could only fully appreciate when one stood back and took the painting in as a whole. He liked it enormously for that trick of the eye – close up, a mass of small brushstrokes, but from further back it was a glorious red bloom. Jane must have felt a kinship to the painting to have given it pride of place above her desk, where she sat to think, to sketch, to consider her orders and perhaps write her letters.

He heard the front door opening and Harry's voice welcoming in their visitor. It crossed his mind to send Harry away but he thought better of it; it might help him to accept the inevitable if he was part of the process. He went downstairs to greet them.

'Doctor Bramley?'

'Indeed,' the man said with a kind smile. He held out his hand.

'Like the apple,' Guy added, unable to help himself, as he shook the doctor's hand.

'Yes,' the doctor said.

Guy realised it might not have been the first time he'd heard that. 'I'm Guy Attwood, a family friend.'

'Harry tells me William's taken a turn for the worse.'

'He has, I'm afraid. Harry, would you like to take Doctor Bramley's hat and coat, please?' Guy turned back to the doctor.

'Did he ask for me?'

'He did.'

'That speaks volumes,' the doctor said, gazing meaningfully at Guy over the top of his thin spectacles – the unspoken message that the end was near, if not upon them.

Guy nodded. 'Harry, you and I are going out. Be ready when I come back downstairs. Is there anything you need for a night away? A beloved teddy bear?' Guy teased.

Harry snorted with amusement. 'Where are we going?'

'Just let me show the doctor upstairs. Get yourself some pyjamas, that kind of thing.'

'I know the way,' Bramley said gently. 'Off you go, young man. And you too, Mr Attwood. Have you, er, said your . . .?'

'Yes,' Guy said, not wanting any further farewells.

'Does William know I'm going out?' Harry asked, sounding plaintive, as he shrugged into his coat.

'He does.' Guy smiled. 'He told me to take you out for the afternoon.'

Harry's face lit with a grin. 'Just us?'

'Looks like it,' Guy said, cutting the doctor a look of sadness.

'I'll take it from here,' the man said kindly. 'Er, is Miss Saville around?'

'She's away at the moment, which is why I'm looking after Harry,' Guy explained. It felt close enough to the truth.

'All right. So . . .' He glanced at Harry and dropped his voice slightly. 'Shall I make arrangements, if necessary?'

'Yes, please. I'll, um, sort things out when I can get hold of Jane.'

'Right, I'll wait to hear from you. Here's my card. I have a telephone now – strange and fancy contraption that it is. So do feel free to telephone me.'

Guy nodded. 'Good day, Doctor Bramley, and thank you.'

The doctor looked at Harry. 'Goodbye, young man. Take care of that fine voice of yours. You made my old friend William very proud, you know.'

It was exactly the right thing to say, Guy thought, as he watched his young charge stand straighter, chest a little puffed.

Harry solemnly shook the doctor's hand. 'Take good care of William.'

'I'll do my very best for him, Harry.' He glanced at Guy. 'I'll lock up on my way out.'

Guy walked Harry out into the Close and before long found himself seated next to the youngster in the cloisters. It was a cold day, so not many people were around. It pleased him to have the space mostly to themselves.

'Mummy and I come here most days,' Harry murmured.

'I can understand why. I would too if I lived here.'

'Why don't you move here, then?'

346

'It's not that simple,' he said, with a smile of apology.

'Why not? Pack a bag . . . pack your teddy bear'—he smirked—'and move in with us. You could marry Mummy and we could be a family.'

Guy cleared his throat. 'I see you have it all worked out,' he said, not knowing what else to say to such a direct statement.

'Guy, if I ask you something, will you be honest with me?'

'I try not to lie, Harry,' he replied, feeling guilt all over again for the lies already told. 'They come back and bite.'

Harry nodded. 'I know that sometimes people lie to save hurting others, don't they?'

'Indeed they do. You're a smart boy.'

'Well, I don't want you to worry about hurting me. I want you to tell me the truth.'

Guy frowned, knowing what was coming. 'I promise.'

'Will William die before I see him again?'

Guy blinked. It wasn't the question he'd anticipated. In his surprise, he was brutally honest. 'Yes, I believe he will.'

Harry nodded, his face serious. 'And that's why we're together now.'

'It is. William does not wish us, especially you, to have to be around when he passes away. Some people like their loved ones gathered around, and others, like William, want to pass into the next life quietly and without tears and upsetting others.'

'So he won't see my mother before he dies either?'

Guy shook his head and took Harry's hand. 'I think that's how he wants it. Your mother and William have said their farewells.'

Harry thought about this and then replied, 'But I didn't get my chance to say goodbye properly.'

Guy sighed, reminded once again of his father. What could he say to ease the boy's mind? 'It's how he wanted it, Harry. William loves you so much, and he wanted you to remember him playing

347

chess with you and going out for walks, or watching you sing in this great cathedral. He really doesn't want you to remember him lying frail in bed in a darkened room.'

That led them into a long silence and Guy allowed it to lengthen, giving Harry time to ponder this and the inevitable loss of someone he adored. It was a lot for a youngster to take in, but Guy could almost sense the cogs and wheels of Harry's mind turning and processing the shock into something he could understand and box up neatly.

Guy finally broke the silence. 'Are you hungry?'

'I was. I don't think I am now.'

'Well, we have to eat or we can't function or think straight. Shall we find a tearoom?'

Harry nodded dejectedly.

'Come on. Let's raise our cups to a wonderful man and your best friend.'

'You're my best friend, Guy. I don't want you to leave as well.'

'I'm not going anywhere. I'll be here at your side.'

'For how long?'

Guy shook his head. 'I don't know. Let's get something to eat and talk about finding your mother.'

Harry hung back, looking down. 'Aunt Charlotte insists *she* is my mother.'

Guy hesitated for only a second. 'Your aunt is not a very nice person, as I'm sure you've discovered. But, Harry, just because families can be cruel to one another at times, it doesn't mean they're not worth saving or pursuing or loving.'

'What do you mean?'

'I mean, talk to the mother you know about Charlotte, and I'm sure she'll tell you the truth about all of this.'

'Why can't you tell me?'

'Because it's not my place. But I will share what I can. Is that good enough?'

Harry nodded.

'Good lad. Come on, I know just the place.'

Guy took Harry's hand and led him away from the cloisters. He had decided that he would no longer hide the unfolding problem from Harry. The boy deserved honesty, and it would serve them all much better not to shield him entirely. He wouldn't share with Harry his greatest fear, but he needed Harry's help and couldn't avoid some truth about his mother's disappearance.

'Come on, it's not far away. Let's move swiftly so we're not seen by any of your schoolmasters or friends – they're going to wonder why you're not in London . . . or at school!'

34

Tomorrow Jane would go up onto the heath and remember happier times with her father. Right now, though, she remained seated in the small tearoom, nibbling on a delicious scone studded with sultanas and feeling better by the minute.

'Enjoying that?' the waitress asked.

Jane smiled. 'It's such a treat. This cream is like no other I've tasted before.'

The waitress grinned back. 'You can't beat our clotted cream from the west. Top up?' she asked, nodding at the small teapot in front of Jane.

At Jane's grateful nod, the teapot was whisked away and returned within a minute with refreshed boiled water. 'I put some fresh leaves in too.' The waitress winked. 'On holiday?'

'Mmm, more like a trip down memory lane. I used to come here with my father.'

'Aw, my love. Well, you're lucky it's not pouring. Weather's not too bad, eh?'

'Not at all. I thought I might go up onto Godlingston Heath tomorrow.'

'Good heavens, whatever for?'

'My father and I did a walk across the heath more than ten years ago.'

'Well, you'll need sturdy boots. They've forecast rain tomorrow.'

Jane laughed. 'I'll be fine.'

'Don't make us send out a search party for you.'

'I'll dodge the rain, I promise.'

The waitress moved on. The teahouse was busy with the day-trippers cramming in for afternoon tea before they returned home on the steamer.

Jane had still not experienced any inspiration about how to approach Charlotte, but it was decision time. She'd decided she was not going to just accept Charlotte's evil plans. Proof or not that she gave birth to Harry, Jane was without question his mother, and she was going to fight hard for him. But how? She needed to clear her mind of all the recent pain. The walk on the heath should help.

———————

Guy was back in the Red Lion – this time with Harry – and being greeted warmly by the staff, many of whom waved and smiled as they noticed him.

'It's nice to have you back, Mr Attwood,' one of the regular waitresses commented. 'Take a seat by the window and I'll be there in a moment to take your order.'

'Thank you,' he said, unnerved by the easy recognition and attention.

'Everyone knows you and likes you,' Harry remarked as they made themselves comfortable in the room used for meals.

'Yes, I got to know them a little when I stayed here. It's lovely in the courtyard when it's not so cold,' Guy said, making idle conversation to buy time before the more difficult one. 'That vine we walked under?'

Harry nodded, wide-eyed.

'It's hundreds of years old. Apparently one of the oldest in the whole of Europe. So, what do you feel like having with your pot of tea, Harry?'

'A lardy cake, please.'

Guy frowned. 'Lardy cake?'

'Don't you have those where you come from?'

Guy shook his head. 'Never heard of it.'

The waitress arrived; Guy remembered her name as Wendy.

'Well, we know we both want tea, Wendy,' he began.

Harry looked at her. 'He doesn't know what a lardy cake is,' he remarked, still surprised.

She laughed. 'Well, my lovely, we do the best ones here,' she said. Guy suspected every bakery and tearoom in the district would claim the same. 'Where are you from, Mr Attwood?'

'Warwickshire,' he replied, hoping all this banter would improve Harry's mood. He seemed to be enjoying himself.

'Ah, well, you lot definitely wouldn't know, then. Lardy cake, sometimes called lardy bread, or rather strangely fourses cake, is made in the south, but especially the west. People from Sussex and Hampshire claim theirs is the true recipe, but don't believe them, sir. The best lardy cake is made right here in Wiltshire, though I will say that in Berkshire and Gloucestershire and down in Dorset they know how to make a mean one.'

Guy nodded politely. 'And what's in it?'

'It's a rich tea cake made of rendered lard, flour and sugar, and then it's spiced and studded with currants and raisins. We roll ours more than any other establishment I know.' She looked at them proudly.

'You roll them?' he asked.

'Oh, yes, Mr Attwood, many times. That gives them their layered texture.'

'Well, we'll have a couple of those with our tea, please, and I think we may need some sandwiches. What do you fancy, Harry?'

'Um?' the boy looked bewildered, unused to being in a tearoom, Guy guessed.

Guy looked to Wendy for help.

'Cheese and chutney? Ham and pickle? Er, we can do egg and cress, or—'

'Cheese and chutney, please,' Harry confirmed.

'Times two,' Guy added.

'Right. Thank you, gentlemen,' Wendy said, making Harry giggle. She beamed at them and left.

The difficult conversation loomed over Guy. He couldn't avoid it. 'Harry, no one seems to know where your, er, mother has gone.'

Harry watched Guy carefully, his expression serious after the earlier amusement. He frowned. 'It's all right, Guy. We both know she is not my mother.'

Guy resisted the urge to clear his throat. Straight into it, then. 'Yes, we do,' he agreed. 'But if we consider that term – mother – who does it make you think of?'

'Mummy.'

'Her name being . . .?'

'Jane Saville.'

'And you're Henry Saville.'

Harry looked confused. 'But Aunt Charlotte—'

'I know what she told you, Henry. And she didn't lie, but the fact is you have been raised and loved since the very moment of your birth by Jane Saville, not Charlotte. She said what she did to hurt your mother.'

'Why? She's her sister.'

Guy blew out his cheeks. 'Why do people do anything that hurts others, Henry? It's usually envy. Envy of what someone has, how someone looks, how much money they possess, whom they're married to, where they live, what they own. And they're prepared to hurt that person, whether it's through theft, greed, anger or plain jealousy.'

'Why does Aunt Charlotte want to hurt Mummy? Is that why she took me to London?'

'Not exactly. She claimed you because she thought you were going to make her life easier, and I also think because she's jealous.'

'Jealous of what?'

'Of your mother, who despite her modest ways, seems to possess what your aunt does not.'

'What's that?'

'Your love for starters. But also happiness.'

'She says she never wanted me, and neither did my father,' he said sadly. 'Why didn't she?'

'You'll have to ask her, or better still, your mother – the one who truly loves you.'

The tea, sandwiches and lardy cakes arrived. 'There you go, Mr Attwood and young sir. Those cakes were made fresh today, and very delicious they are, too.'

'They look it,' Guy said. 'Thank you.' He admired the shiny, layered treat that looked like a cross between a cake and a bread, studded with dried fruit.

She nodded with a smile and left them.

'I'm asking *you*,' Harry persisted, sounding just a fraction petulant. Guy sensed the boy's patience was at a minimum, all the vagueness of the adults around him not helping the situation.

Guy was feeling cornered, but Harry deserved an answer and he had promised to tell him what he knew. 'Well, it's my understanding that you arrived on this earth unexpectedly, and at a time when your Aunt Charlotte could not look after you. Her sister, Jane, loved you on sight, and so she decided to devote her life to you and making sure you were raised in a safe home of love. And, because it was only you two, it was obvious that she would consider you her son and you would consider her your mother. It's natural that you did.'

That seemed to satisfy the boy for the moment, and he began to eat his sandwich, staring out of the window as though contemplating what had been explained. Guy waited, full of expectation.

Finally Harry spoke. 'So why has my mother left me?'

'Er . . .' It was the right and most damning question. Guy reached for the teapot to buy himself a few moments. 'Well, she thinks you're holidaying in London, remember? She has no idea you've run away,' he said. 'She probably took herself off for a holiday.'

Harry frowned. 'I don't think my mother can afford that.'

'William might have encouraged her to have a break to do some painting, especially as you were not around needing meals and help with homework, and so on.'

'But he needs her when he's so sick.' His rationale was sound, Guy thought, but definitely that of a child, with no shades of grey.

'Harry, sometimes adults do things that don't make sense to a child. This is probably one of them. I don't think your mother wanted to watch William die, and I doubt very much that he would accept her being at his side as he did so. They obviously reached an agreement. He has sent both of us away for the same reason. He wants no tears, no heartache.'

Tears began to roll down Harry's face, and Guy felt as cruel as Charlotte for speaking too candidly.

He tried again. 'I think he wanted to have you in his mind singing in the cathedral, and your mother painting at her easel, or remembering the three of you laughing around the dinner table. He didn't want his last memory to be of you both weeping. Can you forgive him that?'

Harry nodded and sniffed. Finished with his sandwich, he picked up his lardy cake and took a bite.

'Well, that's very mature of you, Harry. I'm proud of you. So what we have to do now is find your mother. She needs to know you're back and that we've called the doctor to William.' Guy had almost convinced himself of that summary: no need to mention that his mother had fled her sorrows in the same way that Harry had fled his nasty aunt.

'Where do we start?' Harry asked.

'I was hoping you might help me by telling me some of her favourite places. Can you think of anywhere that she might go?'

Harry looked at him blankly. 'We never went anywhere.'

'Surely you did sometimes? A picnic, fishing in a nearby stream, a family day out? Stonehenge?'

The child before him, sugar coating his mouth, shook his head. 'Picnics on Choristers Green, or once at Harnham Hill. No one I know fishes – certainly not William – and since I've started at the cathedral school, my weekends are taken up with choir practice. The school took us to Stonehenge for an excursion.' He shrugged. 'I don't need to see it again.'

Just for a heartbeat, Guy felt sorry for Harry. No memorable childhood family picnics or big days out to the funfair or circus.

'You know, Harry, when we sort this all out, I'm going to take you fishing, I'm going to take you to the seaside with a bucket and spade, and I'm going to take you walking up moors in Yorkshire. We will take a canal boat on the Norfolk Broads, and we will visit Windermere in the Lake District. We will see if we can find the great sea serpent of the Scottish Highlands . . . have you heard of it?'

'The creature of Loch Ness?' Harry asked, his eyes wide.

Guy nodded.

'Some of the boys at school have spoken about it,' Harry said, his voice stretched with excitement.

'Well, we'll row a boat out onto that Loch, and we'll see if we can catch a glimpse of one of its humps,' Guy promised, smiling at the joy on Harry's face. This Scottish mystery had captivated his own attention when he was just a bit older than Harry. 'Every boy needs these experiences.'

Harry's whole demeanour had changed. 'You do mean all this? It's not one of those things that adults say to shut a child up?'

'No. I give you my word. Listen, Harry, how do you fancy a real holiday?'

'What do you mean?' he said, licking the sticky residue from his lardy cake from his lips. Guy could see the boy was desperate to lick his fingers too, but he reached for his napkin politely.

'Well, you still have some time away from school, don't you? What if I sent you up to my family home? You can run wild there.'

'Who will look after me?'

'An assortment of people – my mother, for one. She would be pleased of your company, I imagine. But the people who work around her would enjoy a child in their midst. You can certainly count on some fishing.'

'But you won't be there?' Harry asked.

'No. I'm going to find your mother. I think she must be told that you are back from your aunt's.' It wasn't the truth, but this was an occasion when it was kinder to lie a little.

'I don't mind a few more days off school,' Harry admitted, making Guy grin.

'Good decision.' He pretended his hands were scales balancing the decision. 'Fishing, riding a bike, building a bonfire or . . . maths?'

Harry laughed. 'I've never built a bonfire.'

'Right, well, a man called Sid would appreciate your help.'

'I have no clothes.'

'Don't worry, they'll find some for you.'

'How do I get to your home?'

'Well, I need to make a phone call. Can you wait here while I do that?'

'Can I have another cake?'

'What would your mother say?'

Harry sighed dramatically. 'She'd say definitely not, but you are not my mother, Guy.'

He felt the urge to ruffle the boy's hair; he was becoming fonder of him by the moment. 'No, which is why I'm going to send a waitress over for you to choose another, but Harry . . .'

'Yes?'

'Any tummy ache is your own problem.'

This made Harry laugh as Guy walked away and asked the waitress to bring the menu over for the lad by the window. He made his way to the reception desk and asked the manager if he could use the hotel telephone.

Miss Farmer crisply answered the call in her no-nonsense yet welcoming way and he explained the situation. He could almost see the smile on her face; it was evident in her tone as they spoke. 'I didn't know that was part of my job description, Mr Attwood.'

'It wasn't until this moment, but it would mean a great deal to me if you would help me in this regard.'

'I have no experience of a child.'

'You don't need it. When you meet Harry you'll understand why. And he's charming, as are you. You will hit it off instantly.'

'So what will you have me do?'

'Warwick and Salisbury aren't too far by train. Could you come and meet him?'

'You mean now?'

'Yes. I'm afraid I have a very pressing matter that must be attended to, so I need the boy in safe hands.'

There was a marked silence while she considered his words and then he heard her take a low breath. 'Tell me how to help, Mr Attwood.'

Relief relaxed his shoulders. 'Thank you. Can you travel

down on the next available train, please? I need you to take Harry to my home and leave him with my mother to be accommodated. But, Miss Farmer, Harry's seven, and he needs playtime and entertainment. He can't be left to his own devices. Can you plan some activities, some outings?'

'That I should accompany him on?'

'Please. My mother will help. I shall speak with her in a moment. But she will organise some excursions like fishing that I don't expect you to worry yourself with.'

'And how long am I responsible for Harry, Mr Attwood?'

'Just a few days. You'll save my life, Miss Farmer, if you can take him safely off my hands for the next seventy-two hours.'

'Consider it done,' she said. 'The next train to Salisbury leaves in . . .' He heard the rustle of papers. 'Forty-two minutes.'

'I'll meet you at the station in roughly three hours then, and I shall have return tickets for you and Harry.'

'Right. I'd better get going if I'm to catch that train.'

'One more thing . . .' There was a pause. 'I'm not in the habit of making such an unusual request, but I want you to know that I am incredibly grateful for your generosity in saying yes to this.'

'You're welcome. I've been pondering how to repay your generosity in my employment and accommodation, and perhaps this is it. Now, I shall see you later, Mr Attwood.'

He smiled as the phone clicked off. Yes, he liked Miss Farmer immensely. She had his measure, and while polite and proper, she didn't act subserviently, and there was a sense of humour in her tone that suggested she was always vaguely amused. His mother would adore her, of course. He had to hope his mother would adore Harry, and Jane Saville, just as much.

But he had to find her first.

35

Guy spent the next few hours amusing Harry with stories of his own childhood and how, as an only child, he too had had to make his own fun. Playtime and mischief tales soon turned into accounts of life at boarding school, including memories of everything from having his head pushed into a drain by the older boys to breaking his shoulder on the rugby pitch.

'Did it hurt?' Harry asked.

'Like the very hell it did!' Guy replied. 'But back then you couldn't show it. You had to grit your teeth and tell sir you would be fine as you hobbled off the field with your collarbone sticking out wrong,' he said, gesturing with his hand at the point where his bone had snapped.

Harry winced.

Guy shrugged. 'Anyway, that got me out of rugby for a whole term.'

'I don't like rugby either. I like cricket,' Harry said.

'Me too. I'll take you to see a match sometime.'

'William took me to see a match in the minor counties championship of 1907.'

'I'll take you to see a test with Warwickshire in the main county contest. I reckon we have a good chance next year of taking out the Honours.'

Harry nodded, enthusiastic. 'I'd like to see England playing Australia.'

'Yes, me too. That's a date, then.'

They shook on it as Miss Farmer's train arrived into Salisbury Station. Guy watched eagerly until he saw her familiar figure alight. 'Ah, there she is.'

'Guy?' Harry tugged on his sleeve. 'Are you just getting rid of me?'

Guy squatted so he was at eye level with the boy. 'No, Harry. But I need to find your mother, and I don't know where I'll need to go to do that. I'm going to start back in London, I think, and then I'm not sure where that might lead. I need to move fast, and I'll go quicker alone. Besides,' he said, standing, 'Miss Farmer here is going to see to it that you have a lot of fun. I promise you she is not like Aunt Charlotte.' He beamed as his private secretary arrived beside them.

'Good afternoon, Mr Attwood,' she said, smiling widely at them. 'And you must be Harry.'

'I am. You must be Miss Farmer.'

'You can call me Alice if that pleases you, Harry. Er, I brought you this,' she said, handing him a paper bag. 'Look inside,' she urged, cutting Guy a look, who gave her one of total gratitude in return.

'It's a comic . . . no, it's *two* comics!' Harry whooped in shocked delight.

'Hope you don't mind, Mr Attwood. I figured Harry needed entertainment for the long journey back. *Illustrated Chips* seems to be the preferred reading for boys especially.'

'I've read about Weary Willie and Tired Tim in a friend's copy, but I've never had my own . . . and now I've got two!' Harry exclaimed.

'You're an angel, Miss Farmer,' Guy said.

'Inside that bag is also some—'

'Chocolate!' Harry finished for her, more delighted still.

'Oh, I think you two are going to get on famously. Here are your return tickets,' he said, and she took them.

'First class?' she asked, looking up at him.

'Absolutely,' Guy said. 'You both deserve it. Now, I've telephoned my mother and she is having a room made up for Harry – I know it will be very late by the time you get there. She will have her driver meet you both at the train and bring Harry home and then drive you home, Miss Farmer. The driver will be at your disposal, should you wish to take Harry anywhere tomorrow.'

'Well, that's all very kind, but—'

'But nothing. All the thanks are mine. My mother will be thrilled to meet you. Anyway, she's already agreed to mastermind Harry's entertainment until I can get back so you may not be required to escort him anywhere.'

'I didn't mind.' She smiled.

'No, but this is exactly what's needed to help distract her. It will do her a power of good to have a youngster around her again.'

'All right. But I'll tell her not to hesitate to telephone me and call in the cavalry.'

'Excellent. She likely won't need to – she's got plans aplenty for young Harry,' Guy said, casting a glance at the boy, already engrossed in his comic with a wide smile on his face.

'Then you get going. It sounds like you have a mission.'

'I do. I'll contact you as soon as I can.'

She nodded. 'We're under control in Warwick, so please don't worry on that account.'

'Not with you there, I shan't.' He grinned. 'See you, Harry. Mind your manners, and I promise my mother will make sure there's not a dull moment in your life while you're with her.'

He ruffled the boy's hair, and Harry managed to tear his gaze away from his comic to smile his farewell at Guy. 'Seems you brought the perfect diversion, Miss Farmer. Thanks again.'

Guy left the station, feeling satisfied that Harry would be safe and happy; this allowed his mind to race free now. He headed for the post office to make another telephone call.

The voice on the other end sounded put out. 'I shall fetch her for you, sir, but I must tell you this is her time for—'

'It's urgent. Tell her it's about one of her daughters.'

'Right, sir, if you'll be kind enough to wait.'

He heard footsteps disappear and then silence for what felt an age, before a lot of shuffling and a woman's voice.

'This is Eugenie Saville.'

'Mrs Saville, this is Guy Attwood and I'm sorry to—'

'Of the Attwoods of Merton?'

He took a breath. *Stay polite. Of course she's going to know the name.* 'One and the same,' he admitted.

'Mr Attwood, what a pleasure. And how curious that you should call. I met your parents a long time ago, but I don't believe we've met, have we?'

'No, Mrs Saville,' he answered obediently.

'Please accept my sincere condolences on the passing of your father.'

He swallowed. 'News travels fast.'

'He was very well known in business circles. And I still read the morning papers.'

He knew that was code for she read the engagements, marriages and obituaries pages. His mother did the same. 'Of course. And thank you. It was sudden but peaceful.' It was easier to just say that and end that path of conversation.

'And how is your mother doing? It is not at all easy as a new widow.'

'She is stoic, Mrs Saville, as I'm sure you yourself have been.'

'Indeed. It wasn't easy raising two daughters without their father.'

He left that one alone too, although it gave him the opening he needed. 'It's about one of your daughters that I'm calling, actually,' he began.

'Oh, really?' He could hear the intrigue immediately enter her voice. 'Charlotte didn't mention that she'd met you.' She began to tinkle a laugh. 'How wonderful. I—'

'Forgive my interruption, Mrs Saville, but I'm not calling about Charlotte. I need to talk to you about Jane.'

'Jane?' she repeated the name as though it were a strange and unfamiliar word.

'Yes.'

'Jane in Salisbury?' she said, sounding entirely perplexed.

'Your daughter Jane, yes,' he confirmed, wanting to laugh, and yet it was no laughing matter.

'What would you want with Jane, Mr Attwood? How do you even know her?'

'I met her while I was travelling in Wiltshire, and we have become, um, good friends,' he said, which both understated their closeness and overstated the current state of their friendship, which was seemingly in tatters.

'I see,' Mrs Saville said, although he could hear only confusion. 'And what is it that you need?'

'Well, I need to find her.'

'Mr Attwood, I am completely at a loss here.'

'Mrs Saville, your daughter Jane has recently left her accommodations with Mr William Angus. She is presently travelling, whereabouts unknown.'

'In that case—'

'Hear me out, Mrs Saville,' he interrupted. 'Please,' he added firmly, then waited. He heard her sigh at being shut down, but she said nothing. 'I'm sure you're aware that Charlotte paid Jane a surprise visit, with a shocking ultimatum.'

The silence between them felt like a third person on the line.

'Mrs Saville?'

'Yes, I knew of the visit. And?'

She had probably orchestrated it, he thought. 'Well, Jane has since left her home, left no word of her whereabouts, and her friends are concerned for her.'

'Friends? Which friends?'

'Well, William and myself, certainly.'

'Mr Saville, what is your interest in Jane? I'm not sure I understand.'

'Let me be plain, then, Mrs Saville. I intend to marry Jane, but—'

'Marry her!' she exclaimed an octave, or perhaps two, above her normal voice.

'Yes.'

'Are you mad?' She sounded deeply offended. 'Guy Attwood . . . one of the most pursued and eligible bachelors in all of England, is planning to marry Jane Saville? She's a . . . a fallen woman, as she's been called.'

'Wrongly, as you well know. And Mrs Saville, if I ever hear you speak of Jane like that again, I shall take this matter to the authorities.' He had no idea what he meant by that, but it sounded threatening, and he was sure the woman on the other end felt unnerved by his statement. He pressed his advantage. 'You cooked up this extraordinarily cruel plan to trap Eddie Cavendish. Perhaps you'd like Melba Cavendish to learn that – she's no doubt still grieving over the early death of her only child. No?'

Silence.

'I thought not. Mrs Saville, I did not ring you today to cross swords with you, but I'm aware of all the sordid background that now has an innocent child – your grandson – in the centre of it, being desperately pushed around from pillar to post, and Jane in a mood that, frankly, concerns me. She loves that boy as her own. She has raised him without any help from you or Charlotte. Your older daughter is as ruthless and calculating as you – you've taught her well – but I don't care about either of you. I don't care about what you've done or what your reasons were. I care about Jane and your grandson. So if you don't want the wrath of the Attwood family descending upon you, I suggest you start helping.'

He wasn't finished. 'Jane couldn't care a whit about money or society's notion of her, but I know you and Charlotte care a great deal about appearances. Imagine what one of your daughters marrying into the Attwood family might do to lift your reputation. I can assure you that many other mothers have tried and failed, Mrs Saville, where you could be seen to have succeeded with almost no effort. Take a pragmatic view for your own best interests, if not Jane's.'

There was a pause, and then a nervous titter. 'Right. Well, I . . . How can I help you, Mr Attwood?'

'Please, if we're to be in-laws, do call me Guy.' He almost laughed at the casual tone he now adopted, a stark contrast to just a moment ago.

'Guy. How can I assist you to find Jane?'

'I need you to think hard about places she might flee to. Her mood is low – desperate, in fact – and may worsen still if she learns that William Angus has passed away, which I suspect he has by now. I saw him today and the doctor could do nothing more for him except ease any discomfort. If Jane learns of this, she will feel she has no one left who loves her, not with Charlotte having taken Harry away.'

'What about you?'

'That's another story, Mrs Saville, and I don't have time to explain. I have to find her quickly.'

'Where is the boy? Charlotte said—'

'He's safe.'

'Does Charlotte know?'

'Not yet. But feel free to inform her. I can't imagine she's wringing her hands,' he said, unable to help himself. 'Charlotte and I had a long conversation and we've reached a mutual understanding about Harry and her future. Right now I want you to think. Where would Jane go? She obviously hasn't come to you.'

'She wouldn't.'

He wanted to say he'd guessed as much but he didn't want to provoke her further. 'Is there somewhere she feels a kinship for?'

'I couldn't tell you of the contrariness of Jane. She isn't easily understood.'

Guy sighed in frustration. He was getting further from Jane with every minute he spent on this call. 'Did she know Wiltshire well?'

'I hardly know her. I don't know what she knows or doesn't know. She didn't have the means to explore Wiltshire, if that's what you're asking.'

'Was it a place of enjoyment from her childhood?'

'No. She and her sister went to Salisbury because an aunt lived there. She's a relative of mine, but they didn't have a warm relationship with her, even though we visited.'

'You'd go as a family?'

'Now and then, out of duty.'

'What did you do when you went there?'

'Well, we were visiting, Mr Attwood . . . Guy. We took tea, we made conversation, we attended the cathedral services, we walked the Close, although Mr Saville was never much interested in all of that. In this he and Jane were most alike. They'd try and escape together.'

Guy was nodding, not really paying attention.

'They'd go off on rambling excursions that couldn't interest Charlotte and me any less.'

'I see.' He blinked. 'Rambling?'

'Yes, he'd take his walking stick and hike around places with his precious Jane in tow. They were like peas in a pod, those two. Charlotte and I always felt left out of their conversations and the little trips they shared. Not that we wanted to go rambling, mind you.'

He could almost see her pulling a face of disgust. 'Where would they go?'

'They got as far away as possible . . . into Hampshire or Berkshire. I remember once they went to some far-flung spot called Godlingston Heath, wherever that is! Apparently they went in search of a flower. Can you imagine that waste of time? Two whole days searching for some strange, carnivorous flower that only grows in that part of England. They weren't even sure it existed. It was a mystery hunt, they said, which they both found amusing and fun.'

Guy felt two sensations as she said this. The first was empathy. Of course it was fun. It was what he loved; the challenge of finding a potentially lost apple was energising – exciting even. The second sensation was visceral; he felt it throughout his body as he stood there, momentarily silent, as something began to coalesce and take shape in his mind.

'Guy? Are you still there?'

'Yes, I'm here.'

'I thought you'd dropped out.' She gave that irritating laugh again.

'Did they find it?' he asked, his tone urgent. 'The flower?'

'Oh, yes,' she said with boredom in her tone. 'There was a ridiculous amount of excitement between them, and of course Jane had to set to and do one of her silly paintings before the wretched flower dried out. She used to cut them up, too.'

'That's what a botanical artist does.'

'Jane played at art because she didn't really like moving around in the real world.'

'You mean the real world like dances, theatre . . . lunching with ladies?' He disguised his sarcasm well enough.

'Exactly!'

He couldn't be bothered trying to stand up for Jane in this instance; it wasn't worth it. 'Was the flower red, Mrs Saville?'

'Pardon?' She sounded dumbfounded. 'Er, red? Yes, yes, it was. As I was told, it was only found in Dorset.'

Was this the clue he needed? The flower she had painted as a youngster, prized because of its rarity? Although it was less refined than her present-day work, for obvious reasons, she had kept it close. He believed this was less to do with the flower and more to do with her father and happier days . . . cherished time spent with the parent she loved so much.

'Did Mr Saville encourage Jane in her artistic pursuit, Mrs Saville?'

'Yes, more's the pity. There was I, trying to get her interested in social activity and young men, while her father was inspiring her towards much lonelier pursuits that would do her no good at all in life. He was fond of Charlotte but didn't understand her. Whereas he and Jane were extremely close. He didn't hide his enormous affection for her. Don't get me wrong, Mr Attwood, I admired my husband, but he's the reason Jane is such an outcast.'

He desperately wanted to reply with *No, Mrs Saville. You're the reason she is lonely and without family*. Instead, he choked back the admonishment and said, 'I have to admit I am deeply grateful to your husband's attitude, because I love Jane for precisely all the reasons you find to criticise her.'

'You amaze me. Jane is certainly a fortunate girl to have caught your eye. She is so plain by comparison to her sister; I really don't know what it is you see—'

Plain! 'I know, Mrs Saville. But isn't that what makes the world so interesting?' he asked, deliberately trying to wrong-foot her. 'If we all found the same sort of person fascinating, the world would lack interest or variety.'

'Well, that's a charming attitude indeed. I'll say again, she's a lucky girl. I do hope she's said yes to you, Mr Attwood.'

'Not yet.'

Mrs Saville sucked in a breath. 'That girl is deliberately contrary.'

'No, I think she's in pain, Mrs Saville, and I am part of that pain, I realise. And now I'm going to fix it. Good day, Mrs Saville, thank you for speaking with me.'

'Mr Attwood . . . er, you will inform me of any arrangements, won't you?'

'That will be up to Jane. Thank you again.'

He hung up before she could ask anything more. He let go of the talking piece as though it might sting him, realising he was putting all of his hopes for his future life and for the safety of Jane on a hunch. But his hunches had served him well so far, he decided. And now he knew where to start.

36

DORSET

The waitress at the teashop had been right about the stormy day. The weather gods seemed intent on driving Jane back off the heath, though they were using minimal weaponry right at that moment, amusing themselves with a stiff breeze straight off the sea that cut through her ineffective cloak. But Jane was carrying nothing more than her burdensome thoughts, so both gloved hands were free to wrap the cloak tightly around her.

She glanced up towards oppressive clouds. Their heavy bellies seemed to jeer at the pregnancy she had never experienced. She tried to dismiss their bleakness and overlook the threat of imminent rain by focusing on their colour. 'Payne's grey,' she said aloud, needing to hear a friendly voice. The hue had a dark blue quality and Jane forced her mind to consider its make-up of Prussian blue, ochre and crimson lake. The watercolour had been mixed by William Payne in the eighteenth century as he strived to achieve a colour less intense than black but dark nonetheless. Her thoughts leap-frogged further, taking her to a colour known as Eigengrau, which was German for 'intrinsic light'; the near-black grey that remained when there was no light. The clouds here had not achieved that depth, because above them shone a painfully bright sky of luminous white, made more intense by the bruised clouds below. They would not hold their water for very much longer, she was sure.

The heath was silent, save for the breeze through the dwarf gorse that covered vast tracts. It was in full bloom, dressed in its golden yellow pea-like flowers, its spiny needles bent in submission to the wind, which was picking up more power with each passing minute. Jane defied it, though, tipping her chin to cast a gaze across the wild, open terrain. It was boggy underfoot and yet could switch without warning from dense scrub to peat bogs, from pools of shallow water to bare, dry ground.

From this vantage, she could see all the way across to Poole Harbour. If she were to paint the scene, it would appear in layers of green as she identified the saturation of chlorophyll. She could pick out everything from the lightness of apple green through fern green, artichoke and evergreen and into muddier greens like olive, laurel and myrtle. What a colour it was, she thought, knowing she could spend weeks identifying all the shades of green to depict what was in front of her. The heather was already showing signs of winter browning, adding a scorched look to the landscape as it stretched to the boggy flats and down to the silver slash of sea, where the lighter coloured clouds seemed to hover. Somewhere nearby was Agglestone Rock, which she'd seen with her father. She would like to see it again and touch it, as though she were touching the past, but she wasn't inclined to go roaming in this weather. The myth went that the devil had hurled the anvil-shaped sandstone from the Isle of Wight with a view to smashing Corfe Castle, Salisbury Cathedral or Bindon Abbey. No one knew why.

It didn't matter. No one was listening or waiting to learn. Her father had shared it with her, but she had no one to share the same knowledge with.

It had been more than a fortnight since Guy had kissed her, won her heart, made her believe in his love and then ruthlessly left her. She couldn't understand it. Couldn't contemplate how someone could be so cruel. She took the blame, though.

'You allowed him into your heart too fast,' she murmured to herself. 'You let your guard down and you gave your trust to someone who hadn't earned it. You're the fool!'

It was as if he had summoned every bad thing that could happen with his arrival into her life.

Charlotte. Jane grimaced; she was still trying to wrap her mind around the viciousness of her sister's shock arrival. Jane shouldn't have been surprised after what had occurred seven years earlier, and yet she was hurting as though Charlotte had rammed a blade into her back. Marriage, her own suffering or even the years had not chipped away at Charlotte's selfish view of life. It didn't matter for a moment to her that Jane had cared lovingly for the son Charlotte had cast aside. She hadn't softened towards Jane, and she saw only how Harry might be useful to her; she held no affection for him. What was troubling Jane even more was what Charlotte might do once he'd served his purpose as bait for her mother-in-law. What then? Jane would take him back, of course, but she couldn't fathom the damage that might have occurred. She didn't trust Charlotte to keep the secret. She couldn't if she was going to parade her long-lost son to Melba.

Harry. Every part of her ached for him. It was probably wrong, she realised now, to make a child the reason to breathe, but Harry was all she had. He was her life, right or wrong, her laughter, her love, her recent past and her only future. And he'd been snatched away without warning.

Adding to this swirl of despair was William. Was it watching her dissolve into those heartbreaking tears that had galvanised his sickness? She couldn't know, and yet she'd watched him change into a hollow, trembling shadow of himself. She'd imagined they had a few years together still, enough to see Harry into his grown-up school. By twelve or so, he would be better equipped to live without William, who was all he'd had as a father figure – until Guy had come into their life.

She hadn't meant to let it happen. She was not prone to opening herself up to people. The years had taught her to be secretive, and that secrecy had led to the quietest of existences. Guy had been like a bright blazing light of promise, something she'd never had, never thought about, because it had not occurred to her that love, marriage, children – other than Harry – would ever be part of her life.

That kiss in the orchard and his admission of loving her had opened up a new world . . . and she'd trusted it.

She'd trusted him.

And he'd abandoned her and Harry.

All of these thoughts had begun to crush her. No Guy, no Harry, no William . . . She closed her eyes against fresh tears. In her heart she was sure William was already dead.

'It was his choice to send you away,' she said aloud, needing to hear someone – even if it was her own voice – remind her of that. She hadn't wanted to leave him, but part of her was grateful that he'd had the strength to make her go, to save her the anguish of watching him fade even more, and to push her to fight.

She'd been away three days now. And Harry had been gone for more than two weeks. How would she be when he'd been gone a year? What would she be doing?

'Painting, I suppose,' she murmured to the wild grasses, knowing this was likely untrue. She would probably give up painting, give up on life because it had constantly tried to hurt her. Each time she put herself back together, the forces that seemed to enjoy taunting her would return. They would find some other way of tearing her down.

So fight! It was her father's voice, his spirit up here on the heath with her. *I surely taught you never to shrink from speaking out against anything that's wrong.*

'He's *her* child,' she yelled back into the winds.

And she'll raise him badly. Harry will go to the dogs in one way or another if you don't reclaim him. Charlotte has no time in her life for a child. He is but a device for her.

'How do I get him back?' The breeze whipped her voice away as easily as it whipped her hair from its pins. Was she going mad talking to herself in this way?

Think, Jane. You have an agile mind. Use it!

She walked back down the hill and sat on the side away from the harsh breeze. In relative shelter, she stretched her thoughts, taking herself back through her life with her sister. All the milestones they'd shared, their petty disagreements and Charlotte's regular smirks and taunts. They lived within her and she dredged them up now, not minding the pain as she looked at the maze of those memories, searching for a pathway.

She wasn't aware of time passing, other than in her mind, as she recalled being with Charlotte in Salisbury, her sister heavily pregnant and acidic. Jane had taught herself to rarely think of that time, painful as it was, but now she allowed herself to unlock those memories in full feeling, full colour.

'Let the pain come,' she whispered to the dancing wildflowers.

Carefully, she picked over those days until it wasn't the breeze, or the cold autumn air that stole her breath. It was her gasp, eyes widened, as though someone had just landed a full-fisted blow to her belly. She stood and immediately doubled up.

She'd punched through the gossamer barrier that had kept this tiny reminiscence in the dark. She had never once recalled the words Charlotte had spoken while she laboured, until now. It was as if she had packed them up and put them in a box, never to be opened, because she was so horrified by Charlotte's rejection of her child. But now she set the words free in her mind, her gaze as far away as her sister's had been through the chloroform vapours and the pain of her contractions.

The scene coalesced as vividly as if Jane was right back there at her aunt's house.

'I wonder who it will look like,' Charlotte had murmured.

'Well, sister, you're exceptionally pretty so I'm sure your good looks will shine through in your child.'

'No! You don't understand. He wouldn't accept it.'

'Talk to me . . . Tell me, why wouldn't he accept it?'

'John . . . Hopefully he'll never see it.'

Jane actually shrieked, covering her mouth even though there was no one around to hear her.

'John?' she hissed aloud, deeply alarmed as the truth began to seep into her consciousness. Her sister had surely been referring to John Fogarty, the second son to one of the richest men in Britain. Harold Fogarty was involved in finance and after his first son had been killed in the Boer War, John became the heir. He was not unlike Eddie in his demeanour and tastes, although rumours swirled that John didn't only lie with women.

In their looks, the men differed markedly. Eddie was dark and slim, not especially tall, not especially handsome, but he carried himself in an arrogant way that meant he couldn't be missed. He didn't have good teeth and rarely smiled. John, in contrast, was fair-headed, broad-shouldered and stood to six feet. His teeth were even and bright. He had the bravado that all handsome men, at least those who traded upon their looks, possessed.

The bile rose. Jane hadn't eaten much for breakfast, but the little she'd had now glistened unhappily on the grass beside her.

Harry was tall for his age.

People commented on his strong shoulders, how well his choirboy cassock fell from them and how well he wore his school frockcoat.

And how many times had she washed, dried and combed that blond hair, which lightened through summer to be streaked with gold.

Harry did not look anything like Edmund Cavendish, and only now did she realise how perfectly spaced his teeth were, and beautifully bright.

He was his father in miniature.

'That's why you looked so unnerved when you first saw Harry,' she said to the winds that might carry that revelation to Charlotte. Jane paced, no longer caring about the cold or the breeze. 'It was because you immediately saw John, not Eddie. And you've been steadily convincing yourself that Harry looks like you . . . but I see it now, Charlotte. I see handsome John Fogarty.'

There it was. The gap in Charlotte's armour.

Jane asked herself if she had the courage to make the accusation that would topple Charlotte's world.

For Harry's sake, the answer was a fast and unequivocal 'Yes!', which she growled into the wind as she balled her fists.

37

Jane was seated in the manager's office of the Swanage hotel she had booked. 'I'm sorry for the urgency,' she began.

'No, no, don't mention it, Miss Saville. Life is rarely neat, and it doesn't respect holidays,' he said, smiling kindly. 'Do you need any assistance in making the call?'

'I shall be fine, thank you. Please add the cost to my bill.'

When the door closed behind him, she took a deep breath. The knowledge that had suddenly consumed her when she'd unlocked that secret door was fuelling an anger she hadn't known she possessed.

The operator put through the call and she waited.

'Cavendish residence.'

'May I speak with Charlotte Cavendish, please?'

'Who may I say is calling?'

'This is her sister, Jane Saville.'

'Please will you wait? I shall see if Mrs Cavendish is available.'

She waited, listening to muffled footsteps recede. There was a pause before faster, clacking footsteps approached.

'Jane,' her sister said. She sounded smug, even just with that one word, Jane thought.

'Hello, Charlotte.'

'To what do I owe this pleasure?'

'There's really only one topic that you and I have in common, Charlotte, so—'

'Before you go on, dear Jane, you should know I've had a visitor, appealing to my sense of sisterhood on your behalf.'

Jane felt like scoffing. 'I didn't know you had a sense of sisterhood.'

'I don't. But he tried to find it all the same.'

'He?'

'Don't play dumb. I mean your lover-boy Attwood. I don't know how you've pulled this off, Jane, but he seems rather smitten. I might even be jealous, which is quite the revelation for me.'

'Guy was there?'

'Hmm,' Charlotte cooed in a tone of intrigue. 'You don't sound too pleased.'

'Guy Attwood has nothing to do with Harry and why I'm calling.'

'He seemed very concerned about Harry, almost paternal. I get the firm sense he believes he'd be a good father to the boy.'

That would have been nice, Jane thought, but she knew that was no longer possible. 'I'm glad you've raised the subject,' she said.

'He can't have him. Not yet anyway.'

'No one is having Harry except me, Charlotte,' Jane replied. There was nothing playful, nothing even vaguely sarcastic or dry in her tone.

Charlotte laughed. 'I've already told you, we have proof. He's mine, Jane.'

'Really? I think I'll fight you on that proof. I suggest you start gathering it, because my instinct tells me you will come up wanting.'

'What are you talking about? You know the midwife will corroborate my story – in court, if necessary. I gave birth to a son more than seven years ago in Salisbury, in your presence . . . and in hers.'

'It's not who gave birth that I will challenge you on, sister.' Jane heard the hesitation; she could imagine Charlotte frowning, quickly assessing what information Jane might have. She took the opportunity to press her point. 'There is no fallback position for you. Harry will be coming back to Salisbury – to his home, to the only home and the only mother he's ever known.'

'That's presumptuous. Guy hasn't even negotiated yet.'

'I have no idea why you keep bringing Guy Attwood into this conversation. Let me be plain.'

'You already are.' Charlotte cackled at her jest.

There it was; the arrogance that had got Charlotte this far in life. Jane had learned that people were often beguiled by someone who spoke with authority and confidence. But secrets could be hidden behind that facade.

She really didn't know what her sister meant about Guy – negotiating what? – but she ignored her. 'Have you told Melba about Harry yet?'

'I have and—'

'Pity,' Jane said.

'And why's that?'

'Because, Charlotte, I've finally worked you out for the liar and manipulator that you are. I can forgive you in some respects; I don't think our mother made it easy for you. But I imagine even darling Harry has reached a not-so-sparkling conclusion about you, what with the way you tried to buy his affections. He's not stupid. He'll have worked you out by now.'

'Doesn't make him not my son, though,' Charlotte sneered.

'Doesn't make him Eddie Cavendish's either.' Jane let that sink in.

'What's that supposed to mean?' Charlotte said finally, her voice faltering.

'You know exactly what I mean. And unless you want me to let the world know that you slept with John Fogarty to get him on the hook while trying to win Eddie Cavendish's ring on your finger, then I suggest you rethink your position.'

The silence felt like a wraith, drifting between them, both sisters clutching a handset that connected them over miles. Jane waited. So she was right! She wanted to yell her triumph, but she would not break this tension. She imagined Charlotte's mind nearly bursting with rage.

'What did you say?'

'I will break you, Charlotte, as you have broken me, but you can save yourself the pain and the humiliation if you give back what belongs to me. You were simply the vessel that held him until he was born. Harry is mine.'

'So you're threatening me with gossip you've fabricated?'

Jane let out her breath with a choked laugh. 'I am threatening you with the one weapon I have: your greatest secret. You've obviously forgotten how you shared your fear about who might have fathered your baby – Eddie Cavendish or John Fogarty.'

'I did no such thing, you wretch!'

Charlotte was almost shrieking now, and Jane knew she finally had the upper hand. 'Then how do I know? In the depths of your labour, half-drunk on the pain and the chloroform, you admitted it, Charlotte. And, frankly, as much as I loathe to say it, Harry is the dead spit of John. It wouldn't take much convincing for either of the Fogarty men to see the resemblance. My advice is that you keep your secret, and I will too, but it will cost you, dear sister. You knew from the very outset that your child could be a Fogarty, so you lied to Eddie, to our mother . . . to me!' Jane's voice broke slightly but she fought the tears and steeled her tone. 'Imagine what John Fogarty will do.'

Charlotte scoffed. 'Nothing, I imagine. He's married with children. He doesn't want his bastard creeping out of the woodwork.'

'Well, at least you're being honest now. But be assured, I have nothing left to lose. I will tell John's wife and his father as ruthlessly as—'

'You'd ruin his marriage? His relationship with his parents?' Charlotte asked, sounding incredulous.

Her astonishment only served to fuel Jane's fire. 'In a heartbeat. Did you even once consider me as a victim in your grand scheme for marriage? You didn't care who you hurt, as long as you got what you wanted. And let's not even explore your abandonment of your child.'

'Jane, you know full well my pregnancy was not planned.'

'I don't know what you think might happen if a man and woman lie together, Charlotte, but you certainly tried it at least twice, so please don't bleat about Harry being some sort of accident. And *you* will ruin the Fogarty marriage, not me. Unless you return Harry.'

'Give me a week, Jane, to think this—'

'No. I'm tired of everything being on your terms. No more time to scheme, Charlotte. You have until tomorrow morning. I shall pick him up in London, or I will visit the Fogartys, who aren't that far away from where you live, as I understand it. Mayfair?'

'Jane, I need time. I've struck a bargain with the most unlikely person to—'

'I said no, Charlotte. You see, I don't care who has suddenly arrived to save you – although I doubt anyone can. I can't believe I ever let you back into Harry's life. I am ashamed that I once again allowed myself to be bullied through a sense of family duty. I really don't care what the law says, sister. A top barrister would give me a fighting chance of retaining care of Harry, and I should have fought you harder weeks ago. I should have made you tear Harry from my fingers, bring in the police, rain merry hell down on my head. I kept telling myself that I had to protect him from the ugliness and the only way to do that was to give him up. I don't see it that way any more. He's a strong boy, and he will bear the burden of know-ledge when it is explained to him.' Jane paused for breath. This was sinking in for Charlotte, she could tell.

Jane continued. 'I shall see you tomorrow morning. And if you refuse, then I shall go straight to John Fogarty – please do not think I am bluffing. Have Harry packed and ready to leave.'

'I can't.'

'You certainly can!'

'No, Jane, you don't understand. Harry's gone. He's run away!'

38

Jane could hear the strain in her voice as she forced herself to stay calm. 'What did you do to him?'

'Nothing.' Her sister sounded sulky, wounded even.

'Charlotte!'

'I told him the truth. He had to know. But it's all right, he probably got the train back to Salisbury, at least that's what—'

'But why? You promised me!' Jane interrupted as her heart sank. It wasn't as though it could remain a secret forever, but she hadn't been ready for Harry to be slammed with the facts, especially the way Charlotte would have delivered them.

'Well, Jane, life is rarely neat, as you well know. And as it turns out, Melba Cavendish doesn't give a fig that I have produced a grandson for her.'

Why wasn't she surprised? 'Even less if she saw him, Charlotte. You're an idiot for thinking she'd buy your story in the first place.'

'Why wouldn't she?'

'You're the one who lived with her. Surely you know her to be a stickler for appearances. This whole charade occurred because you and Mother were stupid enough to believe you could hide a pregnancy and that the truth of it would never come out. And with Eddie dead and unable to corroborate your story – not that it proves anything, given you were also with John – well, that's even more reason not to trust you. Let's face it, she's right to take that attitude. You're lying to her anyway.'

'Yes, but I didn't know that until I saw him. The baby could have been Eddie's.'

'That's what gave you away. I could see it written in your expression when you met him. I just didn't understand it until I gave myself time to think.'

'Well, you always were the clever one, our father said.'

'Don't bring Papa into this.'

'Why not? He's the reason for all of this.'

'Charlotte, that's ridiculous.'

'He never loved me.'

'He did love you. I don't think he liked you much, though. I feel exactly the same way. You behaved in a way that he didn't understand or appreciate.'

'Well, of course, Little Miss Perfect was always there on his lap or acting like his pet.'

'I refuse to feel guilty for showing my affections for Papa or enjoying his company.'

'But you left no room for anyone else, Jane.'

'You didn't try! You took no interest in any of the activities he wanted to share with us. Neither did Mother. You were both more interested in such shallow pursuits that I think he gave up.'

'Not on you, though.'

Jane's voice turned acid, scorching its way through the telephone connection. 'It's all Papa's fault that you became pregnant out of wedlock? That you discarded that child and forced me to raise him for you? And that you wanted him back purely to use him?' Jane didn't wait for an answer, giving a mirthless laugh.

'You're pathetic. He would have given anything to share happy times with you. But you were too preoccupied with yourself and your selfish pursuits. Anyway, I'm not interested in talking to you on this any longer. You said you believe Harry was catching a train for home? I refuse to panic, because Harry's smart and he'll make it to Salisbury Station safely. He knows how to walk home from there. Has someone gone after him?'

'Guy Attwood has.'

If Charlotte had said the man in the moon, Jane might have believed her more readily. She had to repeat it, feeling stupid for doing so.

'Yes! Are you deaf? He seemed to know which route a petulant boy would take and he's given chase.'

'Petulant? I can only imagine the things Harry had to listen to, and I don't blame him for trying to escape you. If anything happens to him, Charlotte – I mean so much as a scratch – I will blame you.'

'Guy will find him.'

'Oh, Guy, is it now? What on earth was Guy doing at your house, anyway?'

There was a slight pause and then Charlotte's voice turned cunning. Jane had heard that shift so many times in her life and recognised it as the moment when her sister had decided to go on the offensive. 'He came with a marriage proposal, and then the news about Harry's disappearance got in the way.'

'A marriage proposal?' Jane's tone had a squeakish quality of disbelief.

'Don't be so surprised. Anyway—'

Jane never heard what her sister was going to say next. She placed the phone receiver back on its cradle in shock and cut the line to London.

Guy was working on a lone thought; even he knew he was drawing the longest line of chance, from a childhood painting of Jane's to where he hoped, with all of his heart, she had fled. His rationale was simple. It was a place where, according to her mother's memory of Jane's childhood, Jane had been incredibly happy. He knew he couldn't rely solely on Mrs Saville's recollections, tinged as they were with bitterness, but there was the painting itself. That's what he was counting on.

No, it was more than that. He was relying on the notion that he and Jane were kindred spirits. It was as though when they'd kissed, they'd glimpsed each other's soul. With this conviction burning brightly, he trusted his own instincts that from the painting in her study – the only one from her childhood – and her mother's confirmation that finding that plant had been a time of great joy, maybe, just maybe, it was where she might flee to.

Why not? It was as good as any other place.

Godlingston Heath, in Dorset, wasn't that far from Salisbury.

It was where she'd had one of her best experiences with her father. She evidently held that memory close enough that she gave the naive artwork, primitive in terms of her adult skills, pride of place in her life. It had to count for something.

And so on arriving at Swanage, the closest point as far as he could tell from which to reach the heath, he first checked the local hotels. He tried each one near the beach, and then the eateries, in the hope that someone might recall the lone woman travelling. He drew a blank at all venues. No one recalled serving a woman of the description he gave, although one tearoom owner with a swooped-up hairdo reminiscent of some Victorian lady of leisure remarked that she couldn't be expected to remember all her passing trade clients.

'Is she memorable in any way, sir?'

He blinked, considering this question. 'Only to me,' he said.

'Then I can't help you, sir,' she said, and although the smile was there, he heard the slight cut of sarcasm. 'My girls serve dozens of people each day. And, you can see, it's busy. Everyone trying to come in from the cold. Which day do you think she might have come in?'

He had been surprised and touched that she'd bothered with him any further. 'Um, at a guess, probably Wednesday.'

She considered this. 'Well, two of the girls who worked that day come on at midday if you care to step back in. Perhaps enjoy some of our hospitality?'

'I shall.'

'Good. I'll send them over when I see you.'

He was impressed with her clever way of generating business, but grateful for the chance to ask again about Jane. He spent the next hour trailing around the town, stopping at every possible souvenir or postcard shop. He purchased a packet of mints and a local newspaper, reading it on a bench near the pier. The cold seeping through his coat chilled his bones, matching his mood. Dejected and fast giving up on the idea of heading to the heath, he saw it was midday. He decided a rejuvenating pot of tea was called for, over which he might consider his options, and with any luck the waitresses might have spoken to Jane. He stepped into the tearoom and didn't even have to raise his hand in greeting, as the older woman saw him.

A waitress found him a small table by the window. 'Just you, sir?'

'Yes. A pot of tea, please.' She nodded and left.

'Sir?' an older waitress came over. 'Miss Watson would like to know if you found the person you were looking for.'

He shook his head. 'I'm afraid not.'

'I'm sorry to hear that, sir. I was working on Wednesday. We did have some ladies in on that day who were alone, but I can't say

I recall the woman you mention, because she sounds . . .' She didn't finish, clearly not wishing to offend him.

'I know, my description is poor and I do make her sound like everyone else. The truth is, she has no remarkable features at a glance.'

'I'm sorry. Is she your sweetheart?'

He was surprised he answered that. 'Yes.'

She grinned. 'Lover's tiff?'

'Something like that.'

'Just give her some time. She'll come round. Oh, here's Janet – she worked that day too. Bye, sir, stay hopeful.' She let Janet ease into view.

She was an older woman too. 'Now, my lover, Miss Watson asked me to come and speak with you.'

He enjoyed her greeting, with that delicious curling 'r' at its end. The phrase was delivered so routinely he knew it was not deliberately spoken to flatter; she probably said it to all the male customers. 'Yes, thank you. I doubt you can help, but I'm looking for someone.'

'She told me.'

'I can't imagine you—'

'I do recall a woman with striking eyes. I'm not sure what colour to call them, sir. I don't have your obvious education, but saying blue just doesn't say it right,' she said, her West Country accent pronounced.

'The woman I'm searching for does have rather bright blue eyes. She often wears a skirt of the same colour.'

'I can't say I recall that, sir,' she said. 'Can't forget those eyes, though. I served her a pot of tea. We got chatting, only briefly, but she was going to stay in town for a couple of days.'

'Did she say where?'

She nodded. 'At the hotel that's a little way out of town. She wanted somewhere quiet.'

389

Guy nodded, realising he hadn't looked further than the immediate accommodation houses.

'And she was going up on the heath to find some plant or other.' That last 'r' rolled spectacularly. '"In this weather?" I remember saying.' She laughed, her 'r' on full display now. He adored it. 'But she said she'd come from Salisbury to visit a place from childhood. I thought that was lovely and told her so.'

'Well, Janet, you've been more help than you can know.'

'Oh, I'm happy to hear that, sir.'

She explained where the hotel was. Guy quickly finished his cup of tea, then paid, leaving a large tip in the jar on the counter and thanking the owner. 'Janet did recall her.'

'Good,' she said, noticing the tip. 'Thank you, sir, do come again.'

Guy left the tearoom and had to stop himself from running. He realised the hotel really wasn't that far away, but it was secluded, up one of the steep alleys and hidden behind the town. No wonder he had missed it on his rounds. It was more of a large guesthouse, but it had a dining room attached.

'Good morning, sir.' The man twisted his head to check the electric clock on the wall. 'No, it's afternoon,' he said with a laugh. 'Time flies. Looking for a room, sir?' His r's curled too.

'Er, no, actually. Looking for someone who may have stayed here.' Guy gave the man the description.

The man looked him up and down. 'Are you the lady's husband, sir?'

Guy was impressed the fellow was protecting her. 'I hope to be, if she'll have me.'

The man closed the guestbook that was open in front of him. 'Well, she did stay here, sir, but you've missed her.'

'I see,' Guy said, disappointment racing through him like a current.

'Not by much. She left about twenty minutes ago. Very nice lady.'

'Do you know how she was travelling?'

'I don't, sir, sorry. The next ferry is due in . . . ooh,' he paused to glance again at his clock. 'Forty minutes. She might be planning to take that.'

Doubtful, Guy thought. Why go to Bournemouth? His bet was that she would be heading back home. He had to hope that was her plan. 'Do you know when the trains run to Salisbury?'

'Well,' the man said, looking once more at the clock and puffing out his cheeks, 'I believe the next train from Cornwall calls into Swanage in just under an hour, but you'd better check with the stationmaster.'

'I'll do that, thank you.' Guy left the hotel at a steady jog this time, uncaring that people might be wondering what the hurry was.

39

Jane was back at the station, waiting on the platform. She couldn't think of anywhere else to go that was lonely enough for her heartbroken thoughts, so she was going home. The train to Salisbury wasn't due for a while, so she was the only person around.

'All right, madam?' the stationmaster asked, approaching her with query in his expression. His accent was even broader than Janet the waitress's. It was so easy to like.

'There's a waiting room just there,' he said, pointing. 'Can't have you catching cold now.'

She'd thought it would feel claustrophobic inside. 'I'm fine, really. I prefer being outside.'

He looked baffled, and she wondered if he was worried she might do something silly like step off the platform into the path of an oncoming train. It was not unheard of.

'I'm a writer,' she began her lie. 'And I'm trying to work through a scene in my mind that is set on a railway platform.' She smiled. 'It's for research purposes.'

'Oh, yes? I hope you'll set your chapter in Swanage, then?'

'Of course.' She grinned. 'Please don't worry. I'll come in the moment I begin to shiver.'

'You do that, miss. I'll be happier to know you're by the merry fire I've got going in there.'

She smiled in thanks and was glad to see him leave. As he stepped back into his office, she saw an all-too-familiar figure arriving on the platform, looking harried and breathless. He saw her immediately too.

She stood in shock. Guy Attwood was hurrying towards her, his handsome features relaxing with relief. She looked around for an escape. There wasn't one.

'Jane,' he breathed, arriving within six feet of her.

'What are you doing here?' She was still in shock that he of all people was in front of her. 'How did you know I'd be here?'

'I'm very good at hunting.'

She didn't smile. 'Why are you here?'

'I'm here for you,' he said.

'I can see that. But why?' He reached for her, but she warded him off by raising her hand. 'No, don't.'

He frowned. 'Jane, there's so much I have to tell you. The note I sent on the day I left, it—'

'I don't want to hear anything you have to say, Guy. I know that Harry has run away from Charlotte's. I am on my way back to Salisbury, as I presume he's trying to get home.'

'He *is* home. He got back safely.'

She blinked through her relief in fresh confusion. 'You've seen him?' He stepped forward and again reached for her. 'No, Guy, don't!' Again she lifted a hand. 'Please.'

He retreated a step and looked wounded. She didn't care.

'He's safe,' he said.

'And William?'

'He made me leave him and take Harry with me. I have to

393

presume he has either passed away by now, or is very close to doing so.'

She looked down and swallowed back the animal cry she felt loosening from her throat.

Guy spoke gently. 'We called Doctor Bramley before we left.'

'Is Harry here?'

'No.'

'Where is he? Please don't tell me he's back with Charlotte.'

'No. I arranged for him to be escorted by someone I trust to Warwick. He will be at my family home by now.'

That startled her. 'How very presumptuous of you.'

He stared at her, and she could see confusion in his eyes. She really didn't care; he deserved all the wrath and bitterness she could fling his way.

'I'm not sure I understand your—'

'Attitude?' Jane said. 'No? Well, yours leaves a lot to be desired.'

'Yes, so William assures me, but Jane, as I explained to him, my f—'

'Guy, Guy . . .' she said, as if speaking to a simpleton. 'Not only do I not need your explanation – you're a free man – but, frankly, I don't want to hear what you have to say. I clearly took the wrong impression from your behaviour, and while I can forgive myself for doing so, I won't forgive myself if I give you any more of my time. Please go away.'

Guy looked distraught. 'But Jane, I feel I do owe you the explanation.'

'All you owe me is Harry. I'd like him returned home. I can see you've tried to do the right thing, and I thank you for that. He certainly didn't need to watch William die any more than I did. Can you arrange for Harry to come back to Salisbury? Or if you prefer that I travel and pick him up, that's fine. That's all I ask. Leave him with the stationmaster at Warwick Station, and I shall meet him there.'

'I shall do no such thing.'

'Guy, if you don't leave me alone, I shall call for help.'

'Against what?' he demanded.

'Harassment!'

He stared at her, even more dumbfounded. 'I came here to help you, to explain about Charlotte.'

'I don't need your help, and I certainly don't want to hear about you and Charlotte. I've spoken to her. I know all about it.'

She watched his forehead crease, his expression becoming stormy. 'I asked her not to say anything to you about the arrangement.'

She gave a cruel laugh, one she didn't know she possessed. 'Well, she did. You can't trust my sister. She probably crosses her fingers behind her back each time she makes a promise. She promised she wouldn't tell Harry that she's his mother . . . but she did. If there's a way for Charlotte to strike a blow against me, it seems she will.'

'Look,' he began again. 'I've been trying to find you—'

'So you can tell me to my face about your *arrangement*?' she interrupted, loading the word with so much disdain it made him frown. 'Guy, ever since we met, my life has spiralled in every way. In the short time I've known you, I've lost everything I love.'

He frowned, deeper this time. 'And you blame me for this?'

'I blame myself for befriending you, for trusting you, for allowing you into my life . . . and for loving you.' She looked away, but decided she wasn't embarrassed for saying that out loud. 'But I am past caring about you, as I told Eleanor. Yes, Eleanor visited me. You leave a trail of broken hearts behind you, don't you, Guy? But not mine, not now I've seen through you.'

She watched him flinch at her words. But when it came to Guy, it was as if she'd lifted her heart from her chest and given it to him to keep for eternity. And instead of cherishing it and protecting it, he'd shattered it into tiny pieces when he'd abandoned her without word, and then crushed those pieces underfoot to a powder when he had come to the 'arrangement' with Charlotte. *I hope her beauty makes you happy, Guy, because you'll soon learn that beauty does not run deep with my sister. Beneath her outer skin, she is an ugly person with every attribute I would have thought you'd detest.* 'How wrong could I be?'

'Pardon?'

She hadn't meant to say those last few words aloud. 'Walk away, Guy, and leave me to my sorrows, please. I really, really don't want you here.'

'Or what? You might say something you regret?'

She fixed him with a stare. 'Thank you for doing what you have for Harry. But right now, please, I beg you, leave me alone.'

He met her gaze and she watched the man she loved take in what she had said and accept it. It was very hard to look upon him and believe that, with the kindness he had shown her and Harry, he could do what he had. *Well, Jane, be strong,* she told herself, *or the danger is that you'll walk into his arms and feel them around you one more time.*

'I have important things to say to you, Jane. Won't you hear me out?'

'How many different ways can I say this? Let me be very direct now. I don't ever wish to see or speak with you again.'

'I thought I was immune to words that could hurt, but it seems you have that power over me.' He cleared his throat. 'Harry is safe with my mother and being entertained royally as we speak.' He took out a card and handed it to her. 'If you would call that number, a Miss Farmer, my private secretary, will make all the necessary arrangements for Harry's safe delivery in whichever is the most convenient manner. You will not have to see or speak with me again.'

She died a little inside. 'That's acceptable, thank you. Goodbye, Guy.' She didn't hold out her hand; she didn't trust its steadiness.

He noticed, she could see, giving a short bow, dipping his head to her. 'Goodbye, Jane. Good luck.'

He turned on his heel and she watched him stride away, before disappearing around the side of the station building.

Jane sat on the bench and was very glad she had arrived early, because no one needed to see a grown woman sob again on yet another railway platform.

———————

Jane returned to the house in the Cathedral Close, which smelled of wood polish and other waxes, suggesting the house had been thoroughly cleaned. It was all very tidy, free of dust and the spiderwebs that always seemed to appear in corners, but there were no flowers, no perfume of nature that normally scented the hallway.

Standing in the doorway of William's room, Jane looked at the neatly made bed. She walked across and smoothed the coverlet unnecessarily before sitting on the edge and breaking into soft weeping. She missed him so much already and she'd barely been indoors for more than a few minutes.

Finally she stood and walked aimlessly through the house, feeling untethered. It had been the kindest home to her, but now there were no voices here, only ghosts. She unlocked the doors in the parlour to escape outside, drawing in fresh air and the earthy dampness of the walled garden, with its luscious ivy covering the brick, and the scent of the brave camellias blooming through the cold autumn, their icy white petals and richly yellow middles reminding her of poached eggs.

She began to feel calmer. She walked on, passing the middle wall covered in wintersweet; its pale yellow flowers come December would be fragrant enough to dominate the perfume of this part of the garden. William had always been proud of his honeysuckle, which climbed over the arbour in summer – she was glad he had been able to inhale its sweetness on the air one last time. Who would tend to this garden now?

She caught herself. The tears and the self-pity had to stop; there was no future in either. Harry was coming home, and Charlotte could go to hell for all Jane cared. She wouldn't answer any wedding invitation or accept any olive branch that her sister or Guy might offer, she thought, glancing around her, and realised she was standing at the apple tree she now thought of as his.

The apples had ripened since she'd been away and she plucked one, biting into it angrily. It annoyed her enormously that it was sweet, with a perfect tartness, and filled with a scented juice that made her think of her kitchen in happier days, when she'd made William and Harry apple crumbles and tarts, or apple sauce to go with a roasted joint of pork. It also made her think of her father, who'd loved apples served in any way, including the toffee apples he would buy his girls each bonfire night and at Christmas time. But most of all it made her think of Guy, of kissing him and dreaming about being together for the rest of their lives.

She turned away from the tree and all of the images it provoked; instead, she tried to fill her mind with Eleanor and Charlotte – both with a claim to the man she loved. It worked. Jane stomped back indoors and into William's study, where she found two letters: one from the doctor, which she wasn't ready to read, and another from William's solicitor, asking her to contact his office. She picked up the heavy telephone receiver and the solicitor's secretary put her straight through to Robert Gladstone.

'Ah, Miss Saville, thank you for calling. I have been waiting to hear from you.'

'Yes, my apologies, I've been away since . . .'

'Of course. Well, arrangements have been made for William's cremation. This is what he wanted – er, no graveside vigils or visits by you or your son.'

Jane swallowed. 'He warned me of this each year, I think.' She could almost see the man's gentle smile; she'd met William's solicitor and liked him on first meeting. His direct but still kindly manner was appreciated.

'Miss Saville, there's the formal reading when you feel ready, but essentially William has left his entire estate to you.'

Jane swallowed hard. 'I see.' She didn't know what to say; that was William, always looking after her.

'There was no one else left alive of his blood relatives, which pleased him, because he said you were the only person who had ever made him feel like he had family.'

She closed her eyes. She felt the same. 'He was so very good to us.'

'As you were to him, Miss Saville. You added years to his life by taking such good care of him. Anyway, I shall arrange for his ashes to be delivered to you, and you may wish to make arrangements for how to disperse them.'

This Jane knew how to respond to. 'In the garden, I think, Mr Gladstone. This was his favourite place. Harry and I will plant a cluster of rose bushes in his honour. He liked roses to be displayed in the house each week.'

'Very good. As to a service . . . do you have anything in mind?'

She felt more in control now. 'I'll organise a small memorial at the cathedral. Harry can sing a solo, perhaps.'

'Excellent. You'll be sure to let me know?'

'I will.'

'Right. Well, you have my deepest condolences, and perhaps you might contact us soon so we can carry out William's wishes as per his last will and testament.'

'I shall.' She had kept her voice tightly steady and could feel it wavering now, glad that the conversation was closing. 'Thank you again.'

Jane remained in William's creaky, worn leather desk chair, losing track of time until the chill of the afternoon began to make itself known in the room. She shivered out of her thoughts. She was still in her overcoat and hours had passed.

She retrieved the card Guy had given her. She planned to telephone the private secretary he'd spoken of before the business day closed, but first she felt she ought to contact her mother.

The operator put her through, her mother answering more quickly than Jane expected.

'Jane. Normally I'd say what a surprise,' came the still familiar voice. 'But I suppose I expected to hear from you.'

'Where's your housekeeper?'

'She took ill. She's been gone a couple of years now.'

'Oh.'

They both held the awkward silence.

'Why did you expect to hear from me?' Jane finally asked.

'Because I've heard from your sister.'

Jane had anticipated Charlotte would immediately contact their mother after Jane's call. 'And?'

'And I've been made aware of your cruel and ghastly threat.'

Jane shrugged, even though her mother couldn't see it. 'She left me no alternative.'

'She'll be destitute!'

'No, she won't. I hear she's already made a fine plan.'

'What are you talking about?'

'She didn't tell you?'

400

'She told me you'd given her an ultimatum and that she has no choice but to bend to your nasty demand.'

'Nothing about marriage?'

Her mother tittered. 'Oh, yes, I heard about that.'

Jane blinked with fury. 'Mother, I don't wish to play games. Please make arrangements to have Charlotte stay with you, because while in the short term she may have no roof over her head, that should all change by Christmas.'

'Yes, well, I'm hopeful she won't have to leave at all if your friend comes through for her.'

'My friend?' Jane didn't know what her mother was talking about.

'Yes, he's going to intervene with Melba on her behalf.'

'Who is *he*?'

'Guy Attwood! Who else? You certainly hide your light under a bushel, Jane. You might have said something.'

Her mother was maddening; why couldn't she be clear? 'Said something about what?' Jane asked through gritted teeth.

'About the marriage proposal.'

'I just did. But do let Charlotte tell you all about it, Mother.'

'I realise we don't have a close relationship, Jane, but nothing will change the fact that I am your mother. The very least you could do was seek my permission in the absence of your father. Even just as a token.'

Jane let out a cold laugh. 'I can't imagine even Charlotte would wait for your permission in this instance, Mother.'

'To do what?'

'Good grief, what is wrong with you? I feel as though I'm talking in circles.'

'I could say the same. What does Charlotte need my permission for?'

'She doesn't,' Jane huffed, 'but if you want to do things the old way, then insist that she and Guy Attwood pay you a courtesy visit. Make him squirm, Mother, although I suspect you will not hold back on granting marriage for longer than a few heartbeats. All that old money coming Charlotte's way? Perfect. I hope you're all very happy.'

There was a pause. 'Jane?'

'Yes?'

'Have you been drinking alcohol?'

'Don't be ridiculous.'

'Smoking opium or taking anything odd – a camphorated tincture or some such?'

'Why are you asking me this?'

'Because you are behaving very strangely.'

'Mother, I am as dependably straight and sober as ever.'

'Then why such curious references to Charlotte and your Mr Attwood?'

'He is not *my* Mr Attwood, quite the opposite.'

'When I asked him to inform me of any marriage arrange-ments with you, he said that would be entirely up to you. The very superiority of it!'

Jane was aghast. 'To me?'

'Yes, to you! Who else?'

Jane faltered. 'You've spoken to Guy Attwood?' Her heart lifted in hope.

'Yes. He hoped I would help him to find you. He asked me all sorts of questions about your childhood, your favourite places. I ended up talking about that silly red plant that you and your Papa were so fond of and excited by. And he suddenly needed to rush off. I presume he found you?'

Jane's heart plummeted, as she remembered how cold she had been towards him. 'Yes.'

'Well, I hope you said yes to his proposal, Jane, because the likes of Guy Attwood will come into your life only once, if you're

402

lucky. I can't imagine why he has chosen you or how you've caught his attention, but you must be the most blessed spinster in England right now. There will soon be women wringing their hands to learn that one of the most eligible bachelors in all of Britain has made his choice.'

'Me?' Jane felt stupid for saying it out loud.

Her mother continued as if she hadn't heard. 'Of course Charlotte would be the better choice, and we could make provision for you, Jane – and the boy, of course – but he seemed hellbent on you being his bride.'

Jane's throat turned so dry, it was as if she hadn't tasted water in days. 'Mother, I have to go.'

Jane could hear her mother's distant voice saying her name as she replaced the receiver on its cradle. The room went silent. She sat as still as the furniture surrounding her and in her shock went back over the conversation with Guy.

She'd been hateful, but that had been her only protection.

Had he actually said he was marrying Charlotte?

No. It was Charlotte who had led her to believe in their engagement. What had she said? Jane went back over that too.

'He came with a marriage proposal, and then the news about Harry's disappearance got in the way.'

And Jane hadn't let Charlotte say any more, as she had leapt to the wrong conclusion, it seemed. Her mother had said Guy offered to intervene with Melba on Charlotte's behalf. But why? And then understanding filtered through like sunlight through the leaves of his apple tree.

Guy had gone to Charlotte and made her an offer. Not of marriage, but of assistance, to speak to Melba Cavendish and persuade her to reverse her decision about Harry. Melba would take his call, of course; there was no way she would ignore any of the Attwoods, not with their ties to the royal circles. And that's why Charlotte had pleaded for more time. She needed Harry for leverage or she couldn't force Guy to follow through.

Jane stood, as despair at her appalling behaviour towards Guy took root. She'd seen the shift in his expression as her demands to be left alone had hit their mark.

'And now he's gone,' she said into the quiet of William's study. 'You've pushed away the only man you've ever loved romantically.'

Repair it! The ghost of William Angus demanded.

'I don't know how,' she whispered.

Yes, you do, the ghost replied softly, and then left her.

40

When Jane's carriage drew up alongside Merton Hall's main door, she was already holding her breath. Just coming up the driveway took minutes; it was flanked by parkland and an avenue of trees that in summer would provide a leafy canopy like an arbour of welcome. In autumn they provided a carpet of russet, greeting visitors at the home they stood sentinel for.

A footman met her and helped her down and a kind-faced butler welcomed her with an expression of puzzlement.

'Good afternoon. I am so sorry, we were not expecting any guests or I would have—'

'Please don't fret. I have arrived without warning unintentionally, but I am Jane Saville.'

'Miss Saville,' he said with dawning comprehension. 'Harry's mother!' He beamed.

'Yes,' she said, pleased he made the connection and called her Miss. Had Guy explained? 'My apologies for not—'

He gave a tutting sound and ushered her in. 'Be welcome, Miss Saville, and do come in from the cold.' He went to help her take off her coat, gloves and hat. 'Although I imagine you'd like to see Master Harry? He's playing out by the fountain.' He gestured down the garden along the side. 'It's not too far, or I could fetch him if you prefer?'

'Oh, thank you, but I would love to go to him, please. Down there, you say?'

'Just follow your nose, Miss Saville. The staff made him some paper boats this afternoon that he's enjoying.'

'That's very kind.'

'I think he's won all our hearts.' The man winked.

'Um, will the family understand if I—'

'Of course,' he said warmly. 'I shall let Mrs Attwood know.'

'Thank you.'

He gave a neat bow and she blushed; it had been a long time since anyone had treated her with any deference. His graciousness was warming. Jane stepped off the gravel onto a neat pathway that wound slightly away from the house, past a small copse into a more private, formal garden that opened up behind a tall hedge. At its centre was a glorious fountain of marble with a statue of Cupid, a gentle arc of water spouting from his arrow held aloft in his bow.

And at the edge of the marble pool bent another beautiful young boy, his golden hair flopped across his brow as he reached in to give one of his paper boats an extra shove. He was singing to himself, in that angelic voice of his, the solo he'd sung on the day Charlotte had taken him from her.

Her heart filled with joy and warmth to see her son looking so at peace, lost in his playtime and so happy that he was singing to himself. *That's how childhood should be. I want this for you every day, my love*, she thought, feeling that she'd somehow let him down, that he might have spent even a moment feeling unloved and unwanted while he was with Charlotte. Never again! They would not be parted from now on until he was a man old enough to make his own decisions.

'Harry,' she called gently.

He whipped around, recognising her voice immediately. 'Mummy!'

That one word.

She'd needed to hear him say it.

And then he was running towards her, holding a wet paper boat, his hands dripping, and she bent to welcome him into her arms. There he was, in her embrace again, exactly where she needed him to be. They hugged, and they hugged longer still. Jane wept silently over him and knew those tears must dry fast; she did not want Harry to see her weep.

She stroked his hair and kissed his head, swallowing her tears. 'Hello, darling Harry.'

He hugged her tightly. 'I've missed you.'

'I'm pleased to hear that,' she admitted truthfully. 'Now, let me look at you.'

He seemed to have grown an inch. His upturned face showed cheeks that were pinched by the cold but also in robust health. His eyes shone and his hair needed a comb and even a trim. He was in old wellington boots and some strange, old-fashioned motley of clothing they'd obviously cobbled together for him.

'These are Guy's clothes from when he was little,' he said with great glee. 'Mrs Attwood gave them to me as I only had one set of clothes with me. Oh, I love it here. Mrs Attwood is so much fun, and Miss Farmer is very kind. And everyone here has been making me things and taking me places. Mummy, we went fishing and Mrs Attwood insisted I sit on a horse. It was extremely scary at first, but she said we should get a pony for me, so I can learn to ride properly.'

'A pony,' Jane breathed, swallowing down a sob. 'That's kind.'

'They're all so kind to me. Not like Aunt Charlotte. She was horrid. I'm sorry, Mummy, I know she's your family, but she was really unkind to me, and she told me something that—'

'I know she did. Shall we sit here on this bench?' Jane asked, pointing to a small love seat set amid a gloriously chequered bed of autumn herbs. The fragrance of thyme lifted above them as Harry followed her to the bench.

'Harry, shall we talk about what Charlotte told you?'

'All right, it was unkind but . . .' He trailed off. She could see he was struggling to find the right words.

'But it's the truth,' she finished gently. 'Aunt Charlotte gave birth to you.'

There was a pause while Harry stared at the herbs and swung his legs back and forth. 'But you're my mother,' he finally qualified.

'Yes!' Jane said, nearly crying with relief and pulling him close again. 'I am your mother. And you are my son.'

'And is that all right with everyone?'

'It is.'

'I can stay with you forever?'

'Yes.' She took his hand and placed her palm against his. 'We are glued. No one can come between us. We're how we've always been, Harry. Just you and me.'

'And William?'

She placed her hand over her heart. 'William has left us, darling.'

Harry simply nodded. 'Guy told me he had probably died. He says I have to be very brave about it and then hold him in our hearts and minds forever.'

'Wise words,' she admitted.

'Can it be you, me and Guy now?' Harry looked up at her with such innocence and earnestness that she didn't know what to say.

She faltered. 'Er . . . I don't know, darling, but I do know he thinks the world of you, so you will always have him as your close friend.' Although she might have ruined her relationship with Guy, it didn't mean Harry had to lose him too. She could imagine him having some happy summer holidays here among his new friends. 'So, shall we go home?' she asked, smiling.

He nodded.

'It's a bit quiet there, but we'll soon make noise again. We'll light a fire each night through winter, and we'll cook together and play chess, and do all the things you love. We'll miss William, but we're going to plant some roses in his honour. I'll let you choose them.'

'He loved red roses,' Harry said. 'He told me that red smell the best.'

She smiled. 'Red it shall be. Come on, it's very cold out here, and your hands look oddly blue,' she said, kissing his head again.

He looked at his fingers. 'No, this is from picking blackberries with Guy's mother.' He laughed.

'We'd better thank Mrs Attwood, and maybe we can catch the four o'clock train.'

The butler met them at the house. 'Did the boats sail well, Harry?' he asked, beaming at the boy.

'They were perfect, Mr Jones. I left them floating around the pond of the fountain.'

'Excellent. I hope mine lasts the longest.' He grinned. 'Miss Saville, please, come into the drawing room. Mrs Attwood shouldn't be long.' He led Jane and Harry into a tastefully furnished room, drawing the curtains slightly and stoking the fire. 'You'll warm up quickly if you'll allow me to send up a pot of tea, or would you prefer cocoa like Harry?'

'Tea would be perfect, thank you,' she replied, allowing herself to enjoy the warmth.

'Let me get that organised,' he said, pulling on a cord. In a blink, a maid arrived and he gave instructions. She smiled at Jane and hurried away. 'There. Sarah will bring you a tray. Harry, would you like to come and wash your hands?'

Jane smiled as Harry followed him obediently. 'You're most kind, thank you, Mr Jones.'

'Warm up,' he said and left, Harry in tow.

Jane looked around her. The room was large and glorious, painted in beautiful colours that felt like a happy assault on her senses as she tried to tease out names and how they might be formulated. Someone of great taste, in her opinion, had decorated this room, with just enough furniture to interest the eye without adding clutter to the space or the mind. Vases of roses gave her pause as she thought of William again, but they filled the room with a beautiful scent of the garden.

A tea tray was served by Sarah in no time, together with some homemade shortbread biscuits that looked irresistible.

'Would you like me to pour, Miss Saville?'

'No, thank you. I'll be happy to do that.'

The maid gave a curtsy and left.

Two sips and the door burst open, and Harry came rushing back in.

And then Jane saw her. Standing in the doorway, tall and straight, was unmistakably Guy's mother. She was a handsome woman who had surely been extremely beautiful in her youth. Her hair was still dark in places but streaked thickly with silver, which she did not hide but complemented with platinum or white gold jewellery. The pieces were small, few but creatively fashioned. She wore a mud-spattered skirt and a simple black blouse, but she somehow managed to make the austere, somewhat rough outfit appear elegant.

'Miss Saville, I'm Adele Attwood,' the older woman said,

moving across the room gracefully – in a pair of men's socks, it appeared. 'You'll have to forgive my appearance; it's muddy out there,' she explained. 'And we're in our oldest clothes because our dear Harry insists on picking a bowl of blackberries each time we head out. I gather you found him playing at the fountain? I meant to go and change but got caught up dead-heading the last of the roses.'

Jane nodded, a little lost for words.

'Harry, do you want to let Jones know that you're ready for your cocoa?' Adele urged.

He raced off, seemingly well aware of how to find Mr Jones.

'Harry runs everywhere,' Adele remarked with only affection. 'Guy was the same, I recall.'

'He's in a hurry for life,' Jane admitted, having not moved.

Adele stopped in front of her and held out a hand. 'It's lovely to meet you, my dear.'

Jane took it, and it was warm with a friendly squeeze. 'I'm Jane.'

Adele smiled. 'I've been dying to meet you since my son told me about you.'

'He did?' Jane was surprised, given their last encounter.

Adele sat down opposite Jane. 'Well, as much as Guy is prepared to say. He's like his father and plays his cards far too close to his chest. I hope you'll change all that. He clearly adores Harry.'

'Harry adores him back.' Jane's heart was beating faster than usual. What did this woman know?

'Oh, I'm glad Mr Jones organised a pot of tea,' Adele said, eyeing the second cup and saucer. 'Don't expect to see Harry anytime soon. He'll head to the kitchen and see what can be pilfered.'

'He seems very happy,' Jane said. 'I'm so grateful that you've taken such good care of him while . . .' She trailed off.

Adele poured herself a cup. 'Well, we've tried in the short time he's been here to make him feel safe and welcome. He's been fishing, he's collected firewood and built a bonfire, and he's been playing with Guy's train set, among all sorts of activities.'

Jane smiled faintly, hating herself for getting everything so wrong. This man had made sure her son had everything he could dream of; how could she have thought he was cruel?

'I do hope you won't rush off with Harry. I think I'm quite in love with him. He's made such a difference to how I . . . oh well.' She seemed to stop herself from saying more. 'You should know we've all loved having him. The sound of a child's voice around this place has made us all feel young again, especially after my husband passed away just recently. Guy rushed home from Wiltshire but missed him, my poor darlings. They still had so much to say. Guy's quite broken, not that he'd show it.'

Jane felt ill; there had been so much misunderstanding on her part. 'I'm so sorry about your husband, Adele.'

Adele nodded. 'Thank you, dear. It's a deep ache. But it's mine and Guy's. And Harry's arrival has brought some sunshine into the house. I hope we'll hear his fun for years to come.' She frowned. 'You know, my wicked son didn't even say you were coming, or I would have made some preparations.'

'Oh, please, I really just came to fetch Harry.'

'Fetch him? So you're not staying?' She looked genuinely saddened.

'Er, no.'

'Jane . . . does Guy even know you're here?'

Jane shook her head. 'Only that I was arranging for Harry to come home.'

'I see.' She watched Jane closely. 'Has something happened between the two of you?' Adele asked gently.

Jane looked at her hands. 'I've upset him.'

'Oh, tosh! Guy's got broad shoulders, and I've never known him to hold a grudge. Besides, Jane,' Adele said, squeezing her wrist, 'nothing in the world about you could upset him.'

'I, um . . . I'm afraid I made some accusations based on presumption.'

Adele gave a sympathetic smile. 'Always dangerous.'

Jane nodded. 'I know, and it's not something I'm in the habit of doing but, oh, if I could tell you what I've been through recently, it might explain how I've jumped to all the wrong conclusions.'

'Why don't you?' At Jane's surprised glance, she continued. 'I mean, why don't you tell me? I realise I'm a stranger to you, but I'm invested in you because of Harry and how Guy feels, so if listening helps, let me assure you, I'm good at it.'

Over their cups of tea and more biscuits, Jane poured out her heart to Guy's mother. She couldn't remember being so open. She was in the midst of recounting the terrible conversation at Swanage Railway Station when the door opened, and the subject of their discussion appeared.

'Good afternoon, Mother, I thought I'd take an early—' He stopped still. The smile on his face faltered as he took in the scene.

Desperately embarrassed, Jane stood. 'Hello, Guy.'

The silence lengthened horribly, and it seemed even Adele wasn't prepared to step into its brittleness.

'You said never again,' he finally remarked.

Jane blinked. 'Pardon me?'

'You said you never wanted to see me or speak to me again, and yet here you are, less than twenty-four hours later, in my home.'

She swallowed. 'I should leave.'

'You'll do no such thing!' Adele said, also standing now. 'Guy, where are your manners?'

He stared at Jane. 'Forgive me, Mother. I was simply following Jane's all too clear instructions.'

'I apologise for my intrusion. I simply came to pick up Harry.'

'Miss Farmer has been waiting for your call.' He clearly wasn't going to make this easy for her.

'I thought this was quicker,' she lied, realising any hope she'd had to mend things with him was dying by the moment. 'Besides, I needed to see my son. I couldn't wait for him to come to me.'

'Right,' Adele said into the awkwardness. 'I am going to leave you two to talk. Jane, do share with Guy what you told me, and Guy, please don't let me down. You know what your father and I hold dear. I'm going to find Harry.'

And with that she departed, leaving them to face each other.

Jane shifted uncomfortably. 'I shouldn't have come unannounced. I'm sorry.'

'No, but you seemed to be getting on famously with my mother.'

'She's been very kind to me.'

'Why wouldn't she? I told her you were the woman I loved and I was going to marry, but I got that so wrong, didn't I?'

'Guy,' she appealed. 'It was I who got it all wrong. But Charlotte as good as said you'd come to her house with a proposal of marriage.'

'I had. To *you*.'

She nodded, feeling sickened. 'The way she said it encouraged me to believe it was to her.'

He looked like he wanted to shake her. 'Why on earth would you believe such a thing?'

'I don't know. I'm in a mess, Guy. Losing Harry, losing William . . . losing you. It felt like I was drowning.'

Guy's hackles softened slightly. 'I went to Charlotte to broker a deal.'

'I realise that now, but I didn't ask you to do that.'

'I know.'

'And what's more, while I might have jumped to the wrong conclusion about your intentions, I think you were rather presumptuous.'

'I was trying to help,' he appealed.

'My knight in silver armour?' That made him look uncomfortable. 'I've never had one, Guy, and I've never wanted or asked for one. What's more, I don't need one. It's a fallacy that women need men to solve all their problems. I loved having you in my life, brief though it has been, but I didn't need saving. I needed companionship, conversation, laughter – and love of the romantic kind. I've never experienced that kind of love before and it . . .' Jane closed her eyes and smiled. 'It made me breathless, weightless . . . but not helpless.' She watched him look down. 'But you weren't there when I needed you. I admire your rush to solve my problem, but it wouldn't have been solved. You could have cornered Charlotte only for a limited time. Then she'd want more, and she could still wield power over me.'

'So you give in?'

'Didn't I just tell you I am not helpless?'

He frowned, baffled.

'Charlotte will not be making any further claim on Harry. You see, I've solved my own dilemma.'

'How?'

'By playing Charlotte at her own cruel game.' She sighed. 'I presume your deal was to intervene with Melba Cavendish?'

'Yes. It escalated slightly today. I ended up buying the house from her.'

'You did what?' Jane was shocked.

He shrugged. 'It was easier than hoping to persuade her to look on Charlotte kindly. She simply wouldn't; I could hear it in her tone.'

'You are *not* giving Charlotte that house. As I say, it will only embolden her.'

'Jane, are you sure Harry is safely back in your care?'

'Completely.' She smiled. 'Although I'm not proud of how I achieved it.'

'And you're not going to tell me, are you?'

She shook her head. 'Some things are best left unsaid, but Harry and I have talked. He seems at peace about who his mother is – and who gave birth to him.'

'Then the house I've purchased shall be given to Harry.'

She looked at him, astonished. 'You're serious, aren't you?'

Guy shrugged again. 'It's his by birthright.'

'I don't know what to say. "Thank you" doesn't seem enough. He seems so very happy.'

'My mother adores him, of course,' he said. 'We all do.'

Jane smiled, reminded of just how cheerful and relaxed Harry had been when she'd arrived. 'They came in here smiling like a grandmother and her grandson.'

Guy gave a nod.

'And Harry clearly adores her back. He's got more colour in his cheeks than I've ever seen. And your mother in muddy clothes was a wonderful sight to behold. I love that she doesn't care about how she looks.'

'Oh, she cares. She just doesn't care what anyone else thinks.'

Jane nodded. 'No doubt that's what Harry feels so safe around. No judgement.'

'Given the right chance, he could run wild here.'

'Like you did?'

'Yes. It's certainly a carefree place for a young lad to grow up.' He looked at her carefully, waiting for a reaction to his underlying meaning.

She met his stare in silence. Was this stalemate, or could they find their way around what stood between them? He had made his apologies. He had shown his remorse with his actions, which meant so much more to her than if he'd used words. He'd helped

William, he'd helped Harry, he even believed with conviction that he'd helped her. The fact that she resented that intrusion was actually her problem to navigate and not his, she realised.

It was her pride that was blocking them.

He spoke first. 'Jane, look, I was going to have Harry escorted to you down south, but now that you're here, let me organise a hotel room for you both and a car to pick you up tomorrow and take you both back to Salisbury. You can always stay here tonight, of course. I shan't be here. I shall get out of your way and—'

'Oh, fight harder, Guy.'

He blinked, confused. 'Pardon?'

'Come on. Fight for me.' She opened her arms wide, palms up.

'I don't know what you want.'

'I want you! Do *you* want *us*?'

'You know I do,' he said, his voice taut, and in a single stride he closed the gap between them, which had felt like a ravine only moments earlier. He took her hands. 'Jane, marry me. Marry me tomorrow!'

'That might be a little hasty,' she said with a chuckle, suddenly shy.

'Next week then. Next month!' he said with urgency. 'Just say you'll marry me.'

All the fractiousness within her fled. Feeling his touch banished the anger, and his gaze chased away the fear. As he searched her face it felt like it was cleansing her of the guilt she felt about using a secret against her sister.

She would use their love to forgive herself . . . and use her good fortune in meeting and loving Guy Attwood to try to find forgiveness for Charlotte and her mother. For Harry's sake. Now there might be hope for Harry to have a family beyond her after all . . . two families even – one in Warwick, another in London.

'What about Eleanor? The way she spoke about you . . .'

Guy squeezed her hand. 'I'm sorry she visited. She shouldn't have done that. We met earlier today; I needed to make sure she understands that there is no future at all for us as anything other than friends.'

'Then I will marry you,' Jane said with a broadening smile.

He opened his mouth in silent surprise, as though hardly daring to believe she had agreed, and then she was swept up into the kiss she had longed to experience again. Everything about being in Guy's arms felt familiar and right, but, more than that, it felt like the comforting warmth of laughing with her father in his study, or chatting quietly with William by the fire on a winter's night after Harry had gone to bed, or listening to Harry sing his solo in the cathedral.

Within Guy's embrace was her rightful place. She was home. She was loved. She was in control of her life at last.

EPILOGUE

A Festival of Empire had opened in May to celebrate the upcoming coronation of King George and his Queen, Mary, which involved a month of exhibitions of British and Imperial trade and culture. British women up and down the country devoured all news relating to the Queen's attire for the coronation; it would be made of cream silk satin and include the floral emblems and symbols of Great Britain and the British Empire, from the Tudor rose and Scottish thistle to the Star of India. The task of its creation had been awarded to a London couture house, Reville & Rossiter.

A temporary coronation annexe was built at the west front of Westminster Abbey to allow the easy forming of processions before entry into the grand church. Meanwhile, inside the Abbey, the traditional ceremonial spaces such as the sacrarium had to be constructed, along with galleries to accommodate the congregation, which would be limited to six thousand.

Along the route of the procession, something in the order of fifty grandstands were erected for the spectators. All through the night of the twenty-first day of June, the ordinary people of London began to gather, taking the best position they could to view the coronation procession of King George V. By two o'clock on the morning of 22 June, the whole of Whitehall and Trafalgar Square was teeming with excited observers, keen to catch a glimpse of their new monarch, who, though he had been King since the previous May, was now to be made official with a crown on his head.

The 1911 season had sparkled with parties, balls, sporting events and social engagements. The summer was hot, with soaring temperatures, the likes of which the British had not experienced in living memory; the good weather had begun in spring and didn't let up. Rain was scarce, but while the farmers fretted, the country basked in the glorious weather.

Reported by *The Tatler*, the magazine that cost its greedy readers sixpence, among the personalities who had taken to the great gardens of London to find fresh air and hopefully a cool breeze were Mr and Mrs Guy Attwood of Warwickshire. Mrs Jane Attwood, nee Saville, was seen to be heavily pregnant with her first child, although the magazine didn't fail to mention that the recently married couple, with strong ties to the royal court, had formally adopted a son from within the Saville family. Henry, known fondly as Harry, was a former soloist for Salisbury Cathedral and was now attending Warwick School, his parents choosing for him to be a day scholar near their family home at Merton Hall. The magazine remarked that they had overlooked boarding at Harrow, which his adoptive father, Guy, had attended alongside his close friend, Winston Churchill, presently the youngest member of Cabinet in more than four decades.

Mrs Attwood, the magazine continued, was due to give birth in August and, despite her delicate condition, she and her husband, among the King's close friends, would be in attendance at Westminster Abbey for the coronation and the small private celebration afterwards at Buckingham Palace.

The royal coach was drawn out of the grounds of Buckingham Palace by cream-coloured horses, to the sound of artillery salutes and the strains of the national anthem. When the newly crowned couple left the Abbey some hours later, still with sceptres in hands and crowns on heads, they drove by the Mall, St James's Street and Piccadilly to enormous and rapturous crowds.

Although Guy and Jane had begged off the small, celebratory lunch that the royal couple hosted for a few guests, they did enjoy some private moments with the King and Queen.

'My gosh, Mrs Attwood, you look very ready to have your child,' the Queen remarked, all formalities finally done with.

Jane smiled serenely. 'It has to be a boy the way this baby is kicking. Please forgive us leaving early, Your Majesty.'

'Don't mention it. Get home and rest. Oh, whatever has Guy brought?'

Jane smiled wider. 'Something very simple for his King. He told me there was nothing he could give his old childhood friend but this curiosity, which he holds so dear.'

'Is that an apple?' Queen Mary, affectionately known as May, sounded astonished.

'Yes, do come and share it,' Jane said, and they joined their husbands.

Guy was about to present his precious bounty. 'Anything I give you is pointless, old chap, so I'm giving you something that means everything to me. I hope this is a gift for Britain.' He handed the King a single polished fruit from the small basket of them at his feet.

'An apple!'

Guy explained its story, adding, 'We've had them stored in tissue, wrapped like babies, since last October in readiness for this day.'

The Queen chuckled. 'I adore this. Do you mean this humble little thing was brought over by the French hundreds of years ago?'

Guy nodded. 'And nearly became extinct, if not for the couple of trees I found in Jane's garden in Salisbury, beneath the cathedral's great spire. Its original name, Your Majesties, is the Scarlet Henry, but Kew has agreed to change the name to the George Rex in your honour.'

'Good grief!' the King said, sounding greatly amused. 'I'm impressed, old chap. Quite the novelty.'

'We have another harvest coming along beautifully for this year,' Jane added, looking proudly at Guy.

He smiled, turning his attention to the Queen. 'And for you, Your Majesty,' he said to May, 'in your honour, Jane and I will plant an orchard in Wiltshire where this brave apple hung on until I found it. We will also see if we can get a grove of this fruit growing in Warwick, to be called Queen Mary Orchard.'

'Oh, but that is marvellous, you two. I can't think of a better, more novel or appropriate coronation gift,' Queen Mary said, smiling widely.

'Well, well,' the King said, laughing and blowing smoke from a cigar to one side. 'I must say I find it rather fun.' He twisted the apple in his hand. 'You were always something of an eccentric, Guy, and now you've confirmed it.'

'Darling, I think an apple for the King is rather romantic,' his wife admonished him.

'Don't get me wrong, my dear. I'm enchanted, and the country thanks you, Guy, for your endeavours with its apple heritage.'

Guy grinned. 'Oh, and there's one more thing. My clever wife painted this for you, Your Majesties,' he said, presenting the study she had laboured over, newly framed. He spun it around and lifted off the soft covering.

'Jane,' Queen Mary breathed. 'This is exquisite.'

'I don't expect you to hang it in your drawing room, Your Majesty.'

'I shall certainly hang it somewhere I can enjoy it. Thank you, my dear.'

Later, realising the crowds were still thick despite their gradual dispersal, they decided to stroll home rather than take a cab. Walking arm in arm away from the palace, Guy sighed. 'It's done,' he said. 'I've never felt happier.'

Jane squeezed his arm. 'I'm pleased for you. Seeing it through and finally placing the apple in his hand is something to celebrate.'

'I nearly gave up several times.' He shook his head.

'But you didn't.'

'No, but it's not because I was able to give the King the apple that I have never felt happier, Jane.' He covered her hand. 'It's because if not for that driving ambition to find the apple, I would never have found you. And I can't imagine life now without you.' He stopped walking and kissed her gently.

Some soldiers stood nearby, now off duty. Earlier, some of them had broken rank to lift their helmets onto their rifles and wave as the newly crowned royals gathered on the balcony at Buckingham Palace. Now, they gave wolf whistles.

Guy grinned as he broke away. 'I hope I didn't embarrass you?'

Jane shook her head. 'No. Being the fallen woman of the Salisbury Cathedral Close has toughened me up. I can take on all stares and critics.' She smiled back at him.

'I believe you, Mrs Attwood,' he said.

ACKNOWLEDGEMENTS

Learning about watercolours and ancient apples for the writing of this story has been a great joy . . . A tower of books has been greedily consumed and I've made several visits to the west of England and a quick jaunt north. I had hoped to include Bath in this story, but there simply wasn't room, so I'll leave that research for another tale.

So many people have had something important to do with this book, most of them dedicating their precious time and expertise so that I could ensure the most authentic read for all of you.

Diana von der Borch-Garden is one of my readers and before I began writing fell into an email conversation with me about Blenheim Palace. Before I knew it, I was deciding to weave both Winston Churchill and the place where he was born into this tale. At her encouragement I made contact with curator and historian Antonia Keaney, who couldn't have been more welcoming or kind. I flew to England, drove to Oxfordshire and met Antonia, who kindly walked me through this extraordinary palace, owned by the Dukes of Marlborough. What a history it has. As it turned out, and the way editing goes, I only needed it for one small scene, but the fact that I had been there and learned about that secret staircase and scary precipice at the top of the great hall made the whole scene come alive in my mind – and, I hope, yours. I'm sure Blenheim Palace will sneak into my stories again – there is just too much to love about it to only feature it once. My thanks to Antonia for her generosity and knowledge.

Sally Pond is a watercolour artist and teacher who specialises in botanical subjects, and it was at her side, in her gorgeous cottage in Cathedral Close, that I was able to enjoy close up the process of mixing colours and working out how to approach depicting a petal with paint. She used some apple blossom for her demonstration and suddenly I felt very connected to my character Jane. I am so grateful to Sally and her family for their warmth during my regular visits.

Cindy Barfoot follows my Facebook page and saw that I was making a dash for Dorset in the UK, having never been but knowing I had to find a grand outdoor setting for a scene in this book. She could tell I was concerned that I may never find it and offered to help . . . Two strangers met on a cold railway platform but hugged as though we'd known each other for years. I was in awe that she would take a day off work for me, and she was excited to meet the writer she followed. Off we went in the car with her two lovely Labradors for a crash course about Swanage in Dorset and the surrounding heath. Wow, what a day! That's all it took – we found our location, we walked it, we slipped in mud and sank in the bog and touched the gorse and took photos of the incredibly far-reaching view towards the horizon. In those couple of hours, I had my scene in my imagination and we even had time to visit a fabulous place for hot chocolate. Cindy, I could *not* have found this place easily without you or had my crucial scene on the heath.

Anne Monyhan is the owner of the house in the Cathedral Close at Salisbury that I chose, unbeknownst to her, for Jane, Harry and William to live. How kind she was last year to invite me in for coffee and to stroll around the entire house with her and learn about its history, its exterior paint colour and to get into that all important back garden that features so impressively in the story. I know people are already taking selfies outside her house to say, 'Found it, Fiona,' and I'm in Anne's debt for finding it as amusing as I do.

There are others to acknowledge. Chris Barnard from the guides at Salisbury Cathedral for his magnificent private tour around this most glorious of buildings, David Donovan for suggesting I get hold of a particular book about paint colours that I have spent many lovely hours with, Pip Klimentou and Sonya Caddy who have read my first draft of every book I've written and helped me knock it into shape . . . and of course my terrific team at Penguin Random House, who offer so much support out of every department, but particularly my publisher, Ali Watts and my editor, Amanda Martin.

To the booksellers. You are amazing. Thank you for the endless support, whether you're one of the team in our favourite retail chains or you're kind enough to check out the back for my books at one of the big department stores. You might be the owner of a beloved indie store or on the end of a phone order at one of the book warehouses. You love books and you love customers who love books. Thank you for stocking mine and recommending them to your clients. Ever grateful.

Can I add that the Wall's ice cream cart in this story appears a little earlier than perhaps its true date of around 1913? And I know with the Red Lion Clock I've taken a liberty of ten years.

A first grandchild was born during the research and writing of this story, so I've dedicated the book to him because I couldn't believe he was given the name of Henry and I was already well advanced in crafting the lovely Henry Saville. Welcome, our dear Henry, into the McIntosh family, and thanks to all within it for the constant support and love.

Fx

RIVERTON ORCHARD
APPLE JELLY

Apples, as this story attests, are arguably the world's most versatile fruit. They work with sweet or savoury dishes with the same elegance.

I make this apple jelly most years from the fruit trees in our small orchard. I use the red apples because they give a beautiful, jewel-like ruby radiance to the jelly. The key to achieving the translucent quality is to resist – even when temptation is at its most keen – to press the fruit to get as much juice as possible. Put the mush on your compost heap if you have one and let it go back into the earth, because the moment you start pressing, you are committing your jelly to turn cloudy.

I usually bottle this jelly in small jars. It's fantastic with cheese or cold meat plates, for deglazing or in sauces, a real treat with scones, as a little sweet surprise in cupcakes, or for adding shine to sweet pies and pastries. Or just slather it on toast and butter and enjoy!

First you'll need to sterilise your jars and lids so they are ready to go.

Equipment
Large stockpot
Muslin/cheesecloth
Mesh colander/large sieve
Thermometer

Ingredients
3.75 kg apples
10 cups water
6 cups sugar
¼ cup freshly squeezed lemon juice
3 tsp Calvados, brandy or Cognac (optional but lovely)

Method
Rinse the apples and cut them coarsely into chunks, then put them, including the cores and seeds, into a very large stockpot.

Add the water, cover and bring to a boil. Once it is bubbling, reduce the heat, leave the lid askew and cook for up to 30 minutes, until the apples are tender and cooked through.

Line a mesh colander with a piece of muslin cloth or a few folds of cheesecloth (or use a jelly bag and stand) and set it over a deep bowl, then ladle the apples and the liquid into the colander. (I used two lined colanders since it was a large amount of apple pieces.)

Allow to stand for at least 3 hours (but the longer you let them drain, the more juice you'll get), and during that time, no matter how tempting it looks, *do not press down*.

The next day, measure the juice. You should have approximately 8 cups but may get a little more.

Pour the juice into a large, non-reactive pot fitted with a sugar thermometer, add the sugar and lemon juice, and bring to a boil.

During cooking, use a ladle to gently skim off any white foam that forms on the surface.

Cook until the temperature reaches 104° C (220° F), then turn off the heat and put a spoonful of jelly on a chilled plate. If it wrinkles and holds its shape, it's done. If not, continue to cook and re-test it at intervals. My batch set at 110° C (230° F).

Stir in the liquor, if you're using, and ladle hot into sterilised jars, then cap tightly. This will keep on pantry shelves, but refrigerate once opened . . . if there is any left once you twist off the lid and dig in.

Book Club Notes

1. Do you think Jane Saville really is a 'fallen' woman – or a fortunate one?

2. Discuss the different ways in which Jane and Guy respond to their familial duties.

3. In the eyes of 'society', Jane and Guy might seem an unlikely couple, but in what ways do they make an ideal match?

4. 'Truly, what more could a boy wish for?' Despite the obvious hardships Harry has faced in his young life, William believes him to be an extremely blessed child. Do you share this view?

5. 'For me to give entirely of myself, I would need so much more in a person than how they look or sound, or their station in life.' How is this comment from Jane reflected in her relationships?

6. What is your view of Eleanor? Is she a victim or a villain?

7.   In what ways has William been Jane's 'guardian angel', and in what ways is she entirely responsible for her own fate?

8.   Discuss the significance and symbolism of the apple in this novel.

9.   Do you have any sympathy at all for Charlotte's actions? Why or why not?

10. What did you make of Guy's gift for the King?

11. Who would you cast in a film of *The Fallen Woman*?

12. Fiona McIntosh writes across a wide range of genres. Have you read any others, and if so, how do they compare?

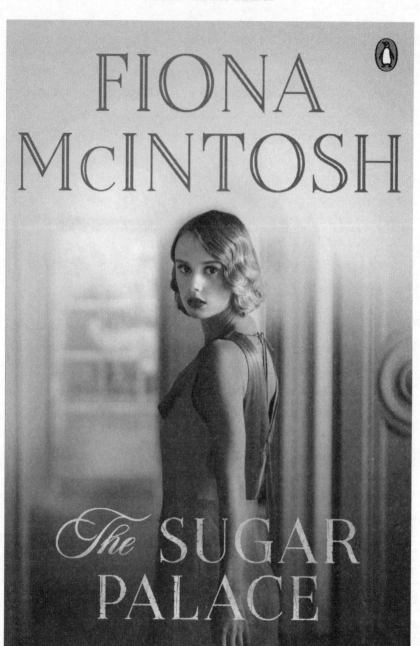

FIONA McINTOSH

The SUGAR PALACE

Under the clamour of the Sydney Harbour Bridge being built nearby, Grace Fairweather is working in her father's grocery shop in The Rocks when she begins making her own confectionery. Her colourful creations of toffees, lollies and chocolates soon become crowd favourites, and Grace begins to dream of one day opening her own sweetshop.

When the roguish but irresistible Londoner Alfie Sweeting comes to work for the Fairweathers, his ambition for her success thrills her – so much so that she begins to question her engagement to Norman. Perhaps the 'safe' option in life isn't the right thing for her after all. Alfie encourages her to open not just a sweetshop, but a delightful destination for young and old – a sugar palace!

With Grace's natural business acumen and Alfie's creative sales skills, it seems like they could be the perfect pairing – in work and in love – but when Alfie's criminal past catches up with him, both their lives come under threat and Grace is forced to make the most difficult decision of all.

Moving between the colourful world of a carnival-like confectionery store and Sydney's organised crime world of brothel madams, gambling dens and cocaine dealers, this is a thrilling romantic adventure that shows not everyone is to be trusted, and life isn't always as sweet as it seems.

'A fast-paced romance filled with secrets, adventure, and plenty of twists.' *Weekender*

FIONA McINTOSH

The ORPHANS

Orphan Fleur Appleby is adopted by a loving undertaker and his wife and she quickly develops a special gift for helping bereaved families. Her ambition to be the first female mortician in the country is fuelled by her plan to bring more women into the male dominated funeral industry.

Raised in the outback of South Australia's Flinders Ranges, Tom Catchlove is faced with a life-changing tragedy as a young boy. He works hard but dreams big, striving for a future as a wool classer.

A chance encounter between the two children will change the course of their lives.

By adulthood Fleur finds herself fighting for the survival of the family's business, while her widowed father drinks away generations of prosperity and a new, conniving stepmother wants Fleur gone. When Tom emerges from the isolation of the desert to find new work at the port woolstores, his path crosses with Fleur's again – only to be caught up in a murder investigation, in which they can only trust each other.

At once tragic and triumphant, *The Orphans* is an unforgettable story about a unique bond between two children that will echo down the years, and teach them both about the real meaning of life, of loss, and of love.

'Flawless.' *Australian Women's Weekly*

Powered by Penguin

Looking for more great reads, exclusive content and book giveaways?
Subscribe to our weekly newsletter.

Scan the QR code or visit penguin.com.au/signup